ANY
ONE
OF
US

ALSO BY MARTYN FORD

Every Missing Thing
All Our Darkest Secrets

ANY ONE OF US

MARTYN FORD

THOMAS & MERCER

Text copyright © 2022 by Martyn Ford
All rights reserved.

Published by Thomas & Mercer, Seattle

www.apub.com

Amazon, the Amazon logo, and Thomas & Mercer are trademarks of Amazon.com, Inc., or its affiliates.

ISBN-13: 9781542034517
ISBN-10: 1542034515

Cover design by @blacksheep-uk.com

Printed in the United States of America

ANY
ONE
OF
US

Chapter One

A text message. Electric words on glowing glass, guiding her eyes away from the horizon, away from the stripe of sundown red that loops around half the world, fading out to fresh black behind her. Those early outback stars that should leave anyone breathless and daunted seeming to thrum above, pulsing billion-year-old photons across the void and into a mind, a speck, a being just sitting here experiencing the near-impossible state of existence. Wow. The beauty, the sheer wonder of all the things she could be looking at. But, no. Her eyes were drawn down to the table, down to the light, down, yet again, to her phone.

Remember Mary Talbot from school? it said. *Apparently, she's dead. They think it's murder. Crazy. Just thought you should know x*

Ruby stared, frowned, turning her head now to read the message again. It was from Elizabeth. Surreal to hear from her like this, after—

A second message arrived.

Premium gossip, hey, Elizabeth wrote. And then up popped a third. *Sorry, shouldn't joke, it's awful really. Anyway, hope you're well. Must catch up sometime x*

Ruby paused for a moment, listening to the constant hiss of weird night-time bugs and the whispered wind you hear but never feel.

Maybe her phone *was* the most beautiful thing she could be looking at. What might an archaeologist make of it a million years from now? They wouldn't be impressed by the fossilised bush shrubs, the long rocks and splintered flints. But the phone? They'd say, "Wait, what's this thing?" Someone *made* this. Was it created to appease their gods? Was it a portal through which they appreciated the distant adventures of anonymous cats? Or both? Or, maybe, it was a device to share information. Gossip. *Premium gossip* about death.

She *did* remember Mary Talbot from school. Curly hair. Tall. What did she do now? Was she a doctor? Or a nurse? Something medical. A vet? Was she a vet? Animals? Horses? Ruby knew this, but her mind refused to recall.

Too much wine, too much sun. That's why she couldn't remember. That's why she was having these big, distracting thoughts about space and her meaningless place within it.

"Reminds me of when I was young," Eduardo said. "The sky seemed like it just went on and . . ."

It was only when he stopped that Ruby realised Eduardo, sitting opposite her at the rickety camping table, had been talking this whole time. Tuning back into the conversation, she lifted her head and pretended she was still engaged.

"Yeah," she said. "Like a painting."

But, from his face, it was clearly too late. Eduardo didn't seem to mind, though he paused, offering her a chance to explain.

"Sorry, I . . . I just got a strange message." She put her phone face down, fanned the notes out and gave him her full attention. Pen ready. "Want to go from the top?" *Click.*

Another brief silence. He didn't want to talk about work. Or sunsets. It was his turn to be rude.

"What did it say?" Eduardo asked, smiling.

Maybe he did have a free pass.

"Someone from my secondary . . . my high school, they've been murdered." Ruby shrugged. "Apparently."

"Oh, I'm sorry to hear that," Eduardo said, taking a sip from his plastic cup. "Were you," he swirled the wine, "friends?"

"Not really, no." Ruby shook her head. "But she was a nice girl."

He placed his drink down, then sighed.

"Right," he said. "Let's see."

Eduardo stood, carried his foldable chair around the table and stretched it back out with a quick flick. Then he sat down, the arm of his seat pressing against hers. Ruby frowned, hesitated. With an overly inquisitive flair, he lifted his glasses to his face and waited.

One lapse in politeness and now all social norms were gone? OK . . . She unlocked her phone and showed him the message.

He read it, nodded and hummed. "Well, I suppose it is quite strong, as far as gossip goes," he admitted.

"Shall we go back to the speech?" she said. "You want the opening statement to be tight."

They were preparing for next week – Eduardo was due to give a lecture on organised crime and, while he knew a great deal on the subject, he seemed dangerously blasé about the whole thing.

"Nah, enough of that." He waved his hand across the notes on the table – the work – the work they were *meant* to be doing. "This is far more interesting. What are you thinking?"

What was she thinking? Ruby was sitting in the middle of the Australian outback, next to a faintly rippling tent, surrounded by miles and miles of nothing, discussing a crime she'd learned about just moments ago. A possible murder that had happened on the other side of the planet. It actually couldn't be further away.

"I don't know," she said. "I know nothing about her. She was quite popular at school? I think she's a vet?"

3

"Army?"

"No, a veterinarian." Now she said it out loud, Ruby was almost certain this was wrong. She'd definitely seen a photo of Mary in a white coat. That's all she could remember. It didn't even matter. "We should—"

"Married?" Eduardo asked, thumb on his chin. He looked older with glasses – more sophisticated.

"Uh. Yeah," she said.

"Usually the husband, right?"

"Well—"

"Let's check him out." Eduardo gestured for her to pass him the phone.

"No," Ruby said. "Really. We should carry on."

"You're not curious?"

She exhaled. "Fine."

Swiping to her third page of apps, Ruby thumbed the Facebook logo. Maxed out notifications in the bottom right-hand corner. She clicked. Dismissed them all. Boring. Then she went to the search bar, typed the first three letters of Mary's name and tapped on her face.

Mary Cassell (Talbot). Practice Manager at Bright Shine. A *dentist*. And there it was, that photo of her in a white coat. Looked like a stock image – she was standing next to an empty chair, arms folded. Well-lit. Professional. Still had that curly blonde hair. But she looked different now – not quite the pretty girl Ruby remembered from school. Twenty years of aging and fading memory will do that to any face.

"You have animal dentists in the UK?" Eduardo asked, reaching back across the table for his drink.

"It was medical. I was in the right ballpark."

He laughed, slouching back into his seat. She was already regretting what she'd told him about her memory. Lost keys, misplaced phone, forgetting where she'd parked. Normal stuff. She'd mentioned it in passing, blamed fatigue, kept it light-hearted. But now it was a thing. Real. Something he could joke about.

Relationship status, married to—

"Sebastian Cassell," Eduardo said, now literally tapping on her phone. Some more madly intrusive behaviour there, but Ruby didn't care.

This, weirdly, felt refreshing – this camaraderie. The shared experience of insatiable, relentless curiosity and speculation. For a profession so grounded in the realms of hard evidence, hers still offered plenty of room for imagination, creativity. Especially in the very early days. Or, here, in the very early minutes since hearing about a crime.

Sebastian's profile picture was of him standing on a beach, topless, sunglasses, tanned, actually red, burned well into the realms of skin cancer. Ruby looked closer at his muscles, at the tribal tattoo on his shoulder. Eyebrow piercing.

The caption read, *Livin the dream, haters be crying. Lol.*

Then there were loads of hashtags. Gibberish mainly.

"Hmm." Eduardo poured more wine into his cup. "Seems like a dickhead. He did it. Case closed." He lifted the drink, a celebratory toast.

Ruby swiped Sebastian's photo away, then scrolled down to his most recent post.

My heart is broken. And a little broken heart emoji. There were a hundred and fifty comments – loads of those sad face reactions. Some of the creepy hug one. And, oddly, three likes.

"What kind of lunatic would give that a thumbs up?" Eduardo said, clearly thinking the same. "Ah, I feel bad now. Still, dickhead or not, he's our man."

The top comment was Sebastian. *And my flight's been delayed,* he wrote. *So I'm stuck in Thailand until Monday.*

Ruby tilted the phone so Eduardo could read. "Guess again."

"OK," he said. "That seems quite solid. I'm stumped. When did this happen? Who messaged you about it?"

"Elizabeth, she's—"

"Ask for more info."

"No. I haven't spoken to her for years."

Ruby went back to the text, scrolled up to see the previous message was a "happy birthday" from Elizabeth – and not even her most recent one.

"See," she said. "I'm a bad friend."

"Hold up, look." He sat forwards, placing his cup on the table. "She's typing."

Both she and Eduardo stared down into the phone, like teenagers, hungry for details. Two people, side by side, huddled over the white glow. A tiny glimmer of blurred light in the encroaching cosmic black. There really was nothing else besides these three blinking dots on the screen. Words forming miles away.

But then Elizabeth stopped. And that was it. No more information tonight.

They sat together, neither speaking. Just the static chirp of those insects, the quiet of the night – loud when you listen. The sun was below the horizon now – the silhouettes of shrubs, arid plants and black spindle trees, like driftwood battered by dust, sanded down to sticks. The colour fading, draining from the sky as red warmth shifted to something else, something dark.

◆ ◆ ◆

Dawn. The ungodly camping hour before the sun, when the world is still blue and you can barely tell the difference between cold and damp. Again, modern technology tore Ruby's attention away from some dream state of primal wonder. The timeless peace of those final sleeping minutes snatched and replaced with vibrations, harsh and tactile against the tent floor. She rolled over onto her elbow and squinted at her phone – incoming call.

Elizabeth Gregory. Her old friend making contact once more.

Ruby sat up, legs still together in her sleeping bag, wiped her eye and hit the green answer icon.

"Hey, hi," she said, emitting a strange sound that explained, no matter what she was about to claim, that she had just woken up.

"Sorry," Elizabeth said. "What time is it there?"

"God knows. It's fine. How are you?" Ruby asked, looking around for some clothes. "Sorry I didn't message back, I was . . ." she turned to see Eduardo sleeping silently next to her, "working."

This was half true. Though the camping trip had steadily become a holiday, despite Ruby's best efforts to keep it on track.

"I'm OK, I think," Elizabeth said. "Things are weird here, though."

Realising that she was still fully dressed, Ruby stopped searching for her clothes. She pulled the sleeping bag open. "Sad, about Mary."

"Yeah, well, that's why I'm calling. I just heard that Scott's dead."

"Scott?" Ruby shuffled to the bottom of the tent. "As in . . . ?"

"Yeah. Scott Hopkins."

"Shit." Kneeling, she unzipped half of the door, then passed her feet straight out and into her cold shoes. Damp shoes?

"You know the last murder in Missbrook Bay was in 1994. Then two in a week. Both from our year."

Ruby strode outside into the morning air, pacing as she listened.

"Apparently, Mary was killed on Friday," Elizabeth said. "Right after the reunion."

"Did you go?" Ruby had received an invite online but was obviously unable to attend. Though, even if she had been close by, she probably would have given it a miss. Standing around, cringing and lying to taller, fatter, greyer versions of her classmates was not exactly her idea of a good night.

"I did. It was fun, actually. Mary and Scott were both there."

"Was he still . . . ?"

"Yes," Elizabeth said. "He was doing coke and being, well, Scott."

"I assumed he'd be in prison by now." In fact, the truth was that Ruby hadn't thought about Scott, or Mary, or any of these people, for years.

"Surprisingly not."

"Have they arrested anyone?" Ruby wondered.

"I don't know. I saw it on the news, just now. Two bodies identified as former Missbrook Heights students. I think they're connecting them, probably because of the reunion."

Ruby didn't respond. She was thinking about home. The UK. Grey, small and so far away.

"Sorry, this is all horrible," Elizabeth added, like they'd forgotten some formalities. "What's new with you? Are you keeping busy out there? You still based in Canberra?"

"On and off." Ruby sat down on one of the canvas chairs, elbows on her knees. "Working out of the British High Commission, with the international liaison folks."

"Sounds fancy."

"It isn't."

"Do you still do murder? Not do them, you know what I mean."

"Well, it's all sorts. Broadly organised crime." She leant back, crossed her feet, swapped ears. "Though for the past few years I've been consulting, I guess you could call it that. Basically, just teaching officers some of the more nuanced, psychological stuff. And recently working on an educational thing with," Ruby looked back at the tent; Eduardo was still fast asleep in there, "rehabilitated offenders."

"You used to do profiling, though, right?"

They never used that word, but normal people did, so, "Yeah."

Behavioural investigative advisor, which was technically still Ruby's job title, doesn't sound cool, but definitely captures the lack of romance and excitement. Her role at the National Crime Agency had always been closer to maths than to drama, much to the disappointment of anyone who asked.

She could hear that Elizabeth was near a thin roof – maybe a conservatory. The patter of rain echoed from the phone's earpiece. Evening rain for her. Ruby picked up her empty, plastic cup, tilting and rolling it on the camping table.

"Where are you?" Ruby asked.

"At home. In my office. Can you hear the storm?"

"Yes."

"I think it's going to get worse."

Ruby looked across the open landscape, the rocks, the dust tracks, the monochrome light of dawn – no long shadows yet. The idea of rain seemed almost supernatural.

"I'm sitting in the middle of nowhere," Ruby said. "In the bush."

"Camping?"

"Yeah, with . . ." she turned to the tent again, "a colleague."

"Just a colleague?"

She smiled. "We'll see."

"Some great straight lines there I imagine?"

9

Ruby laughed, standing and pacing again, scuffing her shoes over pebbles. Elizabeth knew all her strange quirks. "Everywhere you turn."

Growing up on the outskirts of Missbrook Bay, Ruby and Elizabeth lived next door to one another. They used to go on these walks together. The game was to see how far you could go in a straight line. Absolutely as the crow flies. Stand in the garden, close your eyes, spin round a few times and then point.

They'd hop fences, crawl through hedgerows, even climb over buildings, crossing fields and roads and woodland, just to see where they could get before they'd have to stop or change course. They discovered that north-east was the best direction – sixteen miles. But then the tall chain-link border, razor wire and warning signs. A military base. Even as adventurous teenagers, the risk of getting shot was enough to turn them back.

Ruby worked out that if they tried again, but altered course just a few degrees, they might miss it. But, still, sixteen miles remained their actual record.

Here, though, most points on the compass could take her in a dead-straight line for, she looked around, what? As far as she could see. The outback was up there with deserts, tundra, the frozen poles or grassy plains of truly empty places. But insurmountable obstacles wouldn't be the problem. Mother Nature would kill you long before you needed to climb. All lines, especially time, must come to an end.

"Those were the days," Elizabeth said. There was a distant shriek of children's laughter in the background. Domestic sounds. Somehow nostalgic, this brief glimpse of her life. Ruby hadn't realised how much she missed her.

"How are the kids?" she asked.

"Loud." Elizabeth sighed. "Are you coming back this way any time soon?"

No. That was the honest answer. But Ruby said, "Maybe next year."

"It's great to hear your voice. Sad that it took this to reconnect us."

Ruby smiled. Is that how far she had strayed from her hometown? People literally had to die before she had a conversation with her friend. Her best friend. Ruby still thought of Elizabeth as that, despite all the callous things distance and time had done to their relationship.

"Want me to keep you posted on how it all pans out?" Elizabeth asked.

Ruby stopped pacing. Did she? There was conflict here. It was no coincidence that she was this far from Missbrook Bay. Her escape, though at the time subconscious, was by design. A huge part of her did not care about things back home. About the gossip, the pedestrian lives of people still stuck in that strange little town. But she definitely cared about Elizabeth. In fact, now she thought about it, Elizabeth was the only person there she would genuinely love to see.

"Sure," Ruby said. "Tell me everything."

And so that's what Elizabeth did. For the next three days, she and Ruby exchanged messages – only a small proportion of which were discussing the murders.

Eduardo kept asking questions but Ruby was unable to provide any answers. Though, judging from the sparse updates online, she suspected the police were not making much progress either.

Most of their communication was reminiscing about old jokes, retold stories embellished again and again. That day, that party, that trip and, oh, haha, remember when . . .

Elizabeth explained who's doing what, where and how. Auditing marriages, successes, failures, pregnancies. There were countless moments where Ruby was too busy smiling into her phone to concentrate on work. As Eduardo said, this was way more interesting.

Ruby even suggested Elizabeth and her family should come out here and visit.

You'd love it, she wrote. And she wasn't just being polite.

But that was yesterday and Elizabeth still hadn't replied. Perhaps she was thinking of a nice way to say that a thirty-hour flight with three kids might not be worth even the most overdue reunion with an old friend from school.

It was Tuesday now. She and Eduardo had just finished packing up the tent for the final time. Ruby opened the back of his van, slid a bag inside. She looked right, down the long stretch of straight road and left at their journey ahead, looking forward to getting back to civilisation. Routine. Sharp, controlled. Reinstating all of her rules.

"Ready?" Eduardo said.

"Sure—"

But, once more, voices from home found their way to her. This time, words arrived with the stern, official tones of professionality.

Calling from London, from the NCA headquarters, Deputy Director Don Larson.

He opened as he usually did, with questions about how she's getting on. Small talk on the international pilot role she'd been so keen to accept.

Then he got onto the topic of the day.

"Don't know if you've heard what's going on in Missbrook Bay?" he said.

This was unnerving. These two disparate circles – work, personal. Two sets of a Venn diagram she'd always kept apart. Coming together. Colliding. How had this gossip – premium or otherwise – found its way into his mind? This had *nothing* to do with her.

"I have."

"Local team has put in a request for assistance as it's all a bit, well, strange," Don said. "I can't think of anyone better suited."

"Than me?" Ruby laughed, holding her phone with her shoulder as she crouched down to pick up her final bag. "I can't think of anyone worse." She stood, dropped it into the back of the van. "You do know where I am, right?" She slammed the door shut, all packed up.

"Contract's due for renewal."

Ruby had been out here for more than a decade now. While it had technically been an interim position, it was on a rolling extension. In practice, it felt permanent. Especially given the new training programme she was putting together with Eduardo. She had roots here. Of course, she could be posted back to the UK. But it usually went without saying that she wouldn't be.

"And I understand that it will be renewed?" She stepped onto the empty road.

"You know the place. And all that's connecting them is the fact they went to Missbrook Heights School. All from the class of '99. That's your year, isn't it?"

"It is. I just . . ." This was an unusual feeling – a slight insecurity. The idea of going back home, working there, it made Ruby uncomfortable. She was here. Safe here, far away. "Are you asking me or . . . ?"

"I am asking you," he said, in a sincere tone. "Honestly, I'd get it. Conflicting interest – I can see how it's not appropriate. You might be rusty; it's been a while. Plus, it could all be over before you even landed."

"Then, I'm afraid, the answer is no."

"Ah, well, I'm sorry to hear that, but I appreciate you being straight with me. We'll figure something out. They've got themselves all tied in knots. The core force there, it's not exactly geared up for this kind of thing." She heard a smile in his voice. "Serial killer is quite a diversion from damaged flowerpots and graffiti on cobblestone walls, you know."

"Serial killer? Stop reading the news, Don."

"Call it what you want."

"I wouldn't call it that," Ruby said, pacing across the tarmac, back onto the dusty roadside. "I'm out of the loop, I've only spoken to a friend, but it's possible they're not even connected."

"That seems unlikely."

"I knew them. I can tell you, aside from school year, the victims . . . you couldn't find two people with *less* in common."

"*Two* people?"

And then a silence, which Ruby broke with a sigh. "There's been a third," she stated. Not a question. This was a fact.

"Yeah, late yesterday afternoon." Don cleared his throat. "Similar to the others. It's rough and, well, they have no idea."

She took a breath and heard herself say, "Who was it?"

But as Ruby asked, she felt like she already knew the answer. Hope whispered in her ear, there are at least a hundred and sixty people in her year, so it *couldn't be*. But fear replied. And her heart began to hurt, the empty anticipation of inescapable pain. Eyes stinging, she blinked. Tingling their way to the surface, tears she would not allow to fall.

"Elizabeth Gregory," he said.

Ruby nodded.

And again, she found herself staring out across that flat horizon – shimmering now in the heat, the belt of land and sky blurring, inviting. Every route from here leads back home. Back to the UK, all the way to Missbrook Bay. She could spin and spin

14

but it was inevitable. On a straight heading, like those crows, it did not matter which path she chose. Actually, no. Ruby looked down at the ground, at the dusty red earth beneath her feet. It was that direction. That was the straight line. And the entire world was standing in her way.

Chapter Two

Eyes open, precisely one minute before the alarm was due to go off. The incredible reliability of her internal clock strikes again. Though, from late-wake experience, she'd discovered it paradoxically needed the fear of sound to work – the alarm must be set – which rendered the skill largely useless. A lazy chauffeur, dutifully following the bus schedule.

She turned it off, then reached for the bottle of pills on her bedside cabinet. Every day started this way. Substances to keep her sharp – 20mg of dextroamphetamine combined with amphetamine, more commonly known by its trade name, Adderall, followed by coffee and filtered water from the fridge. Ruby was irretrievably addicted to all three and not in the order one might suspect. But never mind. This was a problem for another day.

First, she sat at her small kitchen table, opened her laptop and made sure she had all the case notes downloaded, anticipating the upcoming stretches of being offline.

And then, here it comes, the morning begins to spark. Grand thoughts fall away as focus takes the wheel. Each and every obstacle, all of today's problems, lined up, waiting in an orderly queue. Let's go.

Breakfast. Orange juice. Cold. Scrambled eggs. Warm. Shower. Hot. The roar of the hair drier. Clothes. To the bed. Suitcase bouncing on the springs. Packing. Items placed in zip-lock bags, arranged inside. Small stacks. Neat. Pleasing. Phone. Charger. Headphones. Stop for a moment, consider the window. No clouds. Pure blue. Take this image, keep it safe for later. Shoes. Sunglasses. Baseball cap. Door.

Outside into the clean, glaring light. The taxi waiting on the road. She put her suitcase in the boot herself, despite the driver swooping back to help. He held the passenger door for her. Ruby looked at her watch and climbed in. *Thud.*

Airport. Looped tarmac, a strip of grass, tall glass at the drop-off point. Planes lifting off and banking above, others falling slowly in from the other side of the sky – reflected in the glossy windows. Bright enough to sting her wide-open eyes. Pupils no doubt the size of pound coins, black holes hoovering up the sunlight.

Inside, Ruby queued for boarding, showed the attendant her pass, passport, passing her second carry-on bag to another shoulder. And then, up metal stairs, the runway's hiss lost to the wind, she was on the first of three planes. The rest of the journey was a blur. An old flicker strip of stop-motion clouds rushing past endless stretches in no man's land, eating shop-bought sandwiches, reading case notes, enduring bench naps with half an elbow or the corner of a rucksack for a pillow, waking and waiting in the unique and lonely company of a hundred fellow travellers. All their dreary-eyed solidarity, chins propped up with nothing but hope that the numbers on those screens will change any, minute, now.

Finally, she was coming down through a thick layer of grey, into the rain-dappled murk over London. Droplets shaking, crying down the side of the window as the plane landed with a bounce and a shudder. Lights came on, things were beeping and everyone was up and reaching for their bags.

A broken version of Ruby climbed into a taxi on the road outside Heathrow. She pulled back her sleeve to check her watch. Door to door, forty hours.

Leaving the airport, the taxi came off the roundabout and joined the motorway traffic. Swaying with the corners, Ruby held her phone and looked at the recent messages she and Giles had exchanged. *I'll let you know when I land*, she'd written. Sent two days ago. But it didn't feel like it. The biggest issue with all this travelling was the total shake-up of time. That dutiful ticking clock inside her was truly lost, even the threat of an air-raid siren wouldn't see a pre-emptive strike. She was on her own now. Ruby had slept briefly on the last plane – pure survival mode, short, confusing dreams. But the next stop was surely a real bed. It had to be. So, she held off on the stimulants.

And there it was, simmering away. Some feeling. Worry? Something else. Something blue. Seemed insufficient, simplistic. But it was true. Ruby felt sad. Elizabeth was dead. She chewed her thumbnail. Three people from her school year had been murdered. This was a problem. Her job was solving problems. That one's big, though, overwhelming. She breathed.

Ruby reached down, rummaged inside her bag, found the bottle. Popped the lid. She stared at the orange pill in her palm, hesitating as a voice inside asked her, quite politely, not to take it. *We need sleep. Optimal performance needs rest. Come on. Exhaustion is the most pressing problem. The others can wait.*

Can they, though? Every minute counts, right? Today is already a write-off.

But then why ruin tomorrow too?

Any addict will recognise this back and forth, this lingering sense of being on borrowed time. In her more reflective moments, she did suspect she was hurtling towards some terrible judgement day. Because she was.

That's the thing with catastrophising. That's the therapist's dirty little secret. It is not an irrational pursuit, no matter what they claim. The sense in your heart that something awful is going to happen can, should, must be disregarded to function. It's true – that thing you fear almost certainly won't happen. But something equally bad, or worse, absolutely will. Your body will stop working. Everyone you love will die. It is going to hurt.

Stupid, tired thoughts. Always death. Ruby *always* ended up thinking about death. Like Elizabeth, her friend, who was, there it is again . . . On these drugs, though, she was simply too busy for rumination. The rambling fog of sobriety has a cure. And, with a gulp, Ruby swallowed another 20mgs of it.

She looked out the window. They were sandwiched between two lorries – thundering wheels just a few feet away. And then the taxi changed lanes, slowing down for the slip road. The first sign for Missbrook Bay passing by on the left.

"Lovely part of the world," the driver said, looking back at her in the rear-view mirror.

The landscape was already changing. Trees holding strong above them, bus-shaped tunnels carved out. But every now and then, the flickering foliage opened up long enough to catch a glimpse of the sea. There was, despite the fact Ruby hated this place, an objective beauty that defied her baseless disdain.

So, she nodded. "Yeah."

"Is this a holiday, or?"

She'd already told the driver where she'd come from. But not why. "Um, business."

"You feeling it? Jetlag?"

So bad. "Not too bad," she said.

The driver fiddled with his phone, propped up on the dash-board near the wheel. "Seems the Beachside Hotel road is closed. Market day. So you might have a short walk, I'm afraid."

But different priorities now. She'd removed the option of sleep for a while. Checking her watch again, she made a new plan.

"Actually," Ruby said, "can you drop me off at Missbrook Heights? The school?"

He started tapping into his sat-nav.

Today didn't really count. The routine would start tomorrow. Clean.

They came round the final corner, at the top of the hill, the approach to Missbrook Bay she'd seen a thousand times. Misty, cold and bleak.

As the trees thin, the first thing you see is the ocean – dragging out all the way to the horizon where it joins forces with the overcast above. Sealed, like a giant room. And in this tiny, gloomy corner of it, below them now as the car came over the peak and down, the highest points of town come into view – the church spire, the square hospital on the left-hand side and then every conceivable angle of roof. Below, a warren of stone walls, narrow lanes, steep inclines, the whole place crammed in, seemingly designed to confuse. Like a claustrophobic fairground funhouse – without any of the colour, or any of the fun.

The taxi pulled up at the school just after 4pm. Ruby didn't even attempt to work out what time her body thought it might be. The time, as it always was on these drugs, was irrefutably *now*. She just paid the driver, took her bags and stood at the side gates.

Here she was again, back at school and, right on cue, the marrow in her bones felt as heavy as lead.

Tall fences either side of a short road that led up into the staff car park. The sign was new, maroon like the uniforms. A few kids were still lingering around, some in PE kits, others carrying musical instruments or oversized art folders.

Ruby did as she'd promised and phoned Giles.

"Nice journey?" he asked.

"Pure hell. I'm ruined."

He laughed. Speaking to her stepdad felt different now there was only a mile between them. She was no longer a world away.

"Kettle's always on here."

"I'll settle in and recalibrate," she said. "Probably in a couple of days – imagine I'm going to be pretty busy at the front end of all this."

"Oh, I'm sure. Let me know when you have some down time. Whenever suits."

"Will do. Speak soon."

She went straight in, across the playground, her suitcase wheels vibrating on the concrete. Past a few afterschool clubs in session – the disjointed drums and strings of a big band rehearsing in the hall, shouts echoing from the sports field over on the other side of the science block.

As she stepped into the main building, Ruby realised she probably should have called ahead. Her ID was buried deep in her suitcase and she just knew they'd want to see it. She turned into the carpeted foyer and found the front office still open, but quiet. Ruby approached the counter, parked her suitcase, peering through the sliding window. There was no one here.

Thumbing her rucksack off her aching shoulder and setting it down, she placed her hand on the visitor book. OK. She flicked back a few pages. Random people, builders, someone giving a talk, external tutors, but then, there, two days ago. Police titles next to names she didn't know. So, they'd definitely made a start here. She picked up the pen to sign herself in, tugging the string from under the book's spine, but then decided, nah, this was a waste of time.

Instead, she just grabbed her luggage and headed off inside. Her suitcase wheels smooth on the shiny corridor floor – rolling past silver lockers on her left, dark red doors dented and peppered with half-peeled stickers. It was all a bit cleaner than she remembered. New fittings. Better lights.

She wrestled her way through a pair of heavy, swinging doors, using her back. Now, turning, she was at the English department. Looking through the internal windows, she saw mostly empty classrooms, though a detention was in silent session in one at the far end. Bored, tired kids slouched, doodling, one had his head on the table, arm stretched out – plausibly asleep.

A teacher came down the corridor and smiled at her. No one cared who she was, Ruby thought, watching her approach. Schools, like hospitals, are remarkably open places. You can just walk in. Have a snoop around. She could be anyone, she could have a gun in—

Oh, no, never mind, the teacher was slowing down.

"Can I help you?" the woman asked.

"Yeah, I'm looking for—"

"Ruby Eleanor Shaw," a male voice said.

She turned to see Will, standing in the doorway behind her, wearing a pair of smart black trousers and a green shirt. Tucked in. He was holding a folder. Wow, she thought, he looked just like his dad. Staring into each other's eyes in the school corridor again. But now they were old. Now they were working.

"What's going on?" he asked, fascination in his darting eyes.

Ruby stepped towards him. Will hesitated, first going to kiss her cheek and then abandoning it for a hug. Less formal. More intimate. It lasted longer than it should have.

"I thought I'd find you here," she said, hand firmly on his back.

Realising all was in order, the other teacher disappeared.

"I don't understand." Will released his grip. "Are you . . . ?"

Somehow, she knew he was asking if she was here in an official capacity, so she nodded. "Yeah," she said. Problem number one. "I want to get a copy of our photo. Our full school year pic."

"They are . . ." Will thought for a moment. "They're all on the wall." He pointed over his shoulder. "In the staffroom. Follow me."

When they arrived, Will held the door open and, as she wheeled her suitcase inside, Ruby felt like she was somehow breaking the rules. He'd spent more years as a teacher than he ever had as a student, but she couldn't help but regress. The last time she was here, she was sixteen years old. Back then, entry to the staffroom usually required some extraordinary misdemeanour or a bizarre privilege awarded for good behaviour. A sacred place reserved for the very best and very worst students.

Behind the scenes now. The watercooler, the kettle, the sink, the cupboards each marked with a laminated paper label. That weird blend of workplace and homely comforts – domestic appliances, personalised mugs. The world's best mum worked here. A toaster. Passive-aggressive notes pinned at various spots. Teaspoons *do* belong in the teaspoon drawer

The year 11 photos, dating back to the 1980s, were displayed chronologically on the wall at the back of the staffroom. Nearby, a similar series exhibited past headteachers – these went back to the 1960s – black and white, retro collars, big glasses, questionable haircuts.

Ruby found their full-size photo at chest height on the bricks. The class of '99. Will took it down off the wall, folded the back of the wooden frame away and slid it out. He left Ruby alone and went to the photography suite. The three low coffee tables had been freshly wiped – smelled of lemon and bleach. Ruby sat down at the closest one and waited.

Returning, Will presented her with three double-size colour copies of the photo rolled up into tubes. They spread one of them out on the table, pinning the corners with a few mugs like a treasure map.

"Look at us," he said, smiling as he sat down next to her, peering into the picture. "Reckon you could still name them all?"

Ruby nodded, shuffled forwards on the red foam chair. "First names, probably."

Her eyes were drawn to herself, just left of centre. Sweet sixteen, her well-rehearsed smile, hair in a ponytail, school blazer, tie. Hands clasped at her waist. Just a child. You have no idea who you are, she thought to herself. Then wondered if she'd think the same another twenty years from now. Physically, nothing much had changed. Ruby still wore her hair tied back like that, darker now, dyed a close fit to her natural colour, which was apparently, according to the manufacturers, intense urban chestnut. Brown would do, though, if she was reporting this girl for a crime. Those cherub cheeks were gone, her face was a bit longer, skin creased with half-remembered frowns, few smiles here and there. But other than that, she looked the same. Yes, officer, that one, just older. And tired.

She saw Elizabeth on the left-hand side of the same row, two spaces away. Will must have seen her gaze stop, because he let out a sympathetic sigh.

"I'm sorry."

"Yeah, sad," she said, still concentrating on the faces. She turned to him. "Do you have a pen? Ideally red."

Will stared, seemed to carefully consider his next words. "Are you OK?"

"Uh, yeah, you?"

"Just, Elizabeth and you were close. You seem . . ."

"Fine? What do you want me to say? Yes, it hurts." She shrugged. "It's horrible and tragic and it causes me physical pain, but I don't see how exhibiting that feeling is going to help matters."

His arm was behind, awkwardly, like he had considered putting it round her but then changed his mind at the last moment. Instead, he brought it forwards and placed a hand on her knee.

"Seriously, don't worry," Ruby said, patting his fingers. "It's cool. Relax."

She leant down into the photo again.

"Look at Little Adam," she said.

Adam Ward was sitting on the bottom row, pulling a ridiculous face – eyes crossed, tongue pressed into his lip. Slipped under the radar, immortalised mischief from the closest thing they had to a class clown.

"He was a little weirdo, wasn't he?" Will said. "Funny, though."

"Offbeat."

"Very."

Leaning across to another table, he grabbed a red pen from a pot.

"So, go on," Ruby said, taking it, removing the lid. "Fill me in. Who's dead?"

"Well, obviously—"

"Aside from Mary, Scott and Elizabeth."

"Let's see." He sat back down, started pointing. "Tim and John. Both car crashes."

They were on the top row. Ruby drew red crosses over each of their faces. Below them, she saw Carly Brown.

"Carly," she said, marking her face too. "What was that?"

"A rare brain thing. Genetic. Killed her mum too."

"Jeremy and Elisa," Ruby added, tongue between her teeth as she drew two more crosses.

How could they forget – these were, until recently, the most exotic deaths. That plane crash was the talk of the town. Two local families among the hundred or so passengers slammed into the hard earth and turned to dust.

Will surveyed the photo. "I think that's it. There's just— Oh, no. And big Sam."

This one was news to her.

"Last Christmas," Will explained. "Drink and drugs. Misadventure. I don't think he was ever OK."

Ruby marked him as well.

"So, let's park the murders," she said. "We have a hundred and sixty students, all thirty-six to thirty-seven years old." She nodded at the freshly annotated picture. "And *six* of them are dead. That's bad going, right? Statistically?"

This was an unusual and morbid thought. Ruby wondered what age you had to reach before death became the norm in your peer group. When the living are a minority.

Will shook his head. "I don't know." He got his phone out and googled, *Odds of being dead at any given age.*

The website had graphs, lines, numbers. A complicated diagram with causes broken down, each shown as different colours. Heart disease had a strong lead, but appeared to be falling into second place in recent years. Dementia was roaring ahead in some demographics, leaving cancer in its wake. We're living longer – that was the explanation given. And suicide was still doing well in younger groups. An ironic quirk of the first world – the ride's never been smoother, and yet we can't wait to get off. If you're a *man* under forty-five, the biggest risk is your own mind, your own hands. It was no surprise to see murder was rare. Violent ends so unlikely they didn't even have their own colour. All covered in a grey section marked "other".

"OK," Will said. "The maths is a bit tricky but, yeah, dividing it as a percentage – let's pretend we had a hundred students . . . seems about right. Maybe slightly high, plane crash is an anomaly, I guess. Though, look how steep it gets over the coming decades."

The age line swept up at the end – the inevitability of it all. Literally vertical.

"Not long, hey." Ruby waved the pen over the photo. "This little red cross is going to get us all."

Will let out a short humming sound, still looking at the figures. "Yep."

"How about staff?" she asked.

"Oh." Will put his phone away, speaking as though this was an easy question – some of these people had been both his teachers and his colleagues. "Mr Jones, Mrs Hunter." He pointed. "Bobby – Mr Parks. The rest are still going strong as far as I know."

Ruby marked the short row of faculty sitting at the bottom of the photo. Took a real chunk out of them.

"How on earth is Mrs Spall still alive?" Ruby said. "Genuine witch? Looks about a hundred here."

"Cigarettes and adultery?"

Ruby drew a line from Mrs Spall across to PE teacher Mr Lamar. Then she wrote *Notorious swingers* beneath, which made Will laugh out loud.

Funny how persistent these silly rumours are – still common knowledge twenty years later. Same too with knowing these people by their formal titles. Ruby would still feel compelled to call their headteacher "sir" if he walked in right now.

"So, let's go," she said, "who's your money on?"

"For what?"

Ruby looked at him and frowned. "The killer."

"Oh." He laughed again, somehow disbelieving her tone. Even Ruby was surprised how free, how childish she felt around him. She stared into his brown eyes – almost black. Despite the creases, the stubble, the hairline creeping back, dark and speckled with grey, he was still Will. She was still Ruby. They were both just kids. "Well," he said, turning his hand over. "If you'd asked me to bet on who's most likely to become a murderer, I'd have said . . ."

His finger landed on Scott's face.

"Same," Ruby agreed, wide-eyed. "However . . ."

27

She crossed him out – bigger, thicker, bolder lines for murder. Victim number two. Then, two places to the right, she put an X over Elizabeth's face. Victim number three. There was a silence and Will seemed to shrink back into himself. Sorry. Mournful. Treating this seriously once again.

"She was so happy," he said. "It's just . . . it's bad, isn't it?"

"Yes, Will, murder is bad."

But then he changed gears and smiled.

"Or, of course, Mr Phillips," he said. As though, all jokes aside, Mr Phillips was easily capable of killing someone.

"Yeah, what a nasty piece of work." Ruby looked at him sitting there in his grey suit, mean eyebrows – even a dated film photo like this couldn't hide it. Souls that dark shine through. "But I'm guessing he's . . . what?"

"Old as fuck."

"Got to be eighty-something, right?"

"Easily."

"I have a sneaking suspicion this isn't going to be as simple as a hunch," Ruby said.

"Have you got any?"

She sighed. "Probably someone local, someone who attended the reunion. Probably our year, so they're in this photo. Someone who knew the victims in some capacity. Obviously, a man."

"Whoa." Will pretended to be offended.

"Don't worry, you guys can still run faster."

"I'm almost certain you can run faster than me. I get out of breath eating nowadays."

"Oh, without a doubt," Ruby said, looking him up and down from the corner of her eye. "But this isn't about individuals."

"I have my trainers in my car. We can go to the track right now."

"It's about groups," she explained, thinking out loud. "It's probability. At the extremes, men are just over-represented . . . Violence is just more your thing."

"Suspicious." Will squinted. "Definitely not a woman, you say?"

"Not definitely, *probably*."

"Maybe it's an outsider? Someone who's returned. Maybe she's always hated this school, this town."

"Good," Ruby said, as though he was right to be openminded. "But I landed this afternoon. My alibi is gold-standard." She paused, added, "Maybe it's *you*."

"Yeah." Will tilted his head. "I'm ticking most of your boxes. But no motive?"

"Aside from luring me back? And, hey, look, it worked. I came straight here."

There was an odd silence, like maybe Ruby had struck a chord. Gone a bit too dark with the jokes. Was this it? Was *this* crossing the line? Making fun of their past?

"Honestly, Ruby, there was a time when I would have killed for you," he said. "But those days are long gone."

"I'm putting you down as a maybe." Ruby drew a question mark above his head.

Will considered her suitcase on the carpet the other side of the table. "Are you staying at your dad's?"

"Absolutely not."

"Why? I'm sure he'd love to see you."

"I'm sure he would too. But I need . . . I have to be professional, detached. Focused. I don't want to get into all that."

"All what?"

It was uncomfortable enough working in this town, but staying with Giles would add an extra layer of pressure and scrutiny that Ruby didn't need. "Just don't want him breathing down my neck."

"Where then?"

"Beachside."

"You came straight from the airport?"

She looked at him, looked to the luggage, back to him. "You're wasted here." She pointed with her pen – her little red wand of death. "We could use a mind like that around the office."

"Aren't you tired?"

"I'm not even sure what I am."

"You can stay at my place if you want."

She held the pen like a cigarette, twirled it. "That might be awkward?"

"The hotel is not quite what it used to be."

"I mean, it's never been nice."

"It's much worse now."

Will knew that absolute silence and total darkness were required for Ruby to achieve any measure of sleep.

"I've got my earplugs."

"Offer stands."

"But I'd accept a lift, don't fancy walking down there with all this."

She looked out the staffroom window, into the courtyard – the pond, the tarmac paths snaking their way towards classrooms on the other side. Birds sang, but sunshine melodies were rare – it was crows and gulls round here. Gothic shrieks, seaside gloom.

Ruby leant back over the photo, adding the final cross to Mary's face.

"Huh," Will said. "Look at that . . ."

And she realised what he had seen.

The victims were all on the second row from the top, Mary, on the far left, then Scott and then Elizabeth. Three red crosses. Arranged in order of their demise, every other person along that line.

"Seems a bit arbitrary, for a pattern," Will said. "Could be a coincidence, right?"

"Let's hope so," Ruby added, counting along the row.

If this was the sequence, if it was every other student, Gavin Monroe would be victim number four. And two spaces to the right would be victim number five. Ruby Shaw.

She stared into her own teenage eyes again.

Maybe there was no method, no meaning. Or maybe they were all a target, every single person in this picture. Either way, she had a strange feeling. A rare feeling. Only for a moment, but it was definitely there.

Placing the pen carefully on the table, Ruby sat up straight, surprised at the thought. Of all the things she expected to feel during this trip – anxiety, grief, nostalgia, dread, exhaustion – she genuinely hadn't seen this one coming. True fear. The unmistakable sense that she might be in danger.

Chapter Three

Will dropped Ruby off at the top of the Beachside Hotel road a little after 6pm. She checked in and found her room on the third floor. The hallway was narrow, warped floorboards felt thin beneath the frayed carpet. Inside. Lights on. Sea view. Old window frame, thick with coats on coats of white paint, metal handle flecked with rust. Cold, thin glass – clearly the kind of window that does not open.

Ahead of her, the ocean, fading back to mist where gulls and shadows hovered in the wind. Missbrook Bay had a population of around twenty thousand people but, in this dusk chill, she could only see three on the flat beach below.

The coastline curved and disappeared off to her left, where the town's postcard beauty remained a well-kept secret. A smudge in the fog for the old lighthouse, the pier a streak of watercolour black dashed out with a fast hand towards the invisible horizon.

Turning back to the room, Ruby threw her suitcase onto the firm bed. She was probably still forty-eight hours away from optimal performance but decided to at least try and read the latest batch of case notes. There was a small desk in the corner, where she sat and, elbows on the wood, stared into her phone.

Detective Inspector Jay Simmons, another familiar face from the past, had been bombarding her with files over the last few days.

His name now dominated a full screen of her inbox. The most recent message had an attachment called "Head trauma analysis".

Trust you had a nice flight, briefing at 10am, he wrote at the foot of the email.

But her vision, blurred and swimming, kept splitting the screen in two. It took three strained attempts to get Jay's words into her mind. She opened the file and began to read. Time continued to misbehave, teaming up with her slipping memory to land her, somehow, in the 9pm glow of the desk lamp. She'd been reading this whole time and quite simply could not remember any of it.

No more, she thought, rising to her feet and kicking off her shoes. She went into the pitch-black bathroom. Click. With three desperate flickers, light appeared. Old Victorian-style toilet with a chain flush. And a small bath. But there was a limescale watermark and – she leant down – what was that! Grit of some kind. Bits of bugs. Wings and legs.

A shower, then. The tap squeaked and the plumbing shuddered a drumroll for the initial flurry of near-boiling water, which, within seconds, sputtered and ran cold. But Ruby was too tired to care.

That's it, enough was enough. Now clean, dry, she got into bed. Earplugs in, eyes well covered, she put her head on the pillow and pulled her knees up high. But her mind droned on in the dark and foetal silence. Too wired to sleep, too tired to keep this endless day alive for even a moment longer. She'd done this to herself – why did she take that pill in the taxi? It was too late in the day and she knew it.

Though, even at the best of times, sleep was a precarious commodity. The one aspect of life that can't be conquered with effort. How cruel, she thought, that the most desirable thing exists utterly outside of her control. Worse than that, relaxation rejects endeavour. The harder she tries, the more she fails. The more she fails, the harder she tries. And on she goes into the night.

She kept thinking about all those people from the school year photo. But more than any, she thought about herself. Standing there in the middle, on the left, all those teenage insecurities she'd tried to hide.

These uniformed children were adults now. Married. Kids. Careers. But still, those red Xs mounting up, scattershot over the coming decades – it'd be a neat crosshatch pattern before too long. That little red cross is going to get us all, she thought, echoing her own words as her mind's favourite topic took hold yet again.

And out there in all this death and shame, the seagulls circled, hours passed and, somehow, it was suddenly loud. Her internal clock had dropped the ball. The morning alarm was like a siren, guttural and deep under the pillow – a movie trailer foghorn announcing that the day is ready. Wake. The. Hell. Up. So she did.

Day one. Morning routine. Horrifying buffet breakfast in the hotel's sprawling, soulless restaurant. Haunted eyes of elderly staff who looked both alarmed and grateful to have guests.

Outside. Fresh light. Fog gone. Gulls. The sun adding a glow to half of the overcast sky. Huge beach puddles on the flat sand, so still, perfect reflections indistinguishable from the clouds above. Like portals down into the earth. And she walked along the pavement, the seawall rails. Turned left, across the road. And up. Always up. Her thighs soon aching. They used to joke that, no matter which way you were going, every route in Missbrook Bay would take you up a hill.

Half a mile later and she was turning into the car park at the side of the police station. Or, rather, the office that remained. The reception was long gone. Budget cuts had closed the door to members of the public years ago.

It was an old building. Taller than it needed to be. Lichen on every brick, crumbling moss between. Overgrown plant life on the back walls, thick ivy hanging down to crawl – like some ancient ruin. Tree roots bulged beneath paving slabs at the front, nature shrugging the town off its back, reclaiming what we stole.

Ruby had arrived fifteen minutes early. She typed the code into the side door, which beeped and clunked open. She was simply never late for anything. So, as she went in through the corridor, she was annoyed to hear Jay's voice coming from the briefing room. He'd already started. Had she misremembered the time? Was her memory failing her right out of the gates? These concerns disappeared when she checked the email. Instant vindication – 10am. Her phone had even added it to the calendar automatically.

The door was propped open, so she slipped in and stood against the wall. Jay, mid-sentence, gave her a quick nod and an expression that could have meant, "Oh, shit, yeah, I told you 10am, sorry about that." But she was probably reading too much into it. Especially as she knew Jay well enough to bet that he *wasn't* sorry.

There was a long table, with ten or so detectives sitting around it. White shirts, lanyards hanging from their necks. Between them, coffee mugs, watercooler cups, paper and folders strewn across the pale wooden surface. She vaguely recognised a few of the officers. Though, like everyone in this town, there was always a glimmer of familiarity.

"—Missbrook Heights alums," Jay was saying, in his low monotone voice. "And all attended the recent reunion." He was sitting at the head of the table, a laptop in front of him, the screen beamed up onto the wall for all to see. "As are some of us." He made brief eye contact with Ruby again. "Inquiries at the school are ongoing but there is still plenty more to be done."

The screen behind him changed. A close-up photograph of what looked like blue string. But, zoomed in, the tiny fibres were as thick as rope.

"Forensically, we have been running a bit thin on the ground," he said. "However, we have now firmed up the clothing fibres, which you can see here. These appear not to belong to the victims or, it seems, their close relatives. As long as that remains the case, it's reasonably safe to assume a dark-blue jacket is all we've really got." Jay still spoke like a robot, no intonation, no up and down – just a constant flow of words, like he was reading from an autocue. "Fibres were found near Scott Hopkins' and Elizabeth Gregory's bodies, though no similar trace on Mary Talbot. Nevertheless, we are proceeding as though they're connected."

The recap that followed seemed to be for Ruby's benefit. Or maybe other people at this table were also fresh. Either way, she listened intently, even though she knew this story well.

It went like this. Thirty-six-year-old Mary Talbot was walking home across the Sammer's Lodge park grounds on the night of the Missbrook Heights class of '99 school reunion. She was approached, most likely from behind, and was struck eight times with a blunt instrument. Her death occurred around 1am with an elderly hiker discovering her body five and a half hours later.

Four days passed and then almost precisely the same thing happened to Scott Hopkins. Out near his family's farmhouse, he was alone, walking at least three dogs. Again, the attack appeared to come from behind. Which meant either he did not see the assailant or, more likely as it was still daylight, he trusted them enough to turn his back. He too was hit in the head, though how many times remained a mystery. The damage was described in the notes as "catastrophic and comprehensive", which, while unusually descriptive for a coroner, painted an adequate picture.

Elizabeth, the third victim, was jogging through the woods just five hundred metres from her home and, unfortunately, wasn't killed quite as efficiently as the other two. There was evidence of a struggle. At any rate, something blunt. Something fast.

Despite what may well have been noisy encounters, there were no witnesses, no suggestion of sadism, nothing sexual and no obvious evidence had been left behind. Which meant whoever did it wanted them dead as quickly and as discreetly as possible.

A new slide appeared. A photograph of Elizabeth, lying face down on the woodland floor, in the mulch and twigs, leaves clinging to her scuffed, muddied clothes. Black leggings, white trainers, a fluorescent pink gym top – dressed for her evening run. The wire from her headphones snaking off into the undergrowth.

"Interestingly," Jay said, "the head injuries are consistent across all three. However, it appears going from the overview that some of the damage to Elizabeth Gregory's skull was inflicted posthumously. This, I'm sure I don't have to tell you, is strange. Sufficient time had elapsed after the first few strikes, which were to the face and neck, and appear to be the primary cause of death. It seems the perpetrator waited, turned her over, and then struck her repeatedly. Perhaps they hadn't realised she was dead? Perhaps they had second thoughts? Either way, it seems that the ferocity came a little later. Hesitance would be consistent with the idea that the suspect knew these people well."

Ruby looked at the photograph, at poor Elizabeth on the ground. Then she pictured someone smashing the back of her skull with a blunt object. A hammer? Caved in like a coconut. Blood streaming off over their shoulder on the backswing. It had speckled all the way up to the tree branches above. Bad, hey, she thought. Emotionally, though, Ruby felt nothing. Less than numb. This information was simply part of a larger problem that she had to solve. The most efficient thing now would be to listen, absorb the details and set aside any negative emotions associated with her friend's death. Gentle, kind, loving Elizabeth. *Thud, thud, thud.*

It was hard enough with strangers, but this? Ruby did wonder whether she would be able to navigate such vivid imagery with a sober mind. Or would those rambling thoughts take hold and drag her down into some panicky place filled with all the horror any rational person should feel? Probably.

Good job she was absolutely wired, then. Very much online, despite the jetlag, which lingered somewhere behind her wide, stinging eyes.

"In other recent developments," Jay gestured towards Ruby, "the NCA has been kind enough to lend us one of its best and I'm sure Ruby's unique insight on this will be welcomed around the table. We'd love some behavioural science advice. Big-picture stuff."

She stepped forwards, notepad clutched to her chest, and sat down at one of the empty chairs, between two older male officers. After an awkward introduction, with a few polite waves and smiles, she looked around the room.

There was a long pause. And Ruby realised that all eyes were on her. As though she was going to provide a well-rehearsed speech about the offender. What kind of person they are. What gets them off. The type of creatures they probably hurt when they were young.

But, having read through every single piece of evidence, made reams of notes and speculated for days, she had found no answers. Nothing aside from the obvious conclusions they'd no doubt spotted themselves. The perpetrator was violent, the kind of person capable of smashing three human skulls in a series of evidently premeditated attacks. But this was not exactly news.

So, she just slowly shook her head. She wanted them to understand that she really didn't have anything extra to add. Not yet. There was nothing firm enough to be any more than good old-fashioned conjecture.

"I have no idea," Ruby said, eyes on her notepad in front of her. She looked up, around the room again. "It would be difficult to overstate how unusual this is." Another silence, they wanted her to at least have a go. "But . . ." she took a breath, "if I were to bet, then . . ."

She echoed what she'd shared with Will – the basics. Someone local, someone who attended the reunion, someone who appears to be both lucky and alarmingly competent, judging by the lack of evidence and eyewitnesses.

Jay clicked the mouse and now the full school year photo she'd emailed him last night was glowing on the screen above his head. Though this version did not include Ruby's red crosses.

"So," Jay said. "The class of '99." His eyes always half-dipped like he didn't have the energy to care. "Thanks to our collective knowledge of offender behaviour, the many decades of experience we have in this very room, we have narrowed it down to one hundred and sixty people."

There were a few smiles – this was said in jest, an amicable jab. If anything, it seemed to be camaraderie; Jay was relieved that Ruby had reached the same empty conclusions as them. They really hadn't missed anything. At least, nothing obvious to her.

She knew it wouldn't help the situation much, but still felt compelled to add, "No. Nine of the students in the photograph are dead, including the three victims. A further three members of staff are also deceased. There are approximately twenty others we can firmly rule out. Some who live abroad, for example."

"So, one hundred and, say, thirty?" Jay asked. "That's a lot of work. Any other patterns or theories? No judgement, go wild."

"I was thinking," another voice, "Mary, Elizabeth. Names of queens."

The officer opposite Ruby snorted, a stifled laugh that ironically sounded deliberate.

"Queen Scott?" Jay shook his head.

"Mary, Queen of Scots?" someone else suggested.

"What the *fuck* are you talking about?" Jay said. "This is embarrassing."

"Sounds like judgement."

39

Enough, Ruby thought. Business. "If I had to pick a priority, it would be anyone with a history of violence from that school year, which could get us a viable shortlist."

"How short?" Jay wondered.

Ruby checked her notes, read out a few names. Among them was Frank Enfield. She made a point of pronouncing his full name. Frank Enfield, or Frankenfield, as he was known at school, was Scott's best friend. And, although he lacked the intelligence, Frank was equally unpleasant.

She could tell that some of the detectives had heard of these people. Particularly Frank.

But, "Listen," Jay added, "not everyone here has the benefit of attending the school, can we . . ." he drew a few circles with his hand in the air, "simplify the name situation."

"Yeah." A younger officer opposite nodded, pen in hand, notebook out. "I'm losing track."

"Sure," Ruby said. "Speak to Gavin Monroe."

"He wasn't on your first list." Jay frowned.

Ruby sighed. She felt slightly uncomfortable with this. For her, motive mattered more than almost any other consideration. What, when, where and how are usually clear from the outset. The question mark hangs over who. But that often falls into place if you can just crack why. Even when the job is done, it's always enlightening to know. Allowing people to explain themselves in their own words is invaluable. Justice is not satisfying if you don't understand reason. Something all too often left out of crime and media reports.

The question, "Yes, but why?" should follow any guilty plea.

And this was why the idea that someone would kill fellow classmates based on something as arbitrary, to coin Will's phrase, as every other person in a line of their school year photograph seemed . . . well . . . ludicrous.

Still . . . "If we look at the photograph," Ruby said, turning in her chair. All eyes followed hers to the screen. "The three victims are positioned on the same row, in the order of their deaths."

"Oh yeah," Jay said, frowning into his laptop. "So they are. Every other person."

"If this is an explanation," Ruby added, holding up a tentative hand, suggesting a pinch of salt, "then Gavin Monroe would be next."

"And after that?" Jay said to himself, squinting and then leaning back, slight surprise in his eyes. "Well, if I'm not mistaken," he dragged out a square with the mouse pointer, framing Ruby's face in the photo, "this young lady is you." And he looked up over his laptop, across the table, making eye contact with her again.

"Yep." Ruby nodded. "There I am."

The female officer opposite shuffled in her seat. "Why are you so sure it's someone from this year, someone in the photograph?" she asked.

"I'm not." Ruby sighed. "I'm not sure of anything."

"Enlightening," Jay said. "Anything else?"

"The only other thing I would say is that given the nature of Missbrook Bay and the school itself, it would be wise to keep your ears open to rumours. These victims are connected in some critical way we haven't seen yet. People like to talk. Let them."

Jay wrapped things up, allocating some tasks across the table. Then people started gathering their things, closing folders, laying pens flat on the table, putting phones into pockets as small talk broke out either side of her. They all seemed to know each other. But Ruby, as always, stood alone and felt like an outsider. Like she did not belong.

"Ruby, hey, hi," a man said from behind. She turned. "I'm Ian, from the press office."

He was standing slightly too close to her; she stepped back, slid her chair under the table.

"Hello." They shook hands.

He was young, mid-twenties, dressed in dark chinos and a short-sleeved shirt, a little more casual than others in the room.

"Can I grab a quick picture of you?" He held his phone, landscape, index finger ready to start snapping. "We're putting together a press release, want to highlight the NCA's involvement."

"Why?" Ruby asked, following Ian towards the wall.

"There's an impression that the lack of progress is because we're not taking it seriously."

"Is that the reason?" Ruby smiled. "As opposed to?"

"Incompetence," Jay called out, standing now at the head of the table, placing paper in a folder.

"No, no," Ian said, waving his hand and looking at Ruby again for a third, stern, "No."

His job was, of course, public relations, which almost always boiled down to giving the impression the police were doing their best and were worth every penny of taxpayer money or, ideally, more.

"It's just to keep things ticking over," Ian added. "Getting national interest now." He winced. "We just need to engage a little bit. Investigation ongoing, witnesses welcome. You know the kind of thing."

"OK, sure." Ruby stood against the white wall, holding her notepad and a neutral expression – the professional, objective arrangement of facial muscles she'd chosen years earlier. Now was not the time to show teeth.

Ian took a few pictures. "I'll email it over shortly," he said, swiping to check he'd got a good one. "Maybe you could tag on a quote?"

"Why don't you write what you think I'm going to say, and I'll let you know how close you get?"

Ian laughed. "Good idea."

Once the room had cleared, Jay approached and gave Ruby a more formal welcome.

"I realised I mixed up the timings," he added.

Ruby noted that he hadn't apologised. But, still, "I forgive you."

"Here's a swipe card for the door." He handed her a laminated piece of plastic. "Your details are already on it."

Ruby pocketed the ID card.

"Got a workstation set aside through there," he said, pointing towards the main office. "Should have everything you need. Excuse the mess, we're winding it all down, building's closing later this month. Leaves us two weeks. Plenty of time, right?"

Police forces selling off their estates was not exactly a new concept, but Ruby was still surprised to hear this place would remain the base of operations. Given the farcical theme of that briefing, fourteen days seemed an ambitious timeline.

The desk, directly opposite Jay's, was obviously a temporary measure, cleared for the occasion. Old boxes and clutter piled up either side. The surreal and eclectic items that inexplicably appear in the untouched corners of any office space: a single shoe, a coat hanger, a peacock feather, a Christmas biscuit tin full of spent printer cartridges and all the dust and crumbs between.

Ruby sat down and plugged in her laptop. Then she poured herself a cup of ice-cold water from the glugging cooler, which she could reach without standing up, and took her second dose of Adderall.

Headphones in, notebook ready, she spent the afternoon listening – *really listening* – to interview recordings. The old hiker who found Mary, the tree warden who followed Scott's barking dog back to the scene and, finally, the three teenage girls who saw Elizabeth's "red hair" catching the evening light through the twigs of a fallen tree.

When she heard this her hand froze, the pen stuck on the first letter of "red". It was 7pm and she was beginning to feel a little more than she'd like. Her sigh came out high-pitched, like a half-hidden whimper. She cleared her throat and exhaled, stayed composed. Focused. But focused now on the fact Elizabeth had *blonde* hair. What they had seen was blood. The last pill was waning, though, despite her temptation, it was too late to take another. Ruby was back to the routine and she would stick to it. Discipline and structure lead to optimal performance. Even when the world starts to hurt. Or perhaps, she thought, especially.

Ruby checked her watch. It was time to relocate.

Exercise was the next essential activity on her checklist. Like sleep, and to a lesser extent food, exercise was rarely worth skipping in lieu of more hard work.

So, Ruby decided to take the long way back to the hotel. She packed her things, pulled her coat tight, flipped her hood up and left the station building.

The road outside was empty, the tarmac black and wet with streetlight streamers stretched long into the ground like plumes of fire from rockets. But, right at the end of the street, a single car was parked up, as though waiting. The driver's head was less than a shadow. A featureless shape hidden beneath the urban amber haze.

Ruby turned away from it and began to walk, looking back over her shoulder when she heard the engine start. The black car approached from behind, slowly at first, but then picked up speed, the gears shifting, exhaust booming as it revved and passed fast enough to graze her jacket with warm wind and fear. She felt the same with passing trains. There was always a part of her imagination ready to envisage what impact might look like.

Does everyone do this? she wondered. Are all minds afflicted by sudden jolts of the very worst-case scenarios? Obviously, she wasn't going to jump in front of a train, or a car, or off a cliff, but for some reason she often imagined what would happen if she did. The damage would be catastrophic. Comprehensive.

Down and down the hill, Ruby walked the full length of the curved coastline. From the old navy dockyard, along the low cliffs with their narrow zig-zag paths that veer off the main streets and disappear below. The rocks, the waves splashing down there in the dark.

Back on the seafront road, past the benches and the fixed pay-to-use telescopes, which all seemed to be looking as high into the night sky as their rusted hinges allowed. They weren't interested in the silent ships floating out in the black horizon, or in the white dots on the protruding cliff that hovered like low-hanging stars.

Past the amusements now, the arcade machines, bright lights around the sign like a Hollywood starlet's make-up mirror – gold and radiant. Mad, looping music – frenzied horse race commentary in a jostling chorus with electric coin-fall sounds. All this dazzle, all this electricity, but not a single customer in sight.

Insanely, this was the setting of her first kiss. Ruby and Will, hand in hand, crossing that unchanged bingo hall carpet and stopping at the pick-n-mix machine.

"You do the grab button, I'll do the directions," Will had said.

Now, more than twenty years on, Ruby stood and looked through the wide-open doors. She imagined two fourteen-year-old kids, small cups of coins clutched to their chests, butterflies busy in their flat, young stomachs. About to win some sweets. About to celebrate with a sudden, awkward kiss that seemed to surprise them both.

But something dragged her from the memory. A reflection, shifting and glistening in the angled window. That black car. The same black car she saw earlier. Making a special effort not to look directly at it, Ruby turned away from the amusements and carried on down the pavement.

At first, she'd thought the sense that she was being watched was just small-town paranoia or the baseline anxiety of any evening walk. But now she was sure. That car was following her.

She carried on towards the Beachside Hotel, just a hundred metres ahead on the right. The car crawled behind, on her left, picking up speed as though the driver knew she'd seen. As it passed, she clocked the number plate, repeating it in her mind as it took a corner and disappeared into the night.

Ruby stopped, stepped sideways into a doorway. Quickly, quick. Phone out, she went straight to the note app.

G, she typed, *U*. Then she tensed her jaw and looked back up the road, her hands juddering. Shit. She couldn't remember the next number. It had been less than ten seconds and it was fading, dissolving, almost as good as gone. She was fifty percent sure it was a zero; she typed it in. But doubt about the rest grew exponentially. Sixes could be nines. Any rhyme might switch "P" with "C". Phonetics, shape, similarities, even differences distorted each failed attempt at recollection.

Within the next minute, the number plate was effectively blank. As though she hadn't even seen it. Worse. A random guess, uncontaminated by bias, would now be a safer bet.

Behind her, the bright yellow light glowed on the pavement, the arcade music repeating and repeating and singing to the sea. She could remember the t-shirt Will was wearing, she could taste the sticky sweets they'd won, smell the copper coins in their cups. She could feel those butterflies swimming, see herself, eyes closed, arms at her sides – head up and fists balled for their kiss. The kiss, like a movie, the camera swooping round them, full circle – the lens flaring at the sunny window and round and stopping, zooming, close-up as they both opened their glassy eyes and smiled. She could remember all of that.

But she couldn't remember a fucking number plate she'd seen just seconds ago. A car. First letter was better than nothing. A car was following her. She'd have to describe it. She hadn't seen the driver, she hadn't even tried. Just the car. The car. She'd describe the car. She'd say—

And Ruby scrunched her eyes shut, pushed a tensed fist into one and groaned. Was it even black?

Chapter Four

Walking up to her room, Ruby composed herself and stomached the anger. The ongoing concerns with her memory had been easy to dismiss because, until recently, they hadn't affected her work. Jetlag would have to carry the burden of blame – Ruby couldn't let this issue and its justifiable anxiety derail her attention. Rationality now. Why would a car follow her? Who would be driving? What do they want? Presumably they were hoping to see where she was staying. It was logical then to assume they knew it was here, at the Beachside Hotel.

She dropped her rucksack on the bed, stepped to the window and peered down, moving the thin curtain aside, leaning round to check. The street was empty, bar a couple sitting on a bench and a few kids standing in a circle on the beach.

It didn't make sense. She'd only been here for a day. How would—

Looking back into the room, Ruby got her phone out and checked the news. She paced. The words "Missbrook Bay" in a headline. She clicked. Then, once more, she was looking at a photograph of herself. Maybe it was the neutral expression, or the lighting, either way Ruby realised she'd been unduly optimistic yesterday. This woman did not look just like that teenage girl smiling in her uniform. The story had been online for six hours and most national outlets had something on it. But the gist was the same as Ian's press release. Some sites were running his words verbatim.

Scrolling down, scanning quickly, she found her name.

"Ruby Shaw, from the NCA's Major Crime Investigative Support unit, is assisting local officers investigating the recent murders.

"A former Missbrook Heights pupil herself, behavioural investigative advisor Ms Shaw added: 'These are shocking crimes and we are committed to seeking justice for the victims.'"

Empty, formulaic words. Exactly the kind of thing she would be expected to say – Ian had nailed the quote.

But six hours was enough time for someone to see it and take a keen interest. So, just as she'd feared, or perhaps hoped, this story was all about her.

Ruby sat down at the small desk in the corner of her room and opened her notebook. Longhand notes were slow by design – a meditative way to process information. This gave her subconscious time to assemble foundations. Scaffolding. Because ideas need a firm base if they stand any chance of housing the truth.

Her strict 8pm limit on liquid had passed thirty minutes ago, but there was no denying it – she was thirsty. Fatigue interfering with every bodily process. Sleep would be impaired by dehydration as much as a full bladder, so she had half a glass of water. Even the small rule breaches were frustrating. Tomorrow the jetlag would improve. So would her memory. Or maybe it wouldn't. If only she could forget to worry about it.

Distraction was another unpleasant side-effect of the evening fade, as her blood dutifully cleared the chemicals away. Those children on the beach. Teenagers. Ruby could hear them laughing, tinny music from a portable speaker. Back in her day, under the old lighthouse was the place to go. Somewhere kids could huddle together, drink cheap cider and smoke hash through weird homemade contraptions. The lighthouse was the backdrop to all the best stories, from famous fights to fabled fingerings, from infidelity to criminality and every teenage misadventure beyond.

Even with her earphones in, Ruby could follow their drunken conversation. But now the rowdy little bastards were yelling and – *come on* – singing right outside her window.

Another irritating issue was the dripping sound. It was above – a pipe somewhere was leaking. In a way, it was more annoying than the kids. They'd go home eventually. But this? It seemed here to stay. If anything, it was getting worse. A constant drip, drip, drip and—

Wait. Ruby winced, tilted her head and slowly removed her earphones. Then she looked over her shoulder, turning in the chair, standing now. The ceiling was stained. And she spotted a drop of water – a little silver gem – as it fell straight down into the centre of her bed. She touched the covers. Not damp. They were wet. A literal puddle on the mattress.

And, as though they knew, a triumphant cheer echoed outside on the beach.

Nah, she thought, reaching back to the desk for her phone. Her thumb hovered over Giles in her contacts. He knew she was in town and she'd visit him eventually. But, again, the idea of staying in the house she grew up in unnerved her. This was already, in every sense, far too close to home.

So, Ruby called Will, pacing as it rang. If she was sticking to her rules, the structure, the order, the countless curated habits that optimised performance, including very specific hours allocated for work *and* sleep, this place would simply not suffice.

He answered and she explained the situation. She didn't even have to finish – Will knew where this was going.

"Oh, yeah, um, yeah, of course," he said, with all the hesitance you'd expect.

His offer was clearly never at risk of being claimed. And yet, here she was, taking him up on it. But a mildly awkward intrusion into Will's life was the lesser of two evils here. Ruby had to get out of this hotel.

An hour later, she'd packed her bags and walked to the edge of town. Will's house was at the far end of a cul-de-sac, with trees and fields behind. But now, just silhouettes, a jagged canopy almost unseeable against the night clouds.

It looked especially affluent in the dark, with brand-new lantern-style streetlights lining the road, and neat hedges enclosing homes, black iron fences and tall swing gates. Clean cars tucked in well-swept drives. Neighbours with names like Beverly and Clive, Hugo and Camilla – the doctors, the consultants, the senior executives of companies that make things you own.

Will was waiting beneath a warm porchlight hanging above his open doorway. The house, which used to belong to his grandfather, was at least twice as big as a state secondary school teacher's salary should allow. Ruby entered and he took her suitcase, pushed it against the wall near the stairs then closed the door behind her. Looking around at the high ceiling, Ruby followed him through the living room and into the kitchen at the rear of the building.

"This is nice," she said. "How long have you been here?"

"A couple of years now." Will stepped across the tiles, picked up the kettle. "Overlapped with Grandad's death. It's meant to be temporary – the plan is to sell it, just needs some work."

Ruby leant against the solid oak dining table in the centre of the open-plan kitchen. "Hotel's seen better days."

"I did warn you," Will said, filling the kettle with water. "The spare room's ready." He glanced up to the ceiling. "It's silent and dark."

Ruby looked at him for a moment. Seeing him dressed in casual home clothes was oddly intimate. Thin sweatpants, a black t-shirt and his square-framed designer glasses. Yesterday, in his ironed shirt, smart trousers and contact lenses, he'd seemed like an acquaintance. Or even a colleague. But now? Ruby watched him open a cupboard – he was facing away so she was free to stare.

He was still handsome. Maybe even more handsome? His small, boyish wrists were fuller now, his jaw and neck settling into the proportions of a man. A fully grown, human man. Stubble, creased eyes. Slim Will from school, standing in his kitchen, making a cup of tea. Driving around in his car. Reading newspapers. Going to bed at a reasonable time. Nodding and humming at an engaging political memoir. It was all very strange.

In the living room, she could see paperwork spread on the coffee table. An empty glass and a bottle of red wine. Half gone.

"Marking?" she asked, nodding towards it.

He looked over his shoulder and gave her a tired, eye-dipped nod. "Coursework."

"Can you just stick B plusses on the last pile?"

"Oh, I wish. They've changed the system. Really tricky now. You actually do have to read it."

"That's terrible." Ruby smiled. "Still, having the summer off and finishing at three? Swings and roundabouts."

Opening a drawer, Will laughed. "And yet all we do is moan." He turned around, teaspoon in his hand.

"Is it weird?"

"What?"

"Working there."

"Kind of." He leant on the counter opposite, mirroring her posture. "But it's changed so much. Feels like a different place."

But to Ruby, this all felt exactly the same.

Will stepped past, stopped at the fridge by her side. She felt the air move.

"I know you were being polite," she said. And she reached out and touched his forearm with the back of her fingers. "I do really appreciate this."

He smiled.

On the walk over, Ruby had wondered if the noise and dripping had pushed her here. Or had something pulled? Did she *want* to stay with Will? There was probably no one on earth who knew her better than he did. He knew her insecurities, her secrets, nightmares and dreams. Which was a slightly sad and unsettling thing to consider as they'd not really spoken for the best part of a decade. Still, it was comforting. Liberating. Even now, all these years later, when she was in his company, Ruby was so very nearly herself, whoever that might be.

"Really, it's not a problem," Will said, opening the fridge.

Ruby spotted some dairy-free cheese inside, an open packet of vegetarian sausages, milk made from cashew nuts.

"You a vegan?" she asked.

"No, that's . . ." And there was a sound. Will pushed the fridge door half closed and looked back through the living room, towards the porch. "I probably should have said."

Ruby heard a key, saw the top of a woman's head in the glass, lit by that warm, welcoming light. Then, as the front door opened, she felt a thousand others close, options, chances, possibilities falling away. And it hurt. Though she couldn't say exactly why. What had she expected? Was she hoping that she and Will would hang out, watch movies and fall back in love? No, she didn't want that. Not at all. But it hadn't been impossible. Just unlikely.

Now, though, a woman was walking into the hall, coming through the living room towards them with a smile that barely masked her surprise.

She was pretty, moving as though this was her home and—

Holy shit. When Ruby realised who it was, her fleeting disappointment became something else. Initially disbelief, then fascination, finally settling on humour. This wasn't just a woman. It was Lauren.

"Ruby." Lauren looked between her and Will.

"Long time." Ruby laughed, opening up for a single-armed hug, which Lauren – *Lauren Coates from school* – politely accepted.

She seemed flustered, fresh from the cold, from work – handbag coming off her shoulder as she unravelled a scarf and stepped back.

"Will said you were in town," she added, dropping her keys on the dining table, hanging her jacket on a hook where it clearly belonged.

Below, Ruby saw high-heeled shoes, clues, obvious things she'd have spotted if only she'd looked. In the silence that followed, all three seemed to be making a conscious effort to act as though this wasn't awkward. Everyone here was totally comfortable. Why wouldn't they be?

"When did, uh, you two get together?" Ruby asked, which didn't help the situation much.

Lauren and Will made eye contact – here we go again, let's tell this story. "Christmas before last," she began.

Less than two years, then. Whereas she and Will were in a relationship for six. Ruby even thought, briefly and madly, that this meant she'd somehow won.

Nodding, Will added, "Few days after my birthday. Both single, both local."

"What more could you ask for?" Lauren said.

"Plus, hey," Ruby spread her hands, "if it goes well, marriage, divorce, get half of this house?" Now why on *earth* would you say that, she thought to herself.

"Exactly." Lauren kept a straight face – indulging the dry humour, to Ruby's relief. "The long game."

"Lauren's a surgeon," Will said. "A brain surgeon." Ruby must have looked confused, because he gestured to his head.

"Neurosurgery," Lauren clarified.

"She literally gets on your nerves."

They smiled – some kind of inside joke that Ruby didn't find quite as funny as they did.

"Central nervous system . . . Either way," Will said, setting down a mug for her. "If this goes to the wire," he pointed to himself then to Lauren, "I'm laughing."

To an outsider, Will might have seemed rude not offering Ruby a drink. But it was actually endearing – he'd remembered her rules without even commenting. It was too late for liquid.

Despite this frivolity, the air was still heavy. Ruby cleared her throat.

But Lauren cut through it all, aimed the spotlight right at the elephant. "Well," she said, wide-eyed, holding her cup of tea, "this is almost unbearably weird."

And somehow, after another short silence, it suddenly wasn't. It was fine. A simple acknowledgement, permission to admit it, that was the cure. Besides, any reasons for this to feel uncomfortable had been around long enough for a reasonable adult to ignore. And a reasonable adult was exactly who Ruby was striving to be.

Following another hour of catching up in the kitchen, small talk about the last two decades, family, careers, old names and new deaths, Will took Ruby upstairs to the spare room. He leant in to flick the light on, already treating it as her space.

She stepped inside, parked her bags next to the double bed. The room was tucked at the back of the house, overlooking the garden. There was a desk in the corner and a huge space on the white wall where she could pin up the school year photo. It was perfect.

Though, going by the hushed conversation she heard through the door, her staying here was a source of tension for Lauren. Ruby didn't catch the specifics, just the tone.

She had considered offering to leave. But, then again, what bearing did Will's relationship status have on her? That's all that had changed. Why should it be any less appropriate now? Remaining here proves that it is and always was going to be platonic. The irony was not lost on her. Like an arms race. All parties behaving in a way that results in a mutually undesirable situation. Neither Ruby, Will nor Lauren wanted her to stay. And that was exactly why she had to.

But these concerns faded away the moment she climbed into her bed. Clean sheets, skin still soft from a warm shower as the effortless comfort of overdue sleep pressed down on her chest. Her final thought was about Eduardo. She felt she'd been somehow unfaithful to view Will, even though it had only been for a few seconds, in a plausibly romantic context. And she realised Lauren's arrival hadn't closed those doors. They were never even open. Because Eduardo, ten thousand miles away, was here in her mind.

Ruby woke up eleven minutes before her alarm. Eye mask off. Ear plugs out. She rose. Curtains open. A long garden, trees at the end, all leaves shaking, chaotic in the wind, fields stretching out behind – green squares, yellowed grass, gridded hedgerows.

Day two.

Adderall. Coffee. Work. Things streamlining. Busy. Focused. Able to ride the wave of embarrassment when she told Jay about the car that followed her. "No," she'd said, "I didn't catch the number plate." If anything, the fact she couldn't remember specifics was a greater source of fear than the car itself. Its significance dwindled. A symbol of incompetence that would only distract. Still, Ruby checked over her shoulder from time to time and did not venture outside alone after dark. She was listening to recordings. Reading notes. Learning. Speaking to each and every detective on the case. No progress. But plenty of theory, speculation. Ideas. Pure clarity as she navigated these brainstorms. Bed. Day three. The same. Bed. Day four. Again. Bed. Day five. All traces of jetlag had now disappeared. Ruby was back. Her true self.

The stagnant nature of the case was disheartening, but her accommodation was turning out to be ideal. Will and Lauren were working most of the time, as was she. It was only in the evenings that their paths crossed. And usually even then Ruby was up in the spare room, pressing on with the more time-consuming, aimless elements of research.

As she'd planned, she had the school year photo pinned up on the bare wall. She'd marked it in a lot more detail and was now standing, staring at the faces. Each like a window on a memory, an incident, a vague or drunken exchange of words or bodily fluids. Over those five formative years, she'd had various interactions with all of these people. School is a uniquely social exercise. That shuffling and mixing as people organically gravitate towards one another to form bonds, the vast majority of which do not last. But those that do are among the strongest possible outside of blood. She thought about Elizabeth's face, her smiling eyes and every message Ruby hadn't replied to over the last—

There was a gentle tapping on the open door.

"Hey," Lauren said, coming in slowly. "You have plans for dinner?"

Will appeared behind her, fiddling with his shirt's cuffs, hair wet from the shower. "Oh, nice," he said, spotting the photo as he entered. "You've updated the system."

All three looked at the picture. Ruby standing in the middle, Lauren on her left and Will on her right. They both smelled good. Perfume, aftershave, vanilla, wood, citrus. Nostalgia.

"Red crosses for the dead," Ruby explained, hands on hips. "Blue circles for anyone with violence in their past, people who were nearby at the time. And, I'm afraid to say, anyone . . . iffy."

Lauren scanned across the students, nodding, humming. "Yep, yep. Definitely. Oh, yes. Frankenfield was the king of bad vibes."

"Yeah," Will agreed, "but, obviously . . ."

Ruby turned to him.

"You didn't hear about that?" he added. "There was all this shit with his parents – they tried to sue the police."

"Why?"

"They wanted to file a missing persons thing, but apparently there wasn't enough evidence of foul play. Think maybe he moved somewhere? Ran away. Or, I don't know. He just disappeared. About, maybe, ten years ago?"

"More than that," Lauren said.

"Weird, though, because he was always around and then, well, he just wasn't." Will hummed. "Hadn't really thought about him."

"Were he and Scott still close after school?" Ruby wondered. She picked up her notebook and jotted "ask Jay about Frank Enfield" at the bottom of a page.

"As far as I know, yeah, best friends."

"What are the green crosses?" Lauren asked.

"People we can rule out," Ruby said, returning the notebook to the desk, looking back to the picture.

"Michael Rush gets a green cross?" Will pointed. "Come on. Definite school shooter material. He was a weirdo."

"Harmless, though." Lauren was still fixated on the faces. "But, yeah, eccentric."

"What was that . . ." Will smiled to himself, clicking his fingers to remember something. "The rhyme."

"Don't," Lauren said, hiding her smile behind mature disapproval.

"Ducks, ducks . . ." Will closed his eyes. "No, no. Geese, geese, chicken and ducks, this is all that Michael fucks." And he laughed to himself, stifling it as best he could, wiping tears away. "Oh, Jesus."

Will seemed to have completely relaxed about the severity of all this. Whereas Lauren was, Ruby could tell, tiptoeing. She wasn't particularly close to Mary or Elizabeth. And obviously she wasn't a fan of Scott. But Lauren still seemed to treat this with the respect it probably deserved. In a way, though, Ruby preferred Will's irreverence. Laughter was a safer bet. The alternative would not be conducive to progress.

"Actually, kind of mean, if you think about it," Lauren said.

"Absolutely," Will agreed. "Poultry can't defend itself."

"He lives in China," Ruby said. This research had been painstaking and seemed almost absurdly vague. Though with such a big pool of possible victims, possible suspects, the legwork was always going to be laborious. "Unfounded bestiality aside."

She smiled at Will. So silly. All that casual cruelty and mischief that's commonplace in any school. When adults turn their backs, children say the most outrageous things. One slip-up and you've got yourself a reputation that'll last for decades. Michael had a pet duck. And so, in turn, it was common knowledge that he had sex with it. School really is a snake pit.

"Hang on," Will said, frowning now. "You've given yourself a green cross?"

"Well, yes." Ruby sighed. "We've been through this."

"You get a green cross, but I don't?" He put his finger on the picture, then slid it down to the bottom row. "And neither does Lauren?" He tapped her face.

"She can't rule either of us out definitively," Lauren said, indifferent, leaning in. "Look at my eyes." Will laughed again. Lauren had been halfway through blinking when the shutter clicked. "Oh, I'm wearing the hairband. I've still got it."

"Dee's?" Will said.

"Yeah." Lauren had water in her eyes. "I had it on for the individual pictures too. She was so annoyed that I'd taken it."

Ruby felt Will's hand reach behind her to touch Lauren on the shoulder. Swallowing, Lauren blinked a few times and forced a smile, looking back in time to when her sister was still alive.

The atmosphere shifted gently back to reality. This photograph contained so much. Love, death, joy, grief. There was only one reason they were looking at it. Something sad was happening to these people.

"Anyway," Will said. "We're going to the Anchor. You hungry?"

Ruby was tempted to say no. But some social interaction was, unfortunately, vital for wellbeing. If that base level falls too low, it can dramatically affect performance. Isolation is quite literally deadly. The prison guard's last line of defence, only solitude can punish the punished.

"Sure, give me ten."

Just off the seafront road, up a narrow lane, the Anchor was a wonky pub with burnt-timber driftwood beams slanted across the white façade. The rustic charm carried on inside – low ceilings and creaking floorboards. A plaque on the wall still claimed it as the oldest surviving building in town.

It was busy, so they sat in the corner at a small table presumably meant for two, which seemed fitting. Ruby opposite Lauren with Will tagged on the side, their knees almost touching. Once they'd ordered drinks, the obvious subject came up.

They'd spoken briefly about Ruby's role, but Lauren asked, "What exactly does a behavioural investigative advisor do?"

"What it says on the tin," Ruby said, slightly surprised she'd remembered her title.

"BIAs provide advice by evaluating the actions of an unknown offender from a behavioural science perspective," Will said, quoting something he'd no doubt read online. "It's profiling," he added, layman's terms that he couldn't help but tag on the end.

Ruby nodded. "Basically, look at a crime, then think about the kind of person who could have committed it."

"Huh." Lauren shook her head. "Blows my mind that it's not Scott."

"That's exactly what we said." Will gently flicked Ruby's arm. "Of all the people from our year who could become a serial killer."

"Who says he wasn't?" Lauren shrugged. "Just not the one Ruby's looking for."

"Plus," Will spread his hands, "I suppose in real life stereotypes don't always . . . come true?"

The waiter arrived with a bottle of red wine. Their conversation stalled while he turned over three glasses and half-filled each. Then he tilted the candle on their table and sparked a lighter.

"Thank you," Ruby said.

"Sometimes they definitely do, though," Lauren added, as the waiter left. "He might have fallen short of murder, but you could see in Scott's face that he was a bad egg."

Will slid a glass towards Ruby, then picked up his own drink. "I meant more the unhealthy relationship with their mother, living in a basement, collecting knives." He sipped his wine. "Hmm, that is lovely."

"Or the sophisticated psychopath," Lauren said. "Eats in fancy restaurants but also, I don't know, kills prostitutes."

They both looked to Ruby, keen to hear her view. "No, you're not far off. It's not politically correct but sit in on some Crown Court sentencings and, often, you see the defendant and, well, they look exactly like the kind of person who would do whatever they've been found guilty of doing. Stereotypes start somewhere."

"OK, so, we're in London, a young man has been stabbed," Will said, palms up, painting a picture. "No, wait," he pointed, "a plane gets hijacked. Describe the offender."

Ruby sighed. "You're trying to make me say something racist. The point is, in both of those cases, it's *probably not* the little old blind lady in a wheelchair."

"So, paedophiles *do* have a beard and glasses?" he added.

"*You* have a beard and glasses," Ruby said.

And Lauren, fiddling with the candle, laughed.

"It's stubble, but I'm . . . If I put on twenty kilos and wore sweatpants at the play park, then, yeah, arrest me."

"No." Ruby tapped the table. "Again, we're not talking about single people. When it comes to behaviour, the differences between individuals generally varies more than between groups."

Will looked confused. This wasn't his first drink of the night.

"Virtually all sex offenders are men," Ruby explained. "But you wouldn't dream of not hiring a man for a job because he's more likely, on balance, to be a sex offender than a woman is. That'd be insane. This applies to any over-representation. Sex, race, ideology, age."

"It's almost as if we should treat everyone as an individual," Lauren said.

"Exactly. Equality is actually a good idea." Ruby felt like she should give them something exciting – some romantic insight that normal people always crave. "And an open mind is essential. Because there's a much scarier, much rarer breed of offender. They have by far the most dangerous trait of any – *competence*. We have no clichés for them." Ruby paused for dramatic effect. "Because they don't get caught."

Will had his hand on his chin, transfixed by what she was saying. Then he seemed to come round, focusing on their situation. "Well, you said they left hardly any evidence."

Humming to herself, Ruby thought for a moment about the three deaths. Over these past few days, she'd felt a slight tension between the need to remain professional and the informality of conversations like this. She knew the confidentiality of an ongoing investigation still applied. Even when chatting with old friends from school. Or perhaps especially given that they were, like her, potential victims.

"It's plausible Mary was not planned," she said. "Could have even been impulsive. But the other two. There was research, they knew where each would be. And yet they made absolutely no effort to hide the bodies."

"So they don't care if they get caught?" Lauren suggested.

Ruby drew some air in through her teeth. "They were careful in too many other ways for that to be the case. It's not random, these three died for a reason. It could be that they're working through a list. And once they've ticked all the names off, they're done."

"Maybe they already are?" Will wondered.

"Maybe." Ruby winced.

"Would that be bad?" Will laughed. He took another big swig from his wine, then he stopped, seemed to realise something. "Ah, I see," he added, placing his glass carefully back onto the coaster. "Is that what the police are doing? Waiting for it to happen again?"

"No, of course not," Ruby said. "But . . . you know. Additional evidence would help."

"So, you think there's going to be more before you catch them?" Lauren asked.

Ruby looked down at the table, at the warm candlelight on her fingers, flickering shadows in her cupped hands. She took a long time to consider this. Finally, she nodded. "Yes."

Full of food and wine, all three walked back to Will's place around 10pm. He opened the front door and went straight into the kitchen for another bottle of wine. Ruby had already exceeded her strict four-unit limit so would have to decline.

She'd worked out that this was just enough alcohol to fend off the social taboo of not drinking at all, while retaining enough sobriety to sleep well and wake up close to normal.

Will, on the other hand, drank with exponential enthusiasm. He would go and go until either the alcohol or his ability to move was gone. Luckily, he was a friendly drunk. A few hours in and there would be declarations of love, newfound fascination for any topic and a sudden realisation that something or someone was strikingly beautiful. Only now, in this blurring, slurring warmth, he had the courage to say it out loud. Again. And again.

Although he seemed to respect it, Will never understood Ruby's discipline. But it was a simple concept to grasp. Have you ever opened your eyes after a heavy night and wished you'd drunk *more*?

Lauren entered the living room and began to clear things off the coffee table.

"Open the nice one," she said. "We have company."

"Actually," Ruby added, standing in the doorway, "I'm probably going to head to—"

She stopped.

There was a sound upstairs. Lauren froze. Will stepped back into the living room and stared at them both, alarmed – eye contact all round that asked and answered the unspoken question. Yes, they did all hear that.

Lauren lifted a finger to her lips as they looked up at the ceiling. And then, once again, another noise. A creak.

"What the fuck?" Will mouthed, turning the bottle and holding it like a weapon now.

Then they both seemed to appeal to Ruby. Which was a bad sign – they clearly had no idea who or what it might be. But she just shrugged – what could she say?

"Is it a person?" Lauren whispered.

"Next door's cat?" Will said, more hope in his voice than conviction.

But then, unmistakable, *thud*, *thud*, footsteps. *Thud*. Someone was upstairs and Lauren looked terrified. Before any of them could say another word, a window smashed.

"Fuck me," Will said, now no need to be quiet.

A rumbling sound at the back of the house. Ruby looked towards the kitchen window and saw a shape, a person, fall fast into the garden. The hooded figure rose and took off running – a blur of dark clothes – long gone by the time they tentatively approached the back door.

Just the patio light, creeping halfway down the grass. The thick trees at the end were a mass of black, the intruder dissolving into the shadows.

Lauren unlocked the back door, but Will put his arm across her, ensuring she didn't go outside. This was mildly sweet, though Ruby noted he had no reservations about her stepping into the garden to check. Standing on the patio, she turned and looked up at the second storey through the glaring light above the back door.

A window – the master bedroom's dormer window – was smashed, the splintered frame hanging out at a strange angle. It would have taken a lot of force. A few feet away, Ruby saw broken glass on the paving stones and traced the route across the grass.

When Lauren and Will came outside, Ruby held up a similar border with her arm – keeping them away from the damage, for different reasons.

A faint howl as the air moved. Nearby, bamboo wind chimes swayed and sang.

"Anything valuable up there?" she asked.

Will shrugged. "TV?"

"My sister's jewellery?" Lauren suggested. Though that sounded doubtful – probably not expensive enough to justify burglary.

Back inside, they went upstairs and surveyed the scene. Ruby waited on the landing while Will and Lauren checked various rooms. They both emerged at the same time, shaking their heads. Nothing was missing.

Similar situation in the spare room. Everything was exactly as they'd left it.

"Must have spooked them," Will said, following Ruby inside. "It's a crime spree."

Although it appeared the intruder hadn't come in here, Ruby was careful not to touch anything. Her laptop was still there, on standby, lid down. Her suitcase seemed untouched on the carpet and the desk was—

"Wait," Ruby said, eyes darting around the floor, stepping back, even checking herself in the confusion.

"What?" New fear in Lauren's voice. "What is it?"

"My notebook. It's . . ." Then she crouched, put her cheek on the carpet to check under the bed. Looking back up at Lauren and Will, she whispered, "It's gone."

Ruby's eyes were still now – no more searching. Kneeling on the floor, she just stared at the wall, lost in thought.

"What should we do?" Lauren asked in a hushed tone – like they needed to hatch some scheme together. But this was a straightforward situation. Ruby had no grand plan beyond the obvious.

"Call the police," she said.

Chapter Five

At the end of Will's garden, Ruby stood in the dark beneath the trees and looked out through gaps in an old fence. Mossy stakes with horizontal poles, half of which were rotten, the other half gone. Careful not to step on the path, she pointed her torch into the field ahead. Sweeping left to right over the long grass and bobbing seeds, shadows fanned, turning away from the beam.

The intruder's escape route was obvious. Even with a cursory glance, Ruby saw a freshly snapped branch just a few feet away. But the garden's grass ended with a sunken border of neglected flower beds – messy, woodchip twigs and mulch – so a clean footprint seemed unlikely.

Turning back, she looked towards the house. Forensic officers had erected lights around the patio where they were busy collecting and bagging shards of glass. The broken window's curtains fluttering above. With nothing but her notepad taken, this was already far more than a burglary. Every few seconds there was a flash of light, followed by the charging hiss of a camera. Though she might have only imagined that sound.

At her side, near the fence, a figure wearing white-hooded overalls was leaning over, bent at the waist. Another flash of sudden trees, stark trunk bark glistened like metal. And then, with a jolt, he stood up straight, rigid.

"Uh, Ruby," he said, from behind his mask. He sounded alarmed, maybe even excited. "Check this out."

She lowered the torch and sidestepped between trees to get to him.

"What?" she whispered. He pointed at a protruding knot in one of the old fence poles. She aimed the light, leant closer, squinted. "What is that?"

Lifting his digital camera, the officer zoomed in on the screen with gloved fingers, tilting it so she could see – so she could *clearly see* the high-resolution image glowing in the dark.

"OK," she said, checking over her shoulder – Will and Lauren seemed small all the way back there, giving statements in the kitchen.

Obviously, they'd need to confirm it, but the picture was undeniably familiar. Three thin threads hanging from the side of the fence pole, sticking out like tiny whiskers. Clothing fibres. *Blue* clothing fibres. She was right, that was a dark-blue jacket she'd seen.

Ruby returned to the house and, at the edge of the patio, looked up towards the broken guttering, the steep patch of tiled roof the intruder must have slid down. Those bamboo wind chimes tapping away to the breeze sounded like a xylophone. But the gentle night had no rhythm, no order, no music beyond the soft, simple notes of chaos.

"Well," Jay said, arriving at her side, "this seems significant." He sniffed, looking up, snarling his nose.

"Very . . ." Ruby leant closer to quietly explain the photo she'd just seen.

Jay kept his hand in his pocket while he listened, fiddling with his keys, nodding along. He was twitchy like this, fingers always busy. Often, it seemed as though he was compelled to make a sound at every opportunity. He'd click his tongue, drum his thighs before he stood, tap his nails on any available surface. A constant, annoying and, at least she hoped, subconscious effort to test every-one's patience.

"Shall we," he said, glancing at the trees then turning back to the house. "You want to tell them?"

In the kitchen, Will was at the dining table, speaking to a uniformed officer sitting opposite. Lauren was leaning against the countertop between them, one arm across her chest, nervously chewing on her thumb. Despite all this drama, or perhaps because of it, Will was still cracking on with the wine, although he held it well enough to answer questions.

All three seemed instantly aware that Ruby had news when she came in and stood next to the fridge. The conversation stopped mid-sentence, every eye fixed on her.

She took a breath, then told them about the only physical evidence linking two of the murders. Threads from a dark-blue jacket. As soon as she added, "And out there . . ." everyone in the room knew what she was going to say.

"Oh, great," Will said, with a sarcastic smile.

"Listen," Ruby raised her hand, "this doesn't necessarily mean—"

"What's that saying about having an open mind, but not so open your brain falls out?" He pulled his glass closer and poured more wine. "It seems a fair assumption." Will tilted the bottle. "Only one thing taken, right?" He turned to Lauren. "You checked – all the jewellery's still there."

"It is," she said.

Will seemed more frustrated than unsettled – this was inconvenient. His bedroom window was smashed and he had to get up for work in a few hours. But Lauren looked shaken. Sober. Again, treating this situation with the correct amount of respect.

"Is it definitely from the same jacket?" Will asked.

"The lab will need to check," Jay said. He was standing in the doorway, the garden bright behind him, the forensic glow of white canopies. Realising this was the first thing he'd said to them, he added, "Jay Simmons, I'm the senior investigating officer."

"Of which case?" Will said. "The murders or the burglary?"

Jay smiled, jacket pocket bulging, jingling his keys inside. "Yes, I think, on balance, in the immediate term, a connection is reasonable. Let's assume the worst."

"Or the best?" Will said. "If he's nearby, out in those fields somewhere?"

"Yeah," Lauren added. "You can track him, right? See where he went."

"You sure it was a male?" Jay asked.

Ruby nodded. "Maybe six-foot, medium build. But we only saw his back. Dark clothes."

"Dark blue?" Jay suggested.

Ruby nodded again.

"You didn't answer her question," Will said. "You could be searching."

"It's dark and he's had a good head start." Jay was just on the right side of polite, but still openly dismissive.

He spoke differently to them than he did to Ruby. It was subtle, but there was slightly less respect. She was a colleague. Will and Lauren were just members of the public. Victims of a crime – the kind of plebs he'd dealt with a thousand times.

Ruby had never worked this closely with Jay before. They'd crossed paths earlier in her career and his reputation, which he seemed to enjoy maintaining, was on the money. A kind of pragmatic, no-nonsense superiority that he probably thought seemed professional or even, and this was particularly misguided, cool. But there was no justification, he wasn't *that* good at his job. Bang average. So it just made him seem the worst kind of arrogant. Like every room he was in was the last place he'd choose to be. He was just so far above it all.

His face didn't help. He'd had Bell's palsy in his youth, so now half of his features drooped ever so slightly. Like a waxwork near a sunlamp. When the left side of your entire face sits out of every expression, both good and bad, the content of what you say is all that matters.

And Jay said things like, "You guys do your job and we'll do ours, yeah?"

"What about sniffer dogs?" Will said, as though this was obvious. "A helicopter?"

"Please." Jay seemed amused by that idea.

"It's been over an hour." Ruby softly translated Jay's stubborn tone. "The ground is dry. It's extremely unlikely he's still local. He's got what he came for."

"What was in the notebook?" Jay asked, lifting the eyebrow that worked, as though Ruby might have done something wrong. As though the police had a single piece of information interesting enough to be confidential. Ruby could have plastered those pages on a billboard and it still wouldn't have mattered.

"Nothing that would be useful," she said, inadvertently mimicking the snide drone of Jay's boring cyborg voice.

Hand on chin, elbow on the table, Will frowned, then turned to her. "How did he know you were here?"

It seemed to click into place, a puzzle piece that so obviously fits. "The car," Ruby said, now speaking solely to Jay. "The one I told you about, after my first day at the office. Looked like it was following me."

"The dark car that was too fast to catch the number plate? Did you at least—"

"I didn't see the model," she added, getting ahead of his question.

71

A slight squint – Jay seemed to clock that this wasn't quite right. Again, he regarded Ruby with some suspicion. The mildest hint of distrust. It was, after all, a lie. But the truth, that she saw the number plate, the model and forgot both within moments, would open another line of questioning that she really didn't fancy going down.

Again, no matter how she cut it up, Ruby was the common denominator. Somehow, in ways she just could not figure out, this was all about her.

"Maybe I shouldn't stay?" she said.

"I mean . . ." Will shrugged, agreeing that, yeah, if she hadn't been here then none of this would be happening. "But it's your choice."

Ruby remembered that image – that shape of a man falling out into the garden. Disappearing beneath the windowsill, then rising and running. It all happened so quickly.

"Is there any other damage?" she thought out loud. "He smashed a window to escape, but you said all the doors were locked?"

"They were," Will said, standing, sliding the chair under the table. "I unlocked the front door when we came back, you saw me do it. Same with the back door."

"One of the windows upstairs?" Lauren said. "The trellis on the side wall?"

This was everyone else's suspicion too, hence informality here. The crime scene investigators didn't seem interested in the ground floor.

"How about *that* door?" Ruby turned.

There was a gloomy utility room at the side of the kitchen. It was cluttered with washing baskets, a few tools, vacuum cleaner parts and other abandoned items. Crucially, at the back of the narrow space, in the deepest part of the shadow, there was another entrance.

"That's always locked," Lauren explained, stepping forwards, leaning round to trace Ruby's gaze.

Will nodded. "Grandad lost the key years ago. It's never opened. Think of it as a wall."

Still, Ruby walked towards it, through the tight passage. A light came on, a single buzzing bulb hanging above without a shade. She looked back to see Will standing in the doorway, hand on switch, Jay behind him, peering over his shoulder. Will's face already had a told-you-so expression ready to roll. But, nonetheless, he gestured – go on, see for yourself.

It was cold here, the chill of unused domestic space radiated from the tiled floor and the bare white walls, scuffed and dirty. Dead, dusty, cobweb corners dancing in the air she moved.

At the door now, Ruby hovered her fingers over an old metal handle – thick wood and a cool draught creeping from the frame's edge. And she grabbed it, lowered it and, clunk, pulled the door open with a long creak.

She closed it again and cautiously released both hands, like it was a freshly disarmed bomb. Turning around, Ruby looked down at the floor, at all the potential evidence they were trampling through.

"Maybe we should . . ." She gestured for everyone to move back, towards the living room.

This revelation turned the volume of their conversation down a few notches. As though now it was an altogether more serious situation.

Ruby, Will, Lauren and Jay huddled between an armchair and the TV.

"Is it possible they . . ." Lauren whispered, sighed. "Could they have the key?"

"How?" Will asked.

"It's an old lock," Ruby said. "I'm guessing he picked it. Sometimes leaves scratches, we could look."

"Hmm." Jay nodded.

The idea of a hapless burglar, even a potentially murderous one, was unnerving. But adding a picked lock into the mix seemed strangely worse. Somehow more nefarious. Professional. This man had been willing to smash a window to escape. But he'd entered with meticulous caution and diligence. Low, silent and unseen, yet, like the best predators, all too ready to erupt when explosive violence is necessary.

Will was staring hard at Ruby – glaring now. No more jokes. He took a deliberate breath and echoed what she'd said at dinner, the most dangerous trait of any: "Competence."

She looked back into his startled eyes and nodded.

"The good news is, I doubt he'll return any time soon," Jay said. "But, of course, we'll keep some officers on you." He held a hand out to Ruby. "At least for a day or two."

Then Lauren seemed to realise something – making eye contact with Will.

"On *her*?" Will frowned, thinking the same thing. "Not on the house?"

"She was . . ." Jay sighed. "Ruby was obviously targeted."

The four of them stood in silence.

"Well," Lauren finally said, "then maybe you should stay . . ."

Will nodded. "Safety in numbers."

Ruby agreed that it was probably a good idea. Though, to give the crime scene investigators some space, the three of them were asked to stay elsewhere for at least a night. So, much to their amusement, she, Will and Lauren ventured down the hill to the Beachside Hotel. Camaraderie gave the experience a welcome sense of fun and adventure, so it wasn't quite as bleak as Ruby's initial stay. Besides, a sound night's sleep had not exactly been on the cards for any of them.

All the evidence, thin though it was, proved consistent with her suspicion. The lock had been picked, the dark-blue clothing fibres were, pending further tests, "tentatively" matched to those found near Mary and Scott's bodies and the only item missing was Ruby's notebook. And the fact that there was virtually nothing of use written in those pages was bittersweet. Sure, it wouldn't help the killer, but it might well embolden him.

◆ ◆ ◆

Day seven. Adderall and caffeine pulsing through her veins, Ruby was running. An hour of cardio in the morning. The routine, which called for this at least twice a week, was still lagging. But she pushed on when she could. Like today. Now. Right now her shuffled playlist was screaming some fast, aggressive music into her ears and she found herself sprinting on the beach, feet pounding into the flat, damp sand. The waves crashed, the grey ocean on her right splashing and sending spray up into the wind that may well have been howling.

Ruby came to a stop, hands on knees, catching her breath. She checked her smartwatch. Her heart was going. Going crazy. Going, going, going perhaps, she breathed, to explode. She breathed. Jesus. All this instant data on her wrist and she still couldn't help but run right to the limit.

Walking now, she clambered up the stone steps to the coastline road, pulling herself up on the cold metal banister that stuck out from the weatherworn rockface, rattling like a loose tooth. On the pavement, Ruby stood across the street from the Starfish Café – looking at her reflection in the window. The sea behind her, the monochrome gulls circling. Looking past herself, through herself, she looked inside.

There were mirrors on the backwall, plastic chairs connected to the tables in pairs, ketchup and mustard decanted into plain, unlabelled containers. Sticky. The décor that seemed old even twenty years ago.

She paused her music and the relative whisper of the sea air and slow traffic returned. Pedestrians stepped round her – but she was too focused to move.

It was quiet in the café. Two heavyset men wearing high-vis jackets were sitting in the window seat – builders enjoying their heart-attack breakfast. But beyond them, she spotted an elderly man at the back, a mobility scooter parked at the side of his table.

Breathing gently as her heart rate dropped, Ruby stared at the man and realised she was right. She *did* recognise him. It was Mr Phillips. He had less hair, seemed shaky and sagged. Smaller, thinner. But, yeah, it was definitely him. He was dressed in a brown jacket and beige trousers, sporting that uniquely timeless fashion elderly men so often adopt. Ruby had never even seen clothes like that for sale. Where do these pensioners buy them? And, crucially, why?

Even there, sitting alone, Mr Phillips had a scornful, bitter frown. His teeth together, his lips peeled back as though everything about this wretched world disgusted him.

Ruby crossed the road and went inside, a dangling bell above the doorway announcing her arrival. She strode across the spongey linoleum floor, past the counter, and approached his table. Even though she was standing at his side, quite clearly about to speak, Mr Phillips just sat there. Like a statue, staring across the café towards the window, through the white-net curtain border – looking out at the rough sea, the rolling waves.

Ruby leant down slightly, trying to catch his eye. It was hard to tell if he had even noticed her.

"Why are you standing so close to my table?" he said, his gaze still tracked on the horizon.

Then, turning on an exact horizontal axis, his old, blood-shot eyes landed at her waist, then tilted with frankly psychopathic precision up to her face.

"Mr Phillips, my name is Ruby Shaw. Do you mind if I sit?"

"You can do whatever you want." Back to the window.

She lowered into the chair, sitting slightly side on to show that she was just passing, not here to stay. Now she was directly opposite, he had no choice but to look at her.

"But I'd rather you didn't," Mr Phillips added.

Ruby smiled and sighed. "I'm already down . . ."

"Yes."

A waitress arrived and picked up his plate, which was smeared with baked bean sauce and the crispy fried edges of eggs, which he'd left in perfect, hollowed circles.

"How was the food, Dave?" the young waitress asked, balling up a napkin, sweeping spent sachets of black pepper off the table.

Dave. Ruby knew that was his name, but he was still Mr Phillips to her.

"As good as you'd expect for four pounds," he said.

"Well, I'll extend that to the chef. We'll have more sausages tomorrow, OK? Sorry about that." She spoke a little louder than normal, then smiled at Ruby. "Can I get you anything?"

"More tea," Mr Phillips said, sliding his empty mug towards her without looking.

Sympathetic, Ruby tilted her head, and the waitress nodded with wide eyes. *You don't know the half of it.* A tricky customer indeed.

"I'm fine," she said, adding, "Thank you," in a deliberate voice.

When the waitress left, Ruby picked up the laminated menu. It felt slightly greasy. Photos of food, faded colours and dated prices. "You eat here a lot?" she asked.

"It's not any of your business."

Ruby laughed. "Sorry, I . . ." She put the menu down, slid it aside. "You've probably heard about the deaths?"

"Hmm, yes, I did catch wind of something."

"You may recall that, back in the day, all three were in your tutor group."

"OK."

The espresso machine roared behind the counter, steam billowing up. Then the *thump, thump, thump* of coffee grounds slammed into a bin. When it stopped, Ruby asked, "Do you know who they are?"

He shook his head. "People don't speak to me much anymore. And I have no interest in the news."

There was a pause. "Would you . . . like to know who they are?"

Mr Phillips sort of half shrugged, groaning. "Go on then."

"Mary Talbot," she said, but he clearly had no recollection of her. "Elizabeth Gregory." Again, nothing. "And Scott Hopkins."

And Mr Phillips laughed – a single, mocking, "ha" sound – dry gravel in his throat. This seemed like a rare and genuine spark of joy. Really warmed his heart. Then he hesitated, as though realising he was being inappropriate. But, instead, he hammered it home. Holding Ruby's gaze, he nodded. "Good." There were no doubts about his views.

"You didn't like Scott?"

"Scott was . . ." He thought for a moment, tutted, apparently annoyed at having to put this into words. "Scott was a little shit. I taught for forty years and he was, by some margin, the single worst pupil I ever encountered. Maybe the worst person. Fuck him. And fuck you for pretending to care."

Ruby laughed again. "Wow." She wiped her eye. Mr Phillips had a certain charm. "It's my job," she said. "So, when did, um . . . when did you retire?"

"Again, this is none of your business. Look, are you going to arrest me?"

Although he still exuded power and dominance, disdain and repulsion, he was obviously frail. His hands thin, liver-spotted skin webbed over tendons and bones. In fact, Ruby was surprised to see he was still going. Probably months left. A year at a push. He seemed like he was ready. As Will observed, Mr Phillips caving someone's head in would be entirely plausible if not for what the cruel erosion of time had done to his failing body.

"No," Ruby said, "we're just having a conversation."

"Why are we having a conversation?"

"I'm helping the police investigate the murders. Speaking to anyone local, you know. Thought maybe you'd have some insight."

Really, now she thought about it, Ruby was sitting here out of raw curiosity. It was fascinating to interact with Mr Phillips as an adult, on equal footing. Was he really that bitter old geography teacher? Or was there something human, something normal, something vaguely relatable hiding behind those spiteful eyes?

Ruby paused, thinking, remembering all those mean comments he'd made to students over the years. One moment shone out. They must have been in year 8, possibly year 9. Rachel Timpson was crying because someone – quite possibly Scott – had said she looked like she "belonged on a farm".

Mr Phillips crouched at her desk and whispered, in a reassuring tone, "That is because you are overweight and, as such, resemble a pig."

There were a hundred stories like that – outrageous to think he got away with it. This behaviour was unacceptable even then, though perhaps it had been par for course back when he was allowed to use a cane. Those "good old days" that he'd openly reminisce about, disappointed in the "silly PC laws" that meant he had to rely on words to hurt his students.

She and Eduardo had spent hours in the tent reminiscing about their respective school days on the night of that first text. Ruby did *try* to explain Mr Phillips. But Eduardo just laughed, assuming she was exaggerating. "Surely he can't have been *that* bad?"

"Is that your plan?" he grumbled. "Walk around town asking random people questions?"

At this stage, pretty much. But she said, "It's a complex investigation. You knew the victims; I wouldn't call this encounter 'random'."

"I remember you." He looked her up and down. "Straight As. Always handed your homework in on time."

"Well, what can I say, students were scared of you." She meant this as a compliment, but it didn't land.

"It was pathetic, to be perfectly honest," he said. "You had nothing better to do with your spare time? Bit of a try-hard."

He was not the first person to say this. Young Ruby did try hard. She was a bizarre combination of insecure and analytical. She'd tried, tried very hard in fact, to figure it all out. In the early years of secondary school, Ruby remembered writing notes on how "popularity" worked. She did her best, excelled in every subject, academic and physical alike. She was polite, kind and, on the whole, honest. And yet, she found herself with relatively few friends and not even a glimmer of respect from her peers or, it seemed, some members of staff. Of all the insults levelled at her, "try-hard" was the one that stung the most.

And it confused her. How was trying hard a bad thing? Later she came to realise that the effort was not the issue. No. It was the *perception* of endeavour – appearing as though you are exerting effort to achieve your goals. This, and she appreciated the sentiment now, is a sign of weakness. Expertise is more impressive when it looks easy.

To further complicate the dynamic, the expertise cannot appear to be consciously made to look effortless. If you are acting as though you find it easier than you do, you risk appearing arrogant or, worse, looping right back up to the start and being considered a try-hard. A meta try-hard. Trying hard to appear as though you're not trying hard. Thirteen-year-old Ruby wrote detailed, rambling notes to this effect. Diagrams. Theories.

But it wasn't until she was well into adulthood that she finally understood the social hierarchy of a secondary school is not science but art.

So, she cleared her throat, and pretended his comment meant nothing. "Schoolwork is important," she said.

"No it fucking isn't."

She smiled at him for a long time. Part of her respected this – Mr Phillips was, if nothing else, consistently unpleasant. But, as fun as this had been, Ruby realised it was probably not destined to be fruitful. She sighed, preparing to leave.

"To be clear," Mr Phillips said, holding up a hand to keep her in place, "this is not why I hate him, but were you aware that Scott Hopkins was a friend of Dorothy?"

Ruby settled back into her plastic chair. "What do you mean?"

An exhausted grunt. "You know what I mean."

"That he was gay?"

"Yep." Mr Phillips nodded. "Got no problem with it, long as they steer clear of me."

"What, uh, what makes you think that?"

"My son is also gay. He's married. To a large man." He shook his head, swallowed. "It might surprise you, but I'm OK about that."

"Sounds like it."

"They talk to each other, the homosexual community. There were rumours. Apparently, Scott was deeper in that closet than any man alive. Chains. Whips. Riding gloves. The dark side."

Ruby frowned. This seemed unlikely. Although she was mindful not to be swayed by stereotypes, Scott really didn't fit the image. Then again, now she gave it some thought, she couldn't picture him with a woman either. But the reality was, "He had a girlfriend."

"I just said that he was in the closet," Mr Phillips snapped, slapping the table, clinking the cutlery. "Why don't you listen?"

The waitress made eye contact and Ruby showed her a hand – it's all good. A bottle of ketchup had fallen over. Ruby carefully put it upright again as she considered her next question. Had to be straightforward.

"Let's say that's true," she said. "Why are you mentioning it?"

"His family – his brother, his dad." He licked his lips, flexed them into a sort of twitchy kissing shape. Sniffed. "Chavs."

"They're not really, Mr Phillips, they—"

"Whatever they fucking are." He waved his hand, as if he was batting away a fly. "Live in trailers, I don't know the word. Trash. Poor people."

"Scott lived up at the old farmhouse in Brettwood." Ruby pointed vaguely in the direction of the village.

"Either way. Low income. Working class. Rough folk, you know what I mean."

"I'm not sure I do."

"Old-fashioned values, not as tolerant and liberal-minded as you and I."

Ruby covered her laugh with a cough. "Sure. So . . . ?"

"So, they're not the kind of chaps who would take news like that lightly."

"You're suggesting someone found out that he was gay and then murdered him?"

"Are you deaf, girl?"

"I just want to be sure what you're saying here."

"Yes, that's what I'm saying."

Ruby turned in her seat, scratched her neck, elbow on the table. "What about the other two then? Mary and Elizabeth."

Mr Phillips shrugged again – not like he didn't know, more like he didn't care. "I'm sure you'll figure it out. You're clearly a bright spark."

Absurdly, this compliment felt good. Ruby hid it well, but praise from a man like this was surely rare.

"Thank you," she said.

"I'm joking," he added. "You haven't got a fucking clue what you're doing and it is glaringly obvious. It's pouring out of you." He gestured to her chest. She looked down at herself. "The way you move, your body language. It's all considered. Overthinking."

"All right, well, thank you for your time." She stood up. "If you have any—"

"You strike me as a deeply insecure person who spends more energy worrying about the thoughts of other people than your own."

She just stood there and waited. "You finished?"

Mr Phillips turned his head and looked up at her. "Life will hurt a lot less if you'll just . . . be yourself."

Ruby had wondered if now, retired and waiting for death, he was better or worse than he used to be. But now she could see that Mr Phillips, like so many other things in this strange little town, was exactly the same. He was a bully.

She took a long, decisive breath. "Dave," she said, placing her hand on his shoulder, "from the bottom of my heart, fuck you."

And, for the second time, she saw warmth in his eyes. As though he craved it, as though abuse was his life force. This had been the trick all along. Just give it back to him.

"Yes," he said. "Yes, yes. That's much better." He patted her fingers, squeezed them like a long-lost member of his family. "Good luck with the case, Miss Shaw."

Chapter Six

Back at Will's place, Ruby was standing in the spare room staring at that school year photograph yet again. It was busy now, scribbles and notes – arching lines darting from face to face. Friends, lovers, life, death. One hundred and sixty people, connected by the random whims of age and geography.

She remembered the day the photo was taken – that smile she'd practised the night before. Her well-rehearsed posture – the angle of her shoulders, the height of her chin, the crease of her anxious little eyes. And she cringed at the memory, at that awkward girl she used to be. Maybe Mr Phillips had a point.

As a teenager, Ruby used to spend hours alone in her bedroom, in front of the mirror, adjusting herself. She even took hundreds of photos on her old Polaroid camera, posing in various positions. Profile. Front on. Smiling. Waving. Formal. Casual. This was years before the word "selfie" entered the dictionary – Ruby was well ahead of her time. She thought about sad things, happy things, anything that might seep through and expose itself in her body language. And then she would analyse each posture and consciously adopt the best. The sweet spot between attractive, confident and, ironically, natural. Are all teenagers like this? They can't be, right? Or maybe it's worse nowadays? Now these contrived images are broadcast to your peers. You don't need to speculate, acceptance is quantifiable. Is there more self-doubt or less, she wondered, now that the data is right there in your hand?

Mr Phillips was just trying to get under her skin. And, despite her best efforts to focus on work, she kept repeating what he said in her mind. Calculated. Deeply insecure. Was it slipping? Could people tell how unsure she felt? How any glimmer of confidence was an act?

Deeply insecure. Did she spend more time worrying about the thoughts of other people than her own? No. She genuinely did not care what he thought of her. But, still, she couldn't stop thinking about it. And then she realised that it wasn't the insult that had got in. It was the fact he said she *looked* like she was deeply insecure. Being deeply insecure is fine. Being weak is fine. Being scared is fine. But appearing so? That was absolutely unacceptable.

It was late now and she was getting tired, her temper shortening as distraction nipped at the heels of attention. She sat down at the desk, twirled her pen, bounced her knee. And, with the muscle memory of a well-conditioned lab chimp reaching for a sweet treat, Ruby thoughtlessly picked up her phone.

She landed on Facebook. Scrolling through social media elicited two distinct and dissonant responses. On one hand, Ruby looked at any given post and thought, quite aggressively, Oh, who cares?

But, all the while, she would keep reading, watching, scrolling. Hours could pass, torn between two incompatible states of mind, suspended in a strange superposition of apathy and fascination. Scrolling and scrolling. Pulling that slot-machine lever *just one more time* in case a blip of serotonin might roll up between the cherries and diamonds and bells. *Ding, ding, ding.* The finely catered content sweeping up and up long into countless glowing nights but still, as every gambler knows in their heart, the house always wins.

Like a slave. She tensed her jaw. A slave to this stupid—

Ruby was momentarily tempted to throw her phone but instead went to Eduardo in her messages. She opened his profile picture. Tilted her head, smiled. They'd been texting every day since her arrival and had even reached the dizzy heights of three kisses in a few. She thought about calling him. It'd be nice to talk to someone far away about something else entirely. But this was just more procrastination. She locked her phone, dropped it on the desk, closed her eyes.

Wait. No. She picked it up again. There was a reason she'd opened Facebook. She went back to the app and tapped through to the Missbrook Heights Class of '99 School Reunion group. There were a lot of photographs already, but she found a new gallery posted at the top.

Held at the school, in the sports hall, the event was a sit-down dinner affair – reminiscent of the year 11 leavers' do twenty years prior. Swiping through the pictures, she saw round tables of six and a dancefloor at the back of the hall, complete with a small stage for a DJ. Above this, a banner read, "The Class of '99". It actually had more of an office Christmas party vibe and Ruby was sure there had been scandalous encounters that night, though these had been entirely eclipsed by Mary's subsequent death. In the age-old game of gossip, violence beats adultery every single time.

She stopped on a photo of Kendall Robson. He was sitting in his wheelchair, glass of champagne in his right hand, giving a thumbs up to the camera with his left. The room behind him was cast shadowy and black thanks to the flash. The next picture was similar, but now Mary and Scott were either side of the wheel-chair, leaning low to pose, smiles all round. Another where Mary was kissing Kendall's cheek with all the drunken flair of a frazzled mother letting her hair down for the first time in a long time. Then a close-up of his face, a perfect pair of red cartoon lips printed like a tattoo just below his eye.

It didn't seem to be fancy dress. But going by the narrative of these pictures, which were posted roughly in chronological order, as the night went on and the lights came down, someone raided the drama department's walk-in wardrobe. Simple props began to appear in the photos. Cheap top hats, novelty glasses, canes, Hawaiian necklaces made of flowers.

Now a photo of Mary sitting on Kendall's lap, draping a burlesque scarf over both their shoulders, head flung back, one leg pointing to the sky, drinks held high, pink feathers blurred with motion. Ruby swiped right but realised she'd reached the end of the gallery. This, then, was the last image of Mary alive. Taken just an hour or so before her death.

It looked late. Empty bottles on cluttered tables in the background. A bowl of punch, drained to a red smudge nearby. Sticky ladle resting at the side. And in their faces, the tired, ashen, dreary close of a night – alcohol beginning to leave their systems. Mary, in particular, looked especially pale, as though something vital had already started to leave her body. Maybe the camera had taken it – snatched part of her soul.

It was an unusual photo. At school, Kendall had been a small, shy, timid boy – book-smart and a target for bullies. Whereas popular Mary, blessed with good looks and early development, was far higher up the social ladder. Back then, the idea of her sitting on his lap and kissing his cheek would have made little sense. Though, as drunken adults, it seemed totally reasonable.

This gallery, Ruby saw, was posted by Zoe Parker. A name she did not know. The photographs were, on the whole, quite well composed. Obviously, a curated selection. So, Ruby reasoned, Zoe may have more.

Interestingly, the guest list for the reunion seemed quite strict. Ruby hadn't spotted a single person who wasn't in their school year. Not even husbands or wives broke the rule, aside from where they qualified, and only one sweetheart couple did. So why, she wondered, was Zoe even there?

Still seated at the desk, Ruby opened her laptop. Within a few short clicks, she was looking at a profile on a private care website. So, Zoe was a carer. OK, Ruby jotted down a few lines in her new notebook. Zoe was Kendall's carer? That's why she was there, that's why he was in many of the photographs and she was in none of them.

Ruby picked up her phone, tapped her contacts and scrolled down to Jay's number. He answered after three rings. When she explained that it might be a good idea to speak to Zoe Parker, he sighed.

"Listen," Jay said, "we have finite resources. We know exactly who was at the reunion and when each of them left." His voice was even more dead on the phone. "You have the list, you have the times."

Ruby did have this document. But it did not feature the name "Zoe Parker".

"Presumably, the register of attendees was based on who was invited?" she said. "Not who was actually there."

"What are you getting at?"

"She isn't on it," Ruby said. "What else have we missed about that night? Something might have happened. All three victims were in that room, together. Probably for the first time in twenty years. Certainly, for the last."

She heard Jay's mouse click. He cleared his throat. "All right, then," he said, openly humouring her. "Who is she?"

"It seems Zoe is Kendall Robson's carer."

A long pause as Jay checked something on his computer.

"Wait, wait." He exhaled – tired and heavy. "No. We've already spoken to him. Zoe was there too. You have his statement. Read it."

"I have. But I think it'd be wise to see if she has any more photos from the reunion."

There was another pause. Silence. "Ruby, at this stage, re-treading the same ground would be a waste of time."

She stood, paced over to the full-year photograph on the wall. "Jay," she said, using his name with the same tone he'd used hers. "I'm here to advise."

"Well, thank you. Noted . . . Was there anything else?"

She looked at all the faces. Frank Enfield's had a question mark above it and she remembered the note she'd made for herself. She needed to ask Jay, "You remember Frank Enfield?"

A hesitant sound, as though he was still finding it hard to keep track of all these names. "Who?"

"He went to Missbrook Heights. Disappeared more than a decade ago. People called him Frankenfield."

"OK. Why?"

"I suppose because he was tall and weird-looking."

"No, why are you mentioning him?"

"There was apparently some trouble with his parents?"

"Oh, yeah. Oh, shit, that's taking me back. I do remember."

"What happened?" Ruby asked.

"That was . . . It was a storm in a teacup. A young man just moved away. His mother was mad as a bag of frogs."

"Suspicious, though, right?"

"Is it? You left town. And, trust me, Frankenfield ran in some unpleasant circles."

Ruby smiled at how readily Jay adopted the nickname.

"I'd say leaving without a trace was his best bet," he added.

"I think we should look into that too."

"But why?" Now he sounded exasperated.

"Unpleasant circles. Frank was Scott's best friend at school."

Scott Hopkins. All other names felt irrelevant – forgettable. Ruby just knew Scott was intrinsically connected to this. Of the three victims, he was the only one who arguably deserved it. And there were too many rumours, he was too well known. It wasn't so much what Mr Phillips had said about him, but the fact he had something to say. Scott left an impression on every single person he encountered, a trail of lifelong memories swirling in his wake. Scott Hopkins. Victim number two.

"A lot of these professional boundaries have already shifted," Jay said. "I don't mind if you want to operate outside of your remit here."

"What do you mean?"

"You've got eyes and ears. You're obviously not comfortable on the sidelines. You have my blessing."

So that was where they'd got to, Ruby thought. If you want something done, do it yourself. Initially, this stubborn response had frustrated her. But then, a new and exhilarating feeling. A green-light. The door was open. She could be the one to solve this. And Ruby smiled. Maybe it really was all about her.

◆ ◆ ◆

Day eight. Up and going, caffeine and Adderall. But Ruby was tired, operating at maybe sixty percent capacity. She'd slept just four hours. Half the ideal amount. Kept awake by Mr Phillips sitting there in her incessant mind, telling her again and again that she looked like a deeply insecure person. Never mind, she thought, finishing her second coffee. Onwards.

Getting around town on foot was time consuming but, having recently "got back into cycling", Will had kindly offered her use of his car. And Ruby was grateful as today it was raining with a ferocity that bordered on vengeful. Water not so much falling as being thrown from the sky, turning roadsides to rivers, leaving nothing behind but panic for the last few pedestrians still out in the open.

She was driving through it, hot fan roaring, windscreen wipers on their highest setting, like a drumbeat, faster than her rising heart. Turning left into Kendall's narrow street, Ruby immediately realised there was nowhere to park. These tight residential roads were barely a car width across even without the row of vehicles parked along the edge, two wheels on the pavement, front doors of terraced homes just a metre away.

Ruby drove on towards the old recycling centre, which, although closed down, had wide open gates and plenty of space. The windows were steamed up, almost opaque, as she parked. She turned the engine off and reached into the backseat for her jacket. Will's car was messy – empty bottles, a gym bag, two tennis rackets in the footwell.

She climbed out and walked fast, rain pattering on her hood and shoulders, loud and heavy enough to make the back of her legs wet in seconds. The stress and urgency of this grey weather blurring her peripheral vision, deleting more than half of the world around her. Disorientated, she turned down Kendall's street again, arriving at his small, terraced house. Checking the number, she huddled into the doorway, knocked and then rang the bell twice.

"Two secs," a muffled, female voice yelled from inside.

Ruby just stood there, head bowed, arms crossed tight as though it might make the slightest bit of difference to the water pouring onto her. Like standing in the shower, fully clothed, trying to stay dry.

Finally, after a lot longer than two seconds, the door opened and a tall, broad woman with short, spikey hair ushered her into the house. She was wearing a tunic, like a nurse, but also trainers and gold jewellery. Bracelets and rings.

"Zoe?" Ruby said, pulling her hood back.

"Yes, pleased to meet you. Kendall mentioned you'd swing by." Zoe closed the front door behind her. "Do you need anything? Coffee? A towel?"

"I'm OK, thank you."

"Let me . . ." Zoe put her hand on Ruby's collar and it took her a moment to realise she wanted to help remove her jacket.

"It's fine, I'll—"

"I insist." A stern, almost motherly stare. "It's wet."

"Sure," Ruby said, as she passed the jacket to her.

There was an odd intensity to Zoe's demand, even starker now she'd totally relaxed back to a soft, caring, perhaps default disposition.

"He'll be through there in a moment." Zoe pointed, turning to hang it on a nearby hook. "Go in, take a seat."

Ruby stepped down a narrow, gloomy hallway, turning left at the end to enter a cluttered living room. Old fashioned décor, floral carpet, dark wooden cabinets and a disjointed collection of throws on the sofa.

The curtains were closed and the only light was from an antique lamp in the corner, glowing gold, warm and red through the wonky shade and its knotted tassels. It threw a stretched cone of colour across the ceiling. There was a sense that she'd travelled back in time – to the 1960s maybe. Or earlier. And it sounded like it too. A radio in the kitchen was playing some classic country music, with that distant crackle of something half-heard. An American man singing about road trips, cigarettes and the pretty girl he'll always love.

Ruby stood, waiting. There was a clicking sound and she turned to see Kendall rolling in through the doorway.

"Well," he said, looking up at her from his wheelchair, "haven't you grown."

He had a green wool blanket over his legs, cat hair clinging amid the thick-knit holes. Ruby smiled at him. "You seem to be getting smaller?"

They laughed.

"It's so nice to see you." Kendall beckoned her over – she bent down for half a hug.

They'd seen a lot of each other in school, having both been in the highest sets for every subject. Ruby had sat next to him in English, maths, science and history. And they'd got on quite well. Teachers seemed to post them together, right on the frontline. If anyone was getting a clean sweep of top grades, it was them. Though, in the end, they both fell short. Ruby secured A-stars in every class bar one, which was just a regular A.

She remembered her stepdad's face when she handed him that piece of paper. Giles had looked down at the results, listening intently as she explained that she was still the best-performing student of their year. More A-stars than anyone else. But that didn't seem to matter.

He just nodded, folded the results letter in half and handed it back to her.

"More revision next time," he said.

That had been a formative moment, a crucial discovery. Ruby had always known she was required to be the best, but that was not, as she had assumed, necessarily relative to her peers. No. She had to be the best it was *possible to be*. Winning the race was not enough. It had to be a record.

Since that day, every single academic and professional exam, every single thing she'd done that had a quantifiable score, resulted in her securing one hundred percent. There was simply no other option. Even when it took her three tries. Even when people frowned, confused at her request to resit a test she'd just passed with flying colours.

She sat down on the sofa. Kendall parked his wheelchair at her side and adjusted the blanket over his knees. Then he stared at her, eyes darting as he explored the changes to her face. "You are still so beautiful," he whispered.

Ruby had been surprised by the length of the hug, and now sudden compliments? They'd never been *this* close. "Uh, thank you?"

"Sorry," he said. "I'm on powerful drugs."

"Oh, cool. Me too."

They laughed again.

He'd always clung to her warmth. Other pupils were generally not nice to Kendall, so the basic decency she showed him seemed to shine bright. In fact, you could count the classmates Kendall might describe as his "friends" on a single hand. These included Ruby, Lauren – also a high achiever in academic terms – and Declan Rhodes, the partially-deaf albino kid. There were even rumours that Kendall and Lauren might have, at one point, been more than friends. But Ruby suspected, if there was any attraction, it would have been one-sided – just the longing daydreams of a young boy languishing in the friend zone of a pretty girl leagues above him. It would have been weird if Kendall *didn't* fancy Lauren. There wasn't anything overtly wrong with him, though, he'd just had that unmistakable air of a victim – he was too soft, his glasses were too thick and he was far too smart for his own good. But Kendall was actually quite charismatic and sharp when you got him talking. Though intellect doesn't always help you navigate the more perilous social waters of a secondary school. Because there are sharks. And they can smell a single drop of weakness from a mile away.

"So," he said, "what else do you want to know?"

"I was looking at the photos, from the reunion."

"Oh yeah?"

"You spoke to them? Mary, Scott, Elizabeth?" Named in order. That's what those three were now. Victims.

"I did."

"How was that?"

"Mary was fine," Kendall said. "She was quite drunk. Elizabeth was lovely as always. I saw Lauren too. Lauren Coates. She and Will . . ." He gestured as though they belonged to her. Then he hesitated. "You know they're together now, right?"

"I'm actually staying with them."

"Isn't that a bit . . . ?"

"We're all adults, it's fine."

"If you say so." A sceptical smile.

"You still in contact?"

"Not so much with Will, but I see Lauren from time to time. Still good friends, I would say. And, also, recently, been seeing her in a medical capacity. She performed my last three surgeries. Strange hearing people call her Doctor Coates. But, yes, the night, the reunion, it was good. It was nice to chat to everyone. Nicer than I thought it'd be."

A cat came into the room, stopped on the rug, then leapt up onto the sofa and pressed itself against Ruby's thigh. It felt warm through her cold, damp jeans. Ruby placed her hand above the cat and it lifted its head to make contact with her fingers. Then she stroked the fur, her thumb just behind its flicking ear.

"She likes you," Kendall said.

There was a short silence, just the sound of the cat's deep purr, the faint radio, and Ruby wasn't sure if she should prompt Kendall on that third name.

But then he sighed. "Scott was actually quite civil," he said. "I think he was wasted." Kendall put his index finger on one nostril and sniffed. "Lot of wide-eyed questions, you know."

"Was that the first time you'd spoken to him since school?"

Kendall nodded. Then he looked at the cat, back to Ruby. "I hope this isn't the wrong thing to say, but, when I heard that he was dead . . . I was . . ."

"You can say it," Ruby added. "You wouldn't be the first."

"I . . . I'm not sure if that's really how I feel. I used to think he was, well, evil. But nowadays I'm not sure if there actually is such a thing. Scott didn't choose his upbringing. He didn't choose to be that way. I don't know. What do you think?"

"Well, my interactions with him were not quite as extreme as yours."

Kendall seemed to know this point was coming. "There are a great number of people who had a reason to dislike Scott," he said. "And I appreciate I am high up on that list."

"Yes."

"You may have noticed I am in a wheelchair?"

Ruby looked at the spokes. They were decorated with colourful beads — red, yellow, green, purple, all turned pastel by time and sun. That's why the wheels had clicked when he moved. She imagined sliding those beads left and right, as though playing with an abacus. As though trying, in vain, to add something up.

"There was a story on the news just yesterday about a benefit cheat," she said. "Some guy who pretended to be disabled. There were photos of him playing volleyball on holiday. Rumbled."

Kendall laughed. "Yeah. But then again."

He removed the blanket from his legs — they were withered down to bone. They seemed almost mummified, even through trousers. His knees were like pieces of knotted wood.

"Fair enough," Ruby said.

"You can ask about it all, I don't mind. It's quite a saga."

"Any improvement?"

"Better mobility, no question. But it's been long enough now. I'm not as optimistic as Lauren seems to be. The plan was to have me up and walking in time for the reunion. Few steps in a frame last year. But, alas. Nerve damage is complicated. Then muscle degradation and all sorts."

"So that's a possibility? Walking again?"

"Apparently, according to her. Though I'm not holding my breath. It's the hope that kills you. This isn't ideal, I know that. Just . . ." He sighed. "Christmas before last, my grandad died, OK. Then, a week later, to the day, my mum went too."

"I'm sorry." Ruby wasn't quite sure what he was trying to say.

"The point I'm making is about perspective. Because, believe it or not, this . . ." He patted the leather arm of his wheelchair, then turned his head, showed Ruby the scar. A thick cord coming down his jaw, almost perfectly vertical. ". . . is not the worst thing that's happened to me." It looked like a train track running from his ear to his neck, pale stitch holes either side of the line. "To be honest, I feel *sorry* for Scott. At the reunion, he was off his face. He was a mess, in so many ways. I started talking to him, not the other way around. Really, who knows what was going on behind those eyes, but I doubt being Scott Hopkins was a picnic. Maybe that's punishment enough. Because I bet, despite everything, I'm happier now than he has ever been. Life is . . . it's . . . The universe is out to fuck you and Scott was just another part of it. Honestly, I've got no grudges. Blame is such a dead end."

Kendall had been dealt a tough hand. A childhood of bullying is one thing, but Scott had taken it to another level.

"And funnily enough, after that day, he left me alone," Kendall said. "As though maybe even he realised he'd gone too far."

"Can you remember much?"

"No, not really. Flashes, kind of. It was over something so stupid. He asked me to pass him his bag, which was on the grass. And I said no. Then he just went ballistic. He hit me, but I didn't retaliate. He hit me again and again. Foolishly, I stood up. Again.

98

And again. Then he kept pushing, shoving. Wanted to fight. And he pushed me closer and closer to the edge of the wall . . . Then, a final shove. I stumbled backwards and . . . Five feet. That's how far I fell." Kendall held his hand up just above his head. "That's it. As bad as he was, Scott can't have known that this," he looked down at himself, "would happen."

There were a lot of serious incidents at Missbrook Heights, but Scott attacking Kendall was by far the worst. It was remarkable on reflection that it took a further three weeks before the school expelled him. Senior staff seemed keen to frame the encounter as a fight, rather than an unprovoked assault. Expelling Scott was an admission of fault on their part – something they delayed as long as they could. But eventually downplaying it became untenable. Either way, poor Kendall was in hospital for weeks and received plastic surgery to repair his jaw and save his eye. Half of his teeth were implants. The injuries to his spine, and subsequent complications, eventually put him in this wheelchair.

Ruby thought about Scott at the reunion, posing with Kendall, leaning down to smile. To smile with all of his natural teeth. Inches from that scar, from all the damage he'd left behind. But there really was no malice in the photo. Maybe, to him, that day on the school field wasn't even significant. Victims remember. Bullies are free to forget.

"There is such a thing as evil," Ruby whispered, thinking out loud. "Unfortunately."

After a short silence, Zoe entered the room and stood behind Kendall, just over his shoulder. She seemed keen to join the conversation. "Talking about the reunion?" she asked.

"Yeah," Ruby said, hand on the cat's back, one finger under its thin collar. "I noticed that, uh, you took some photographs."

"That's right." Zoe removed her phone. "I'm guessing you want me to send them? All the ones I didn't put online?"

99

"Yes." Ruby looked up. "Yes, please, that would be helpful. Thank you." She spelled her email address.

"Is this to work out who was there?" she asked, swiping to the gallery. "Because the detectives have already done that."

Ruby could tell that Zoe was a controlling presence. The calm, open atmosphere had changed. Zoe was in charge now.

"No, not necessarily," Ruby said. "Just want to get a flavour of the night."

Zoe's phone emitted a whooshing, email-sent sound. "There you go." Then she put a hand on Kendall's forearm. "Did you mention that you spoke to all three?"

"Yes," he said, with slight impatience. Ruby sensed tension between them.

"Must be hard, for you." Zoe tilted her head sympathetically. "Kendall mentioned that you were good friends with Elizabeth. We saw her from time to time. Spent last Christmas together."

"Yeah?"

"Elizabeth's older brother is married to Kendall's stepsister."

"Small world." Ruby frowned, getting a grip on that connection.

"Welcome to Missbrook Bay." Kendall sighed. "One big happy family."

She thought back to those next of kin interviews, the recordings she'd listened to on her first day here. Elizabeth's was the hardest. Her grieving husband, now a single father. That unthinkable horror of life-deranging loss – it felt all too real in his juddering voice and Ruby had so nearly lost control. She had to pause it and step away.

The topic of Elizabeth seemed to shift the mood in the room again. Now tragedy descended. Kendall put two fingers on his lips, as though deep in thought. Then his eyes began to water and he covered his mouth, first with one hand, then with both.

"Aw, fuck," he said, muffled in his palms. His face fell into his hands and he groaned. Zoe squeezed his shoulder and Ruby reached out to touch his knee. It felt so small, like a child's leg. "It's OK," he added. She let go, leant back onto the sofa as the fickle cat fled across the carpet towards the kitchen. "Elizabeth was so . . ." He sniffed, took a breath, stroked Zoe's hand affectionately. "She was just so nice. It sounds pathetic to use that word. But she really was the nicest person. And those kids . . ." He shook his head, swallowed, approaching anger now. "It's like, Scott was the worst person imaginable, but Elizabeth? Elizabeth was the best."

There was a pause. And Ruby nodded. "She was."

"You are going to catch the person responsible," Zoe said, staring at her.

This seemed more motivational than a question. Maybe even an order. And Ruby nodded again, firmer now. "Yes, I . . . we will."

The three of them spoke for another hour or so and Ruby discovered, as she'd suspected, that they had left the reunion together, around midnight. She had what she came for – more than a hundred photos from that night waiting in her inbox.

Showing her to the door, Zoe stopped in the hallway and stepped close. "Listen," she said, checking over her shoulder to be sure Kendall couldn't hear. "All this has been a lot for him. Not just losing Elizabeth, but bringing all that Scott stuff up too. He's on strong medication and emotionally he's quite fragile. If the police do need to ask any more questions, can you make sure it's you? The other detectives were very cold. I did not like them."

"Sure," Ruby said. "I'll do my best."

She turned to the door.

"Your jacket."

"Oh, yes." Ruby hung it over her arm. "Thank you."

She stepped outside into the cool air. The rain had stopped. Now the late afternoon sun was breaking through the clouds, hitting the wet road. A blinding glare from every puddle – tarmac stars, speckled silver and twinkling. Combined with the rising steam, the ground was fiercer than her eyes could take. Ruby rounded the corner, and went through the recycling centre gates towards the car.

She climbed into the driver's seat. It felt clammy, damp inside, like a greenhouse – horribly warm with the sun at her back. The windows were still fogged up. Taking a deep breath, she slid the key into the ignition. Then she put her seatbelt on and looked up at the rear-view mirror, squinting. But she couldn't see a thing out of the back window, just glowing condensation – a sheet of white, like an X-ray light box.

And as she searched around the dashboard for a button to clear the glass, she heard something. Then, in an instant, she knew something. She just knew. She just *knew* that she wasn't alone. Before she even checked, she actually had time to think the words, *there's someone on the backseat.*

Eyes to the mirror.

And then, eerie and deliberate, a silhouette rose up behind her. Surreal, heavenly light eating into the shadow. A large male shape, backlit with a hood, a halo. Ruby didn't jump. Just the opposite. She froze as a thousand options fell away to leave just one. Get out. Run.

Half a second of silence and then, quick, she swung her hand down to undo the seatbelt but he grabbed her wrist. Then he seized the belt, yanked it back until it was tight across her waist.

Writhing, desperate and manic, Ruby threw her weight forwards and twisted, scrambling, getting the door half open, her fingers slipping off the handle, leaning but then slammed back, back into the seat as he pulled the belt, tugged it until there was no more give.

She tried to yell the word "help" but the last half was lost as he yanked the belt a final time, tearing the air from her lungs.

"Shut up," he said, "shut the fuck up."

Ruby turned to see if she could reach him – his eyes, his face, anything. But every time she moved the seatbelt tightened, like a constrictor, pulling her back, hard into the seat.

Realising she was stuck here, she stopped struggling. There was a strange moment of calm. Peace. Both of them catching their breath. Stalemate. OK. Now what, she thought.

She heard him move, strengthening his position, felt his mass against the back of the seat, imagined the belt coiled around his arm, his hand gripped firm.

His face came up close, just behind her ear.

Then, below, she saw something poke slowly between the seats, hovering above the handbrake. Eclipsing it. The grey barrel of a sawn-off shotgun. A clean beam of yellow light glinting off the metal. He placed the end against her ribs, pointing it up into her armpit.

"Listen to me very, very carefully," he whispered.

Chapter Seven

It was ironic to consider just how strong they make seatbelts. Ruby could hit a wall at top speed and, amid all the instantaneous mayhem that would entail, so many things would break. Limbs, organs, her skull. But not the seatbelt. Its sole purpose, no matter how extreme the force, was to keep her here. Right here, in this seat.

"Start the engine," the man said.

During the tussle, he had unplugged the seatbelt and was holding it behind her. He'd unspooled it to the very end of its runners, so her back was pressed flat against the chair.

Humanise yourself.

"Please can you loosen the belt?" she said. "It's hurting me."

There was a pause. And he did. He gave her an inch. It was still digging into her waist, still cutting against her collarbone, but she had some mobility back. Wiggle room. Not much but some.

Ruby gradually moved her hand to the key, eyes locked on the rear-view mirror. What was she going to do? She needed a plan.

"Quickly," he added.

But she stopped. His voice was familiar. She lowered her head slightly, leaning as far forwards as she could to make him out in the bright reflection.

Backlit and hooded, it was difficult to see his features. But the few she could see jutted out. Distinct cheekbones, wide chin, sharply depressed temples giving him a broad forehead. Pale. Dark eyed. Tall. He was definitely tall. And Ruby was now certain that she recognised him. He looked even more like Frankenstein's monster in this light than he ever had at school.

A young man who disappeared years ago. Now he was here, armed in her car, taking her hostage.

"Frank?" she whispered, staring into his reflection, wincing through the doubt. "Frank Enfield?" Ruby made sure she pronounced it properly, leaving enough of a gap between each name.

But he didn't reply. He just sprang forwards, disappearing from the mirror, but arriving at her side, in her peripheral vision, bashing hard against the seat.

"Drive the fucking car," he hissed, teeth together.

And he really meant it this time. She felt the gun again, pressing into her hip, firm enough to bruise.

The fight or flight adrenaline was dissipating. Ruby took an unsteady breath as she came to terms with the horrendous fact that neither was an option. All that remained was fear. No. Worse. Terror. The kind of claustrophobic dread that threatens to derail every human sense.

Humanise. Buy time.

"Please, Frank," she said, hands on the wheel, clearly visible, "I'll drive," fingers splayed, clearly submissive, "I'll do what you say," clearly scared, "but can you please stop pointing the gun at me."

She saw him checking through each window – looking once behind them, tetchy and fast. "What?" he snapped.

Ruby flinched, head bowed, shoulders tensed.

"What did you say?" He spoke quietly now, maybe in anger.

"The gun. Please can you lower the gun."

There is a third option in fight-or-flight situations. The thing we fear too much to even list. But, no, calm, breathe. Ruby was not going to die. She was going to think.

Do what he says. She started the engine and lowered the handbrake. And then, as though it was a fair trade, she felt him take the gun from her hip and sink away behind her.

"Thank you," she said.

But he maintained his grip on the seatbelt – holding it like a lead, as though Ruby was an unruly dog.

Reversing the car, carefully, slowly, her movements were conscious, considered – she turned the wheel with all the caution of a driving test. Textbook mirror checks. Clutch, into first gear and then—

God. Another spike of cold, goosebump horror. Nausea. Ruby felt a sudden need to lie down, collapse to the ground, curl up, knees to her chest, foetal, as though that might be the only way she'd feel comfortable. Or safe. Safe. The very idea of feeling safe seemed absurd, like she'd been a fool to ever believe it was possible. Stay calm, think. The humble beginnings of a panic attack shuffling her mind. Resetting each train of thought back to clean fear. Trapped. She was trapped.

The car was still. The engine turning over. Rumbling. Idle.

"Go," he said. "Drive to the gate."

Ruby thought about Giles. How would her stepdad handle this? How would he want *her* to handle this? His voice seemed to echo from the past. Remain calm. Even when you're scared. Do not allow terror to cloud your judgement.

OK. She drove towards the car park's gate – along rows of empty spaces.

But she was already breaking a crucial rule.

"If your captor wants to go somewhere else, you shouldn't go," Giles had told her. "Because the destination will be invariably advantageous to them, not to you. All you're doing is travelling to the scene of a crime."

Giles had given her endless hours of self-defence lessons. Military drills for a twelve-year-old girl. They had seemed so ridiculous, a complete waste of time. But now every piece of information was coming back to her, overruling the formal training she'd had since. His was far more thorough, far more focused on self-preservation.

"Resist at every opportunity. If told not to scream, then scream. If told not to run, then run. Every single moment of compliance helps your captor."

Then again, there were caveats. There were exceptions. Like here, now, they were in a quiet car park. The nearest house was a long way away, behind fences and hedges. There were no witnesses.

Ruby needed to get out onto the street – find some eyes. But, as she came to a stop at the open gate, Frank told her to turn left. She blinked slowly, her heart sinking. That direction took them away from the town centre. Still, she indicated and pulled out onto the old coast road.

Driving now, Ruby was able to think clearly. The real questions. Long overdue. What was this? What was happening? Where was Frank taking her? Why was he armed? Was the shotgun even real? Was it loaded? Had she already missed her—

". . . man, on a trapeze." Frank was mumbling something to himself. Whispering under his breath.

She just eyed him cautiously in the mirror. He was sitting back now, her seatbelt plug still in his hand – the rest wrapped around his forearm. She rose a little and saw the gun on his lap. Real enough.

"Very high up," Frank added. "And you can see him swinging. Did you see?"

She swallowed. "I . . . I'm not sure what you mean?"

Frank looked out the window, watched the world sweep past, fascinated like a child on holiday. As though it was all new to him. The sun was gone now – overcast grey had returned. But he still leant down to admire the sky above.

"He goes through the spotlight," he said, pointing at the brightest cloud over the ocean. It flickered in and out of view, between the gaps in the trees. "It's big and white." He smiled – tired but full of joy. "Round. The man in the middle has a walking stick. Welcome. Welcome. And he turns around, looking into the dark crowd."

Hands ten and two on the wheel, Ruby kept a straight face, fixed on the road ahead, her eyes widening ever so slightly. What the fuck is he talking about?

Then Frank made eye contact in the mirror, pulled his hood off his head and came forwards. But not to threaten her. Just to talk. "Does the circus still come?" He spoke clearly now. Normal. Casual.

"Pardon?" Ruby said. She'd heard him but she didn't fully understand.

"The circus *used* to visit. They had the tents on the recreation ground. I'm small so, well, it's obviously in the past. I just wondered if it still happens now."

"Oh, I . . . I'm not sure." Ruby was taking the gentle corners, staying within the speed limit.

"Can you find out?"

They were just leaving the boundaries of Missbrook Bay, turning inland – the scenery changing along the gradual incline, more trees lining the quiet road. Up ahead, she saw a sign for a layby. Three hundred yards.

"I could look online, if we pulled over?"

"No." He frowned. "No." Suspicion in his voice. "We'll look later. It doesn't matter. Not yet."

And Ruby watched the layby slide by the window, disappearing behind, shrinking in the rear-view mirror.

Frank's directions took them towards Brettwood, a tiny, secluded village a few miles outside of town. The roads began to narrow, passing through a tunnel of looming trees, long looped vines hanging down like swamp nooses in the shadows.

But then the woods opened up to sudden, sprawling fields either side of the car and, beyond the hedgerows, farmland that stretched for miles.

"Turn left," he said, urgently. "Up here. Left, left, left."

She slowed down, indicated and turned off the main road. A weaving rural lane now, steep grass banks and rare cut-outs to pass oncoming cars. But there were none. And she felt, once again, completely alone.

Had he been a stranger, Ruby may have already made her move. Opted for fight. But a few visceral scenarios played out in her mind. She imagined grabbing the gun, *bang*, losing a hand. Screaming. Wrestling around the interior of a moving car as he discharges the second barrel into the dash, or into her chest, wheels riding up the verge, rolling over and over in a haze of mud and glass and dust and whipping to a dead stop against a tree. Or simply slamming on the brakes, refusing to go any further and, just, what? Hope he wasn't true to his word? And if he was? The gun might poke through the headrest, like a curious snake, touch the back of her neck. She'd close her eyes. And *bang*.

She also considered deliberately crashing the car. But, even though the seatbelt was keeping her pinned in place, she wasn't properly wearing it. Frank's grip was strong, but it was nothing compared to the unimaginably brutal forces involved in a collision. Any impact would hurt them both. It'd be a fine balance – how much pain was she willing to endure? How much would freedom cost?

But the fact remained. He wasn't a stranger. Ruby knew him. They went to school together. She felt her physiology shift again – she'd weathered her mind's suggestive dance with that panic attack. Not today. Clarity now. She wasn't dead. She wasn't injured. She was just driving. Driving somewhere, for some reason, with Frank. Frank Enfield. Frankenfield from school.

"Where have you been?" she asked, eyes flicking to the mirror.

"Black door," he said, distracted by the window. "In the black door room." He looked forwards. "Where did you go?"

"I was working." Humanise. "I moved to Australia." This was good. Talking. A conversation. "I came back last week. What is the black door room?"

Silence.

"What's going on, Frank?" She sighed. "Hmm?" Eyes to the mirror. "Where are we going?"

"OK," he said. "There's another turning just up here, on the right. See that?"

There was a gap in the hedgerow – a metal gate propped open, sinking into the foliage like it would never close again. Ruby turned, the wheels rumbling over a cattle grid and off onto a gravel trackway.

Ahead, up the shallow hill, the horizon felt close, like a cliff edge, the rest of the world tucked away behind it. The terrain became steadily worse, a potholed track lined on both sides with long grass and brambles, scattershot blackberries, still red, still damp and polished from this morning's rain.

At the top, they came onto a flat concrete area in front of an old building. A neglected, ramshackle barn of some kind, possibly abandoned. There was an array of junkyard debris around the sides, rusted farm machinery, broken trailers, a fridge door, a white porcelain sink smashed in two, half swallowed by the ground – moss pouring out of the plughole.

110

"Park there," he said and the tyres crunched towards the only discernible space.

She turned the engine off. It felt empty, quiet and Ruby got the sense that there really was no one here, no ears to hear the fear that she might scream and yell and shout about.

"Get out," Frank said, releasing his grip.

And the seatbelt was loose, crawling over her as the runners sucked it back into its nest.

"Frank, listen to me, whatever's going on with you, I can help."

"I know you can. That's why we're here. Now get out of the car."

The back door opened. Still in the driver's seat, Ruby watched him climb out and stand at her window. He showed her the shotgun, then grabbed the handle. Hands up, on show, Ruby passed her legs out as he took three steps back, gun tracked on her at all times. She stood.

And now she got a good look at him. Six and a half feet tall. Thick dark hair, sunken eyes with dopey, dead, Addams Family shadows beneath. Frank wasn't fat per se. He was literally big boned. Even his fingers. An archaeologist uncovering his skeleton might wonder if his tribe considered him a giant. A mammoth. A warrior. His heavy brow would have looked right at home cooking hard-hunted meat in the flickering mouth of a cave.

He pointed behind her – she turned to the old building. It had a wooden door, which hung half open, the frame and hinges crumbling.

"Go," he said.

When she hesitated, he came forwards, grabbed the back of her collar and shoved her round the front of the car. Stumbling, Ruby began to walk.

"Go inside." She felt the barrel of the sawn-off shotgun pressing into her lower back, just above her coccyx.

111

There was a weakness in her stomach, hollow, almost like hunger. But the idea of ever having an appetite again seemed unimaginable. Part of her wished he was pointing the gun at her head or heart. Ruby knew about exit wounds. She knew what would happen if he pulled the trigger. What it would actually look like to be shot here, to look down and see it all explode and tumble from her stomach. Ragged strips of viscera slapping out onto the gravel ahead of her, grit and grass sticking to the wet bits. Somehow on the ground, watching gun smoke and steam rise away. But, as educated as her imagination was, Ruby knew it'd be so much worse in real life.

She realised she was slowing down – the door still ten metres away.

"Frank," Ruby said. Calm. Composure will pay dividends. Humanise yourself often. "Why are you—"

"Just go."

Another shove.

Slow motion now. This walk. This final stretch. This was it. The last window. Her last chance to roll the dice and run.

On her left, Ruby saw a footpath that led to an open field. Bare, spindly trees posted throughout, black like claws against the sky. They seemed somehow incomplete when the gargoyle birds perched at the highest points took flight. Now they circled, surveying the world below, searching for smaller things to kill.

On her right, Ruby watched the wind glisten and shiver across the dark green crops, waves stroking the earth. A vast, passive creature big enough to seem perfectly still beneath our feet, unmoved by the endless plight of our tiny little lives.

And there, dead ahead, a half-broken façade of ivy and wood around that open door.

Now just a few paces to go. Time to decide.

She could take off running down that footpath, past those stark and Gothic trees, through startled birds that swarmed like bats. Maybe he'd miss. Maybe he wouldn't even shoot. Or maybe he'd panic and she'd get a back full of shotgun pellets. Maybe she'd fall and it would become something far worse than it was ever going to be.

But Ruby didn't run. She just walked up to the old wooden door and stopped. Then she turned around and faced him. Frank was right there, shotgun at his hip – pointing at her gut.

Again, she thought about the training. About the best places to strike. Throat, groin, solar plexus. Eyes. A thousand ways to hurt a man long enough to flee. Funny how a military veteran like her stepdad had always taught her that physical conflict was an absolute last resort. Fleeing or fighting were at two ends of the spectrum. Two points on a map. One of which you never want to visit.

"The idea is to be strong enough, fast enough, smart enough to never even have to fight," he'd say. "The only violent encounter you're guaranteed to survive is the one you do not have."

But this? Whatever this was, it was surely not what Giles had been preparing her to face.

"Go inside now," Frank said.

Was there another option? Could she survive without fight or flight? Could she find her way to an uncharted place on that map?

Was that it? Ruby wondered, as she turned back around and pushed the door. Hope? Was that what had kept her complying? Hope that she could talk her way to safety? Was her nervous system wrong about the danger? Was the snake really just a stick? Or was it simply fear stripping her of all rational judgement?

Whatever the explanation for her behaviour, Ruby watched herself stride inside the dimly lit space, the ground now dry mud with a light covering of hay. Walking slowly along the planked wall, she stepped past a stack of rotting pallets, a barrel and, hand on a beam, tentatively leant round to peer into the main section of the building.

Above, there was a cramped loft space, a low balcony running the length of the roof, the ladder missing all but three rungs. Along either side of the ground floor, small pens for animals – metal feeder baskets tied to gates with baling twine. Empty. The most recent sign of life was a sleeping bag in one of the enclosures but, as it was covered in brown dust and woodchips, it clearly hadn't been used for years.

The air smelled like cold mud, the tang of old copper and was lit by the slightest lines of vertical white between the planks. Sensory details, future triggers for flashbulb memories she hoped she'd live long enough to make.

Further inside now, she could see the large space in the centre of the barn – the concrete strip between the animal pens. In the middle, there was a clean wooden table with chairs on either side. It looked like a makeshift interview room.

Frank was crouched in the corner, fiddling with a portable halogen floodlight. The square kind you see at building sites, with a yellow cage frame and a curved black handle. Click. It came on, glowing a deep, low-battery orange, barely lighting the space. Table leg shadows long and stretched to the wall.

He turned, looked over his shoulder. "Sit down," he said.

And, still dazed in the fog of hope or fear, she did.

Then she watched as Frank came round to her side, his gait heavy and laboured. He pulled something metal from his jacket pocket. And Ruby sat, eyes wide, as a pair of handcuffs clattered onto the centre of the table.

They were real. Not the fluffy pink kind you see in sex-shop windows, not the fancy-dress toys with safety catches. No. Genuine, heavy, uncompromising handcuffs. This was the red line. This would be the turning point. Ruby had no idea what was going to happen next, but she knew what *wasn't* going to happen. She'd risk both barrels before those cuffs clicked home around her wrists. There is not enough hope or fear in a thousand troubled lives to justify following that order.

All the speculation and indecision faded. Fight. Ruby would go down fighting. She felt her heart rate pick up and breathed carefully through her nose, hands forming fists. Not if, but when.

Then Frank lumbered over to the other chair, pulled it out and sat down opposite her. The shotgun was on his lap, half hidden beneath the hem of his . . . jacket.

Ruby sighed. How had she missed it? Why hadn't she even wondered? It seemed so embarrassingly obvious now the thought arrived. Closing her eyes and bowing her head, she settled decisively and irrevocably on the first thing she'd felt back in the car. She'd been foolish. There was no hope here. The question was, what kind of man had he grown into since those hazy days at Missbrook Heights? Who exactly was he?

And now she had an answer. Frank Enfield was wearing a dark-blue jacket.

Chapter Eight

Unable to fly, unwilling to fight, Ruby had just obediently walked into the jaws of that third, unthinkable, unlistable option. Sitting now in the middle of nowhere, face to face with what? With who? An armed killer? That made as much sense as any other explanation. No, Ruby thought, thinking clearly for the first time since he rose up behind her in the car. It made more.

She looked over her shoulder, towards the door, past the dim orange light in the corner of the barn. Then back to Frank – huge and heavy, seemingly lost in his own thoughts, like he was racking his brain for the next thing to say. And finally, Ruby's eyes tilted down and settled on those handcuffs in the middle of the table between them. Time to go, she thought.

Gently placing the balls of both hands on the edge of the table, Ruby got a firm grip. She planned to shove it, stand, turn and run. And if he caught her? She would fight. This was it. Feet flat on the ground, muscles ready, she swelled with a final breath and—

"What was your name?" Frank asked.

Ruby stopped. Deflating, blinking, she frowned. "You . . ." The phrasing had tripped her up – what *was* her name. "You know my name."

"Answer the question."

Was he toying with her? Was this just foreplay for whatever nightmare he had planned?

"It's the same."

Then he rubbed his eye with the back of his wrist. "I mean, what . . . what is your name now?"

Silence. "Ruby," she finally said.

"Ruby what?"

"Ruby Shaw."

"Where do you . . . Who do you work for?"

"The National Crime Agency."

"Anyone else?"

"I . . . we assist the police."

Frank squinted at her, nodding slowly. "What colour is the sky?" he asked and now he seemed suspicious of her answer.

"Listen, I—"

He banged the table – she flinched. "What colour is it?" He glared.

"Blue."

"Say that it's red."

She could see both of his hands – the sawn-off shotgun still on his lap. Would that extra half a second be enough?

"Why?"

"Say it."

Ruby turned her head, hesitating, confused. "The sky is . . ." she shrugged, "red."

"Say it again."

"The sky is red."

And Frank leant towards her, staring into her face, studying every feature. "One more time."

"The sky is red."

"Now." He tapped the table with his thick index finger. "Now. From now. From *now on*. If you lie to me, even once, I will hurt you. Badly. Do you understand?"

Ruby nodded, realising that it wasn't just the ramblings of a madman. Frank had been looking for tells – trying to detect her lies.

Then he took a long breath, as though building up some courage. Some nerve to ask his next question. The big one. For all the drums and confetti, for the light show and applause. For that one-million-pound cash prize . . . "Where, is, Scott, Hopkins?" he said, a new intensity levelling his voice.

Ruby opened her mouth, but paused. And Frank glared again, as if to warn her. No lying. Was this another test? Was he insane enough to have killed someone and forgotten? Was the jacket a coincidence?

"Do you really not know?"

"I'm asking you. Now answer me."

"Scott is dead," she said, holding his eyes in hers, nodding to be crystal clear about it.

"But . . ." Frank winced, recoiling like he'd smelled something bad. It seemed to cause him physical pain. "Do you promise?"

"I'm sorry," Ruby whispered. "I know you were friends. I know it's—"

"Do you promise?" Desperation now.

"Yes. I promise."

Groaning, he pressed his palms against his temples and, elbows on the table, scrunched his sunken eyes shut. Ruby sat forwards, spotted the gun on his lap. But then Frank looked again, and her eyes drifted back up to his.

"Have you seen the body?" he asked.

"Yes."

"In real life? With your own eyes?"

"I've seen photographs."

"So, that means . . ." He bounced in his seat – excited, hopeful. "It, it means you can't be sure?"

Ruby just stared at him. His broad nose had no bridge, a straight line from his forehead – like a Roman helmet. A gladiator. And he nodded, frantic enthusiasm animating his pale face.

This instability was double-edged. Hope and fear were back again. A lot of things can be found in the midst of volatility and chaos. But plenty more can be lost. Exploitable, dangerous and glinting from his very soul, Ruby was now absolutely certain that she was dealing with madness.

"Right?" he added, his eyes were electric with it. "You can't be?"

"Look, I . . ."

"You just said, you haven't seen his body."

"I know," Ruby held up a hand, "I know, but the police—"

"What? They did what? They *told* you he was dead?"

"I have seen close-ups of his injuries. There is an active investigation. People have dissected his corpse. They've looked inside his stomach."

Ruby wasn't quite sure why she'd highlighted that. Maybe because examining the stomach's contents was the pinnacle of invasion, intrusion – a breach of all dignity and privacy reserved only for surgeons and pathologists. He or she is now a piece of evidence, naked, open, split. The meal they never knew had been their last picked apart with tweezers, inspected, brightly lit under a magnifying glass, written about in detail you wouldn't even find on the packet.

"And it was all real?" Frank said. "Is it possible that it's a trick? Please, please be honest." He reached across the table, offering his hand. But she didn't move. "Please, actually think." Eye contact now, his fingers jittery, appealing, begging, making a fist. "Think. Think. Is it one hundred percent?"

"Why would they lie?"

"I'm just asking you to consider it."

His doubt was infectious. Ruby started to wonder if there could be a conspiracy. Some grand scheme at play. She thought about the very nature of information. Things we know. How much we learn about the world comes, ultimately, from the mouths of other people. From text. Screens. Books. Can we be one hundred percent sure of anything beyond the bedrock of our own existence, in whatever form it actually takes? She thinks, therefore . . .

"It's all on a scale of plausibility," Ruby said. "The earth could be flat. But it probably isn't. You could be a brain in a jar. But you're probably not."

"So, say it. It's possible that he's alive."

She really hadn't expected to be having a philosophical discussion about the fundamentals of truth but, sure, "It is possible," she said.

"How could it be? Speculate."

Ruby thought for a few seconds, looking over his shoulder at the barn's planked walls – the slight glow from outside was nothing but pure white, no detail, just light. The vertical lines shifted, seeming to breathe, brightening, dimming, almost disappearing from time to time as the clouds moved across the sky.

"I . . . I suppose if he faked his death somehow," she said. "But there was a body. And Mary and Elizabeth died in similar ways. So . . ." Blood, dental records, tattoos, his family, the crime scene. DNA. Not to mention the hundreds of people contributing to the investigation. This was ridiculous. "Frank, listen to me, it might be difficult to accept, but he really is gone . . . Scott is dead."

"OK." Frank sat up straight, nodded, upset but acting mature. A brave face, like a little boy who's agreed to be a big one. "I believe you."

She narrowed her eyes and nodded along with him.

"We will say that it's a fact," he added. "And it will always be a fact?"

Ruby wasn't surprised by this anymore; she just dutifully answered his questions. "Correct."

"He can't come back?"

"No. He is dead, so that means he will be dead in the future."

"Forever?" Frank asked, with unsettling sincerity. "Scott was just . . . a man?"

She nodded again. Then she swallowed, feeling oddly unqualified to be having this conversation. Murderer or not, Frank needed to be incarcerated. He required far more help than she could ever provide.

"And the others? Mary and Elizabeth? They're dead in the same way?"

"They are."

"I understand." Composure returned. Next question . . . "Did someone murder them?"

Ruby had learned her lesson about definitive responses. "I believe so, yes."

"Did *you* do it?"

"No." Ruby shook her head, adding an emphatic, "No."

"Are you looking for the murderer?"

"Yes."

There was a long pause and the pendulum of intensity swung back to the table. Frank seemed suddenly panicked, vulnerable. Forgetting his big boy pledge, he hunched over, curled in on himself and looked up at her from the corner of his eye. "Did I do it?" he whispered, horrified by the idea. "Is . . ." And his chin quivered. "Is it possible that it was *me*?" He searched her face again, as though Ruby was his oracle and her answer would change everything. "Am I really that dangerous?"

She felt her own lip judder as she took a shallow breath. Maybe this was why he'd brought her here. To find out if he was a suspect. For the first time, Ruby was tempted to lie. Comfort the beast. Distract with gentle deception and then do what she should have already done, flee, *run*.

But she couldn't. She just said, "It is possible."

"Do you *believe* I did it?" Slight threat behind his eyes, pupils wide and shark black.

What did she believe? "I . . ." What was her honest answer to this question? "I don't know," she said.

"Do you think I *could be* a murderer?"

Ruby looked again at his jacket, considered the fact she'd been brought here against her will, at gunpoint, by a visibly disturbed man who'd been missing for more than a decade. Then she closed her eyes and sighed. "Yes."

"I think . . ." He tilted his head, like he was trying to recall an ancient memory. "I think I might be who you're looking for. I *am* dangerous. I just . . . I get confused about time. Do you think more about the past, the future or the present?"

"I'm not sure. I worry about the future sometimes."

"Are you worried about the future now?"

"Very."

"Why?"

Ruby just gave him a sad smile.

Then another thought came to him. He looked at his hands, lowered his head, eyes darting around the gloomy barn. "What if I'm remembering this?" he said, distrustful of every sight, every sense.

"Remembering what?"

"This." He touched the table. "This conversation. You. What if this is a memory I am having?"

Ruby shook her head. "No. This is now."

"Are you sure?"

"Yes."

"It's hard to know things." He seemed to be speaking to himself. "You can't trust the TV. Or doctors. Or . . . or even your own memories. Memories are created in your mind. That's why I had to ask about Scott. I had to be sure. The news said he was dead but I had to hear it from Ruby directly. Does she understand? Do you understand?"

"Maybe but I'm not—"

"I think you arrest me. Or, you will, or you did? For murder." He turned to the corner of the room, squinting in thought. "But I . . . Can you be charged for crimes you haven't committed yet?"

"Not . . . not unless there is evidence that proves you're going to do it."

"I just, I can see . . . It's like I can feel it. Somewhere . . . Maybe it's in the future? If Scott *is* dead then I would . . . I would *have* to . . . So . . . You want to arrest me?" Pointing at her, his face lit up, this was a significant revelation. "That's it, isn't it?" He wagged his finger. "You *want* to arrest me."

"Please, Frank . . ."

"Answer the question," he said, flashing that menace again. "Do not lie."

"Yes," she breathed, compelled by inexplicable honesty. "I want to arrest you."

Now he appeared to be calm, a new idea reassuring him. It made sense. "OK. Right. I understand." And he nodded decisively. "I understand what I have to do." He put both hands on the table.

"Frank, wait," Ruby's heart hurt – terror surging back, "please—"

He rose. Suddenly so big. Standing, looming in front of her, above her. Tall. Huge. Ruby dwarfed, tiny, frozen in her seat.

"We're done here," he said.

Predator's eyes – empty, looking at her, looking *through* her. Total indifference. The way bears regard meat, moving or still, it doesn't matter.

Then he picked up the cuffs, stepped around the table, coming towards her.

Ruby shook her head. Fuck. It was happening.

"Put these on," he said.

Happening instantly – in one motion, Ruby sprang to her feet, knocking the chair back and, without a beat, she punched Frank in his jaw. Harder than she thought possible. He barely flinched, leant away, frowning in disapproval more than anger. Lifting a hand, he blocked her second strike, grabbed her wrist, then her scruff and tried to—

She tugged her weight sideways.

"What are you—"

Ruby headbutted him – flinging her skull like a hammer into his face, feeling his nose crack against her forehead, so hard it rattled her. Dizzy, tunnel vision, the end of a piano note fading in her ears as she lowered herself to one knee, looking up as he turned, reeled. A blurred shape – a man, a giant – stumbling, hand on one of the animal pen gates, the metal clacking as he kept his balance.

Turning back, Ruby grabbed her wooden chair and, again, she was rising and she spun, swung round to her feet and hit him with it – a deep thumping sound as it connected to the side of his head, spinning wildly, bouncing away, landing unbroken nearby.

He shielded himself and, without even looking, leant over and pushed Ruby away with one hand, hard enough to throw her to the ground – thudding to her back, she skidded across the rough concrete and stopped near the wall. She rolled onto an elbow – level now with the soft sunset glow from the floodlight in the corner.

And there. On the other side of the table. The gun shifted into focus. Right there, just a few metres away, under his chair, and Ruby went to her front and crawled, scrambling, up, up and diving, her shoulder colliding with the table leg as she snatched it, rolled over onto her back, ready to fire, expecting him to be close, above her.

But he hadn't moved. He was just standing in the corner, touching his face, eyes closed, feebly waving a hand as though he was being swarmed by some annoying insects, shocked and rocked but still solid on his feet.

Keeping the sawn-off shotgun aimed squarely at his chest, Ruby went carefully to one knee, then stood. She quickly cocked it, saw a pair of bronze circles neatly in the chambers looking back up at her, then snapped it shut again, angry and relieved to see that it was loaded.

They both panted, neither speaking, a clean line of free-flowing blood pouring from his cupped hand, like he was holding his nose on his face.

Ruby felt warmth trickling onto her eyebrow — her forehead aching.

"Why did you hit me?" he mumbled, leaning down to pick up the cuffs.

"On the ground." She sniffed. "Lie down." She wiped her face with a sleeve.

"What are you doing?" he said. He held the cuffs out with his right hand, his left palm on show — red and dripping — his eyes glassy and hurt. "I want you to put them on. Please." Then he strode towards her.

"No," she yelled. "Fuck you. Lie down." She stepped backwards, clumsy, almost tripping over the chair. "Down." She kicked it aside.

Ruby's forehead felt tight. An egg-shaped pressure – she touched it quickly, ah, flinched, blinked, her eyeballs seeming to throb. How was he still standing?

He came forwards again and she sidestepped, the corner of the table between them.

"Frank," she shouted. "Stop. *Stop*." She jutted the gun towards him, holding it high. "I promise, if you take one more step, I will shoot you." She felt the trigger against her finger and knew it wasn't a hollow threat. One more inch and she'd end it.

Silence. Both of them stood still, the halogen light on the ground behind Ruby made her shadow big, bigger than Frank, big enough to put him in the dark. But Frank, blood dripping, face innocent and sincere, did the opposite. He stepped back, further eclipsing himself in Ruby's fanned shadow, hands lifted above his head.

"But, I . . ." He seemed more confused now than he had during the entire conversation. "I . . ." And then a smile became a laugh. So informal and friendly, as though she was being silly. This was all a big misunderstanding. "Oh, no. No." Then he brought his wrists together and held them forwards, the cuffs dangling from his red fingers. "I meant, put them on me." A kind, submissive offering. "See."

Ruby felt the gun sink, confusion dissolving all the urgency and desperation. She aimed again. "Please lie on the ground."

"I can . . ." He closed one of the cuff rings on his wrist, nodding. "I can lie down. I'll lie on my front so you don't have to worry. I understand, I'm sorry."

Then he knelt down and lowered himself to the ground, lying flat, just like she'd asked. He put his hands behind his back and waited. "You will have to close the other one," he said, arching his neck to see her. "You arrest me. Then I go to prison. I think that's how it goes."

Ruby glanced around the barn in disbelief, frowning, smiling – the sheer incredulity of something impossible, surreal, like that moment when you just know you're dreaming. But she wasn't. Frank really was lying on the dusty concrete floor.

"Stay there . . . stay still."

Stepping slowly out of the halogen light, Ruby approached him from behind. Still apprehensive, she crouched between his legs, held the gun with one hand and locked the cuffs with the other, tugging to check they were secure.

He put his cheek on the ground, one eye looking up at her.

"Thank you," she whispered.

Then she stood a few paces away, ordered him to stand and walk back the way they came, back to the door. Frank, at gunpoint the whole time, dutifully complied.

Outside now, they went across the gravel towards the car. Ruby opened the back door and again, she stood clear, well out of reach, her back to the farm machinery rusting amid the overgrown nettles, the weeds and wilting grass.

"Get in."

And he did. He climbed into the backseat. Ruby realised that, during this entire ordeal, she'd been busy catastrophising, imagining the countless ways this *could* have gone. But leaving here with Frank Enfield in handcuffs had seemed, well, it hadn't seemed like anything. It was literally unthinkable. And yet here they were.

Now he was settled on the backseat, Ruby put the gun on the ground behind her. Then she leant over, closer to his face than she'd like to be, and clicked his seatbelt on. An intimate moment of silence when she realised, even with her throat inches from his teeth, that she wasn't in any danger.

She crouched down at his side in the open doorway and checked his injuries, surprised to see he was remarkably intact. While his nose was effectively destroyed and he had a swelling on the side of his head, none of it called for a hospital visit. He seemed, for want of a better word, fine.

"Where have you been, Frank?" she asked, reaching into her pocket. "All these years?" He just stared dead ahead as Ruby shuffled on her knee and screwed some tissue up his nostrils. It must have hurt, but he didn't react.

"Hmm?" she added, wiping blood off her thumb. "Where did you go?" Still, silence. "Did you kill them?" And Ruby leant round, trying to catch his eyes.

Frank glanced at her once, then bowed his head. "No comment," he said.

Nodding, smiling, Ruby patted his thigh. "OK." With a long sigh, she put a hand on her knee and pushed herself upright.

She went round to the boot and placed the shotgun inside. Slamming it shut, she grimaced at a cold sensation in her hand. The pain was overwhelming, sickening. Testament to the power of adrenaline, which had been keeping what now felt like a broken bone secret all this time. Ruby had punched him so hard. How on earth did he stay on his feet?

Her shoes crunched as she went round and stood at the driver's door. Over the roof of the car, she could see back down the track, the stones gathered in the middle, the shape of tyres tracing two parallel lines – pothole puddles, warm, like pools of light in the earth. The air smelled heavy, of mud, ploughed fields and green leaves, weeds and agriculture. Rural, nostalgic and far enough inland not to hear the gulls or smell the sea. The scenery felt different now, better without the grinding dread of imminent death shrouding it all.

Ruby climbed into the driver's seat, then she pressed the child lock button for the back doors. For a few seconds, she stared at Frank in the rear-view mirror. He seemed like he was somehow gone. All the fever and double-edged madness had drained from his eyes.

But now, with the tables fully turned, Ruby felt reborn, newly grateful to simply take another breath. Even the fresh throb of her injuries wasn't unpleasant in a conventional sense. More like the ache of a hard day's work. Tolerable, because she'd earned the right to rest. She'd earned the right to sit and heal and, tonight, fall asleep in seconds.

It was late. Above the fields and crops, over the flowering ground elder in every hedgerow, dusk was settling in. The sun was low enough to shine onto the underside of the overcast. Clouds set alight, a ceiling of freeze-framed fire that made all those busy birds black.

"Look at that." Ruby squinted out of the window, blinking at the beautiful view. Smiling, she glanced back to check Frank was looking too. And he was. "The sky is red," she whispered.

Chapter Nine

Ruby was at the station building, sitting in the offices next door to the three-cell custody suite. Again, she got the sense that this place was winding down for its scheduled closure in just under a week's time. Most of the day-to-day police work had already stopped, most desks were bare, most chairs sat turned aside and empty. Single pens in solitary pots, kitchen cupboards with no more than one mug per head, entire rooms that now seemed huge and loud without curtains or cabinets. Just sprawling carpets that stretched from wall to wall, dark and depressed where furniture had been, the scuffs and stains of bygone days that may well be nostalgic to someone old. Or someone dead and rolling beneath the earth, angry that the backdrop of a thousand stories from their long, rich, colourful career had been silenced by the echoing acoustics of a truly desolate place.

Ruby wondered whether, if not for all this incongruous death, the station would be entirely dormant. But, then again, it meant that everyone here was here for the same reason, every mind focused on the same task. And today, they needed one of those cells, so the whole engine of processing a suspect dusted itself off and whirred into action.

Frank Enfield had just no-commented his way through his initial interview. He only broke his silence once, not even responding to a question. Interrupting, he said, "I am dangerous, I need to be locked up."

Now Ruby and Jay were waiting while a doctor had a go at assessing him. In cases like this, there is a temptation to stop the Liaison and Diversion services from getting involved too soon. Especially when it seems inevitable the suspect will be deemed mentally ill. But with Frank, it didn't really matter where he ended up, at least in the short term. Besides, a padded room and some medical intervention was definitely a good place to start.

"Here you go," Jay said, approaching Ruby, phone in hand. "Check your email."

Seated at her desk, she refreshed the inbox on her laptop. Before she even read the message he'd forwarded, Jay added, "Anonymous tip. From some teller at the bank. She recognised Frank – called in a few days ago."

"And it's taken this long to find its way to us? What was he doing?" Then Ruby checked the wording of the email. Frank had been in the bank, withdrawing a "large sum of money".

"No word yet about how much," Jay said.

"Wonder what it was for?"

"New marbles?" He went to the desk opposite her and sat down with a long groan. "Nickname makes sense now." Jay slouched back in his swivel chair, still staring at the closed interview room door, and began twisting his wedding ring. Busy hands. "Very unusual man."

"Uh, well, yeah. Yes."

There were a few detectives at work in the office behind him, the building continuing to feel both empty and occupied, stuck in a state of limbo.

Jay sighed, sat up, grabbed a pen. "Remind me of the exact wording?"

"He said that I 'arrest him for murder'. The implication was that he *would* kill someone, though he seemed somewhat confused about the details."

"Strange."

"But I think it fell short of what you might call a confession."

"He's a big boy. Six four, six five?"

"About that."

"And your notebook? The guy who broke into Will's place?"

Ruby shook her head. "No, I think he was smaller. And can you imagine Frank picking a lock?"

"Sound point. He strikes me more as a kick-the-door-down kind of man . . . See he kept looking at the clock?"

Ruby, who'd been a silent observer during the interview, had noticed that. "Yeah, he seems to have a thing with time."

"You think he's," Jay tapped the side of his head, "all there?"

"Absolutely not."

"Doctor Wallace is good, she'll give us something. Happy to sail close to the wind with the whole patient confidentiality stuff."

"Oh, and," she said, "I checked the car – card's not there."

Ruby had used the code to get inside, having, at some point, lost the laminated ID swipe card Jay gave her for the door. It almost certainly fell out of her pocket at the barn. But, if she was honest with herself, she could not recall the last time she saw it. Again, she was unnerved by the fear that she'd simply left it somewhere and forgotten.

"I'm sure it'll turn up, if you were rolling around in there. But I'll get a replacement for you."

Ruby had an icepack wrapped in a damp tea towel resting on her hand and, with a wince, she carefully readjusted it. The pain was dull, pulsing with that unique throb of broken bone. But she hadn't gone for an X-ray. Not yet. She wanted to stay here and see the verdict on Frank. And it went beyond professional involvement.

She actually felt attached, perhaps even a slight affinity, like he belonged to her in some way.

"How is it?" Jay asked.

"Feeling better," Ruby lied. "Thank you."

Of all the things to reflect on from that incident, she kept thinking about her punch. Analysing every detail. Up until the age of eighteen, Ruby had boxed competitively and, if not for some ill-timed injuries, it might even have become her career.

Again, this was partly thanks to her stepdad's influence. It seemed a great way to appease him – learn self-defence while excelling at something. And she was good. Her record was solid. She'd only lost two fights – both on points, both of which she'd inwardly contested. Judges were fallible. Those particular judges were arguably blind.

She replayed it in her mind, leaping up from her chair and swinging, connecting with Frank's jaw, as hard as she could, which, bare-knuckled, was far too hard. Comfortably hard enough to break a hand. Her form was perfect. Her hips rotated with absolute precision. And yet, he didn't go down. Worse, he didn't even wobble. Did this say more about her weakness, or his strength?

Either way, a bizarre insecurity simmered in her stomach. She'd always believed that, if nothing else, she had the ability to knock someone out. Or, at the very least, stop them dead in their tracks. A secret power, like walking around with a weapon that no one could see.

She flexed her wrist, inspected her swollen knuckles, glossy skin, wet and pink from the frosty tea towel – plausibly broken, sure, but the damage seemed correctly spread on her first two fingers. Maybe it landed too high on his face? Maybe the punch wasn't as perfect as it felt? Or maybe Ruby just wasn't as good at punching people in the face as she'd believed she was?

It was ridiculous that she kept dwelling on this, and the pride she felt when Jay commented on Frank's injuries – "You did a number on him" – was followed by shame. She was simultaneously ashamed to be proud and ashamed that she had no reason to be. Why? Why didn't he go down?

"Don't think I'd have driven out there alone with him," Jay said, his wonky, half-drooped mouth locked in disapproval. "No offence, but that was a hell of a gamble."

As though there was an alternative. Ruby shook her head at him.

"I was at gunpoint." She frowned. "What the fuck would you have done?"

"I'm not sure how I would have fared. I'm not trying to offend you. I was just saying, you were extremely lucky."

He just couldn't help himself. This was by far the worst thing about Jay. He had an opinion on everything. He always – *always* – had something to say. But he was right. It was luck, not competence, that meant Ruby was sitting here.

She clenched her jaw. "Have you ever been punched in the face, Jay?"

Still seated at his desk, he held his fists up, as though ready to fight. "You got a taste for it now?"

"No, no, just wondering."

Despite his resoundingly punchable disposition and the palsy melt on the left side of his features, which could pass for damage, Jay had the demeanour of someone who had, by chance, gone his whole life *without* being punched in the face.

"It's a formative experience that everyone should encounter at least once," Ruby added. "Humbling. It's difficult to maintain arrogance when you know it's an option."

"Wow." Jay seemed taken aback and, uncharacteristically, sat perfectly still. "Does sound like fighting talk."

Then she felt another surge of shame, guilt. She was projecting. Being mean. Unpleasant. All the things she hates. "I'm sorry," she said. "I don't . . . I'm just tired. I'm tired and my fucking hand is so obviously broken." She lifted the ice pack. Bright red knuckles. Her eyes stung, right on the edge of tears, watering all by themselves. "I'm really sorry."

"It's cool," Jay said. "You don't need to apologise. I can handle the rough and tumble."

And now she felt even worse. She rubbed her eye and sighed. "I just don't understand."

"Relax. If he's our man, it's over. And you got him." He lifted his arms. "Hurray." Though even this, with his monotone drone, sounded sarcastic. "And if not, we cross him off and carry on."

She focused her attention on her laptop screen, tapping the right cursor key to scroll through the reunion photos Zoe had emailed. They were essentially a selection of the same pictures Ruby had already seen, interspersed with inferior versions. Some blurred, some with a thumb in the corner – a few selfies of Kendall, which looked like they were taken without Zoe's consent. She thought back to those abacus beads on his wheelchair's spokes – that distinct clicking sound, sharp as a ticking clock, but clattering along with all the chaos of rainfall.

"Anything good in there?" Jay asked.

"Nope." Ruby tapped, tapped, tapped. "Same old stuff."

Funny how crucial and urgent this line of inquiry had felt before Frank derailed everything. Now it seemed irrelevant. Maybe even futile.

"What did you think of her?" Jay said.

"Zoe? Bit dominant, maybe, but pleasant. Pretty sure she's more than just Kendall's carer."

"I got that impression too."

"There was also a moment when—"

135

The interview room door handle moved – both their heads snapped to look as it opened and Doctor Wallace stepped out, eyes wide. Ruby and Jay turned in their chairs, awaiting her judgement. She'd been in there for more than an hour and, as she strode towards their desks, looked as though she'd just returned from the frontline of a war that you *would not believe*.

For a good few seconds, she didn't make eye contact, just stood, staring vacantly at the window. "In all my years," she eventually said, speaking to herself. "So . . ." She looked between them. "Which one of you is in charge?"

Ruby held her good hand up, as though grandly presenting none other than Senior Investigating Officer Jay Simmons. Grabbing a nearby chair, Doctor Wallace sat down and wheeled close with her heels, positioning herself at the end of their desks.

"Tenterhooks," Jay said.

"Well . . ." She rubbed her forehead with the back of her hand, then sighed, a heavy puff of tired air. "Right. OK." The doctor reached out and picked up a Post-it note.

Ruby and Jay waited patiently while she jotted down an address.

"You know this place?" She held it up so both of them could see.

Leaning in, Jay nodded. "Sure. Old Hopkins' Farm. That's Scott's house."

"Have you been there?" Doctor Wallace asked.

"Some of our officers interviewed his girlfriend. Or ex-girlfriend."

"So you haven't searched it?" She was speaking to Ruby now.

"No, right?" Ruby checked in with Jay. He shook his head.

"I'd recommend that you do."

"And what about Mr Enfield?" Jay asked.

"He's . . ." Then she lowered her voice. "He's meant to be on medication. Seems he's been off it for a long, long time."

"So, would you say he's . . . ?" Jay pretended to search for the right word.

"Mentally unwell?" She lifted her eyebrows. "Did you really need a medical professional to tell you that? Yes. He needs to go to hospital. Today."

"Let's just take it slow for now," Jay said. "We're going to charge him with something. He abducted you at the very least."

But Ruby hesitated, half-shrugged. "I . . . I'm easy." She waved her good hand. "As long as we know where he is, might pay to hold out for something bigger?" She spoke quietly, as if they were conspiring together in the hushed tones required when operating outside of protocol or law. "Something solid."

"Getting him sectioned, yeah." Jay was fiddling with his shirt sleeve, his tics speeding up. "That could work."

"Honestly, even without all of today's adventures," Doctor Wallace gestured to Ruby's injuries, "he wouldn't be going any-where. I've started the ball rolling."

The three of them exchanged eye contact – agreement all round. But Ruby held the doctor's gaze for a few seconds longer.

"Do you think he killed them?" she asked.

Doctor Wallace did not respond. Instead, she stood, picked up that Post-it note and placed it on the desk next to Ruby's ice-packed hand. She tapped the address twice with the end of her pen. "I suspect you'll find a lot of answers here. And probably a fair few questions too."

◆ ◆ ◆

It went without saying that Ruby would ride along with the units heading out to the Hopkins' family farm. This meant going back through Brettwood, along the same road she'd driven just hours earlier. Now, though, she was sitting in the passenger seat of Jay's car, watching the world glint and glide past the window. Her hand was bandaged and tucked against her chest in a makeshift sling. The bruise on her forehead was also blooming into an obvious injury, her eyes a little smokier each time she checked her reflection.

They drove past the turning and Ruby looked up the trackway that led to where it had all happened. Now it was cordoned off with yellow siren cones, police tape and closed road signs. Officers were up there, picking the barn apart. It was, after all, the scene of a crime. Though Ruby was not quite sure what they were hoping to find. Maybe her ID swipe card at least, which she'd have to destroy as Jay had already given her a replacement.

They pulled up at the front of Scott's house just after 8pm to a fanfare of barking dogs. The building was made of wood, neglected planks that should be white settled to murky grey, flaking to reveal the grain beneath. It looked more like something you'd see out on the American plains, a frontier farmstead complete with a veranda on the front. Ruby imagined it as a faded sepia photograph with a vignette of damage around the edges. A rocking chair would fit nicely on the deck but, instead, there was just a disused oven, the door long gone. And a small annex with a rusted, corrugated iron roof was tagged on the side.

Through the missing slats of a high picket fence, Ruby could see into Scott's garden. Unmown grass, long and thick and beginning to resemble wilderness. Dense nettles at the back, some tall and reaching into the grey evening with all the ambitious glory of a sunflower. A row of chicken wire enclosures, each containing grassless earth and a wooden kennel in the corner. Ruby counted five of these ramshackle cages, but it sounded like there were a hundred dogs back there. All of them barking. A mad symphony of power and fear and rage. Each dog roaring at the cars or at each other. One was simply barking at the sky.

She and Jay climbed out and stood on the driveway.

"Those dogs," he said, bowing his head as if the noise was painful.

Although there was a car parked in front of the nearby garage, Scott's house felt empty, cold.

"Gemma Burnham is on some of the older paperwork," Jay explained, reading something on his phone. "Though she claims not to have lived here for fifteen years."

They had a warrant to search the place, which, Jay suggested, might be simpler if they arrested Gemma. It seemed that Scott's former partner, listed as his next of kin, had quite the reputation.

"But she's in there now?" Ruby asked.

He glanced at the building. "Taking care of the dogs. We know her well. Drugs, violence."

"What about today, though?" Ruby said. "Reasonable grounds?"

"Not yet." Jay seemed excited as he pocketed his phone and leant on the bonnet of his car, eyes on the house.

"Is she big?" Ruby wondered, looking at the van and the six uniformed officers milling around the side of it.

"No," Jay said. "But . . . well, you'll see."

They held back while two of the officers made their way up the wooden steps to knock, which made the dogs bark even louder.

One of the curtains moved. Ruby pointed it out with a nod.

"We see you," Jay whispered to himself.

Eventually, the front door opened and Gemma, standing in the shadow, rolled her eyes. "You lot again?" she said. But then she spotted the extra vehicles, saw Ruby, Jay and seemed to realise this was not going to be a straightforward conversation.

As the uniformed officer began to speak, she flung her head back and huffed. "Let's go then, shall we?" she shouted, pushing through them, knocking one against the veranda railings as she came down the steps.

"Miss." The young officer was flustered, hand on his taser, regaining his balance to follow her.

"Happy?" she yelled at Jay, striding forwards now. Jay didn't move a muscle, but Ruby stepped behind the open car door as Gemma stormed towards them, sniffing, wiping her nose, fast, clearly intent on trouble.

"Miss, please." The officer had his cuffs ready, trailing close behind. "*Miss.*"

"Miss?" Jay laughed, tilting up to his feet, ready to retreat. "Grab her."

And then, just before she arrived, they did – hand on her wrist, then her shoulder, swinging her 180 degrees. It took three of them to pin her to the ground. Now on her front, cuffs clicked home, she stopped resisting. Like it was all a show, a routine, a part she had to play. They lifted her back to her feet and a female officer brushed dirt and grass from her baggy t-shirt.

"That was silly, wasn't it?" she said. "Now, are you going to be nice and go in the car or are—"

"Don't touch me," Gemma shouted. "Fucking bitch. You see this?" She threw herself sideways, stumbling, but they had a firm grip – calmly holding her like a horse that'll never be safe to ride. "You see why people hate the police? Sneaky fucking pigs."

"Is there anyone else in the house?" Jay asked.

"Just ghosts."

Jay smiled.

"Fuck you," she said. Then Gemma spat but missed. And now the officers were done with civility.

"That's enough," someone said as they slammed her against the car.

Jay approached the van and opened the back doors, exposing the cage. They bundled her inside. Again, she seemed well versed in this – sitting on the low bench, leaning round to shout more insults and something about human rights as they slammed the doors. There were some thuds and muffled protests but, after a few seconds, Gemma fell silent.

They walked across the driveway, stepped up onto the veranda and Ruby turned to watch the van drive in a wide circle then head back towards the station, wheels splashing in and out of puddles, Gemma safe and sound in the back, dogs singing her off.

"Told you," Jay said at the door. "She's her own worst enemy."

Ruby realised now that the apparently gratuitous police presence, while cautionary, was also a tactical decision. Just the mere sight of the resources required to bring Gemma into custody had been enough to provoke her. She was resisting an arrest that might not have even happened if only she'd stayed calm.

"Sneaky pigs indeed," Ruby said.

And, with half a smile, Jay agreed.

Inside, the house was dirty. Black mould crept up from the skirting boards, water stains crawling down the walls to meet them. Ruby leant round the doorway of the kitchen to see cluttered worktops, unwashed dishes piled high, a bin full of disposable plates and tissues. Flies buzzed.

The open-plan living room wasn't quite as bad. Messy, sure, but not a health hazard. The sofa cushions were torn, the uprights of all the furniture gnarled and chewed through to the bone by dogs, strips of foam lining ripped out, springs and wood exposed. She also noticed a few transparent bags and three syringes on the coffee table.

Ruby carried on down the hall, stopping at a small round table in the corner near the foot of the stairs. It looked as though it might have housed a phone years ago. Now, though, there was a bundle of chains – shiny and new. And amid the snaking mass was a vaguely familiar metal device.

"What is that?" Jay asked.

It had two horizontal pieces, with long bolts and winding butterfly nuts either side. At first Ruby thought it might have been a component from some kind of machine, but then a hazy memory from school. A history lesson. They'd been learning about the slave trade.

"Thumbscrews," she said, turning slowly to look up the stairs.

"Oh yeah," Jay whispered, "you're right. Now why would Scott have thumbscrews?"

Ruby just shook her head, then went up, the wooden steps creaking beneath her feet.

On the landing, she stood at the banister outside the master bedroom. The door was open. She saw a double bed, a wardrobe, old white curtains hanging from a tilted railing. Against the wall, there was a desk with a monitor, a tower PC on the floorboards beneath. The screen was faint grey, glowing on standby. It might have been her imagination, but she felt as though she could hear the electronic hiss. On this side of the house, the dogs were barely audible – almost ambient enough to ignore.

"Pretty good double glazing," Jay mumbled, noticing just how quiet it was in here.

Ruby took one more step, leaving the bedroom, turned and stopped. Her eyes fixed hard on the target ahead of her. A bullseye she hadn't even realised she was aiming at.

Jay came round the corner, standing at her back.

Waiting at the end of the narrow hallway, there was a room with a . . . "Black door," Ruby said, echoing what Frank had told her. "The black door room."

She cautiously approached, checking the frame when she arrived. It was thick, painted metal, with a hatch in the bottom half, a bit like a large cat flap. Ruby pushed it open with her gloved hand. A gloomy space, a stale smell. She reached round to the wall and flicked the light switch.

A bedroom appeared, plain, lacking character, like a prison cell. But very much homemade. It had a single bed against the wall, a cheap pillow without a case, rags for a duvet and a thick woollen blanket that looked itchy, the same texture as loft insulation.

Despite signs of disrepair, it was by far the neatest room in the house. Spotlessly clean.

"What is this?" Jay asked as Ruby went inside.

"I'm not sure . . ."

She stepped towards the window, past a small, old TV, a black box resting precariously on a low wooden milking stool. Ruby hadn't seen a TV like that since she was a teenager.

On the back wall, there was a shelf with a single framed photograph in the middle and a line of candles either side, each sitting in a pool of melted wax. Short, charred wicks curled and black. Before she saw it, Ruby imagined the picture would be of Jesus, or the mother Mary. But it wasn't. It was a photograph of Scott. The display looked, though she didn't want to actually think this word, like a shrine.

She peered outside, through the glass. Below there was a sloped, corrugated iron roof, with a panel missing. This was the top of the annex she'd noticed when they arrived. A six-foot mound of rubbish inside; water bottles, food packaging, all of it presumably dumped out of the window.

On her left, there was a tight, half-width sliding door. Jay grabbed the small handle, pulled it aside. They both looked into an en suite bathroom, a single cabin unit, as though it belonged on a train. Toilet attached to the shower, round light above. Everything was made of plastic, like a festival Portaloo, colour worn away, surfaces pale, scuffed rough from use and age. It reminded her of old toys that had been left out in the garden all summer long.

Two more officers arrived, equally unsure what they were seeing.

Ruby looked back over her shoulder as Jay squatted, checking underneath the bed, hand on the mattress. Then she turned full circle, inspecting every corner, trying to make sense of—

A little red light caught her eye. There was a CCTV camera just above the main door. A black wire came down to the top of the frame, then crawled under and out. Ruby followed it, leaving the room and tracing the cable back down the hallway ceiling. It led to the master bedroom, went inside, down to ground level, then round to—

Ruby stared at the computer.

Hesitating for just a few seconds, she went in, pulled the chair out and sat. She tapped the spacebar and the monitor lit up. Lock screen. She hit enter – no password needed.

And now she was looking at Jay and another officer from above – a live feed. Down on the taskbar, she saw the computer was muted, so she turned the volume up. But no sound.

She minimised the video feed and found a cluttered desktop. Icons, games, documents. The background was a stretched, low-resolution photograph of a dog – presumably one of those still barking outside.

A folder, labelled "FRANKENFIELD", took pride of place in the middle of the screen and Ruby felt offended on his behalf. This was Scott's house. It seemed cruel that his supposed best friend would use this nickname, especially in the private quarters of his computer.

She double-clicked the folder and saw files – she scrolled the mouse wheel – hundreds of them. Down and down. Thousands. Each named with a numerical code. Halfway into the depths of the folder, she opened one at random.

A video began to play. Frank, sitting on the bed, watching TV. She made it double speed, triple speed, clicked again until it was going sixty-four times normal. Frank darting around, a blur, lying down, sleeping, zipping into the toilet, out again, doing sit-ups, press-ups, food sliding in through the cat flap in the bottom of the black door, eating, rubbish dropped out of the small window, into that shack. Pacing, pacing.

Sometimes Frank was just standing in the centre of the room – eerie and still, seeming to judder, the colour gradients shifting around him for hours on end. At one point she thought it had frozen but, no, the clock whizzed on. Frank staring at the photo of Scott. From this angle, it looked even more like a shrine. Especially when the candles were lit. Frank venerated him. Worshipped him. Perhaps this was the reason for his disbelief at Scott's evidently mortal limits. How indeed. How *could* a god be dead?

She opened another. It was the same. Ruby scrolled down further, checking the dates of each file, going back in time. Weeks. Months. She put her hand over her mouth. Years.

Ruby sat there for over a minute. Near silence. Electricity, the wood of the house moving in the breeze, a bang or a creak, police radios and the unmuzzled fury outside.

Had Frank been in there all this time? Trapped in a room, alone, for more than a decade? Her hand was shaking – her heart rate picking up. Empathy, angst or maybe just total bewilderment. Unsettled in ways she couldn't understand. Like those caged dogs in the garden. Something awful but fundamentally beyond comprehension.

Then a sudden thought. She sat up straight, grabbed the mouse, scrolled back up to the crucial dates. Found the file that corresponded to the night of the reunion. The hour window of Mary's death.

Ruby saw Frank sound asleep in that single bed. To Scott's death now. Again, Frank standing in the centre of the cell. Elizabeth's afternoon demise, and here he was, still in this room. The final video she checked was the evening of the break-in. Had it been Frank who stole her notebook, smashed Will's window and ran off down the garden into the night?

She didn't know if she was more confused or less when she saw him there, in that room, sitting on the floor like a child, lit only by the television, arms crossed, hugging himself as though wearing a straitjacket.

He was watching the news. And she crept forwards in time until she saw her own face, the photo Ian had taken, glowing on the screen within the screen. She paused it. A striking, almost cinematic image, his shadow long, his shoulders hunched, the colours stark like a frame in a graphic novel that needed to convey nothing but madness.

Frank could have done many things with his newfound freedom. But he had not killed Mary, Scott or Elizabeth. Nor had he stolen Ruby's notebook.

And, of course, he wasn't in there now. So, her next question was, when did he leave? Ruby isolated the moment. Not long after he'd watched the news, Frank stood, approached the black door and stared at it. From above, Ruby could only see half of his shoulder and the top of his arm. He stood there, not moving, for three full hours. Then, finally, he disappeared from view. A new light glowed on the floor and he was gone, the shadow of the door closing behind him, creaking without a sound across the carpet.

Sighing, she leant back in the chair. Doctor Wallace was right. Answers, yes, and plenty of questions too. But above all these troubling revelations, one stood tall and proud. An alibi, firmly ruling Frank out.

Ruby felt uneasy on her feet when she walked back to the cell.

Officers were searching everything around her as she sat on the small bed, elbows on her knees, staring at the wall, just like Frank had done for so many lonely years.

Jay had been outside. He came back in and perched on the mattress next to her, a tired, end-of-a-long-shift weight to his voice.

"They found a load of guns out in the shed," he said. "Scott's dad seemed to have a licence. Shotguns, even a couple of pistols. Though, some of the lockboxes are empty. Which isn't great news."

On a normal day, missing guns might top the list of significant things.

But, "Listen . . ." Ruby explained what she'd just seen on the computer.

Jay, eyes locked forwards, didn't speak until she'd finished. When she had, he just whispered, "I see."

"Yeah." Ruby's leg was bouncing nervously as she looked around the room. The idea of being a prisoner in Scott's house scared her right up to the limit of her composure. Like a phobia she never even knew she had. Turns out she suffered badly from whatever this fear was called.

"We knew Scott Hopkins was a questionable individual," Jay said. "But . . . fuck. This is dark."

They sat for a while, coming to terms with what it meant. Both reframing Frank as something else. Perhaps just another one of Scott's countless victims.

"His family, Frank's mother," Jay added. "They reported him *missing*. Why would Scott keep him locked up? I thought they were friends?"

"They were best friends." Ruby rubbed her forehead, held the bridge of her nose and—

"Wait." Slowly lowering her hand, she looked to her right, at the window, then panned back to her left. The thick black door. "Oh . . ."

"What?" Jay was curious. He tried to follow her gaze.

"Look carefully at this room. What does it remind you of?"

"Uh. A prison cell?"

"Exactly. But what's missing?" There was a silence.

"I don't . . . I don't know."

"The door, the window . . ." And she took a breath, head hanging, eyes on the floor now. "There are no locks." Ruby sighed, a new layer of regret. "Frank was free to leave at any time."

Jay opened his mouth. But he couldn't find a single word. He was literally speechless.

Chapter Ten

They were unable to speak to Gemma Burnham until the following morning as she was, according to the custody officer, "Off her tits on all sorts."

Her blood was full of heroin, cocaine and, surprisingly, she confessed to smoking "a big fat rock of crystal meth" just before police had arrived at Scott's house.

Though, by the sounds of things, she wasn't necessarily any more serene now. Ruby could hear her shouting down the hall of the custody suite – no discernible information, just the bassline of relentless conflict. But there was a certain melody – every sentence punctuated by the unmistakable beat of her favourite two-syllable word.

"Fucking this, fucking that," Jay mumbled, cheek pressed into his palm, elbow on the table, long numb to Gemma's behaviour.

But hopefully, now sober, she'd at least be willing to sit still.

Ruby and Jay were waiting in the interview room, sitting side by side at the pale wooden table. On top, two thick folders, a plastic cup of water and a voice recorder. Jay idly fiddled with the corner of his notebook, checking his watch from time to time.

Last night, when Ruby told Lauren and Will what she'd seen at Scott's house, they'd looked at her like she'd just openly admitted to eating, and frankly enjoying, human shit. Wincing disbelief, confusion and then finally the dawning of full horror.

"What?" Will had said.

"Yeah, say that again." Lauren seemed almost angry.

"Eleven years, in that one room."

Will's nostrils flared in disgust. Alarm. All the facial expressions you'd expect. "That is probably the most fucked-up thing I've ever heard."

"It's just really sad," Lauren added. She had tears in her eyes. "Frank wasn't exactly . . . he had learning difficulties, he's obviously a vulnerable person."

"And why, though?" Will asked. "Why did he put him in there? Why did he *stay*? Just . . . why?"

But Ruby, wide-eyed, could only shrug – any guess was as good as hers.

And that all-important "why" was exactly what she hoped they'd learn from Gemma today. Scott's ex-girlfriend was estranged but still close enough to take care of his dogs, to sit alone in his dormant house of horrors and consume ludicrous amounts of drugs.

"What was Scott like at school?" Jay asked, now playing with a pound coin – making it stand on its side, holding it in place with his index finger.

"A bully," Ruby said, leaning back in her seat, feet crossed.

"What are we talking?" He pressed the coin down until it fell. "Wedgies and noogies?" He put it back on its side. "Stealing lunch money?"

"How old do you think I am?" Ruby said. "No, Scott was a proper bully. He'd kick the shit out of smaller kids. And bigger ones for that matter."

The coin fell and Ruby sat up and took it, sliding it across the table away from him. "Sit still."

"He ever pick on you?" Jay went back to the corner of the notepad, brushing his thumb over the pages. Always fidgeting. A source of constant noise.

"Occasionally."

"Why?"

God, why? Why? There's that question again. An image of Scott in year 8. Maybe younger. Year 7. He'd walked up to Ruby in design and technology class and, without any provocation, stabbed her in the bicep with the point of a compass. A firm jab, down to the hilt of the thing. Shocked, Ruby had grabbed her arm, taken a step away from him and checked as a small spot of red appeared on her white school shirt.

She was more hurt by the gesture, by the fact he would *want* to inflict pain, than the injury itself. Tears rose up and tried to fall, but she held them in – a skill she'd almost mastered by then. Still holding the compass, Scott had just looked into her eyes, keen to see her reaction.

"Why?" she'd asked. Sincerely, she meant it. Why?

It was as though she'd asked a robot a question it hadn't been programmed to answer. He turned his head slightly, blinking, looking around the floor as he processed the request. Was this really the first time in his life someone had asked him to explain himself?

And then he smiled, like he'd only just discovered the reason himself and, yeah, he liked it. "Fun," he said, enthusiastically nodding at her. He seemed grateful. Then he turned on his foot and walked away.

Kendall was right. Scott was the worst person at Missbrook Heights. By far. But Kendall stopped short of allocating true malevolence. Ruby, who had a keen interest in human psychology even then, had wondered just what was wrong with Scott. What diagnosis she'd give him.

He wasn't a psychopath – he evidently empathised, which made him all the more effective. No obvious signs of depression or anxiety, if anything he was upbeat, chirpy, but not to the extent of overcompensation.

He was an anomaly – mentally ill, without question, but not in any conventional sense. Ruby had observed him with fascination and, much to her dissatisfaction, came away believing he was simply a bad person. Scott *was* evil. That word really did stand up.

And now, she thought, he's dead.

Had he been the only victim, this case wouldn't contain many surprises. Aside from the fact it took the collective restraint of all the people Scott encountered, all the people he hurt, not to kill him sooner.

Ruby didn't believe in heaven or hell, but she knew that if they existed, he would be thriving in the latter. Not only to pay for his sins. But also to complete his homecoming. Because, if there are punishing fires beneath our feet, they surely forged Scott Hopkins and sent him up here to do their bidding.

"Here we go," Jay said, sitting up as the custody sergeant opened the door. He led Gemma inside, sat her down opposite.

"Sorry for the delay," Gemma said, picking up her cup of water. "Requested gluten-free food. Think someone had to go to the shop and get it."

Jay let out a long sigh. "Are you intolerant to gluten?"

"Nope." She sipped, eyes creasing with a half-hidden smile.

Then she looked Ruby up and down, noticed her bandaged hand.

"You should see the other guy," Jay said.

Gemma was thin, wrinkled features and blotchy skin. Scabs. Like the second picture in a before-and-after poster warning about the adverse effects of long-term drug use. She had scraggy hair, make-up smeared around her eyes, not from tears but time. Ruby put her at about forty – maybe forty-five. She looked as though she'd put on a full face of glamour three days ago and smelled like she'd been out on the town ever since.

Jay leant over and pressed the red button on the recorder. He stated the time, the date and every name in the room. And then, they began.

"No," she said, answering his very first question. "I did not know Frank Enfield was in that room."

"You must have discovered it following Scott's death?" he asked.

"Frank was gone by then."

"No," Ruby said, recalling the key moments she'd isolated in the footage. "He left a number of days after that. And he returned more than once. He'd been sleeping there. You didn't see him?"

"I didn't see him."

"Ships in the night?" Jay suggested. "So, you turned up at your boyfriend's house—"

"*Ex*-boyfriend."

"You . . . you went to feed his dogs and didn't look around?"

"I did look around. But Scott having a dungeon wasn't exactly mind-blowing. Honestly, locking someone in a room makes total sense."

Ruby shook her head. "No, it doesn't."

"You clearly didn't know Scott very well."

"Ruby went to school with him."

"I know. I bet he liked you." Gemma's eyes lit up. "So smart. Tucked your shirt in. Skirt always regulation length. I bet Scott liked you. I bet. I fucking bet." She spoke fast, excited. "You got vulnerability in your eyes. I saw it. When you were walking around with your books. Straight As and ironed clothes. Like you're better than everyone. Being the best. Better. I remember. I remember what you were like." She held her fists up, just like she was ready to box. "Olympic team, right? That was you, wasn't it? The shadow boxer. I remember you."

"You went to Missbrook Heights?" Jay asked.

"Yeah, three years below her."

"*Below?*" Ruby said.

"Fuck you."

"Sorry, I . . ."

"See." Gemma pointed. "You apologised. Weak. You should never be sorry. That means you did something wrong. Why did you even say that? Sorry. You're not sorry. You meant it. Why did you say that? Fucking sorry. Why? Such a try-hard. Try-hard. That's what they called you, wasn't it? I remember. Surprised that I was three years below you? Why? Why?"

Because, Ruby thought, you look old as fuck, you horrible fucking little junkie rat. But the sudden flash of anger dispersed quickly and she swallowed it down.

"I thought you were older," Ruby said. Calm and composed. "I didn't mean to cause offence. That's why I said sorry. But you're right. I'm not."

The mood simmered for a while, electricity in the air fading back down to the default animosity Gemma carried with her at all times.

"Then," she said, "you did know Scott. So, you know that he's capable of locking someone in a room."

"There were no locks." Jay was pouting, casual, open confusion, still coming to terms with that fact himself. "Frank chose to be there."

She nodded again, like this wasn't strange. "But I swear on my mother's life that I didn't know."

"How many times have you been to that house?" Jay said.

"A few? I don't know. Twice a day to feed the dogs and clean up some of the shit."

"I meant before that. Before Scott died."

She shrugged, hesitated. "Two. Maybe three times. He always came to my place. Or we'd meet on the beach. Why would I lie? There's no crime. Who cares if Frankenfield's sitting in a room? It's a free country. He's mental. He's fucking gone in the head. See his big old skull and dumb eyes. You remember him?"

"Were you close to Frank?" Ruby said. "Before he *disappeared*." She emphasised that word, hammering home that Frank's own family had reported him missing. They even launched legal action against the police when he wasn't found. This was not some kind of harmless role-playing arrangement that could be brushed aside with the words "consenting adults".

"No. Not really." Gemma sniffed, waved a hand. "I mean, I saw him sometimes when he was with Scott. Drinking and stuff. You know. Getting into trouble. Just being boys. They were best friends. Well, apart from . . ."

"Apart from what?"

"I think they had a fight once. Scott said Frank hit him during one of his," she quoted with her fingers, "'episodes'. Which was not wise. But Frank . . . I think he's, like, mentally not . . . you know. Medically. He took anti . . . antidepressants or antipsychotic pills or whatever, until Scott told him not to."

"Why would he stop him taking medicine?" Jay asked.

"I dunno. Big pharma? Bad doctors? Who can say? Maybe Scott put him in there for his own good. He always said Frank was dangerous."

That was the word he'd used himself. Had Scott coached him to this conclusion? Delusion was clear as day in that barn. Then again, Frank believing he was a danger to the world wasn't necessarily wrong.

Ruby squinted. "Why do you think he would stay in there?"

"Probably because Scott told him to. That was pretty much the only thing you needed to do to stay in Scott's good books. Just do what you're told."

"What if he told you to do something terrible?" Jay said.

"It wouldn't be as bad as what would happen if you said no."

"So," Jay wondered, pausing for effect, "you always did what he told you?"

"Yes. I learned that lesson very early on."

"What kind of things?" Ruby said.

"I don't know?" Gemma looked between them as she spoke. "Shopping? Getting him drugs." She widened her eyes and shook her head fast, side to side, putting on a deep, mocking voice. "Walking the *dogs*."

"You like those dogs?" Ruby asked.

"No. Fucking nasty things. But they don't deserve to starve. Look, if I had to guess, I'd say Frank was being punished for something. Maybe the punch. Maybe he was just disobedient. Scott was into that sort of thing."

"What sort of thing?" Jay said.

"Bondage and shit. Threatening people. You know, said he'd shoot you or whatever. 'Do this, do that or *bang-bang-bang*'." She deepened her voice again, this time to impersonate him.

"So." Jay opened his folder. "You were aware that Scott had access to a number of firearms?"

"They were his dad's."

"That's right." Jay slid a sheet of photo paper across the desk – a selection of guns – rotating it to show her. "Do you recognise any of these?" He looked away, giving her time to check.

Gemma leant forwards. "Yeah, that one." She pointed at a pistol. "That's Scott's gun. Carried it everywhere he went. Old man was a vet. Apparently, he used to shoot horses with it. Poorly ones, though, not in a bad way."

Ruby found her use of the word "poorly" endearing. Made her seem young. We're all just children who got big, she thought. A minute earlier, when Gemma had called her a "try-hard", Ruby imagined punching her in the face, even if it meant breaking a second hand. Now, though, she wanted to hug her and extend a truly heartfelt offer to help. Side-effects may include mood swings, she thought to herself, impossibly echoing the product information leaflet she hadn't even read. She checked the time. An hour until her next dose.

"Scott ever shoot anyone?" Jay asked.

"Nah. Pointed it. But nah. Nah. All talk. Well, I mean, shit. Maybe. But not that I know of."

"Why didn't you tell us any of this in your initial statement?" Now Jay seemed annoyed.

"You didn't ask. Got a knock at the door. This pig . . . this police officer said Scott was dead." Gemma slouched back in her chair, arms folded. "I guess I was still listed as emergency contact or whatever. So, I drove over to feed the dogs. That afternoon, a detective came and took a statement. Asked me where I was and shit like that. Like I did it. I was having my wisdom teeth removed that day. You can check. Why the fuck would I mention that Scott didn't leave the house without his gun?"

"You believe Scott would have been armed when he was murdered?" Ruby said.

"Hundred percent." Her eyebrows shot up. "That's why it's surprising."

But the fact was, his corpse wasn't armed. Which meant either Gemma was wrong or whoever killed him was now walking around with that gun.

"Did you ever—"

"I need to go to the toilet now," Gemma said.

"Can it wait?" Jay asked, eyes closed.

But he didn't even need her response. He just stood, called the custody officer in and watched while he escorted her down the hallway.

Now they were alone, Jay sat again and left a silence, as though Ruby had something to tell him.

"What?" she said.

"Are you all right?"

"Fine. You?"

"What was all that about? She called you 'shadow boxer'? That was a nerve."

"I used to box, back then, back at school."

"And you were good?"

"Reasonably. Lost some technique over the years, though." Ruby lifted her braced hand.

"You were in the Olympics?" he said.

"No, I wasn't."

"Why did she say that?"

Absurd that Ruby still cringed at the memory. It was just one of those ridiculous lies that spirals out of control. In fact, all that happened was that she was enrolled in a youth scheme that had, in the past, provided candidates for the Olympic team.

Ruby didn't explicitly state the lie at school. She just told a young PE teacher that she was training with an Olympic coach and later, when someone said she had been selected to represent Great Britain, she didn't correct them. She nodded. And so, it went around the school.

Ruby enjoyed it. Extra attention. Feeling as though she was exceptional. At the time, she didn't really have the emotional computing power to honestly assess why she did it. But years later, the explanation was all too obvious. Acceptance. Popularity. Points on an invisible social league table that she'd truly believed was below her.

She remembered that pang of fear in her stomach. Like a drug addict, high off their latest hit, knowing that a reckoning is just around the corner. Short-term gains. Hollow and, ultimately, counterproductive.

When it emerged that it wasn't true, *of course* it wasn't true, people made jokes. At any opportunity, fellow pupils would hold their fists up at Ruby, as though they were ready to box. A quick stance. A bespoke gesture meant solely to ridicule her. To be fair, "Shadow Boxer" was quite clever, as far as school nicknames go. Punching nothing but air.

Here she was, two decades on, and something so pathetic and trivial was colliding with something so serious, so real.

It *was* a nerve, one that hurt far more than it should, her hand throbbing along to that stupid feeling in her chest. Shame. Anxiety. Literal fight-or-flight adrenaline coursing through her veins because of an embarrassing memory that did not, by any sensible measure of value, matter. Three people were dead. And Ruby was sitting here, tasked with stopping the killer, and this was what troubled her? The thoughts of other people, from more than twenty years ago? She needed to sleep. Lay off the drugs. Sort herself out.

But Ruby didn't say any of that to Jay.

She just said, "Who knows?"

Gemma returned, still clearly enjoying the inconvenience she was, with her limited means, able to cause.

"Where were we?" she asked.

"Scott," Ruby said.

"Yes."

"You ever hear rumours that he was gay?" she added.

"Gay?" Gemma shook her head, then sat up, came forwards. "Who the fuck's been saying that?" She tried to read Jay's notes, as if the culprit was written there.

He closed his notebook. "When you were together—"

"We weren't together."

"*When* you were," he said. "What was your relationship like?"

"Rainbows and flowers, what do you think? It didn't last long."

"But you remained friends?" Ruby asked.

"Sure."

"Did you . . ." Jay tentatively spread his arms – he came in peace. He meant no offence. "Was it a sexual relationship?"

"Why does that matter?" There was a pause. "No," she added. "Scott was a virgin. He had no nuts. No testicles. Nothing." Then she cupped her hands around her mouth, pretending to shout, but whispered, "It didn't work."

Frowning, Ruby checked in with Jay, who confirmed, with a subtle nod, that this was true. Did she already know? If she had read that, it was definitely a footnote. Castration seemed like something that should have been a headline in the post-mortem report, but Ruby couldn't say why. Just seemed odd. Particularly as Scott behaved like a man with more than the average amount of testosterone, not less.

"How come he had no testicles?"

"Think something happened when he was a kid. Some accident or something. Who knows really?" Gemma scrunched her lip and shrugged with just one shoulder. "Though, I did hear that apparently his old man chopped them off as a punishment. But that was probably bullshit. Doesn't matter either way. No balls. Why do you think he was so angry all the time? Little boys and their little peepees. Fuck you up for life, that will . . . I bet *you* wish you had a dick."

Ruby frowned again. "That's a strange thing to say."

"I was talking to him." And she rolled her head, letting it flop to one side as she stared hard at Jay.

Ignoring her, he kept things on track. "So, Scott was, would you say, heterosexual?" he asked.

160

"Why do you need a label?" She seemed to disapprove of the pen in his hand.

"What label would you use if you had to?" Jay twirled it.

"He . . . I suppose you could call it asexual. Is that the term? People who just aren't interested in sex at all."

Ruby nodded. "But you said he was into bondage?" she asked. "What about all the chains, the leather? He had a whip."

"What about it?" Gemma sighed. "God, you're obsessed. It's all cocks and balls with you. Not everything is about sex."

"So . . ." and Jay set the pen down, "strictly platonic BDSM." He scratched his temple.

She nodded, seeming to enjoy how bewildered they were. "Scott had slave and master relationships with men, women, anyone. Fucking dogs. Say what you like about them, they were loyal. Well trained."

"Well trained?" Jay stifled a doubtful laugh. "I've never heard anything like that racket."

"Dogs were silent when Scott was alive. Not a peep. Now they bark all day and night. It's like they miss him. Or . . . maybe they're angry at whoever killed him. Maybe they know. Shit. Maybe the dogs did it?"

Did Frank fit this description too? A loyal subject, unleashed and lost, searching for meaning in the newfound absence of his master. Just another one of Scott's well-trained dogs.

"If not sexual gratification," Ruby said, "what, do you think, was the purpose of these relationships?"

"You for real? You really don't know? You people?" She looked around the room, pointed at the door. "There are bars on those windows back there. How many handcuffs are in this building? You've picked me up, locked me in a cell." She snarled. "*A fucking cage.*" She showed her teeth.

"Language, please, come on," Jay said.

"You've chosen when I eat, you've filmed me while I piss. You took my laces away. My shoelaces. Where are my fucking shoelaces?" Gemma leant down, tugging at the side of her trainer to show how loose it was. "And now you're asking me that? That question? With a straight face?"

"Sorry, Gemma," Jay sighed, "just meet us halfway."

"What's it about? *What's it about?*" She rolled her eyes, sat back, looked at the wall. "It's the exact same thing that gets you two off." There was a pause and now she seemed annoyed that they weren't getting her point. She came forwards again, chest against the table, both hands flat on top. "It. Is. About. *Power.*"

Another long silence. But now on the topic, Gemma seemed compelled to reclaim what little agency she had left in this situation. She finished her cup, then pushed it across the table with her finger.

"I would like some more water please," she said.

"Of course." Taking the cup, Jay stood. He left the interview room door open and stepped out into the hallway.

Alone now with Gemma, Ruby felt so curious – this unparalleled insight into Scott's strange, deranged life was a goldmine. That awful boy from school who grew into something far worse than she could have ever imagined.

"Gemma," she said, "who do you think killed Scott?"

This was the first question she seemed to take seriously. "I don't know," she whispered, looking at the table. "He did so many terrible things to so many people."

But, once again, Ruby was struck by how incompatible this explanation was for Mary and Elizabeth. Two normal, nice, friendly women who, aside from school year and hometown, had absolutely nothing in common with Scott Hopkins.

"Maybe I deserve to die too?" Gemma said, with every bit of her newfound sincerity.

162

"Why do you say that?"

"Because I . . ." She picked at her fingers and seemed genuinely unsettled. "Because I stood by and did nothing."

Ruby didn't reply, she just sat and absorbed this idea. Guilt by omission. How many chances had there been to change his course? How many sleepless nights filled with speculative regret, playing back things unsaid, actions untaken? But this would imply Scott's behaviour was somehow exempt from the sheer weight of inevitability that's been bearing down on every single moment since the dawn of time.

Maybe believing that things could be different is all we ever have. The alternative, that we're passive observers, simply witnessing every glimpse of beauty and dread unfold before our startled eyes is too much to bear. Or, worse, maybe we don't deserve the comfort of actually feeling the determinism to which we may well be bound. Perhaps our sense of free will, which fuels everything we do as much as everything we don't, is just another cruel curse, another illusion that makes this mad and inexplicable shitshow all the harder to star in.

And now, here, in this interview room, Ruby was beginning to sense her own regrets blossoming in her dark and potted memories. Because something was happening. Outside these walls, a storm had already begun. There were voices. Commotion. Phones rang and rang.

Gemma heard it too, leaning curiously to look out of the half-open door.

"Stay there," Ruby said, holding up her good hand as she stood.

Out into the hallway, she turned to her right and saw Jay, standing at the watercooler, empty cup in one hand, his phone pressed against his ear in the other. He looked up and into her eyes as detectives in the office behind him grabbed jackets and keys. Jay always had something to say, but, once more, there was no need.

Because Ruby could tell, just from his face, that it had happened again.

Everything seemed to be moving, as though an impossible cosmic lapse meant she could feel the earth spinning beneath her feet and, for just the briefest of moments, it felt like the ground might roar off without her, leaving her behind to become just another silent speck in the void.

Whether this fulfilled their inward hope or outward fear, it was obvious that victim number four was dead. And how ironic, Ruby thought, to feel detached at a time like this. Because it would not be a stranger. Whoever it was, it was someone she knew. Someone she went to school with.

And Ruby couldn't help but wonder if, in some tiny way, by some missed opportunity or soon-to-be-obvious manifestation of incompetence, she shared the blame.

Chapter Eleven

Like many big things from her childhood, the Cliff Ridge Recreation Ground didn't feel quite as daunting as Ruby remembered. But, today, the forty acres of sport pitches stretching between the fences and treeline still managed to make her feel small. She slammed the door shut, turned away from the car and walked across the grass, Jay following close behind as they passed the cricket greens, practice nets and looming rugby goals.

Up ahead, all around the wooden pavilion building, blue lights spun in the afternoon gloom. Armed officers, dogs, spreading out and searching. Voices crackled away on ambient radios, half-heard call signs and soundbites, all with a unique collective objectivity, the pleasing and efficient nature of composed urgency whispering through the airwaves.

Ruby arrived, climbed some steps and walked across the stone slabs, along the pavilion's front wall. The wide windows were placed high, tucked up into the eaves of the roof. Darkened glass, like mirrors, reflecting the flat, empty grass at her side. It was as dim as daylight ever gets, grey clouds above, but no rain, just their shapes cast, vast and sprawling shadows sweeping fast across the pitches like the faint ripple of light on a shallow seabed. At this scale, Ruby was just another grain of sand.

Good hand gloved, disposable shoe covers on both feet. Inside now, into the fresh scene. All the lights were off, most chairs were upside down on the tables, the floor cleared and ready to clean. Disturbance was obvious at first glance, like microexpressions on a loved one's face. You could never explain how you know something is wrong, but you'd bet everything you own that it is. But then she looked and saw the signs. A bar stool at an unusual angle, the cool breeze of an open window somewhere behind the bar and then, most notably, the muffled hum and roar of a vacuum cleaner still running. It was on the carpet, near the door to the kitchen, the tube coiled exactly where it had been dropped.

Jay crouched and flicked the mains switch, cutting the place to silence. Rising, he turned back to Ruby. "In there," he said, tilting his head towards the faint glimmer of light glowing from the kitchen.

Remnants of last night's party were spread across the bar. Countless glasses, some half-eaten buffet platters covered with clingfilm and a few paper streamers still webbed over beer taps and light fittings. Behind, a banner dangled vertically from a shelf. It said "Birthday" in multi-coloured bunting letters, though there was no sign of the "Happy" half.

On through the bar's partition, towards the kitchen where Ruby saw that the lock had been broken, barged open, splinters of door frame clinging on, flakes of paint around the floor. Going inside, turning, tentative and slow so that—

She stopped. Stared.

He was sitting on the tiles, his back against the oven door and, maybe because it was so raw, his open eyes still seemed full of life, as though he was pretending and might just take a sudden gasp of air and laugh. But the closer she got, the truer it felt until, now standing over him, the totality of death was undeniable.

There was something particularly upsetting about head injuries. A fractured leg, a severed arm, even the sight of abdominal organs was not as bad as the coconut shatter and ragged pink that peeks out from the shell. Rugby teams would have toasted drinks in this very building, reminiscing about seasons past and present, laughing as they compared scars from a catalogue of injuries sustained on the pitch. But not to the head. Head injuries defy the brave faces and stiff upper lips of gallows humour and resilience. Our minds are just too precious. Generations have to pass before brain damage can stand even the slightest chance of seeming funny.

Adam Ward, previously equipped with a dry sense of humour himself, was the bar's deputy manager. A short boy who'd sat behind Ruby in maths class. At school, his height, while often mentioned by fellow students, didn't seem unusual. With a young face and a bright smile, getting to year 11 and still being four-foot ten was worthy of note but not derision. Even teachers would call him "Little Adam" without any hint of malice. But now, having filled out to the proportions of a full-grown man, complete with a balding head and a thick covering of stubble, Adam seemed especially small.

Ruby had not seen or heard from him since school, so her impression was tainted by nostalgia and youth. The few memories of Adam she had were hazy, an overview more than specific instances. She could hear his distinctive laugh, picture him being boisterous in lessons, not quite the class clown but well on his way. He had an enthusiastic energy – the kind of kid who runs when there's no need to, finds obstacles to jump over and can't be near a wall without balance-beaming along the top of it. No, wait. There *was* a specific moment. In year 10, he'd climbed onto the roof of the music block as a dare but couldn't get down again. A crowd amassed in the playground, despite what teachers said, and cheers echoed around campus when he finally came climbing down that fire engine ladder. If not for the mangled nightmare at her feet, Ruby may have even smiled at this memory.

And now here he was, sitting in the kitchen of his workplace, ready to serve police in their desperate search for his killer. The story of what happened to him still lingering in his glazed eyes, like he'd happily tell her everything if only he could.

It wasn't necessary to remark on the fact Adam was in Ruby's year at school – that went without saying. Equally, she didn't need to check the photograph to know that he was sitting on the bottom row, nowhere near the three other victims. The pattern theory, far-fetched as it was, seemed obscene now it had been so dramatically disproven.

Jay arrived at her side, standing in the doorway as he ended a call and pocketed his phone.

But Ruby, squatting on the tiles to be level with Adam, didn't look up.

"There's a recording," Jay said, sounding like he was talking to the wall, not to her.

"A recording of what?"

She heard Jay sigh. "His 999 call."

Without moving her head even an inch, Ruby's eyes darted around the messy scene. A broken glass on the floor near his leg, a saucepan lid against the dishwasher and an old metal pedal bin in the corner, lying on its side, rubbish spilling across the tiles. And there, half-hidden under the oven, she saw a mobile phone, face down. Something frenetic had happened here. Something loud. Then she settled back on his injuries. They were, to coin a phrase, catastrophic and comprehensive. So, she already knew the answer to her next question, but felt compelled to ask it anyway.

"After he was attacked?" she said. "Or before?"

Had Little Adam from school, desperate and scared, called for an ambulance or for the police?

Jay exhaled through his nose. "During," he said.

Having identified the body, there wasn't much left for Ruby to do here so she rose to her feet, turned around and went back through the pavilion's bar area. Past trophy cabinets and old framed photos of cricket teams on the side wall. The stark eyes of masked officers in white overalls came filing through, carrying cameras, tools, equipment, another waiting at the main door, holding it open for her to leave.

A little way out onto the grass, past the massing crowd, Ruby walked and put the entire scene behind herself. Just empty space now, rows of pitches, scuffed and muddy around the goals. A man throwing a tennis ball for his grateful dog, fast and bounding as all the blue lights flickered faint on the trees in her peripheral vision.

She breathed, staying focused, not letting what she'd just seen get any traction in her mind. Dwelling on the horror was not conducive to success. Adam's frantic fear and faded pain did not belong to her. And yet, her central nervous system insisted on empathy, chemicals having a stab at what it might have felt like. Maybe it was the lack of sleep, or the painkillers she'd taken for her hand, either way the Adderall was not doing its job. Muddy claws of creatures, beasts, a thousand things that should stay buried were pushing up now on the underside of the bulging ground. She could not afford to let them breach the surface.

Something just like that had happened to Elizabeth. A comprehensive catastrophe, Ruby thought, putting her left hand over her mouth, her right hand braced against her swimming stomach as every heartbeat jolted like a sleep-twitch.

And she closed her eyes, travelled back in time to see herself right here on the grass, six years old, trying to ride her first bike. Falling again and again, she'd picked herself up, pulled wads of dirt from the end of the handlebar and, one foot on the pedal, the other tiptoed on the ground, she'd lined the wheels up and tried once more.

The memory was among the clearest she had from her childhood. Learning to ride a bike is formative, a milestone, sure, but its proximity to grief is what gave it all this weight. Trauma has a way of staking claims on the calendar. It hijacks smells, sounds and can even, Ruby was fast discovering, taint what many claim to be the best years of your life. How long before everyone in that photo would be unable to think about their time at Missbrook Heights without death rearing its ugly, inevitable head?

Ruby met her mind's go-to topic at a young age. Just five tender years into all this, too small to understand the implication of her mum's diagnosis. Adults tend to skirt around the truth when talking to children in situations like that. Bone cancer was best described with gentle euphemisms – mum was ill, poorly, she needed to rest. But Ruby had wished she'd read between the lines, clocked all that subtext in those long pauses and cautious bedtime chats. They always started with a sigh, a pat on the leg and the counterproductive instruction to "listen, sweetheart".

So, just eleven months later, when it actually happened and Giles sat her down to explain, six-year-old Ruby had been more confused than upset. She remembered shaking her head, frowning, asking a few follow-up questions to clarify what he was saying. He kept referring to her as Emma. Emma had passed away. Then he'd correct himself and say "your mother" but never, not once, did he use the word "mum". And certainly, the transient days of "mummy" were well and truly over.

They'd been together for three years and got married just weeks prior to her death. Like it was a dying wish Giles had granted. The short tenure of their union made his commitment all the more commendable, though later Ruby came to realise her mum had not needed a husband. The wish had been for a father.

Still, even then, Ruby had a sense that she could be in some trouble. She hardly even knew Giles – he was always away on deployment in some distant place – and she recalled a lingering fear that he might not stick around. Her biological dad was, in some ways, more gone than her mum. So estranged that he wasn't even presented as an option. In fact, Ruby didn't know his name and to this day felt no shame that she'd never sought to learn it.

All she had was Giles. This huge, stern man, as familiar to her as a fellow passenger on a long-haul flight. Mannerisms, smell, posture and smiles but still, despite passive intimacy, a stranger. If she'd had to pick a word to best describe how she felt about him, young Ruby probably would have settled on scared. Giles was scary. The kind of solid, strict adult male who exuded authority and diligence. Like a headmaster who could cut a rowdy class to silence with little more than the threat of his arrival.

Once the news had settled, Ruby remembered turning to him and crying. Almost performatively – tears because she felt that was the right thing to do. Giles would expect it, so she complied. He just hugged her, patting her back with the kind of affection you might expect when one soldier comforts another. He didn't squeeze with any sudden flashes of love or angst or clamouring moments of mutual despair. No, Giles just wanted a six-year-old girl to feel better and so he did what he thought he should.

And she didn't even need to voice her anxiety. He read her mind.

"You are legally my daughter," he'd said. "Your mother's death does not change that. It's important for your psychological and emotional development that you understand I love you, I care about you and I will protect you from harm."

"I love you too." Ruby blurted that quickly, even though it can't have been true at the time. She was just clawing for any warmth she could reach, nurturing a precious flame in a place far too dark for a child to be left alone.

That was the first and last time they said those words to each other. Not that it became less true, but because they both knew. It had been stated for the record. They loved each other. Onwards.

So, they went home from the hospital and, almost immediately, Giles adopted her and took early retirement from the army. Ruby didn't understand that this is what he'd done until years later. He just explained that he wouldn't be going away anymore. And then they settled into that strange period that follows such things, right after the shock has faded. Like when you submerge yourself in an ice bath and your breath goes and the pain feels like it might suffocate you but it doesn't. It just aches. Most people who've lived are dead and gone but you? You're still here.

Unique procrastination comes next. Like, what now? What do you do? Watch TV? Read a book? Box up all her things and, what, throw them away? Keep them? Adults ask how you're doing and you say, "Good". They smile. You smile. And on it goes. Though at her age, Ruby didn't concern herself too much with all this. An afternoon was a lifetime, hours far too long to worry about how they should be filled. But Giles kept his chin up, he was reporting for duty, he was ready for action. His mission? Raise a six-year-old girl he scarcely knew.

"OK," he said, three days later, just as she'd finished her breakfast. "How well can you swim?"

"I'm not sure." Ruby's voice sounded small in her memories. Innocent. Polite. The kind of sincere, endearing noise that would make any reasonable heart ache. "I can do breaststroke?"

"Good. Front crawl?"

"A bit."

"Face in the water?"

"No."

"We'll do that later then. And, I notice you don't own a bike?"

Ruby, spoon still in hand, shook her head.

"I'm going to buy you one. What's your favourite colour?"

"Red?" she wondered, like she was asking permission. Was there a wrong answer?

"OK. A red bike."

"I don't . . ." she began, but for some reason couldn't actually say it.

Again, though, Giles understood. "Can you ride a bike?"

"Not really."

"Put your coat on," he said.

And then here they were, in the middle of this very grass. Ruby and the seagulls, the breeze, the fog hazing out at the edge of everything she could see, her small brain noticing far fewer things than she might later claim to remember in all the shrouded gloom and doubt that overcasts early memories. The sun might have only shone on her recollection, but it was bright and it was warm.

"Foot on the ground, foot on the pedal," Giles said. "Hands here, yes, firm like this. Head up. Good." He stepped back. "Now go."

Ruby pushed off, managed one full rotation of her feet, wobbled, panicked, wobbled and *thud*. She'd looked up at him, resting on her elbow. He just waited as she clambered out from under the bike, stood up and tried again. *Thud*. And again. *Thud*.

"Look where you're going," he said, crouching to brush grass from her leg. "Eyes forward." He pointed ahead of them – at the pavilion off in the distance. "When you look down, you fall."

The anger of hurting yourself and failing at the exact same moment was making her hands tremble, muscles sore with the diminishing returns of unskilled effort. And she threw everything she had into the next attempt, but travelled less than four feet

173

before she slipped, bashed her shin into the pedal's teeth and fell. Sheer stinging pain and *rage*.

"I can't fucking do it," she said, shuffling on her side to kick the bike away.

Then she felt a surge of immediate terror, even surprise that she knew this word, let alone well enough to use it so adeptly. Her head snapped up, checking to see if he'd heard. And, oh no, he had. Giles scowled down at her. A titan, looming tall with all the power and rumble of God and thunder. But he never shouted. It was always calm, the potential for a storm was more than enough to seek shelter.

"I don't ever want to hear you use that word again," he said. "Do you understand?"

"Sorry, I'm sorry. I didn't mean it."

"Get up, and do it again."

But she punched the ground. "I *can't*."

"Ruby." And he glared. "What did I just say about that fucking word?"

Her chin hung, eyes wide – hearing adults swear seemed nuclear, arriving with the force and daunting awe of something that might destroy worlds. Bewildered, she didn't reply. It took her a good ten seconds to understand. Incredibly, this wasn't an act. It wasn't a grand, rehearsed way to make the point. Giles had been sincerely offended to hear a six-year-old girl say "can't". To him, this was the most egregious four-letter word she could ever utter.

She nodded. Stood. And went again.

They were there all day long, hours, until, late in the afternoon, it finally clicked and Ruby just got it. Like spotting the reality of an optical illusion and suddenly being unable to even see the shape that fooled you. She cycled around him in a big circle, solid, confident, her long sundial shadow sweeping as she looked left again and again to see his face tracking her, turning on the spot.

"Look, look," she said. And he was. He was looking.

That expression – Ruby drank it in, felt it fill her, like some vital life force nourishing the marrow inside her hollow bones. There was no clapping, Giles had barely even smiled. It was just the slightest of nods. Less than approval, far less than praise. It was acknowledgement. Giles had seen her and all was in order. She was riding her bike, just like she'd been told to do, as though success was the status quo and harmony had been restored.

From then on, that feeling was all she ever wanted and, luckily for her, Giles explained in a clear and concise way exactly how she could get it. Simple, Ruby just had to be the best. Be the smartest person, the fastest, the strongest. The safety found in superiority is unparalleled because, as he told her, if you're the best in any given situation there really is nothing to fear.

This comfort blanket of excellence that Ruby always wore had been sown here, on this grass, three decades ago. And she didn't need to psychoanalyse herself to appreciate the nuances of the memory, of the moment she finally started riding and her mind was at peace. It was just her, the bike, Giles's face and she realised, as with so many other things, the faster she went the more stable her balance became. That was the first moment of many more that followed where, for just a fleeting period of time, the kind that passes faster than you can ever appreciate, Ruby wasn't thinking about any buried thing that might crawl out from the ground to capture her attention and ruin her day.

So, with a sigh, she turned around and faced the crime scene. Ruby looked exactly where she was going. Eyes forward, a dead-straight line from here, firm and on the goal. Because, as Giles taught her when she was small, if you look down, you fall.

Ruby sat in Jay's car, still parked against the kerb, the tarmac path leading along the recreation ground grass and to the pavilion over on her right. He'd already forwarded her an email with the nineteen-minute sound file attached. Once it had downloaded, she put her earbuds in and listened.

The 999 call began with the normal formalities – Little Adam's panicked voice asking for the police. Even before he said a single word, it was obvious that this was very much an emergency. Close, heavy breath on the receiver as he relayed his location.

"I need— Oh, shit." Adam's voice rising now. "Police, please. Someone— They . . . they hit me and—"

A banging sound. *Bang, bang.*

"OK, sir, are you able to get to a secure—"

Bang.

"Oh, they're here," he said, with unnerving composure. Resignation. "Someone's breaking the door."

The microphone strained, muffled, something brushing against the phone.

"Sir, units have been dispatched, what I need you to do now is—"

A noise loud enough to make Ruby flinch. She turned the volume down two bars, worried about her eardrums. There was movement, but – she squinted – it sounded distant. Ruby guessed he'd dropped his phone on the floor. That was the sound, glass and metal colliding with tiles.

And then, the door now broken through, face to face with the intruder, Adam uttered his final words. "Oh my God," he said, undeniable recognition in his voice. "It's you."

The rest was confusing. It was hard to paint a picture of exactly what was happening – noise, chaos, violence. No talking. Just a few primal grunts. Perhaps both knew they were engaged in a fight to the death. A fight that Adam was destined to lose.

And once he had, there were footsteps. It was done. But the controller left the line open, listening in to the whir from the vacuum cleaner in the next room, which ran through the entire recording. The next sounds, an uncomfortable sixteen minutes later, were sirens and the deep, bellowing voices of men declaring, again and again, that they had arrived.

"Police, police."

This was followed by one officer describing what they'd found. Professional solemnity keeping his voice stable, human shock adding sighs, stutters and all the requisite shame. The catastrophe on the tiles. Now they needed extra support to search the area. The suspect can't have gone far. But, judging by the reports on the radio, their response time had been ample for a successful escape.

Ruby scrolled back along the zigzag lines, her phone presenting the audio as a heart-rate monitor and the encounter itself, spiking and wild, as a cardiac arrest. She looked up, looked right, a shadow approaching the car door. Jay leant down, opened it and climbed into the driver's seat.

"You listened?" he asked.

"Yes," she said, removing her earbuds.

Without any prompt, Jay fiddled with the radio, changed a wire and turned Bluetooth on. Ruby connected her phone so they could hear it all unfold together.

Parked here, not far from the scene, immersed in what happened there little more than an hour ago, she tried again to draw pictures in her mind. The tall order of asking one sense to do the job of another. But an image had begun to form, fading into existence like a slowly developing photograph.

The actual murder itself seemed quick, a hateful act, maybe, but not one fuelled by fury or passion. There was no shouting. No signs of sadism. And no attempt from either party to engage in conversation. If Ruby had to describe the image she'd made, it would be an execution. It seemed, and this was a cold word to use, efficient. They'd just barged in through that kitchen door and got the job done.

A few groans, a tussle maybe, a glass that smashed and a pan that clattered across the tiles. The bin fell over at some point. And a series of thuds. Then the footsteps and—

She tilted her head, frowning. Jay had clearly heard it too.

"What was that?" she thought aloud.

Ruby scrolled back. Played the killer's casual retreat again. Turning, walking and . . . she leant towards the speaker. It *sounded* like whistling? Not wind, an actual tune.

Wincing, Jay shook his head and turned the volume up full on his car's radio. A constant static from the speakers, hissing with the potential for sound loud enough to shake the cavities in your chest, tremble hairs on skin too small to see.

Phone on her thigh, Ruby used two fingers to isolate the segment in question. Just after the violence, three seconds into the relative silence that followed. She played it again, on a loop. A humming sound that became, yes, it was, it was a whistle. The melody grew more and more distant with every one of the last few seconds, tracking the killer as they left the pavilion and strolled back into the shadows of anonymity.

"You recognise that?" Jay asked.

"Almost."

But when Ruby slid the treble up and the bass down, it sang around them, the car alive with music. Jay sat, eyes closed, head gently swaying, almost like he was meditating, orchestrating.

Ruby closed her own eyes to listen. Footsteps. Humming, humming, whistling. She left it playing, the familiarity of the tune just beyond her reach. A song. It was there, skirting around the edge of recollection.

"Dah . . . dah," she whispered, getting two notes.

And then, gradually, she began humming along to it. Louder and louder until she was able to pause the recording and continue with her own rendition. She rolled her hands, nodding at Jay and, eyes wide, he nodded back.

"Dah, dah-dah . . ." he joined in, "dah-dah, dah-daaaah, dah . . ."

Now they were both singing together, abstract sounds replacing the lyrics they still hadn't grasped. Ruby gestured for him to carry on.

"A hymn . . ." she said, "a carol, a Christmas carol . . . Fall . . ."

"*Fall*," he grabbed her shoulder, "on your knees."

"Oh, hear the angel voices," she added. "Yes."

"A thrill of hope, the weary world rejoices . . ." He patted the steering wheel. "Yeah, yeah, that's it . . ."

And they stopped. Sat for a few moments in total silence.

"'O Holy Night'," she said, abandoning the song to state its title. "The stars are brightly shining."

This felt momentous, her first glimpse into this person's life, their mind, the idle tunes they whistle when they find themselves alone. Joining those blue threads of clothing fibre in the extremely sparse collection of evidence. One more thing Ruby knew about them.

"Does it mean anything to you?" Jay asked.

Ruby stared at the scene, her mind busy with options. Trying to remember where she'd heard this carol, whether it had any significance at all. Films maybe. TV. Primary school trips to church. Other than that, she drew blanks, shook her head.

"But," she said, "he'd dropped his phone. They didn't know he'd called. They didn't know we were listening."

"And what do you think he meant? 'Oh my God,'" Jay echoed Adam's final words. "'It's you.'"

This meant only one thing and it wasn't a surprise. "They knew each other," she said. Then she turned to look at Jay. "Maybe from school."

Adam's open eyes had seen. Photons of light had drifted into his pupils just minutes earlier. If only he'd had the presence of mind to say a name. Ruby wondered whether there was any trace left inside him, curious about when information dies. How long before an oxygen-starved brain is just another piece of earthly matter? Just dust from those brightly shining stars.

When she turned her phone's Bluetooth off, the police radio in Jay's car whispered away again with the normal chatter you learn to ignore. Odd words jump out. Units. Numbers. Roads.

But then one line of distant dialogue caught their ears. A name. A suspect. Frank Enfield. They both froze rigid, sitting perfectly still to listen again to something astonishing.

A warrant for the arrest of Frank Enfield. The controller was describing him now. His height. His clothes. And, be warned. He should be considered dangerous and possibly armed.

"—north-east. Suspect last seen in his room at, uh, 11am."

His room. His hospital room. Some back and forth on the black radio. Thought to have exited through a window. Reports of his escape only just called in. An officer close to the hospital confirmed they were leaving a job and were now en route. Ruby pictured a car turning, blue lights flickering on a road somewhere.

Checking the clock, she looked at Jay, who was clearly thinking the same thing. Adam's 999 call was placed at 1.46pm.

Frank was last seen at . . . "11am," Ruby said.

"Plenty of time."

"Why the— why wasn't he restrained? Was no one keeping an eye on him?"

But Jay could only sigh as he removed his phone – his rolling eyes long worn to unprofessional blunders, to humans and their errors. Though this one seemed especially outrageous.

They'd taken Frank to Missbrook Hospital to run some tests, routine for the early stages of committing him, presumably, to a mental health institution. How could the collective will of every necessary legal, medical and law-enforcement body result in this? He should have been cuffed, sedated or an inescapable combination of the two.

Perhaps the severity of it all had been lost in translation. Something Jay put right as he made a call and explained that Frank Enfield was – without any shadow of a doubt – wanted on suspicion of murder. Injecting a whole new layer of urgency into the situation.

Ruby had been so ready to go back to Will's spare room, walk up to that photograph and find Frank Enfield standing tall on the back row. His pale face, his dark hair. The stature that justified his nickname. She'd planned to cross him off, green ink to rule him out.

But then she thought again about all the things he said to her in that barn, right before she broke her hand on his jaw. He spoke about truth. The nature of reality, of belief. Certainty. What can she trust? What could she ever hope to know for sure? The footage of him sitting in that room at Scott's house told many stories. Was Frank's innocence truly the prevailing theme?

Adopting the open mind he'd insisted on, Ruby wondered how it could be possible. How could he have done it? They knew when the files themselves were created, but formally dating silent footage is not straightforward. And Scott's record-keeping was admittedly erratic. The timestamps on the videos could be false, a trick. A way to deceive. But then why would Frank allow himself to be arrested?

Why. That was the biggest question of all. By the end of today, there might be irrefutable proof that he had killed Adam. And maybe the other three too. But, once again, why? Why would Frank do this? It was beyond infuriating not to have an answer. It caused her physical discomfort, far worse than the throb in her braced hand.

But alongside the discontent she'd feel if delusion or insanity was the explanation for all this, Ruby was once more looking down the barrel of fear. The violence was brazen and the aftermath blasé. Was it simply naïve to hope for motivation that made sense? Or did the opportunist mayhem of a madman suffice?

Because, if so, then every single person in that photograph was eligible for a little red cross well ahead of their time. And the idea that she might be waiting in line was just as plausible as any other unsatisfactory explanation. That empathy she'd tried to bury out there on the grass might not have been distraction after all, but premonition. Just a little taste of what's in store.

Chapter Twelve

Despite the sense of momentum, what followed was a period of inertia. There was no meaningful CCTV, aside from four frames of a blurred shape passing the threshold of the car park and, as the pavilion had hosted a party the night before, the prints and DNA were close to useless. A single eyewitness reported seeing someone leave the scene around the time in question. Someone wearing a hooded coat of undetermined colour, "possibly dark". They hadn't seen their hair or skin and, only when pushed, described an individual of average height and average build. Jay remarked dryly that this meant they were on the hunt for "a human being".

Ruby's extensive research on the origin and cultural footprint of "O Holy Night" felt similarly futile and now she was infected with the tune playing on repeat in her head. Between thoughts she'd hear herself think, "Oh night divine" and, when she woke up to day ten's sunrise glowing through the curtains of Will's spare room, her mind whispered, "For yonder breaks a new and glorious morn."

Back to the photograph, a snapshot in time. The whole school year, right here, lined up in front of her. Earlier, Ruby had ceremoniously taken the lid off her thick red marker pen, stepped to the wall and put an X over Adam Ward's face, just like the others.

Bottom row, third in from the right. Four victims now. Four little red crosses.

Maybe whoever was doing this had their own photograph. Perhaps they were using circles, targets, like upcoming appointments on a calendar. Who next? she wondered, twirling the pen. Which one of these people was living out their final few days? None of them, she decided. Ruby would not let another soul fall. She would figure this out. She was going to save them all, she thought, allowing herself a moment of unfounded optimism – glimpses into a hero's journey, a fantasy that, despite everything, still felt possible.

Her gaze fell to the question mark hovering over Frank Enfield's head at the top of the photograph. His escape from hospital was an unwelcome injection of chaos and, considering his far from average appearance, it was an ongoing surprise that he remained at large.

Lauren entered the spare room, came to the desk at Ruby's side and set down a cup of tea. They'd been speaking about Frank and she picked up the conversation right where they'd left off.

"It kind of makes it worse that it wasn't about sex," Lauren said. "But I'm not sure exactly why."

Clearly, she hadn't been able to stop thinking about Scott's questionable pastimes.

Ruby agreed. Even the most obscene and evil acts of sexual perversion are not, despite what your initial outrage tells you, incomprehensible. All living creatures are at the sharpest edge of evolution, billions of years, countless generations whose most potent commonality is that they successfully reproduced. Whether you're discussing desirable bust-to-hip ratios, high-testosterone bone structures or even the indomitable pressure for social approval, evolutionary psychology has an explanation up its sleeve. And if you're short on time, and can't study it like Ruby had, the field can be summarised adequately with a single word. Sex.

Although distorted well beyond reason, and complicated by his apparent castration, Scott was surely equipped with some form of this fuel. But the fact it didn't explain his actions made them much harder to swallow.

"Oscar Wilde said everything is about sex." Ruby turned to Lauren. "Except sex. Sex is about power."

Lauren, frayed from a sleepless nightshift, was still wearing her hospital ID card around her neck. Holding her own mug, she came over to the photo. They stood side by side.

"Scott just cut out the middleman," Ruby added.

"Why wasn't Frank put somewhere more secure?" Lauren asked, finding the question mark above his face.

"He was meant to be sedated."

Doctor Wallace, who was technically responsible for Frank, had told Ruby he'd climbed out of a window, onto a low roof and down a fire exit ladder. Her theory was that he may have been one of the rare people with partial immunity to the sedative drugs he'd been administered. Or perhaps, she wondered, he simply needed a larger dose. A final possibility was that good, old-fashioned medical error saw him hooked up to someone else's drip. Either way, it seemed ironic that a man who'd spent the last decade confined to a room was so resourceful when it came to escaping.

"It said on the news he's wanted on suspicion of murder?" Lauren then looked to Ruby, trying to gauge her view.

But Ruby sighed, answering the question she hadn't needed to ask. "No," she said. "I don't think he's responsible."

"Why?"

"We saw the culprit. He ran down the garden. Only a glimpse, but he was not six-foot five."

Lauren agreed. None of them could be sure about age or race. And even gender wasn't a hundred percent. But the person who stole her notebook was nowhere near Frank Enfield's size.

Most of all, "It just doesn't make sense."

Lauren thought for a moment. "Does it usually make sense?"

"What?"

"Murder."

"Yes," Ruby said. "Almost always. Inexplicable violence is rare, even in dangerous places."

"What about evil?"

"What about it? Pick an atrocity. Pretend you believe what the perpetrators believed and suddenly it's not irrational. Burning witches is quite reasonable if you're certain they're demonic. It's too lazy to shrug and dismiss violent criminals as 'bad people'."

"Maybe you just don't understand Frank's motives yet?"

Ruby hesitated. Tilted her head to concede the point. "That's possible."

With a heavy breath, Lauren stepped back and sat on Ruby's bed. She'd been in surgery all night and was visibly exhausted.

"How did it go?" Ruby asked, turning and perching on the edge of the desk to face her.

"Good. Seven hours. Painstaking but we got there." She put her mug on the carpet near her foot. "Young guy fell off a ladder at work. Landed on some packaging machine, ended up with a metal pole stuck in his back. Firefighters had to cut him out. He shouldn't have even been up there without a harness. All very sketchy. His boss went in the ambulance with him, looked quite shaken." Lauren let out a tired laugh. "Standing there, sleeves covered in blood. He said, and I quote, 'This is my fault'."

"Where there's a blame there's a claim."

"Cha-ching."

"You fix everything?"

"Mostly. I'm not normally on call for trauma like that. I imagine there will be follow-up procedures. Spine was fine, though he severed a nerve in his shoulder so he might have some trouble with his right arm. But a weak hand is better than no hand."

"Quite." Ruby's weak hand was wrapped up tight in a thick, black brace. The fracture was tiny, just below the knuckle of her ring finger. Though, apparently, there was no point in a cast. A prognosis that Lauren confirmed when she inspected the injury and a photo of the X-ray on Ruby's phone. She also explained some technical details about how the bone would fuse and told Ruby she was lucky the break hadn't "spiralled". It was, according to her, a common injury seen in the hands of people who like to fight.

"Bare-knuckle boxing is a bad idea," she'd added, with a wry smile.

They'd been spending more time together over the last few days. At school, Lauren and Ruby had been on the edges of two social groups that crossed over enough to be more than strangers, but less than friends. They were, not that either would have used this word, acquaintances.

Most of Ruby's views on her had been heavily tainted by the events that led up to the end of her and Will's relationship. Ruby painted Lauren as a villain. But really, the betrayal fell at Will's feet and even that, amid the inevitability of it all, hardly mattered.

They were going to break up. That had been clear for months. Will and Lauren's kiss just accelerated things. Made it a far cleaner cut. Though not clean enough for any chance of reattachment.

Strange how significant and formative your first serious relationship becomes in later life. Losing your virginity sits on a pedestal but no one warns you about the whirlwind of genuine romantic bonds. Will was Ruby's first official boyfriend. And, disturbingly, her last too. Six years and two months, crumbling out at the end to climax with that single act of infidelity.

Ruby had suspected there was more of an overlap than Will claimed. But she didn't care. It was the kiss that did it. Drunk at a party, in front of witnesses. People saw it happen. That's what gave the incident all of its finality.

But now, actually getting to know her, Ruby realised Lauren was probably a better suit for him anyway. That initial spark had always been there, simmering in the background. In a sense, it was odd that it took them another decade to get together. She wouldn't say she was happy for them, but there were no hard feelings.

Still, Lauren was almost comically perfect – fitting the cliché of someone she could so easily envy. Pretty, intelligent and the kind of cringey do-gooder who spends three months volunteering, building a school in some African village. Something Lauren had literally done. Twice. But this Good-Samaritan kindness that Ruby had always thought was so hollow, so pretentious, was, to her astonishment, authentic.

Two nights prior, Ruby heard Lauren and Will having a heated discussion. Not quite an argument – perhaps they'd stopped short of slamming doors for her sake – but there had been a firm point of disagreement. And earlier today, on this very new and glorious morn, when she asked Will what it was about, he told her that Lauren had signed up to a scheme, pledging to give away ten percent of her income to charity.

"It's called effective altruism," Will explained, shaking his head. "Do you know what she gets paid? A tenth of that. Every month. Gone."

"Sounds like it's none of your business," Ruby said.

He cocked his gaze to the side and gave her an eyeless smile. "What an interesting point. Any other observations about our relationship?"

Apparently, she'd enrolled over a year ago without telling him. He only discovered it when he saw her bank statement and, given their shared financial interests, believed this to be a breach of trust.

Will then went on to make Ruby promise she would keep it to herself.

Donating vast sums of money to good causes is one thing. But doing so secretly, anonymously, without the glory? It made Ruby smile, suddenly reframing the image she'd had of Lauren. A woman who had run three marathons, hosted glitzy fundraisers for a children's prosthetics charity and dedicated her life's work to medicine. Things that Ruby had cynically dismissed for no other reason than she knew about them. While prestige and acclaim do not diminish the net result – motive is largely irrelevant, a paramedic's salary and social standing doesn't matter much when they're pumping life back into your heart – here was evidence that Lauren's good deeds really weren't connected to her ego. Not even the mortal sin of pride could be levelled at her. She was selfless. Lauren was the real deal.

On one hand, the revelation had Ruby right back to that cartoon of perfection. While the other hand was opening the door to a changing mind. Ruby was probably a fair distance from *liking* Lauren, but respecting her was certainly an option.

"Was there any talk of a diagnosis?" she asked. "For Frank?"

"Not really. But the psychiatrist said she'd never heard anything like it."

"She? Was that Doctor Wallace by any chance?"

"Uh, yeah." Ruby nodded.

"I know her well – she's seen it all. If what Frankenfield said shocked *her* . . ."

"The footage puts him in Scott's house at all the relevant times. Frank . . ." Ruby sighed. "It just wasn't him."

Lauren sat quietly, looking at the wall, drawn to the line-up of faces.

"But you still haven't crossed him out?"

"I . . . I'm not quite there yet."

"Suppose that footage says more about Scott than it does about Frank," she said. "It's always the way, isn't it? The auteur. The man behind the camera."

And Ruby froze. Then she turned to the photo. "Wait." She took a step back.

"What?"

Ruby had been uncharacteristically irrational. Unable to explain, to herself or others, why she was obsessed with this photograph. Crossing the fourth victim off had made her feel sick with the possibility that it held no answers. The killer might not even be in their year. And yet she'd felt compelled, even entranced as she stared endlessly into the eyes of all the possible victims. Unprecedented to know them in advance. These people there, in the playground, on that sunny autumn afternoon twenty years ago. A hundred and sixty students, eight members of staff, four red crosses and one more person who, no matter how hard she looked, Ruby would never be able to see.

"The photographer," she whispered.

A surge of vindication. She was right to linger on this picture. It was as though some deep, recessed part of her mind knew and was keeping her here as it turned and screamed and turned in the dark, clawing feverishly at the walls of her subconscious, trying to push this idea, this name, this very thought into the spotlight of her attention. Don't look away. The answer is right there. And so obvious now she'd seen it.

She spun round to face Lauren. "What was he called?"

"I have no idea. Just some guy who came in to take pictures once a year?"

"No," Ruby said. "No." Firmer now. "The school's photography department was established in 1999. They installed the darkrooms the year we left. He . . ." She groaned. "What was his name? The first photography teacher."

Lauren looked at the carpet, eyes darting. "I'm not even sure I remember a photography teacher."

"He was there for our final term, then the year after we left, there was all that shit. He was accused of something."

"I remember that, but . . . would *he* have taken that picture?"

"Why hire a freelance if there's a photographer on campus?"

"Are you sure he was there when we were?"

"Hundred percent. I know his face. Ginger beard, glasses. You know who I'm talking about."

"The photography teacher who left was called something like Mr Allen?"

"Alfie," Ruby said – the name just coming out of her mouth.

Lauren's face brightened with recognition. "Yeah, Alfie. It wasn't mister."

"No, that's right," Ruby pointed, grabbing her phone from the desk, "he wanted students to use his first name. That was it. Alfie."

Lauren stood and again, they were side by side, staring at the photo.

"I'm *sure* he took this." Ruby swiped her phone unlocked and searched *Missbrook Heights*. She scrolled down old news stories. Nothing. "It's going back a bit. What were those accusations about?"

"I have no idea." Lauren curled her bottom lip, shrugging. "But a creepy-looking photographer at a secondary school? I reckon we could have a pretty good guess . . . Will would know."

Without even looking up from her phone, Ruby went to her contacts and hit Will's name. Checked her watch. It was 2pm. She hoped to catch him before his final lesson of the day. And she did, then she asked.

"You mean Alfie Rogers?" Will replied, clearly distracted.

"Yes." Ruby tilted the phone away from her face to echo the name to Lauren. "When was he hired?" she added.

"I could ask Jenny, in the office. She's been here forty-odd years. Knows everything."

There was a pause.

"Now?" he said.

"Yes, please."

Will sighed, she sensed him thinking about the time, imagined him checking a white wall clock. "All right, hold on."

She heard a door open, then pupils in the hallway – conversations, shouting. The nostalgic clatter of lockers.

"No phones in the hall," a kid yelled.

"Go inside," Will said, over the noise. "What are you doing? Put— no. Put it down . . ." Then the sound of his hand covering the receiver – words overlapping.

"But *sir*—"

"I don't care, go back into class."

Still surreal to hear Will speaking like a teacher. Finally, Ruby heard him arrive at the staffroom. There was a short, muffled exchange, which she couldn't make out. The line crackled, his voice returning.

"—Thanks, Jen," Will said. "You hear that?"

"No."

"Alfie Rogers started working at Missbrook Heights at the end of 1998." A door opening. "That was the year GCSE photography was added to the curriculum." Will's fast footsteps in the corridor. "Then he left under a black cloud in 2001." Another door.

"So, I was right, he might have taken our photo?"

"No, he definitely did." Sounds changing as Will made his way back towards his classroom. "Jenny remembered. All the newer school pictures are digital. But the old ones are film. They wanted to get their hands on some negatives to blow it up for the reunion. Tried to order a copy and couldn't."

"Why not?"

"Alfie moved away after all that stuff. He was accused of misconduct. Taking inappropriate photos." Will stopped walking, she pictured him standing outside the lesson. "Listen, I have to go."

"Why wasn't that in the news?"

"There were no charges."

"Because . . . ?"

"Well, the accusations were anonymous. Think it was a former student. So not even underage."

"Former student? So, could be someone from our year?"

"Maybe, I don't know. Apparently, it got quite nasty. He's framed as a bit of a victim here. Sounds like a witch hunt."

A vendetta. That was the one word that came to mind.

"Does the school have any contact details for him?"

"I don't know. Look, Ruby, I'm late for the last period, I really—"

"Please could you find out?"

He sighed again, then she heard him turn around and go back to the staffroom. Another short round of mumbled questions.

"No," Will said, definitively. "We have no details on record."

"How come?"

"Ruby, this is *twenty years* ago. I'm not in a position to defend the school's admin. I really do have to go."

"OK, thank you." She hung up.

A new theory. Possibilities, scenarios, motives swirling in her mind. A man hounded out of his job, out of his home. She had one sole, absolute aim. The stars were brightly shining. Find Alfie Rogers.

Ruby went straight to the desk, sat down and, phone still in her good hand, clumsily opened her laptop.

"I guess I'll, uh, leave you to it," Lauren said, standing in the doorway behind her.

"Thanks, for the tea." Ruby put her earbuds in and scrolled to Jay's name.

He told her there was record of a short investigation into Alfie Rogers, which was later dropped, though he'd provided a statement to the police after someone threw a brick through his living room window. "In fact," Jay added, "by the look of things, you may be better placed to find him."

"Why?"

"He applied for witness protection."

"What had he witnessed?"

"A town full of angry weirdos who thought he was a paedophile?"

"Did he get it? A new identity?"

"You tell me."

Next, Ruby went through the official channels at the NCA. She knew the UK Protected Persons Service was not exactly renowned for being an open door. But she had to try. On the phone again, she was connected to Don Larson who, she hoped, would shine some light.

Normal small talk with her boss, Don asking those general questions – sitting in his glassy office in London. Just another case on his desk. He seemed so detached that he didn't clock the urgency in her voice. This wasn't just an update call. Finally, she asked and, with a few clicks, he found the file.

"Here he is. Alfie Rogers."

"I need his new name," Ruby said.

"Need, or want?"

Did she have justification for an arrest? Probably not. So, "Want," she said. "Badly."

"To be honest, you'd need something concrete."

There was a pause.

"I'm assuming you do not have that?" Don asked.

"Not really. I . . ." Ruby looked to her right, out of the window, across the treetops at the end of the garden, to the patchwork fields and grey clouds above. "I could possibly find something?" She was careful with her words, skirting around the idea – important not to utter these things aloud.

"I, um, well, I would advise *against* that," Don said. "I've had similar interactions with the service – they're understandably quite cagey about any attempts to make contact. It would need to be ironclad."

It felt solid. But the contents of Ruby's heart, her gut, her unfounded faith, would not satisfy these formalities. What did she believe? That Alfie was responsible? That, in some way, he was con-nected? "I just want to talk to him."

"If you just want to *talk* to him, then I could put in a request?"

"Then what? His handler will ask him if he'll speak to me?"

"Exactly."

"How long would that take?"

"I have no idea."

Ruby paused for a few seconds, tapping her red pen against her laptop. "OK. Ask."

Surprisingly, it took just under an hour before Don called back. "Nope," he said, with an annoying brightness in his voice. "The answer was a resounding no."

Ruby, still speaking hands-free, found herself pacing. She stopped at the window and sighed. This was frustrating and she hoped it had been discussed over the phone. Still, "I suppose now if a reason for his arrest did arise, it might come under extra scrutiny?"

"You suppose correctly."

She'd put it into the system. Made it official. Even if it was verbal, it was there, on record. Now the protection service knew what she wanted. She'd tried to open the door and had, instead, announced her arrival and possibly added another lock too.

"So, what now?" she asked.

"If you come across a legitimate reason, by all means call back. If not, I'm sorry to say, but it's the end of the road."

There was another silence. Ruby stood at the window, hazy raindrops shifting like flocks of birds in the changing wind, light enough to make fog beyond the end of Will's garden. The sound of running water from a gutter above, bamboo wind chimes clattering below. And, leaning towards the cool glass, looking off to the side, she realised that her room had a sea view, right at the edge of the vista, a thin strip of flat horizon.

"What would . . ." She paused. Ruby had always respected Don. Despite being her professional senior, he was happy to speak both as a colleague and as a fellow human being. "What would your advice be?"

Turning, she sat on the windowsill and looked back into the spare room, gloomy now, the only light glowing from her laptop screen.

"My advice?" Don seemed to know that Ruby wasn't going to stop trying. "Be very, very careful."

"Thank you." The call ended and she strode back to the desk.

Now Ruby felt even more compelled to track Alfie down. The old adage is true. The less you want to speak to the police, the more they want to speak to you. But she'd exhausted all legal avenues. And now she had a big decision to make.

Ruby sat alone, elbow on the desk, surviving hand pressed against her chin. Her phone was face-up next to the mouse and she was just staring at it.

Could she? Could she call him?

Years ago, Ruby would have spoken to Elizabeth at a time like this. She was the source of grounded, compassionate wisdom. She'd have listened and explored the options without prejudice, not burdened by the weight of professional obligation, not tethered to the law or fear of judgement or any of the other countless things that stop people saying what they *really* think. Ironic that what she wanted right now, at this moment, at these crossroads, was to speak with her friend. But she couldn't. Because Elizabeth was dead. Because someone had caved her head in for reasons Ruby did not understand.

Finally, she imagined what Giles might say. Clarity. Absolute and direct. Would this course of action help her achieve her goal? And she nodded to herself. The answer was unequivocally yes.

Ruby snatched up her phone and called Eduardo.

"Well, hello there," he said. "How is the UK today?"

"Bleak."

"I saw you on the news – made it all the way out here. I sense it is going slowly?"

"Very. How's the course?"

"You were right. Preparation proved fruitful."

"I'm pleased."

"How's your dad?"

Ruby still hadn't been to see Giles. But she didn't want to think about, let alone explain, why. So, she just said, "He's fine."

"I miss you."

"I, oh . . ." This stopped her. It was a surprise. Not that he missed her, but that he'd said it. Now, on the other side of the planet, she could see it so clearly. You do not spend four nights camping alone in the Australian outback with a colleague. Eduardo and Ruby's time together – which had been so rapidly derailed by all of this – really was nothing to do with work. They'd pretended it was, like teenagers, children, intimacy growing, reaching for the light of unspoken things, nourished in the silence of a glaring secret that was, as they both knew, common knowledge.

Glimmers of another fantasy. A straight line through the earth. As far away from all this as she could get. What if Elizabeth had never called, never died? What if Ruby was still out there, down there, warm in the sun, telling him how she felt with every form of communication beyond words?

"Are you there?" he added.

"I am, unfortunately, very much here." The heart's cruel affinity for absence. "I miss you too." She'd been so close. Right on the cusp of normality. A stable job. A reasonable apartment. An attachment to another human that she would never openly admit to yearning for every scrolling night she slept alone. "I miss you so much."

They spoke for a while about the case. Eduardo clarified that it was the twenty-year school reunion that set it all in motion. Ruby had been with him when she received the invitation and imagined how she'd have conducted herself if she had gone. If she'd stepped into that raging furnace of insecurity and self-promotion.

There's a script for such occasions. Ruby had even rehearsed lines in her mind, well aware of things she might exaggerate. Questions she might divert. So . . . why hadn't she settled down? Would she have children? If so, when? Would the judgemental eyes of her former peers slip down to the drink in her hand and see her empty ring finger? Would she say she was seeing someone? Would Eduardo have to be something more? Was he her partner now? Oh, they might say, hand on her forearm, pray tell.

If, by some improbable geographic glitch, he was there, if plus ones had been allowed, and he overheard her saying this, would he laugh? Or would he smile, put his arm around her waist and agree? Would he tell them he felt like the luckiest man alive?

Are those wedding bells we can hear? Reddening cheeks, eye contact and half a shrug of maybe. Of who knows. Of time will tell.

"Though, now," Ruby said, on the phone, speaking in the real world, "I have hit a bit of a dead end."

She was gradually steering the conversation towards the real reason she'd called. Eduardo's speciality was uncannily fitting for her current situation.

How would they frame his career in those reunion circles? When the pleasantries glide along to their inevitable destination. And what, they would invariably ask, do you do?

Maybe she'd jump in, take the question. Eduardo trains law enforcement personnel. Cyber security, intelligence, tackling the ugly world of organised crime. But they'd probe. Sounds cool, more, tell us more. How does one get into this line of work, Eduardo?

Ruby wouldn't mention his past. But would he? Or would he dance around the truth?

Obfuscate about his very unique insight?

Considering her own expertise in this field, Ruby wasn't actually sure about the social norms when it comes to discussing an extensive criminal record. Perhaps it's like medical procedures or close calls with a disease everyone knows. Rude to ask, but perfectly acceptable to volunteer a life-affirming story. Though criminal rehabilitation does not elicit similar adoration or praise. And sympathy? That's rarely on the cards.

Eduardo didn't seem ashamed of his background. But Ruby imagined he would be keen to establish early on that this was another life. Again, anyone searching for something to say in the awkward silence that would follow may not feel comfortable asking for detail. Like grilling a soldier on just how many people they've shot. Was it fun? Do you feel bad?

Eduardo *did* feel bad. The immorality of what he did was inescapable. In this other life, which ended years before Ruby met him, Eduardo worked for a number of nefarious organisations. His speciality was finding people. Individuals who had left gangs, wronged cartels, informants hiding from the awful consequences of their lawful actions.

And, if he was candid about this, here would be the longest silence of all. People would nod and wonder. They would conclude that, while not having any direct violence on the charge sheet, Eduardo's hand, the very hand they shook at the start of this conversation, in this imaginary retelling of a school reunion she never even attended, had not always been as clean as it was today.

But he'd served his time and he was, Ruby knew, fully rehabilitated. Having waded through the murky waters of malevolence and vice, Eduardo had found clarity in moral virtue. He was now dedicating his life to ensuring that the wrongs of his past could be averted in everyone else's future. To her, he was living proof that people can and do change.

Back in the persistently real world, all this made what she was about to ask incredibly insensitive. She needed his help to find Alfie but a big part of her wanted him to refuse. Any answer would be bittersweet. Was his rehabilitation a façade? Something he would drop for her? And would she think less of him, or more, if he agreed? This predicament turned over in the back of her thoughts as she began to explain.

"So, there's no official way you can reach out to this guy?" Eduardo asked.

"None."

Once she'd outlined the details, the obstacles, the locks on the door, both old and new, there was the longest pause of the call.

"Are you asking me to help?" Eduardo finally said.

It seemed he knew the stakes too. The trust. Everything felt like it was on the line, as though the future of any relationship they might have depended on his response. Ruby looked up to the photograph on the wall, feeling guilty, scared, lost and alone all at once. And she sighed. "I am."

"OK," he said. "With all my heart, no."

And Ruby smiled, eyes closed, she nodded. "Ah," she breathed. "I kind of thought you'd say that."

"I'm really not that person anymore."

"I know. I'm sorry for asking."

"However," he added. "I can give you a name – the kind of person who could assist. This is someone with extensive knowledge. He could set up some online scrapers to see if there was anyone who fits. This would hinge on how seriously the individual in question had been treating their new identity."

"What would that person need?"

"As much information as possible. Old name. Photos, the more recent the better. Connections to any groups, family, where they grew up, hobbies, interests, that sort of thing."

"I can get that."

"I'll give you a phone number. You pay this man enough, he'll find anyone for you. He'll find ghosts. He'll track down your imaginary friend from childhood. But obviously, it did not come from me."

"Of course."

This was the perfect response. Eduardo was not willing to break the law. But it seemed he would not judge Ruby if she did. After all, he still had a long way to climb before he reached any moral high ground. Though he seemed not to like the idea of her falling too far.

"If you did make contact with this individual," he said, "would there be any repercussions? For you, I mean."

She smiled again. His concern was for her, not the ethics involved.

This was a factor. Alfie might not like Ruby turning up on his doorstep. So, she would have to lie to him. And if he was worth investigating, the ends would justify the means. If not, if those ends were dead, then what was the harm? What was the risk? There was none.

"No," she said, definitively.

"And when it's over, when you're finished there, what are you going to do?"

Ruby laughed. "I'm going to sprint to the airport."

"I'll be waiting."

At 4am, just a few short hours into day twelve's dark morning, Ruby was in the spare room, somewhere between awake and asleep, metres from the school photograph that Alfie took all those years ago. And her phone, on the carpet by the leg of the bed, lit up silently with a message from an unknown number. She looked down, squinted and saw an address.

Chapter Thirteen

Ruby parked at the edge of a large square courtyard walled on every side by tall blocks of flats – the one up ahead casting its shadow over patches of grass and tarmac paths. At the car's side, some old play equipment with a green rail fence – the metal gate clunked in its frame, in the breeze that swayed the empty swings beyond, their chains dangerous and cold, twisting ghostly and slow.

Ruby looked up, out of the driver's window, past a fizzing streetlight that had mistaken this day for night, up to the blackening clouds above. She had simply forgotten to bring a jacket. But, she thought, yeah, she remembered seeing one in the boot of Will's car.

As she climbed out, a child cycled past on a BMX bike – pedalling hard, he disappeared into the amber mouth of the closest underpass. At the back of the car, Ruby tried the boot. Locked. Reaching into her pocket for the key, she glanced around this place again, surveyed the community Alfie called home. Those graffitied tunnels that scurried like hollow roots beneath the identical monoliths. The train clattering along nearby, hot and screeching high on a bridge at her side as litter swirled, little dust devils made of ribboned plastic and torn paper.

It had all happened faster than Ruby expected. Eduardo was right. Time elapsed meant Alfie had let his guard down. His online presence was low-key and could be considered careful, aside from a profile on a dating site that included a headshot and his screen-name "Alfred77". The scraper, a relatively simple piece of software, returned a facial match within hours. Alfred77 had a keen interest in photography, literature, poetry and film and was hoping to meet a like-minded woman with a good sense of humour – someone who enjoyed the finer things in life. Someone unique, like everyone else.

Although ethically dubious, the expertise Ruby had employed was affordable and, she was told, "not particularly sophisticated". Considering how easy he'd been to find, Alfie was lucky she did not have malicious intent. The worst she was going to do was arrest him. Though, given that she'd had to drive for hours to reach this address, that seemed unlikely. But it was the photo that settled her fear or perhaps dashed her hope. Alfie was underweight to the point of disorder. Whether or not he had the mind to kill someone with a blunt instrument was up for debate. But he absolutely lacked the body.

Still, Ruby felt compelled to speak to him. On the drive, she'd indulged her imagination and wondered how his departure from Missbrook Bay could be connected. All that ugliness. All those rumours and disgrace. Was there a thread here, something to tug, something to trace?

Perhaps she'd been bolstered by his evident shortfall in physical strength. Or maybe she was simply falling for the sunk cost fallacy. It might even have been her unfounded obsession with the school year photograph. Either way, she was here.

Keys clinked in her hand, she slid one into the boot lock and turned, thinking that, at worst, Alfie was a unique window into the past. A former teacher who'd fled with nothing but scandal and unsated menace in his wake. His memories of Missbrook Heights were, like hers, untainted by recency or presence. They shared the underrated clarity that only absence can provide. Yes, this felt right.

The boot hatch hissed up and away and she looked down into—

Ruby froze. A sudden statue. She stood in the rain and cold staring down at a sawn-off shotgun, just lying there in the boot. Like some piece of modern street art, an unmoving figure, Ruby might as well have been made of bronze.

But then she regained her motor skills, checking over her shoulder, left, up at those countless windows, right – even more on that side. Instinctively, she reached down and hid it, sliding a car jack against the barrel, covering the gun with the coat she'd hoped to wear. Then she slammed the boot closed and took a breath, thought for a moment, be cool, calm, trying to hide her confusion, her panic. She got her phone out, stared down – all a casual performance. Someone might be watching. Specks of water appearing on the glowing glass, bubbled light refracting like tiny blisters.

It took a good few seconds to actually form the thought. The words. The explanation. She'd been driving around with a loaded gun for days. Frank Enfield's shotgun had been in the boot of Will's car all this time.

"Yeah, no, I've processed everything." That's what Ruby said to Jay. All those crimes they could have charged Frank with: false imprisonment, threats to kill and, of course, possession of a firearm.

Regret and fear came on strong. The sheer unprofessionalism of this. Ruby felt her cheeks redden, toying with the humiliation she'd feel if she did what she should have already done and locked the gun in the evidence room. She'd be tempted to lie – say she held on to it deliberately. For protection. A straight-faced admission of a serious offence, *a very serious offence* she'd still be committing even if she confessed the far more embarrassing truth.

Why, Ruby, why haven't you processed this piece of evidence? This loaded gun.

"I forgot." Even imagining that response felt absurd. It was literally unbelievable. She closed her eyes, her heart shifting gears up to a new tempo as she considered the implications of her fading memory once more. It's just the drugs. The Adderall. She was taking too much, burning too brightly, shining like those lyrical stars. Fall on your knees, she thought, oh hear the angel voices – they were yelling at her now. Not about the dear saviour's birth. No, no. They were screaming about *shame*.

Her shoulders were wet. The sleeves of her jumper speckled and damp enough to stick. But still, she was hot. The irony was not lost on her. Driving here to Alfie's flat was a criminal act in itself. But this? And what if the dust settled and then they realised there was no gun? Her claim that Frank abducted her at gunpoint would fall flat. No.

She calmed herself as she locked the car, checking twice that it was definitely locked. If police picked Frank Enfield up, he'd be back in a cell and facing charges. Then, and only then, would she come clean. A simple oversight. It could happen to anyone. She took painkillers for her hand. That's what she'd say. She was drowsy. And she'd just take the ridicule on the chin. No one was going to charge her with anything. But they would laugh. In her face, behind her back, yeah, they'd laugh.

A deep breath in through her nose and, jaw clenched, she buried it. Then, with a new resolve, she flicked her hood up and strode off towards the block of flats on her left. Problems. Solutions. Progress. Yet another layer of pressure added to this deadly situation. Ruby really did need to solve this. Ideally soon. If nothing else, every frayed fibre of her threadbare self-esteem depended on it.

Inside the building, she went straight to the lift. No mirror, just dented silver panels. Black pen scrawled on every wall. She pressed the button for the fifth floor with her knuckle and rose up through the block's spinal column. The pale light from each storey fell down the slit in the metal, she counted: three, four and, slowly to a stop, five. Doors beeped, spread open and the taut cable above seemed relieved to be rid of her.

A long corridor. She walked. Bare concrete and alien cuisine cooking behind closed doors. Boiled things, like school dinners. Steam. She turned a corner. Heard a television, loud music from another flat up ahead. Down the narrow passage, somehow colder than outside, the wind finding its way in through a window at the end, whistling wire-lattice glass smashed with year-round frosting.

And she stopped. Here it was. Flat 313. Alfie Rogers.

She knocked and, while waiting, experienced another wave of anxiety. Doubt. Maybe she was making a—

The door opened. Alfie, dressed in a long-sleeved, black t-shirt and a pair of beige cargo shorts, didn't say a word. He just leant out and looked down the hallway, as though checking she was alone. She saw his collarbone, the tendons in his neck. His skull. Ruby was right – he must be ill. Health hides your skeleton. Alfie's was plain to see.

"That was quick," he said, stepping back, inviting her in like she was a guest he'd been expecting.

All of her rehearsed lies fell away. There was no need. He wasn't stupid. But still, she wondered, "How did—"

"I've seen the news," he said, cutting her off. "I don't get many visitors, then a couple of days ago I get a request to speak to the police – the first real contact with the protection service I've had in over a decade. And now you are here knocking at the door. It's not rocket science."

"I—"

"For God's sake, you're freezing, come in."

He put his hand on her shoulder, strangely caring and gentle. She entered, standing awkwardly against the wall as he closed the door.

Although small, it was a relatively nice flat. Pale wooden floor, expensive furniture. She spotted a gigantic TV in the living room, a surround-sound ensemble of black electronics mounted between wall lights. Alfie seemed to have that modest affluence of finding yourself in late middle-age, childless and, judging by the dating website, single.

"I have a pot of coffee on the go," he said, passing her and heading towards the kitchen.

Ruby followed but stopped halfway at a series of framed photographs on the hallway wall. The first signs that she was in the right place.

"It's the old dock," she whispered, thinking out loud, leaning in. "It is."

"Did you take these?" Then she felt stupid because the answer was obvious.

"Yep. There's more of the bay in the living room. But the dock was always my favourite spot."

The old navy docks at the edge of Missbrook Bay were long abandoned, dangerously derelict, cordoned off with tall wire fences. Two jutting rectangles of concrete, a capital "F" from above, the heavy metal cleats embedded, like anvils, horns, the yellow paint all but rusted away. The dock buildings with their shattered windows, weatherworn façades. Thick ropes, green mooring lines slack and swamped with hanging plant life, clumped like wet hair. Nowadays, its only visitors were adventurous teenagers and late-night drug users.

She stared into the first photograph. Alfie had taken it from high up on the western cliffs, just off the crumbled road. Every surface was covered in ice, a thin layer of snow that made it seem somehow active, like an Arctic sea base. The fierce winter ocean churning up spray from the rolling marbled black of heavy waves below.

Then she saw, next to this, another photo taken from the exact same spot, only in spring. The green sea moss on the underside, furry and wet, everything beneath the tideline caked with shells and barnacles like plaque on teeth. Ruby could almost smell it, she could almost hear the water sucking up and down, echoing below the concrete jetty's cavernous underbelly, splashing, howling, gurgling away in the dark.

The next photo of the docks was taken in summer, blue skies and bright sun – the ocean white with shards of light that would have hurt your eyes to stare. And finally, in the fourth picture, the low and golden glow of autumn setting the calm sea on fire.

Every season on display. The time that marches on.

"Is it still there?" Alfie asked from the kitchen, turning back as he poured some coffee.

"Uh, yeah, they never got round to knocking it down. I think there were plans to make it into a museum at one point. But that apparently isn't happening."

"Go and have a seat," he said, nodding towards the living room.

Ruby stepped inside and sat on a small armchair near the balcony doors. Alfie entered, handed her a mug, then sat directly opposite, an empty sofa on her left, the TV on her right.

"I'm Alan, by the way." He put his coffee down on the low table between them, then rearranged the cushions to get comfortable. "Reynolds. Though you probably know me by another name. Call me that if you'd rather."

"Ruby." She smiled, noticing his initials were the same. Simpler. Easy to remember.

"So . . ." he sat back, lifted a foot onto his knee, "how can I help?"

Ruby had prepared herself for a frosty reception, but he seemed happy, even keen to chat.

"Why weren't you willing to talk to me?" she said.

"Oh, I don't know, I just . . . I don't want hassle and I supposed if it was serious enough, you'd keep trying. And I wasn't wrong. I've got nothing to hide. Fire away."

"I wanted to speak to you about what happened."

"That's a very broad topic. Suppose we'd start with the Big Bang?"

"Fast forward a little."

"Dinosaurs?"

"Bit more."

"My employment at Missbrook Heights?"

"Yeah, let's go with that."

"You know what happened with *that*."

"Not really." Ruby shook her head. "I've only heard rumours."

"I suspect they're quite close to the truth."

"I hope not."

"Well, now I'm intrigued. What's the worst one?"

"That you had a sexual relationship with a student."

"A reasonable leap, I suppose." He shrugged. "But no. That's wrong."

"Go on."

"I took photographs of a *former* student. She was nineteen years old and wanted some, shall we say, boudoir shots for her boyfriend."

"That's it?"

"We kissed." He sighed. "Her partner – who, for the record, was older than me at the time – was the confrontational kind. When he found out, her line of defence was that she'd felt coerced. She said that I'd wanted something besides money for the services rendered."

"Did you?"

"I . . . no. I wanted to be paid as well. But, sure, I shouldn't have done it. It was inappropriate." He folded his arms, lifted his shoulders. "I was a single, thirty-year-old man." He seemed to be distancing himself from that younger, more virile version of himself. "She instigated and . . . there really was no coercion. It was a mistake, but it was not a crime."

"Then what?"

"As you know, Missbrook Bay has a way with rumours. Jump ahead a few weeks and I've lost my job."

"Why?"

"Police arrested me *at school*. In front of a packed playground. I don't know why they did that. They questioned me, no charges. All was well. But shit sticks. Thing is, looking like a sexual predator isn't a million miles away from being one. Teaching there was untenable. The head knew it, I knew it. No hard feelings."

"And what made you move?"

"The threats got a little bit too real." He took a big breath in. "Someone spat at me on the bus. Then I was attacked, but I got away, fortunately. It was a collection of things."

"Serious enough for a new identity?"

"I think maybe the police felt responsible – they were helpful with the relocation. I left everything behind. Once it had all died down it kind of seemed, I don't know, silly. But at the time, they believed I was in real danger."

Ruby could hear the sounds from outside, the whispering urban sprawl behind her. Venturing into any London borough renewed her gratitude for silence – the rural tranquillity of Missbrook Bay, despite the squawking gulls, had a certain charm. Here, constant traffic droned out of sight, horns, a siren – impossible ambient noise that seemed to be coming from above.

"Who was the girl?" she asked.

"I'd rather not say."

Ruby just stared at him.

211

He hesitated, then lifted a hand, throwing the words "who cares" into the room with a groan. "Marilyn Evans."

She didn't recognise the name. "What year was she in?"

"I told you, she was a *former* student. Can we please be clear on that?"

"No," Ruby clarified. "I mean, when did she leave?"

"Oh." He frowned, doing a quick calculation in his head. "She would have left in 1997? Or '96 maybe? She'd left before I was employed. I assure you, I never knew her when she was a student."

Ruby believed him. That was it – the one small straw she'd been trying to clutch – the vague theory that someone was exacting vengeance. But why would this incident result in those four red crosses on the class of '99's photograph? She pictured the origin of this image, iconic in her mind, imagining Alfie behind the camera, opposite her just like he was now, checking light, clicking the shutter to capture that moment in time.

Ruby looked over his shoulder. The wall behind him was taken up with a bookshelf, set into the bricks, spines arranged by colour. A rainbow. Just like the rainbow the sky might produce right now if only the sun would shine.

Her attention lingered here too long – combined with a lack of sleep, stress, fear and an omnipresent sense of failure, the Adderall seemed to be doing nothing. She didn't feel wired, focused and capable. At best, the drugs had elevated her to the dimly low heights of normality. Sobriety. They were right. This *is* a slippery slope.

Alfie picked up his coffee, took a sip and broke the silence with, "So, I'm supposing you believe the murders may have something to do with all that?"

Turning away from his technicolour bookshelf, Ruby chewed the inside of her mouth and shook her head. "I just don't know."

No, she thought, killing the negativity before it took hold again. The sense of stagnant progress was an illusion. The break-in, the black car, the dark-blue jacket, Frank, Scott, the night of the reunion. She was getting closer. There was a connection, she just couldn't quite make it out yet. Like that slowly developing photograph, submerged in fluid, glossy and red. A hazy shape, shimmering beneath the water, shadows forming into a picture of *something*.

"For what it's worth," Alfie said, "I play bridge three nights a week, down at the community centre. It's a very tactical game, it's not just for old people."

"OK?"

"I'm just saying, I haven't been to Missbrook Bay since 2001."

She smiled. "I didn't ask."

Laughing, Alfie rolled his eyes. But he didn't say more. He seemed to realise that resisting suspicion was counterproductive. Putting his mug back on the table, he pointed at her, nodding.

"I remember you," he said. "Had a sideline taking pictures for the local paper. The sport section. About your boxing?"

Ruby remembered that article – the grainy, black and white photo, the referee holding her gloved fist high. A rising star. "Huh," she said, ignoring the spike of shame. "Small world."

"Huge world, small town. I knew your dad too."

Ruby felt no need to correct him with "stepdad".

"Yeah," Alfie went on. "He used to drink at The Anchor. Big guy. Scary. Giles?"

Ruby nodded. "Big scary Giles."

Having been in town for almost two weeks now, Ruby's visit was long overdue. While her excuse, that she was busy, was true, she'd also hoped to have made more progress than she had, so she could at least appear to justify her distance. All this hard work, and what did she have to show? What would she even say when he asked how the case was going?

"Good man." He put the tips of two fingers on his lips and squinted. "I remember," he pointed again, this time at the ceiling, "there was a fight and he just stood between these two young fellas and stared at them. From one to the other. That was it. Just a look. And they stopped. It was amazing . . . Bet you were well-behaved growing up."

"Very."

Ruby was no stranger to this glance – though she rarely saw it aimed at her. The discipline, while strict, received virtually no resistance. Which said a great deal about Giles's aptitude as a leader and as a father. In the army, his job had been to make people achieve certain goals. And he knew exactly how to deploy this skill on a child.

Even in her teenage years, Ruby's most outrageous instances of rebellion were, at worst, mild withdrawal from conversations. She was well-behaved because there was no other option. How could she get top marks in every exam unless she studied? Would staying up beyond her bedtime help or hinder her chances of success the following day? Homework was completed at the earliest opportunity, revision was comprehensive, exercise regimented. She ate her vegetables because vitamins and minerals were mission-critical. And all of it with the least input imaginable from Giles.

Even "the talk" was carried out without red cheeks or ceremony. There were no taboos in their household. Female biology was as matter of fact as any other issue.

"You can have intimate relationships with boys or girls," Giles had explained when the topic came up. "But you need to appreciate the risks involved, including pregnancy, sexually transmitted infections and your overall safety."

It was also around that time the training became increasingly frequent and focused on self-preservation. Ironically, boxing led to her first semi-romantic encounter – a boy called Alex who she'd sparred with at the gym. Ruby remembered the day she told Giles she was going round his house to watch a film. She must have been fourteen, maybe fifteen. Perhaps naïvely as she didn't have many her age, Ruby had insisted it was just a "friend thing", so it would be OK to stay over.

Without even looking up from his book, Giles had said, "No, that's almost certainly not true. Virtually every boy you interact with is trying to have sex with you."

"Every boy? I don't think I'm that good looking."

"Teenage boys . . ." Giles had sighed. "It's a safe rule of thumb. Just keep it in mind."

But he never told her that she couldn't go. Later, she'd wondered if this seemingly blasé attitude was awarded to flatter her. Give her the information and autonomy to make her own mistakes. Whatever the reasoning, she remembered appreciating his stance, his knack of making her feel like his equal. Competent commanders, he said, appear to do almost no work – the hallmark of a great leader is to operate right on the cusp of their own redundancy.

Sure enough, Alex was not particularly interested in seeing how the movie's third act panned out and, when she returned home just before 9pm, neither she nor Giles needed to comment.

What would he have said if nineteen-year-old Ruby had wanted to have risqué photographs taken at the home of a former teacher? Probably nothing. It went without saying.

"Were you sad when you were fired?" Ruby asked, returning to the room.

"It was a joint decision. But, yes, it was my dream job, photography teacher. It was perfect." He paused, seemed wistful, half-smiling at a memory. "Broke my heart."

"What do you do nowadays?"

"Headshots. Weddings. But work has slowed down. I've been . . . unwell."

Ruby just left this floating in the air.

"Better now, though," he said. "I actually got the all-clear at the end of last year. Feels like a new chapter."

He didn't even need to say the word "cancer". "I'm pleased." Ruby meant it.

"Any other questions?"

"Ever married?"

"Briefly."

"Single now?" she asked, even though she was pretty sure she knew the answer.

"Look, you seem lovely," he said, with a smile, "but I'd prefer someone my own age."

"That's not what I've heard."

And he laughed, a warm, easy-going chuckle that faded out to silence. "Very good."

This was not what she had expected. Alfie really did seem like a decent man. She felt comfortable with him. An odd, mutual understanding. The sense that, just by being here, alive, just by existing, they were fundamentally on the same team.

Ruby realised now how obviously lost she must have appeared. Sitting in his living room, reminiscing. Making jokes. He seemed to notice, picking up the topic – the actual reason for her visit.

"The victims," he began, "I must say, I can't remember any of them. Apart from Scott, who I remember all too well."

"He had that effect."

"Can I be honest with you?"

"I insist."

"It'll sound strange, but I am fascinated by all this."

"Murder?"

"Death."

"Me too."

"How were they killed?"

This felt slightly morbid but Ruby owed him candour. "Head trauma."

"Weapon?"

"Not sure. The damage seems to be consistent with a blunt instrument, repeated strikes to the head. A lot of . . ." Ruby winced. "Force." Elizabeth. Splatter on the branches above. No, bury it. Swallow.

"And they're all from your year?"

"Yes. But other than that, they just seem so . . . different. There's a connection. They have something else in common. Something they did maybe . . ."

"Or . . . what if it was a hollowing?"

"Excuse me?"

Alfie put on a stern face – like an actor locking into character. He stroked his stubbled chin, then gestured as he said, "Take sword and axe to peasant or king, cut down even maids afar . . . if no deed done, no fear nor scar."

"What's happening?"

"Be wise," he went on, "for once evil descends, the black heart of contagion already has hold, remove it with vigour, be brave, be bold."

"Are you OK?"

"Not a fan of medieval poetry, I take it?" he asked.

"Can't say that I am."

"There's . . ." Alfie looked behind himself, back at his rainbow bookshelf. Then he rose up quickly and went straight to the right-hand side, where the violet spines shifted to black and brown. He slid a book out, came back, sat down.

Some old medieval history. He perched it on his knees, licked a thumb and flicked through the pages. Finally, he bent it open on one, spun the book round and passed it across to her.

There were gruesome illustrations. Peasants pinned to tables, their brains being scooped out like ice cream from the backs of their open skulls – scalps unfurled on the wood. Cross-hatch shading. Proportions all slightly off, the style of a tapestry.

"See," he said, "it was a strange practice. They would kill them, remove their hearts and, quite advanced for the time, their brains."

"None of their brains were removed. Or hearts."

"No, but, look." He pointed. "They didn't always do that."

"What is it?" Ruby was confused. "A punishment?"

"Kind of. Some sins were believed to be so egregious that even witnessing them was punishable by death." He shrugged, waved a hand towards the book. "Maybe it's that."

Ruby looked back down into the pages on her knees. "Being executed for a crime you didn't commit seems unfair."

"They thought that if the devil had made someone do something bad, anyone who saw it was a risk. Demonic possession was contagious. It actually isn't *that* far-fetched."

"Yes, it is."

"No, I mean, the idea of rewriting history. When everyone who remembers the horrors of a war is dead, how potent do you think its lessons will be? If everyone forgets, it's like it didn't happen."

"If a tree falls in the woods and no one's around to hear it . . ."

"Exactly. Absolute silence. The tree never fell."

"So . . . ?" Ruby wanted him to clarify his point.

"So, maybe it's not revenge for something they did. But something they saw."

There was a long, intense silence.

"Or maybe not," Alfie said in a new, brighter voice. "I don't know. It's not *my* job to figure it out."

He gave her his number and said he'd be happy to answer any more questions. Ruby left, drove back to Missbrook Bay and spent the afternoon sifting through new reports from the scene of Adam

Ward's death. Jay provided her with a couple of witness statements and some notes about the lack of meaningful forensic evidence. He said in passing that he'd met his wife in that pavilion, almost thirty years ago. Jay seemed sad about it. Like a fond memory had been infected, overwritten by something terrible.

◆ ◆ ◆

Day thirteen arrived. Ruby was in the station building, at her desk, when Jay came in and sat down opposite. There were metal-frame uprights where their desks met, but the old blue office dividers were, unfortunately, gone. Without delay, Jay began turning a wooden knob on his drawer, making a barely perceptible squeaking sound – the kind of noise that'd disturb dogs.

Ruby put her earphones in, focused on her laptop screen.

"Why did you get so angry about it?" he asked.

She looked up to see Jay staring at the Velcro splint on her broken hand. "About what?" Ruby removed one of the earbuds.

"The other day, with Gemma. When she said 'shadow boxer'. I've never seen you lose your cool."

"I didn't."

"You *nearly* did, though."

"It's . . ." With a sigh, Ruby removed the other earbud and just told him. Explained the whole stupid story. A silly lie that got out of control. A ridiculous source of embarrassment, even now.

"Were you old enough to compete in the Olympics?" he asked, when she finished.

"No. Maybe. I don't know. It was just one of those childish things. Obviously wasn't true."

Instead of replying with a snarky comment, which Ruby was braced to receive, Jay nodded. It almost seemed sympathetic.

"Do you like me?" he asked.

219

"Um, you're all right?"

"No, seriously." He sat up straight, arms on his desk. "What do you think of me? Be honest."

"I don't know, Jay." Ruby turned her hand over. "I think . . . I think you come across a bit curt at times."

"Curt?"

"Rude." He was waiting for more. The word she wanted to say. So, she said it. "Even arrogant."

Jay was clicking his pen now, click, click, repeatedly pressing it with his thumb. *Click, click, click.*

"And," she added, "your fidgeting is pretty annoying." He stopped. "In fact, sometimes I think you get kicks out of winding people up. It's like you have these tics, but only with company."

"How could you know?"

"I've seen you alone. Sitting perfectly still."

"Astute." He smiled, scratched the good side of his asymmetrical face. "You know, when *I* was at school, children bullied me. Not too bad, they'd just make fun. So, I used to be deliberately unlikeable. I'd irritate everyone, even my friends, as much as possible."

It seemed Jay was telling her this for her benefit, not his. "Why?"

"To get ahead of them. Because unprovoked attacks hurt too much. So, when they made fun of me, as they definitely would, I could take ownership. They would be mean about my mouth, my cheek, children always were, but it would be *my* fault. I didn't care if people hated me. I really didn't. As long as it wasn't because of my face."

Ruby felt guilty now for all the times she'd noticed his features. Even thinking about them seemed cruel.

"Bell's palsy is rare in kids," he said. "Doctors told me it'd go away. But . . ." Jay drew a quick circle around his face and laughed. "I can take the humour, the joshing, from colleagues, friends and

220

even family. But there are *some* people who have never commented on it. Never. Not once. And you're one of them."

"I try not to say unkind things."

"I know. I respect that. Even more than this work ethic of yours. Good manners. You're so polite."

"Thank you."

"See . . . Don't be afraid or ashamed . . . Don't . . . We all have our own fights. Everyone's at war with something. And if they're not, they will be. One day." Jay stood, walked round the desk and patted her on the shoulder. "Get some sleep," he added, turning back for his jacket. He hung it over his arm. "That will help."

Jay left. Now alone, Ruby enjoyed one of those ephemeral glimmers of optimism. A feeling that, for just a moment, tricks you into believing things really might be OK. Like she felt with Alfie – we are on the same side. We're all in this together. Such periods of time were growing shorter, rarer and their opposites increasingly intense. So, when they arrived, Ruby put them straight to work. Psychological comfort was just fuel for the fire. Problems. Solutions.

Opening her notes, she stopped at a page marked "hollowing". She couldn't remember the name of the book Alfie had shown her and refused to take it when he offered, insisting she'd buy her own copy. But now she discovered she hadn't written the title down.

If in doubt, ask. She grabbed her phone, hit Alfie at the top of her contacts. It rang and rang. No answer. She tried again, but nothing. It was 8pm. Perhaps he was busy. Maybe he was taking photos or playing bridge at the community centre.

Ruby put her phone on the desk. What was it called, she thought, tapping a knuckle on her chin, something about—

Her phone lit up, buzzing on the wood with an incoming call. But not from Alfie. Another number. One she didn't recognise.

She answered. "Hello?"

"Who is this?" a male voice asked. He sounded stern. Official.

"You rang me." Phone pressed to her ear with her shoulder, Ruby reached for a pen, leant back in her chair.

"My name is Detective Sergeant Dennis Warren. I'm with the Met Police."

There was a silence. He realised she wasn't taking her chance to speak.

"You've tried to ring Alan Reynolds a number of times," he said.

"Alfie," Ruby whispered, remembering that his new name, his current name, was Alan.

"Are you friends?"

Ruby squinted, sat forwards. What was this? Had Alfie been spooked? Had he spoken to the protection service? "He's . . . an acquaintance. A, a colleague. Why do you ask?"

"There's been an incident." That familiar sigh. It was said to be the hardest thing you ever have to do in this job. "He was attacked late last night and—"

"He's dead," Ruby said, but it didn't sound like a question.

She wasn't moving. She wasn't breathing. Everything had stopped.

"I'm sorry," the detective said. "A murder investigation is underway. Really, I'm so sorry to spring this on you, but he didn't have many recent calls. Would it be OK if I asked you a few—"

Ruby hung up, threw her phone on the desk like it was hot, suddenly radioactive. Backing away, she covered her mouth. She stood, swivel chair spinning empty. She turned. Full circle. Panic. Back to the desk. No. She turned again. Fight or flight. Hand in her hair. Other hand trapped, sweating and strangled in this itchy fucking—

She tore her brace off, tugging the Velcro from her wrist, dropping it as she stepped quickly, barging into the toilet where she stood and breathed.

And breathing, clutching the sink, she managed not to vomit. Managed not to cry. She just kept thinking about him. The new chapter he'd just begun. That hearty laugh. The time it must have taken him to arrange those books by himself. Alone in his humble flat with all that extra colour and life uniformity adds to the world. Chaos was bleak and brown, but order was a rainbow. It had been beautiful.

She closed her eyes. And here it was again, this sense that the planet itself had become untethered from the sun and was drifting free beneath her feet, a mutual dance of gravitational divorce at a scale she was simply unequipped to comprehend. But she could feel it. And she knew there was no way back. No way on or off God's green earth.

Alfie was dead. He'd been on the list. And Ruby had led them right to him. There was no doubt now. No room for speculation, or hope, no confusion about how much blame she had to bear. Because this was, without any question, her fault.

Chapter Fourteen

Ruby, biting her thumbnail, was pacing in Will's kitchen. Having abandoned the brace entirely, she'd already put her broken hand back in service, using it to punch a hole in the living room wall. It hurt, but not as much as she'd feared, or perhaps hoped, it would. Gristly tendons sliding and twanging beneath her skin when she flexed her fingers. But the swelling stayed down, her red flesh tight and bright as she ran it under the cold tap, trembling, numb. Physical pain had plateaued. But psychological pain, it seemed, did not have a ceiling. And if it did? Well, Ruby would just have to punch a hole in that too.

The front door opened, she turned – Will and Lauren mid-conversation as they came in. They'd been out for dinner. In the hallway now. Keys on a shelf. Shoes off. Just going about their normal lives.

"Who did you tell?" Ruby said, meeting them in the living room, her cheeks compressed as though from a sour taste, anguished, narrowing eyes that so badly wanted to cry but never would.

Will frowned, casual, intrigued. "What are you talking about?"

"Alfie Rogers is dead."

"Jesus," Lauren whispered.

"I . . ." Ruby stared at the floor, breathing heavy. "He was hiding. Oh, shit." She looked back up. "He was safe." Her voice juddering. "And I led them there. Someone was following me . . . They killed him."

"But I thought . . ." Will said, shocked. "That means it's not just people from our—"

"*Who did you fucking tell?*" Ruby yelled, startling them both. "At school, who knew? Who knew that I was looking for Alfie?"

Still in a baffled, mumbling state, Will shook his head. "I . . ."

"Why did you tell anyone?" Ruby spread her arms. "What the hell is wrong with you?"

Now, though, Will seemed to be losing his patience. Exhaling confusion, his next breath filled him up with something else. Anger. Indignance. Like he'd done her a favour and she'd thrown it back in his face.

"You made me ask in the staffroom," he said. "Everyone heard. This stuff is all anyone talks about."

"Who?"

"You want a list of the faculty? Their partners? And what about pupils? It's non-stop, online, in the classroom . . . I mean, it is literally the talk of the town. *Countless* people would have known."

They were standing in a triangle, Will and Lauren side by side, the bay window behind, Ruby opposite, facing them down. She felt her teeth grinding as she glanced between them. "You two knew," she said.

Lauren didn't seem offended, but Will's eyes were still on Ruby, solid and scowling.

"Where were you yesterday evening?" she asked, calmer, composed now.

"I was at work," Lauren said. She sounded as if she wanted to help, like she understood this was a formality – nothing personal.

But Ruby needed detail. "At the hospital?"

"Yeah. Covering for a colleague, a consultant's office . . ."

Ruby nodded once at her, then slowly turned to Will. "And you?"

"Are you serious?" he said.

"Does it sound like a joke?"

Will jutted a finger at her, "Fuck you, Ruby," a sudden burst of pent-up animosity and spite in his voice. He really meant that.

Even Lauren clocked that this was not a measured response, no matter how outrageous the implication had been – she stepped aside, turning, alarmed but curious to see where Will's temper was taking him.

"This is typical," he went on. "It's projection. All this . . . it's not . . . You're not upset that poor Alfie is dead." He looked her up and down, shaking his head as though he'd caught her out, like he was feigning disbelief for something he'd always known to be true. And then he smiled. Nodded. Yep. "It's because it reflects badly on *you*."

"Counter-accusations? Obfuscation?" Ruby pretended she was surprised. Even impressed. "Skipped denial, went straight to petty, defensive nonsense. So fast too. Fascinating."

Groaning, Will removed his phone and stepped closer. He scrolled down on the Missbrook Heights School Facebook page, finding a video that had been livestreamed yesterday evening. That *he* had livestreamed yesterday evening.

Footage of the big band on the sports hall stage – the same room as the reunion – a five-minute segment from an after-school concert. He hit play and, while the tinny music sang from his phone's speakers, Ruby felt her anger simmering down, leaving behind, as it so often does, a sediment of shame. He was right. This was a classic case of projection. "That's where I was yesterday," Will said. "At work, doing my job."

Ruby nodded through a new layer of doubt. She hadn't needed these alibis – it was all a performance, a show that *appeared* to be about straightforward deduction, the cornerstone of standard-issue police work. But the subtext, now clear to see, was desperation. Yes, everyone knew that this play was *really* about how clueless she was, scrabbling around in the dim fog of baseless accusation, throwing knives into shadows, blind and scared and hitting nothing but her friends.

"I'm . . . I'm sorry," Ruby said, teetering on a whimper. "You're right, I don't think . . . It doesn't matter who you told. The car, the break-in, my notebook. Someone's been keeping tabs for a while. It predates Alfie. They were already following me."

She'd just not seen it coming, hadn't even considered he might be a target. All other victims had been from her year and she'd had no reason to think the pattern would change. But even that – the only thing connecting them – was gone. They were killing teachers now.

"I just . . ." Ruby scrunched her eyes shut, pinched the bridge of her nose. And there in the darkroom of her imagination, the thick paper, glimmering silver and glossed red beneath the liquid. But it wasn't developing. The picture was blank. It was a photo of nothing. "I need to figure this out before they piece it together."

"Who?" Lauren asked. "What do you mean?"

"Alfie was in witness protection." Ruby opened her eyes. "I tracked him down. The NCA, the service, they knew I was looking. Even Jay knew. The best-case scenario is that I'm suspended."

Now Lauren seemed to understand the situation a little better, she looked at Ruby with something like concern. Or suspicion.

Will sussed it too. "So," he said, "Alfie's death hasn't been formally connected?"

"Not yet. I panicked. But when that happens, in a few hours, or possibly tomorrow, yeah . . . I'm in trouble."

Will laughed.

Ruby stared at him. Hard.

"There's that reputation again, hey," he said.

"No, I'm worried they'll . . ." Ruby sighed. "They'll take me off the case."

"Good," he said.

"Will." Lauren touched his arm.

"People are dying," Ruby said. "I need to—"

"Exactly," Will cut her off. "People are *dying*. And who are you thinking about?"

Ruby squared her shoulders to his, tilted her head. "Have you got something you want to say?"

"Shall we . . . ?" Lauren gestured for them to leave the room, but Will ignored her, stepping even closer to Ruby.

"Nothing I haven't said before," he whispered.

Lauren was politely fading away into the kitchen – a token gesture as she could still see and hear them through the tall, open-plan archway.

"Say it again." Ruby waited.

A short pause. "No." Will snapped out of something. "Forget it." He unzipped his jacket – forcing normality. Then he checked his watch, looked like he was about to change the subject.

"Is it because I didn't trust you?" Ruby said. "Can you really blame me?"

She regretted saying that. Even as the words were leaving her mouth, she wished she'd caught them, swallowed them down with everything else. In a matter of minutes, seconds, all the chemicals in her blood that wanted her to argue with him would be gone. But now she was their slave.

A tired, single laugh from Will.

"Just tell me. Hmm?" Ruby leant for eye contact. She sounded drunk, like an abusive spouse poking around, fishing for a fight.

And she hated it. Already, she could imagine herself later, replaying this conversation, cringing, wishing she'd said almost anything else.

Serene now, Will gave her a sort of you-asked-for-it shrug, and then he said, "Remember, you were telling us about Mr Phillips, in the Starfish Café? What was it he said?"

"He said a lot of things."

"About you."

"I don't know?" she lied. She knew.

"Well, I do. I remember it verbatim, because it was just the perfect summary. A deeply insecure person who spends more energy worrying about the thoughts of other people than your own."

Ruby was annoyed that she'd shared this encounter so faithfully. It had been a casual conversation, over dinner, just small talk about her day. A funny anecdote about a mean old teacher from school.

"With all due respect," she said, "which is almost none, you don't know me."

"I know you so well."

"I don't care what people think. Especially not in this pathetic, shitty little town."

"Ah, there we go." He pointed. "You want people to think you're the kind of person who doesn't care what other people think."

"What is this? You been reading day one psychology?" Not the best comeback, Ruby thought, but he seemed to get her point.

"Even when we broke up." He spoke in a slightly hushed voice that Lauren could obviously still hear. He wasn't lowering it for her, though, but for Ruby. "Can you remember what you said?"

"What on *earth* is happening? Why would you go *there* of all topics?"

"Do you remember? The main reason?"

"Because you kissed Lauren," Ruby said, loud, all too aware of how soap-opera this was getting. How awkward. How immature and absurd Will was making this situation for both of them. That cortisol was almost gone now. There was no justification for this anymore. It was embarrassing in real time.

"Guys," Lauren said, "shall we just dial it down a bit?"

Ruby's memory was failing her at every turn. But she remembered the break-up like it was yesterday. That night Will told her what he'd done, sitting on her bed, clutching her hands, apologising again and again. And he was genuinely sorry, which made it worse. Because he knew it was wrong and he did it anyway. He even promised it would never happen again and begged Ruby to believe him. She *had* to believe him. The strange thing was, she did. But that wasn't the issue. Will had cheated on her at a party, in front of *hundreds* of people.

Like a child, a chimp, totally lacking the cognitive faculties to comprehend the error of his short-sighted choices. Eating that first marshmallow because the promise of two later was beyond him. He just couldn't resist. The real problem was not that he'd lost her trust. Worse, Will had lost Ruby's respect.

Now, fifteen years older, in this new life, Will was speaking gently once again. "That wasn't the main reason," he said.

"Yes, it was." Ruby looked at her feet. "It really was."

"You said, if I'd cheated on you in private, you might have considered staying together."

Ruby looked up from the carpet, smiling ever so slightly, because she knew where this was going. An endgame move, checkmate now obvious and inevitable.

"It was," he added, "because there were witnesses. You were concerned about how forgiving me would reflect on *you*."

Again, Ruby felt the urge to resist this. But she couldn't. Because it was true. That was *exactly* the reason.

"Listen, I love you," he raised a cautious hand, "as a *friend*, but I can see what's happening. You look, no offence, like shit. Like you haven't slept." She hadn't. Not properly. Not for days. "You take Adderall to keep you sharp, you count how many units of alcohol you drink to find the sweet spot. Just enough to be sociable, not enough for a hangover. Optimal performance. You still do it. All these years later."

"You have an issue with hard work now?"

This outburst had initially felt like an unjustified attack. Something she must confront and fight. But now Ruby wondered if she deserved to hear this, *needed* to hear this. Like urgent surgery, maybe these home truths will heal, even though they were almost certainly going to hurt.

"But *why* do you have to work so hard?" There was a long silence. "Whose approval do you need? Is it because you're here? And everyone's watching? It's like I can see you coming unravelled, I can tell . . ." He stopped, frowned, looking over her shoulder. "There's a hole in the wall." Then he spotted her knuckles.

"I am sorry about that." This wasn't helping her case. "I accept it is unreasonable. I'll pay for it."

"This pressure you put on yourself. Seriously, Ruby . . ." Another pause. "They'll figure it out. It doesn't have to be you."

She shook her head.

"Some time off might be good?" he said.

"No, I can't do that." The idea made her feel sick, physically unwell.

Then he said, with genuine, heartfelt sincerity, "Needing to be the best is not a strength. It's a weakness."

But Ruby shook her head again. She felt so small, vulnerable. Like a lonely child. Scared and lost. Her eyes were as full of water as they could get before a single tear fell. They never fell. Ruby hadn't cried since she was thirteen years old and she wasn't about to start now, not in front of him. So, as always, she just blinked them away.

"I saw Adam Ward's brain," she said, quietly. "His skull was broken."

Will looked truly sorry now. They'd both been caught up in that haze, the flurry of their shared past. All those disputes, the personal insights and trivial insults that did not matter, not here, now, set against life and death. There was a moment of camaraderie as they made eye contact and allowed perspective to return, silently acknowledging the nightmare unfolding beyond these damaged walls.

"I can't stop," Ruby said, speaking honestly now. Admitting the truth as accurately as she understood it. "It hurts me. I can't think about Elizabeth. I can't think about Alfie. I can't think about any of them. I can't stop and think."

"Why?"

"It's like . . . I feel as though I've lost something. Something . . . fundamental?"

And she pictured herself on the recreation grass again, cycling in those big circles. Six-year-old Ruby, going round and around. Giles standing, watching on from the bullseye, turning with her, noticing that she'd done it. Not approving, acknowledging. They were just three days into their new life together. Three short days on the wrong side of all that inescapable pain.

Thirty years ago. She frowned. Almost to the day. Funny, when Ruby thought about her mum now, she felt absolutely nothing. She hadn't even noticed the anniversary of her death drifting past last week. Because it had worked. It was true. Ruby had been far too busy to dwell on such things. Head up. Eyes forward. Look where you're going. Because, as Giles said, if you look down . . .

But it was OK to fall, she thought, as long as you get back up. As long as you have the grit, the resilience, the sheer determination to stand up, brush yourself off and try again. And that was it. That was *precisely* the thing she'd lost. Ruby had plenty of options on the table. But stopping simply wasn't one of them.

◆ ◆ ◆

And neither, it seemed, was escape. Arms at her sides, rigid in bed, Ruby made the tragic error of forming the thought, realising and setting in stone the evident fact that she could not fall asleep. She rolled over and checked her phone. It was 3.02am.

She got up and went downstairs, her bare feet on the cold tiles. Staring out of the kitchen window, Ruby felt her glass grow heavy with water and she drank slowly in the dim light. The moon directly ahead, sensationally bright above the black trees at the end of the garden. Her eyes adjusting enough for it to seem like the sun, shining down from some other dimension, the same as ours just lifeless, without detail, colour or sound. A mirror world, where hope is fear and silence is everything but peaceful.

Ruby went into the living room and sat down on the sofa, placing the glass on the coffee table. It was dark in here. Pitch black with curtains drawn solid around the window.

How could she have known? Finding Alfie and leading someone right to him was unforeseeable. She smiled at the thought. The retrospective mental contortions necessary for survival had already begun. It was like driving a few miles per hour faster than the speed limit. A minor moral lapse that only becomes monstrous when a child runs out into the road and you discover, far too late, just how many extra metres have been added to the stopping distance of your hard-pressed brakes. Tyres and pedestrians screaming in harmony amid all the rising steam. Alfie's death, while her fault, was not a proportionate consequence. Karma had been merciless to both of them.

But this was not the only thing troubling her tonight. The gaps in her memory were becoming too significant to ignore. Frank's sawn-off shotgun, *still* in the boot of Will's car. She really had, hand on heart, forgotten it was there. She shook her head. Not only was this an unacceptable breach of duty, it also opened the door to some unanswerable questions.

What other faults in judgement and recollection had there been? If she knew the magnitude of her failings, she could begin the timely process of deferring, projecting and ultimately repressing them. But Ruby didn't even know what she had to bury. And where does anxiety flourish, if not in the dark and fertile soil of uncertainty?

There was a sound and she turned. A figure stood in the doorway, the shadow of a shape she couldn't see, but felt nonetheless.

"Sorry," Ruby whispered, "did I wake you?"

"No, no," Lauren said. "I was up."

She came and sat down at her side, still unseeable in the lightless living room.

"I want to apologise for earlier," Ruby said.

"It's fine. Will gets like that sometimes. Especially after a couple of drinks."

"I didn't mean to insult him."

"I know."

"He's annoyingly perceptive." Ruby sighed. "There's a lot of truth in what he said."

Slight movement on the sofa cushions, maybe Lauren was turning to face her. "You take Adderall?"

Ruby hesitated. Will saw her swallow a pill earlier in the week and, when he read the label, he smiled and said, "That figures."

But it felt worse for Lauren to know, more transgressive somehow. After all, she was a doctor and taking prescription drugs without a prescription was not exactly recommended.

"Sometimes," Ruby said. No response. But, again, Ruby could feel eyes on her. "Every single day," she added. "I know it's bad, I just . . ."

"I'm not your mum. You're an adult. I get zopiclone from a private colleague, so I can't preach."

"Is that a sleeping pill?"

"Yes. Want some?"

"Well," Ruby said, "you being here isn't a good review."

"I haven't taken one tonight. Hence . . ."

Ruby could tell from the direction of her voice that Lauren was facing forwards now, looking at the wall opposite them. Or into the black void where the wall would be.

"Thanks, but no thanks. Taking one drug to wake up and another to go to sleep seems a risky tactic."

"Losing sleep is a risky tactic."

"True," Ruby agreed, wide-eyed, nodding. "Can you sleep without them?"

"Not really. Can you operate without Adderall?"

"I prefer not to."

"Reckon you're addicted?"

"I wouldn't know." Ruby laughed. "Haven't stopped taking it for long enough to find out."

"We'll go with yes."

There was something liberating about talking in the dark. The intimacy of a face-to-face conversation but with none of the subtle cues and microexpressions. It felt almost like a confession, as though anything they might say here, in the dead of the night, was not just confidential but exempt from judgement. The real world was asleep. This wasn't even happening.

"I am right in thinking it's not prescribed?" Lauren asked. "You don't have ADHD or . . . ?"

"I don't think I do, no."

"And you're aware it's amphetamine? Similar to speed?"

"Yes."

"Where do you get it?"

Another shameful pause. Subverting medical convention was one thing, but breaking the law? "A drug dealer posts them to me," Ruby said.

"Oh."

"Good few years ago now, when I was revising for some exams, I read an article about students using it as a study drug. Then, serendipity. We arrested someone with a large quantity of prescription stimulants. All sorts. He told us where he got it. The rest is history."

"Presumably you're not studying now?"

"It keeps me . . . focused," Ruby said, answering the actual question Lauren had asked. "Enhances virtually every valuable trait. Think clearer, faster, *cleaner*, if that makes sense. All problems can be solved and, if not, they can be ignored. Nothing feels overwhelming and," this was the main part but she didn't want to place too much weight here, "I'm not distracted by emotions."

"Sounds pretty good."

"It is. Though, to be honest, I think lately I've developed quite a tolerance."

"Any side-effects?"

There was the longest silence so far. Ruby finally broke it with, "Memory loss?"

This was the first time she'd connected the two issues out loud. And, weirdly, it was reassuring. Like she had an escape route – stop taking the drugs and her memory would, she hoped, restore to factory settings.

"Describe it," Lauren said.

No, this didn't feel like religious counsel. It felt like what it was: a conversation with a medical professional.

"I . . . forget stuff."

"Like what?"

"Small things." The number plate. Her ID swipe card that still hadn't been found. It wasn't at the barn, or in her pocket, or in the car. She was right to worry – she might well have simply lost it. And, worst of all, she tensed her jaw, cringing and wanting to yell the thought away, *the shotgun*. "Small things that are actually huge things . . . Could it be related to the drugs?"

"There's a very simple way to find out . . ."

But what if stopping didn't cure it? Ruby had worried this was something more serious. She knew of a few conditions that become all the more harrowing when prefixed with the words "early-onset". Her relative youth was no consolation. But the truth was, she didn't want a diagnosis. That would make it real. Head up, eyes forward. Go. The crash is coming either way. It doesn't need a name.

"Why do you take zopiclone?" Ruby asked, steering off this uncomfortable topic.

"It's a long story."

"You have somewhere to be?"

Just from the sound of her breath, Ruby knew Lauren was smiling. "OK. Well, I'm pretty sure I have post-traumatic stress disorder."

"From what?"

"It's . . . always been there."

"Then it can't be post-traumatic."

Another shift on the cushions. Lauren didn't like these turning tables. "I think, probably, it's connected to my sister."

Ruby knew about Dee – Lauren's sister had suffered from some rare disease and died when she was just eighteen. "What was wrong with her?"

"A lot. But eventually, her kidneys stopped working. I gave her one of mine. I'd have given her every organ in my body."

Ruby had seen the line on her torso, like an appendix scar, just longer, slightly curved.

"But it didn't work," Lauren added. "It tingles sometimes. You know scar tissue is the same as normal flesh. But in healthy skin, the collagen is woven together and random. Whereas damaged tissue grows in a single line. It is neat. Uniform."

"That why you can't sleep? Poetic thoughts about scars?"

"I haven't slept properly since the break-in. I'm sure you're right, he wouldn't come back, but the idea of a murderer being in your bedroom . . . It isn't particularly relaxing."

"So, you agree," Ruby said, a smile spreading across her face. "Will is a suspect?"

Lauren laughed. "He doesn't even kill spiders. I'd be very surprised."

"Yeah . . . he is a bit too soft."

Plus, Ruby remembered, he was on a residential school trip to France on the night of the reunion. Another reason her earlier accusations were absurd. It was literally impossible.

"But even without the break-in," Lauren said, "I often wake up around this time and it's like someone's kind of . . . flicked a switch in my mind. Before I moved in here, I used to live at the flats on Cliffside Road. Near the old navy dockyard."

Ruby pictured the scene, saw all four seasons flashing up in her memory. Alfie's framed photos on his hallway wall. Soon they'll be taken down, boxed up and passed over to his next of kin. Along with a broken rainbow of books.

"There's a building at the end," Lauren went on, "like a concrete bunker kind of thing – not sure what it was. I used to sneak in at night, by myself, and just sit in there. Sometimes with a candle. Sometimes in the dark. Even now, it's where I run to in my mind whenever I feel vulnerable. It's hard to explain. But it's comforting.

Being alone, hidden from everything. It's my favourite place on earth."

Ruby told her about Alfie's photos, dragging the conversation back to this ugly, inevitable topic.

"Can I tell you a secret?" Lauren asked.

"Sure."

"Last week, at work, I was thinking about how terrible it all is. But then I thought about Scott. And, this'll sound awful, but I think he got off lightly."

This surprised Ruby. Though, having known Scott well, the admission didn't shed doubt on Lauren's apparently universal compassion. It just illustrated how bad he was. Even from his grave, Scott Hopkins drew resentment and ill will from almost everyone he'd encountered, even from someone as benevolent as Lauren. His toxicity was infectious.

"You're not the first person to say this."

"I don't feel like that now," Lauren clarified. "Not when I really think about it. Not at 3am, once the switch has been flicked. Now I just wish someone had been able to help him. Like maybe I could have said something at school."

"I'm not sure you're qualified."

"But that's the feeling. It's not that I *can't* sleep, it's that I don't want to. Part of my brain thinks sleeping is a waste of time. As though I could be doing something positive instead."

"I know exactly what you mean," Ruby said.

"It seems so stupid, simple. But there's so much pain in the world. It feels wrong, unthinkable that you wouldn't spend your life trying to make it better. I know how trite that sounds."

"No," Ruby said. "I get it."

"Imagine there was a starving person in your living room. You'd be a monster if you didn't give them some food. And right now, at this very moment, there are people who need help. There are people experiencing unimaginable suffering, somewhere. The only reason we're not all kept awake by this is because we can't see them. Geography is no excuse."

"But what can we do?"

"Something. We can do *something*."

"Like charity fundraisers?" This sounded sarcastic, but Ruby hadn't meant it to.

"It's a start. It is something. And I know you won't believe me, people are cynical, but it's not about the glory. It's not because it feels good."

Ruby remembered what Will told her. All the money Lauren donates secretly, anonymously. "I do believe you."

"I don't know. Maybe it is all just to get that chemical hit. Milk as much dopamine out of the day to have enough to face tomorrow."

"Does all this affect your work?"

"How do you mean?" Lauren's frown painted in sound.

"Well, for example, Kendall. You've performed surgery on him."

"Yeah, a few."

"And you guys were pretty close back at school."

"We were," Lauren said. "And, yes, it's not good medical practice to provide care for someone you have a personal relationship with. But I know who else was in the running to perform his procedures. I'm quite simply better."

"Modest to boot."

"No, there's no egos. Just facts. I wanted Kendall to have the best chance. I did those surgeries *because* I know him, not in spite of it."

"Exactly. See. You seem to have an oversupply of empathy," Ruby said. "Almost a disorder. It's keeping you awake. Cutting people open must be quite taxing? Especially people you know."

"Hmm." Lauren considered this. "It would make it hard. But I switch it off. It's like my mind realises that, for the next few hours, the best thing I can do is disregard it. Then it becomes mechanical. One of my lecturers used to say that anaesthetic benefits the surgeon as much as the patient. I mean, can you *imagine* the horror of surgery if you were awake? Traumatic for everyone involved. But having someone unconscious, breathing through a machine, face covered, tubes and tape. It is dehumanising. You can ignore the stakes and just do the job."

"Huh, never really thought of it like that."

"And then, after," Lauren's voice brightened, "they're a person again and you get to see their recovery. It's just the most overwhelming feeling. A couple of months ago, we operated on a little girl, three years old. She was so small, and she had these growths, cartilage in her spine, between the vertebrae. She couldn't walk properly. And we fixed her. Her parents gave me flowers, which was nice. But she . . . she kept saying thank you. And . . ." Lauren was clearly on the verge of tears. "Oh, she had this doll. Like a little ragdoll. Basically, her comfort blanket. She clung on to it all the time. Every appointment she held it and hugged it to herself. She even wanted it on her pillow for surgery, which we *pretended* to oblige but I'm not sure it was the most hygienic thing." Lauren laughed. "She came back, a few weeks into physio. Just a check-up. It was all good. And . . . Oh, I can't even say it. She came into my office – walked in, no limp." Lauren was crying. "And, uh . . . She offered it to me. The doll." She sniffed. "Like a gift. She wanted *me* to have it, to say thank you . . . Ah, Jesus, sorry." Lauren gasped, getting herself back under control. Laughed again. Exhaled. "You ever just cry at the smallest things?"

"That doesn't sound small." Then Ruby shook her head. "But no. I don't."

Somehow, she knew Lauren was looking at her again.

So, she added, "I haven't cried since I was thirteen. I actually remember the day. Funnily enough, it was because of Scott."

It was a couple of weeks after the compass incident. Ruby probably still had a scab on her bicep where he'd stabbed her for reasons neither of them could fully explain. She was just closing her locker, leaning down to remove the key when, out of the blue, unprovoked, Scott grabbed her in a headlock and wouldn't let go. It didn't necessarily hurt, but she was trapped. And she did not like it.

Usually, this kind of petty violence was contingent on an audience. But they were alone, which, if anything, made it far more sinister. Either way, Ruby had already had enough of his antics and worried that if she did not retaliate, he'd frame her as a victim. So, she reacted with disproportionate force, biting the tough meat of his forearm until her teeth almost met. He released his grip.

And then as he began the bully's classic tactic of pretending it was all a joke, she punched him in the face. Hard. Hard enough to slam the back of his head into the lockers behind and send blood free-flowing from his nose.

Unfortunately, this was the only part of the incident that Mr Hunter, the famously strict head teacher, had seen. Ruby and Scott were hauled to his office, a fabled dungeon from which he administered and admonished.

But Mr Hunter was far angrier at Ruby than at Scott. He was, it seemed, effectively a lost cause. Whereas Ruby should have known better. She had let herself down. And Ruby burst into tears. Angry, spiteful tears without dignity or control. She just stood there crying at the sheer injustice of it all.

Then, later, her eyes still red and her cheeks still sore, she walked home alone. Sniffing, she sat down at the kitchen table and stared at her knuckles. She'd composed herself by the time Giles entered but he could always tell when something was wrong.

Placing shopping bags on the kitchen worktop, he'd looked over his shoulder. "Are you OK?" he asked.

Ruby swallowed, pressed her lips together and paused long enough to be sure she could recount the story without bursting into tears again. Halfway through, she *almost* lost it when she said "Scott" and felt her throat seizing up. But then she got to the part where she was told off and crumbled. Dimpled chin, cheeks red and eyes wet, she just couldn't stop crying.

Giles, with his stern face, stared at her for a few seconds, having listened intently to the account. "It does sound like you were provoked and, while violence should be a last resort, I can see why you feel it was unjust that you were so severely reprimanded."

"It's not right. It's not. It's not."

"But why are you so upset?"

A tremendously confusing cocktail of social anxiety, hormones, frustration. Ruby tried her best to explain but eventually gave up, realising she couldn't put it into words.

"It's just not fair," she concluded.

But his expression firmed up. "This is all irrelevant. It is done. What matters now is that you never show weakness in front of them again."

"Scott?"

"Everyone."

Ruby frowned. "OK?"

Giles crouched at her knees. Heads level, he turned her chair to face him. Then, wide eyed, he looked into her soul. This was serious. Whatever he was about to say, she had to pay complete attention.

"Ruby, it's normal to feel sad. But you are *naked* when you cry. Do you understand? You should treat tears like you treat nudity. If you wouldn't be comfortable with them seeing you naked, then they should never, *ever*, ever see you cry."

This seemed like quite good advice – shielding yourself, being vulnerable only with those you trust. But then again, a strange thought. Who *could* see her with no clothes on?

She was thirteen. Young enough to need a hug, old enough to go without. The age at which privacy becomes essential and your relationship with your own body is steadily and irreversibly bonded to shame.

The truth was, at that age, Ruby wouldn't have felt comfortable naked in front of *anyone* on earth. Not even Giles. Bath time had been a solitary affair for a few years by that point.

She wiped her wet cheek. "I don't like being naked in front of you nowadays," Ruby whispered.

And Giles paused, giving her a few extra seconds to think it over. But then he hammered it home, looked back into her soul once more and commanded her attention.

"Then stop crying," he said.

So, she did. And, more than two decades later, she was yet to shed another tear.

"That is cold as ice," Lauren said, once Ruby had finished explaining.

"I took it to heart. I'd be naked. I can't let people see. It's not that I don't feel it all. I miss Elizabeth so much. It's my fault Alfie is dead. Because of my arrogance. Impatience. Incompetence. Because of whatever is wrong with me. I feel like a total fucking failure. No matter what I do. I feel it. No matter how good it is, it's never good enough. No matter how *hard* I try. It's like I'm running to the horizon and when I get there I can relax. But I never do. I never can."

There was a long silence while Lauren absorbed this. She seemed to be thinking hard about her next words.

"Do you ever want to cry?" she asked.

Ruby's eyes tingling on the cusp, like they so often were. "All the time."

And then she felt fingers searching in the dark near her thigh. Lauren found her good hand and held it. "Ruby," she whispered, squeezing gently. "I can't see you."

Taking a slow, silent breath in, Ruby let it happen. Her eyes stinging and, as she blinked, as she exhaled . . . a single drop was released. The warm tear trickled down her cheek, down her neck and onto the collar of her t-shirt. It felt neither good nor bad. There was nothing to see, nothing to feel. Nothing at all but peace.

They spoke for hours, the sun rising steadily to deliver them back to the real world, until, somehow, it was 7.30am and they could see each other clearly. The day was beginning to move.

There was a sound upstairs, Lauren tilted her head to look at the ceiling. "I guess we should get ready."

"I guess we should."

"So," Lauren said, summing things up, "what are you going to do today?"

Ruby stared at the warm, golden slice of morning sun stretched across the carpet. She felt recharged. The simple power of a conversation with another human being had given her just enough morale to say decisive things. Bold things like, "I am going to figure it out."

There was a pause. Ruby wondered if this declaration would be met with approval or perhaps a subtle smile, polite and full of doubt. But Lauren's face was blank. Just staring.

"Do you believe me?" Ruby asked.

"I do," Lauren said, nodding. Sincere. "You are going to solve it."

She stood, opened the curtains, then left the room and went back upstairs to get dressed for work.

Alone again, Ruby took a breath, asking her body to hold fire on the torment it had stored up over the years, ready and waiting for a moment just like this. Unleash it tomorrow. Just give me a few more hours, she thought, as she dropped a pill into her mouth and swallowed, standing and turning to face all the light and fear, all the horror and hope of day fourteen.

Chapter Fifteen

Ruby was back at school again, in the playground, the wide buildings of Missbrook Heights behind her. Over on her right, tall
chain-link fences with thick foliage shielding the road beyond. And
up ahead, the pale wall at the edge of the playground. Chest-high
bricks, where students would sit at break-time, perched like birds
in a row. Next to that, the concrete turned to a grass slope, leading
onto the playing fields that stretched off for acres, ending with a
line of trees. Then suburbia, angled rooftops and, further still, out
of sight from here, the ocean.

Ruby walked across the empty concrete, over the worn netball
markings underfoot, or hockey, or both. There were even faded
hopscotch squares, just enough left to play. Like cave art from
another era. The school was more than a century old. Long ago
there would have been little girls and boys in ill-fitting uniforms,
grey skirts cut square and baggy, squatting for marbles, running
with a hoop and a stick, black leather shoes hopping, loud on the
ground. Their full-year photographs were just like today's, only
colourless, with fewer faces, fewer smiles, small monochrome eyes
full of wary innocence that seems misguided from her vantage
point, because when Ruby thinks about this period, the prevailing
theme is war.

She often wondered if future generations might look at us with similar pity. Shaking their heads in a museum somewhere, unable to relate or even comprehend how these people were just going about their normal lives, in coffee shops and offices, a few short years left on an unseeable clock. They really had no idea.

She was heading towards the photography suite, a two-storey, detached building tucked in among the trees at the edge of the playing fields. Square and modern compared to the red bricks and tall windowed façades elsewhere on campus.

Will was waiting for her at the doors, which he'd propped open, ready for her arrival. He sipped from a mug, checked his watch. One sleeve of his smart shirt rolled up, the white material creased from a long day's work.

It was Giles's idea to come here. Ruby had spent most of the morning and half the afternoon with him. Returning to the home she grew up in, like many places in this town, made her feel young again. Small.

Although their reunion had been warm, Ruby noticed how different it was from last night's intimate, insomniac heart-to-heart with Lauren. It wasn't that she couldn't be candid with Giles. Ruby could share any problem with him, at any length, so long as she was ready to discuss and implement the solution.

Maybe it was the bizarre set of circumstances that put them in that living room together, or perhaps the simple honesty you find in darkness – either way, Ruby had spoken at length about her stepdad and their unusual relationship. Giles was, if there was one, the source of all her faults and virtues. Ruby had told Lauren about leaving town, accepting the job on the other side of the world and how Giles's reaction had blindsided her.

Fifteen years ago, Ruby was in her early twenties, so his role as her father had already diminished significantly. But he was still needed. He was still there, on standby. Ready. So, when Ruby told him she was moving away, far away, it exposed something she'd genuinely never seen. Giles looked sad. She had hurt his feelings.

As such a bastion of stoic resolve, Ruby had rarely considered his inner world. The idea of him being anxious, scared or even unsure about anything felt unthinkable. And yet there he was, eyes like a puppy, looking back at her and saying nothing.

Giles had just nodded and, after what felt like a minute's silence, said he understood, stern and formal as though he'd been ordered to stand down from some great cause he'd been fighting for that was, without any ceremony, over. No flags, no gun salutes. His work here was done. At ease, soldier. Ruby hadn't realised it at the time but, afterwards, the hole she'd left behind was obvious.

Giles joined the military at sixteen, straight from school. Then, following the death of Ruby's mum, he'd taken early retirement, worked part-time when he could and focused all his remaining attention on raising his stepdaughter. He had been occupied for every moment of his life.

That day was the first time busy Giles had faced a situation that scared them both in equal measure. There are few things more dangerous to a troubled mind than waking up and having nothing to do.

Or maybe she'd read too much into his reaction – that was the hardest part, the uncertainty. It was no more than a few seconds – blink and you'd miss it. His tall walls, the stiff-lipped frontline he'd always stood behind. She wasn't meant to see what she saw that day. This brief glimpse into his soul, his heart, and Ruby now knew that it was not made of metal or stone.

It had illuminated a fact so clear, so conspicuous that Ruby was astonished she'd never noticed it before. It really hadn't crossed her mind that Giles might need Ruby just as much or, by then, far more than she needed him.

And, once this moment had passed, it was back to normal. His following comments were just as restrained as she'd expected – he did not congratulate her on the job she'd accepted, or offer any exclamations about excitement or trepidation. Just a few general questions on logistics and schedules. But, even though this was totally in keeping with his character, that day it felt especially harsh. Somehow cold.

Ruby had always known his lack of praise was by design. Too much and she might feel satisfied, might believe there wasn't room to improve. The constant sense that she can and should do better was essential for growth. Though, equally, it made achievements feel empty. What water is to food. Vital, but not enough. She had to stay hungry.

Giles had even admitted this himself. He'd told Ruby that he'd never lie to her. He would pin her drawings on the fridge, sure, but he'd never say they were fantastic works of art. They were adequate for a child her age. An acceptable level of ability had been displayed. It did resemble a horse, but anatomically some aspects were not accurate. The legs were too thin, the body too round and the sun does not emit straight yellow lines.

If only she'd had the courage or understanding to say something similar back to Giles. This parenting style is not without merit, but, look, here, these are the things you could change to improve it.

But this honesty, he claimed, meant that when praise arrived – which it so rarely did – Ruby would know it was authentic. Nothing adds value more than scarcity.

She'd told Lauren all of this last night. All the things she wished she'd said to him. That all she'd ever wanted, all she'd ever needed, yearned for, worked for, prayed for, was for him to exhibit pride. Not just feel it, but *show* it.

That was the target, sitting just on the other side of that unreachable horizon.

Even as she walked into her childhood home, familiar and alien all at once, she kept thinking about everything Will had said. Being the best *was* contingent on what other people thought of you. If Ruby was secluded on a desert island, it really wouldn't matter whether her camp was impressive. She probably wouldn't do her hair, wear make-up or consider her clothes. Excellence needs an audience; status needs a ladder. You can win with skill, perseverance or even charm. But winning without a loser is simply impossible.

It wasn't unsettling to reframe her feverish ambition as a weakness. She'd discovered that herself the day she left. Every castle, every fortress, every inch of wall and wire had, at its foundation, insecurity.

Ruby and Giles's relationship was no different. It was not built on strength. There was an unspoken fragility that neither of them had ever been brave enough to confront. But still, all shortcomings set aside, Ruby loved him. Truly. As much as a father. More. She respected him. And, like any sunlit horse she'd brought home from school, his efforts were notable. Giles had sacrificed his career, he'd dedicated decades of his life caring for her and, despite these flaws, Ruby knew that he had tried his best.

And that, for her, was enough.

Ruby arrived around 10am, greeting him with a smile and a long, tight hug. Eyes closed, both of them gripping hard enough to leave everything unsaid. No shared genes, no blood, just unconditional love. You actually *can* choose your family.

Giles felt old in her arms. A smaller, softer version of that towering commander she remembered from her youth. Greyer too, balder, the slightest of hunches forming as age began to deconstruct his once stately posture.

Having made drinks, he sat down in his chair at the round kitchen table. The exact same spot she'd left him in fifteen years prior, suitcase on the floor, tickets in hand. And it felt like nothing had changed. He was still wearing a woollen jumper, sheepskin slippers, a pair of his colourful chino trousers. Green today. As though the image she had in her memories had been plucked out and dropped into reality, perfectly formed. He was just as she saw him.

Ruby sat opposite and enjoyed the small talk. They'd spoken on the phone plenty of times over the years, but this was the first face-to-face conversation they'd had in well over a decade. Although she knew it was an illusion, she liked the comfort of feeling, for just a few hours, as though the outside world couldn't get to her.

"It is really nice to see you," he said, his eyes locked with naked sincerity. The walls were gone. There were no brave faces. They'd both grown out of them.

Again, she was struck by his apparent vulnerability, which she had never, not once, noticed growing up. It's a formative moment when you discover that your parents, these adults you'd always assumed had everything figured out, had all the answers to all the questions any young mind might ask, were just the same as you. Humans. Fallible and guessing. Children who grew up and had to pretend they had the slightest idea what this entire thing was all about. It'd be cruel to act any other way. Kids deserve the charade.

"It's been too long," Ruby said. "I am so sorry."

She'd wanted to say that getting away had been essential for her mental health back then. The opportunity to start fresh somewhere was irresistible and, having arrived just weeks after she and Will broke up, Ruby had no reason left to stay. The truth was, she'd felt trapped in Missbrook Bay, and moving to Australia seemed like a solution, an escape from it all. From all the eyes and names she knew.

The irony, of course, was that Ruby was running away from something that lived inside her. Your mind is the only thing you really can't leave behind.

Most of all, though, she'd wanted to say that she wished she'd visited earlier. That something other than death had pulled her home. The saddest part was, she had no real excuse. Their final conversation was not dramatic. There was no fight, no slammed doors, no angry declaration or disagreement. It was understated, small, subtle and amicable, certainly there was no justification for any estrangement, let alone one as long as theirs had been.

Messages had been sent, things like, *We must arrange something.* Or, *Perhaps next Christmas you could come home?* Ruby had even suggested he fly out to her. But each time the plans just faded away and went cold as life marched on at its exponential speed. Another formative realisation. It's short, they say. A hollow platitude that one day, with a heavy heart, reveals itself to be harrowingly true. Tick. Tock.

Fifteen years, Ruby thought, about as long together as apart.

But she didn't say any of that. Ruby hadn't visited Giles to probe into their past, but into her future. And their conversation did what she hoped it would – injected clarity into her clouded thoughts. While Lauren might have satisfied some dormant and emotional necessity, Giles was on hand to provide raw objective direction.

There, at the kitchen table, sitting right where she'd told him she couldn't ride a bike, Ruby explained everything. Every shameful detail, an open book about the case. Giles just sat and listened.

When Ruby got to the end of her two-week story, she shook her head, looked down at the mug of coffee in her hands and said, "Now, I'm lost. I have no idea what to do next. No idea *where* to go."

"This is quite the pickle." He nodded.

"I feel like, I don't know, like I'm missing something."

As always, Giles cut through the noise.

"What *do* you know?" he'd said. "What connects them? What's the one thing, the only thing?"

She stared at the wall, through it, shaking her head. "Same school year. But . . ."

"What?"

"Not anymore. Not all former students. Alfie was different."

"He should be your focus, then."

It was more complicated, though, given that Ruby had called Jay that morning and told him what had happened, formally connecting these deaths. She explained she was probably followed and that, she knew, it was her fault Alfie was dead.

Jay was speechless. And when he finally began to speak, Ruby hung up. That was a few hours ago now and she had been in no man's land ever since, ignoring his calls and searching for an answer in this ever-narrowing window of time.

Crucially, she could not involve herself in the investigation. As such, the scene of Alfie's death remained largely a mystery to her.

"To be honest," Ruby said. "What I did there is serious. Although the heat had died down, Alfie was still in witness protection."

"Will they fire you?"

"Possibly, yes. And absolutely they will remove me from the case. They probably already have."

"So, what *can* you do?"

Ruby just shrugged. "Ask my dad for advice?"

Hand pressed against his smiling mouth, Giles laughed through his nose. He liked being asked but clearly felt underqualified. Still, as he always did, as anyone ever could, he tried his best.

"I would advise you to go out there and keep trying."

"Go out *where*?"

"You'd assumed it was your year group, the class of '99. But it's not."

"No."

"So, again, what is it? What is the only common denominator?"

Ruby nodded. This answered both questions.

"Missbrook Heights."

And that was why she was here, at school, stepping into the photography suite building. Like so much else, maybe even everything else, this felt like activity for its own sake. Ruby just had to do something. Even something that was, no matter how she levelled her sights, an extremely long shot. No, worse than that. She didn't even have a target.

Turning a corner on the landing of the second floor, Ruby entered Alfie's old office. There had been three occupants since he left under that black and scandalous cloud in 2001. All traces of him were gone.

"So, yeah, this is it," Will said, from the doorway behind, holding the keys.

Ruby stepped to the desk, idly opened a drawer.

"Uh." Will approached. "Maybe best not to snoop too much?"

He was probably right. What was she even hoping to find?

"Look, I've got to pop back to the staffroom," Will added. "You OK here for a bit?"

"Sure." Ruby sat down on the swivel chair, facing the window as Will left.

Through the glass, she could see nothing but a big tree. Thick branches, the wind shaking sun-glittered leaves, so much late daylight making green things white, cold things warm. Some of the thinner branches were touching the window, blocking the view. Spiderwebs, sticky seeds and sap around the frame. Mulch in the gutter. She heard twigs brushing against the building, a few birds outside, quietly singing their songs.

If she leant, she could just make out an after-school sports session on the far side of the pitches, boys dribbling balls between colourful cones – shouts echoing over the occasional blasts from a whistle, too far away to see any faces, any rosy cheeks, just blurred impressions of white t-shirts and blue shorts crisscrossing.

She slouched back in the creaking chair. Everything that had happened seemed to present itself all at once. Like a life review, your memories flashing before your eyes as you breathe your last few breaths. The black car that was following her. The culprit himself. The man who picked a lock, broke into Will's house and stole her notebook.

Frank Enfield taking her hostage, interrogating her about the world, about truth and what it all meant. Her broken hand – it barely even ached anymore. Sharp in certain positions, or when she bumped it, but otherwise a vague throb, low enough to forget. Frank was still out there somewhere. Huge and busy, doing whatever it was he needed to do.

Then there was Scott, victim number two. Pivotal in some way. Different from the others. But not as different as Alfie.

Alfie Rogers. The anomaly. Her eyes swept the room, big arches around the ceiling. A former teacher. The man who took the full-year photo. He'd seen it from the other side. Why was he dead? Why were any of them dead? What did they do?

Maybe, he'd suggested, it *wasn't* something they did. But something they *saw*. What could they have seen? she wondered, staring out of the glass at that tree. What could *he* have seen?

Nothing through this window. Those were old trees, they'd have been blocking the view just like this twenty years ago.

"Helpful?" Will asked, returning. He'd been gone quite a while. Ruby hadn't even noticed that nearly an hour had passed.

She didn't answer, just stared ahead, across the cluttered desk, through the glass, into the leaves. Darker now the sun was below the canopy line.

"I've got to pack up," he said. "So . . ."

"Sure, sorry," Ruby said, standing. "I'll get out of your hair."

She went back outside, onto the playing fields, stood beneath those trees, near the wall at the edge of the grass. Will waved as he wandered off across the playground, heading home for the day.

Down the shallow slope, the rest of the school spread out in front of her. The music department attached, bordering the playground on the right side of her view. Ruby could hear them practising in there, disjointed melodies. Stopping and starting. Five, six, seven, eight. Then muffled drums. A trumpet.

She was alone besides a few seagulls hopping around a bin at the edge of the concrete expanse, more above, squawking, circling over the faded hopscotch. But they were all scared away when a pair of students, two boys, maybe year 9s, came round the corner. The birds fled, flapping off and out of the evening shadow, up into the amber light then over the rooftops and away.

The boys walked past below Ruby, heading towards the gates in the bottom corner of the playground. They were talking, laughing, wrapped up in the haze of youth. Perhaps they'd been in detention. No, wait, Ruby spotted trainers, sports shorts, blazers over their white t-shirts. One of them made eye contact with her, possibly wondering who she was, what she was doing just standing up here.

The pair arrived at the metal hoop stands near the gate, where they unlocked their bikes. They climbed on their saddles and rode in a wide circle before they cycled off and out of sight, rolling down onto the road. Their clicking gears fading to silence.

Clicking like Kendall's wheelchair, she thought, like those beads on the spokes.

Ruby realised she was standing exactly where it happened. This was where Scott attacked him. Nearby, on her left, the edge of the field. A wall. The modest five-foot drop down to the playground. Something they saw? And she looked up at the trees, the thick leaves. You couldn't see down from Alfie's office window. Not now. But in winter?

Still slow and drawn sluggish by a sense of futility, Ruby removed her phone and called Kendall.

"When did it happen?" she asked, once she'd raced through formalities.

"What?"

"Your fight, or . . . when Scott attacked you?"

"It would have been, um, year 10? So . . . 1997?"

Ruby was pacing, looking down at her feet. She put her bad hand against the trunk, thick bark, leant, head bowed. "What time of year?" Pushed against it, found the pain.

"End of November."

She stopped, stepped back, looked up. "No leaves on the trees," Ruby mumbled to herself.

"Um, I guess not?"

"Who was there?"

"I don't know, I genuinely don't. I'm sorry."

She turned back towards the main buildings, phone pressed against her ear. Identical windows spaced equally across the three-storey brick façade – all but one classroom dark now. The sports had finished too. She looked across the empty grass. Long tree shadows now covering the entire field in dusk. Relative peace at every turn, the unique tranquillity found only after school.

"But," she said, "it wasn't just you and Scott?"

"No, no. There were people there."

"OK." Ruby walked forwards, over the grass, stepped up onto the wall, toes flush with the edge. Looked down. "Who?"

"Well, Scott was there, obviously. And . . ." There was a pause, Kendall seeming to realise what was happening. The names she was hoping to hear. "Oh. Oh, OK." She heard him shuffle in his chair. "Um. Mary *could* have been there. But probably not, because . . . they'd broken up by that point?"

"Who had?"

"Well, she was seeing . . ." He paused again, humming like maybe, just maybe, this might fit. "She was seeing Little Adam Ward."

Ruby's mind gave her a flash – like subliminal messaging. Just a single frame of him dead on those tiles in the sports pavilion. And a near silent sound – a few notes of that eerie whistling they'd heard at the end of his 999 call. The cold, casual retreat. But then it was back to here. Back to now.

"So," Kendall went on, "Mary would have been there if Adam was – maybe they *were* still together."

"The others?"

"Elizabeth could have been there, feasibly. We went to drama club together."

Little sparks in her memory. Yes. Elizabeth told Ruby about what happened. That's how she knew. That's why Ruby could picture it so clearly. Elizabeth saw.

"She was there." So, that was four of the five. Scott was definite, the others hovering around the possible mark, Elizabeth fixed firm on ninety, maybe ninety-five percent. "Any staff?" Ruby wondered.

"No," Kendall said. "Well, I'd like to think not. They'd have stopped it, right? Scott hit me a lot of times. My jaw was broken before he pushed me."

Ruby sighed. She'd known it was a vicious encounter. Kendall was in hospital for weeks. And it all started because Scott asked him to pick up his bag. A simple request. And Kendall had said no.

Which was, according to Gemma, the only word you must never, ever utter to Scott Hopkins.

She looked behind, imagined Scott punching him, pushing him. Closer and closer to the edge of this wall. The very wall she was standing on. And then, a final shove, his heels hit these bricks and over he went. She looked down. Wasn't that high. She'd jumped from here as a child a hundred times. But falling backwards? Head first? Onto concrete? Yeah, it was high enough.

Violent, unjustified, barbaric. But also, a crime.

"It was reported to the police, right?" Ruby said. She'd have to call Jay. Get him to check the file.

"*Apparently.*"

Ruby could hear Kendall's radio in the background. Still that vintage country music. The scene sounded just the same as when she'd visited on that rainy afternoon last week. Seemed like a lifetime ago. She could almost feel the cat, see the disjointed sofa covers, his glowing antique lamps.

"Did the police interview you?"

"Once. Literally nothing came of it, though. Insufficient evidence. Whoever was there, they weren't brave enough to testify against Scott. Do you blame them? Look, I'm sorry, but I just can't be sure on any of this. It happened after school; I know that. So, between 3 and 4pm. Or maybe later? It was dark. I remember the lights. Really, it's possible that anyone could have been there at that time. Ruby, *you* could have been there for all I know."

And a strange shiver crawled up her back. Hot, cold, itchy. *Was* she there? Had she stood in this exact spot twenty years ago and witnessed the incident? Could she really have forgotten something like *this*?

There it was again. That bittersweet duet of hope and fear. Incompatible and disparate. If Ruby was on the list, there was a real chance she was racing towards the end of something far more absolute than this case. But, then again, falling into the killer's sights might well be her best chance at catching them. The fact remained that, despite her shifting labyrinth of memories, Ruby was almost certain she *wasn't* there. She'd have remembered. Surely something that potent and visceral would not fade away? The attack was many things, but forgettable was not among them.

"Are you thinking it had something to do with that?" Kendall asked.

"I don't know," Ruby said. And she felt uncertainty creeping in. It was tenuous. Too many dots joined with ambitious, conditional lines that only survive if a list of accompanying things remain true. Things she had no way of knowing. The people she needed to ask were dead. And the list of possible victims ran, as it always had, well over the one hundred mark. No, higher. It wasn't just former students. Not anymore.

She sighed, starting to deflate. Shit, she'd really thought this might be it. Again, she looked back up through those trees.

"You said it was dark," Ruby heard herself say. "But you remembered lights?"

"Oh yeah, definitely," Kendall said. "I saw them glowing through the fog. The lights hanging from the eaves of the music block."

Ruby turned to that building – she could just make out the shape of a teacher sitting at a piano, the top of a double bass at his side.

"Christmas lights?"

"Yeah," Kendall said. "The big golden lanterns they used to put up. And, it's weird, because all the windows would have been shut, right? It was winter. Cold."

"Sure?"

"But I could hear the singing," Kendall said. "I can still hear the choir now. They were rehearsing. Funny, it completely ruined that carol for me. Shame. It's such a beautiful song."

Frozen solid again. A statue on the wall, Ruby just waited. She didn't want to test fate, no leading questions. This, if nothing else, was the one thing he remembered about that day. So, she just stood there, and she waited.

And then, his voice small and distant in her ear, like the voice of an angel, Kendall said the title with such commitment, such unwavering, glorious certainty. "'O Holy Night.'" He sighed. "The stars are brightly shining."

And goosebumps ran across every inch of Ruby's skin as her eyes fell closed all by themselves. A thrill of hope, she thought, the weary world rejoices.

Chapter Sixteen

Ruby was running. Back across the playground, taking the concrete steps two at a time, grabbing the rail to swing around the corner, down past the main building, then turning to arrive in the car park. She got to Will's car, opened the door, climbed in. Out of breath, she called Jay and listened to the rings as she started the engine.

"Answer," she mumbled to herself. "Pick up the—"

"Ruby," he said, as she reversed out of the space, phone on her shoulder, clumsily switching to the other ear, good hand on the wheel now.

"Listen," she looked left, checked the mirror, drove, "I need—"

"I've been trying to call you all day – we need to talk."

"Jay—"

"I've had your boss on the phone."

"Can you please—"

"Why didn't you tell me you were going to Alfie's place? Why on *earth*—"

"Would you shut the fuck up and listen." Ruby came to a hard stop at the car park gates.

Silence. He was listening. She put the phone on the passenger seat, then pressed her earbuds in.

"I am sorry," she added, now speaking hands-free. "I know what's going on." She drove through the gates, down the ramp and onto the road as she explained. Then said, "I need you to look at Scott's file. Around November 1997, he attacked Kendall Robson, at school. There were no charges, but check the notes."

He sighed. "Hang on, I'll need to log in remotely."

He was at home. Ruby remembered the date, that ambitious timeline – fourteen days had passed. The old station building was closed. Doors shut for good.

At some traffic lights, glowing red above the car, Ruby looked through the window. It was getting dark. She turned the headlights on and waited.

"Here we go," Jay said. "It's the very first entry. Officers attended the scene along with an ambulance. Seems . . ." He paused, reading. "Huh, OK. So, an officer – an unnamed officer – wanted to pursue GBH. They interviewed Scott Hopkins but . . ." More reading. "He maintained he was defending himself."

"Bullshit."

Green lights. Ruby pulled away, coming up the high street as Jay added, "This is just what it says. There was a statement provided some weeks later. From a student."

"Who?"

"Anonymous. Just a letter. Typed, it says."

"Is it there?" She waited at a zebra crossing.

"No."

Ruby groaned. "Anything else?"

An elderly man shuffled through her headlights, in front of the car. Infuriatingly slow.

"That's it on the file. Headline is, no real evidence. Nothing concrete from witnesses. Statement was useless without a name. One kid's word against another. Schoolyard tussle that got out of control. These things happen . . ." A couple of clicks. "But . . . wait a second."

The road cleared and Ruby accelerated, driving fast again, indicating at the upcoming corner, palm flat on the wheel as she turned and changed gear and revved up onto Bayhill Street.

"Right . . ." Click, click in her ear. "Scott's statement. Kendall started the fight. Blah, blah, blah, he was acting in . . ." Jay's voice changed, stern now, reading verbatim. "Suspect refused to provide names, but suggested if officers wished to corroborate his version of events, they should interview the eyewitnesses present. Mr Hopkins believed, in addition to himself and Kendall Robson, there were *six* eyewitnesses. One of whom was a member of staff."

"Alfie?"

"Could be. Maybe he broke it up. Doesn't say."

"Six," Ruby said. "So, add Scott to the list, that's seven in total."

"Seven, yes."

"Two left, then," Ruby said. "This is it. They're killing the witnesses. Anyone who saw."

"And Kendall?"

"He's the victim. I'm sure he isn't on the list."

Ruby went over the single-lane railway bridge, slowing to pass a van.

"That's not what I was getting at. Do you trust him?"

She thought about small, shy, intelligent Kendall. Sitting next to her in maths. Both at the front. Top of the class. He was too wise for a grudge. Besides, he couldn't walk.

"I do. He doesn't even know who was there. And he wouldn't . . . Plus, Kendall's stepsister is married to . . . Elizabeth was his sister in-law. They're technically family."

Now it was a straight line, the residential lanes narrow, the engine loud, booming off the close walls, front doors zipping past.

"We're still looking at someone who knew the witnesses, then?"

"Yes."

"Male."

The notebook thief. "Yes."

"Someone dangerous, disturbed . . ."

Ruby knew what he was suggesting. "I agree, getting Frank Enfield in cuffs is still a priority." She indicated at the junction – *click, clunk, click, clunk.* "But this is something. Let's keep a clear—"

"And there's the small matter of the guns."

"What guns?"

"Scott's is unaccounted for, we know that. But I've just been told *another* registered pistol is also missing from his locker. I'm guessing Frank went back for it. Just be careful. Two guns."

Three if you count the sawn-off in the boot, Ruby thought. But she stayed silent, stomached the shame. Then again, if there were three guns in play, Ruby was relieved *she* had one of them.

"Two names left on the list," she said. "We need to figure out who they are."

"Perhaps Kendall might be of some assistance?"

"Agreed." Ruby arrived on his street. "I'm with him right now. Thank you."

Ruby hung up. She parked the car on double yellow lines, climbed out and jogged the final ten metres to his tall terraced house. Knocking, she thumbed the bell. Checked her watch, body twitching impatiently.

There was some commotion behind Kendall's door. And then, with an awkward judder, it began to open. He had to retreat in his wheelchair to allow her inside.

Having assisted, she closed the door and followed him into the living room, sitting immediately as he straightened himself up at her side – his wheelchair spokes clicking, a final bead falling into place when he stopped.

She'd already explained her theory on the phone, now, "There are seven names on the list," Ruby said. "Someone *is* killing people who witnessed the attack. People who saw Scott push you."

"God."

Ruby leant forwards, elbows on her knees. "I think Mary, Scott, Elizabeth and Adam were there. And Alfie Rogers, the old photography teacher, he would have been looking down from his office window."

"And he's dead?" Kendall whispered, his eyes full of shock.

"He is."

"But why . . . why do you think . . . ?"

Wincing, she explained that, "We heard the suspect on Adam's 999 call. As they . . . after he'd killed him, he hummed a tune. And he whistled . . ." Instead of saying the title, Ruby just quietly sang, "Fall on your knees, oh hear the angel voices."

Kendall looked down at his lap and nodded through a long silence, Ruby staring at him the whole time. She didn't need to say anything. He was smart enough to know what she was thinking. But he didn't speak. He wanted her to ask.

"I just told a colleague that you are not personally involved," she said. "Am I being naïve?"

He smiled, eyebrows lifted. "We're back to the elephant in the room." Kendall waved his hand. "If Scott was the only one, this would make a lot of sense. But the others? And why would I care? *They* didn't do anything."

"Exactly. They didn't do *anything*. They just stood by."

"Fine." He hesitated. "So, devil's advocate. There is a moral argument that Scott deserved to die. But I just can't stretch further than that. So, to answer your question, no. You're not being naïve. I promise, Ruby, really, I promise I have nothing to do with this."

She believed him. "We need to think. Together. We need to work out who else might have been there." She got her phone out, opened the full-year picture and passed it over.

Kendall seemed momentarily overwhelmed as he looked down at more than a hundred and sixty faces, all their classmates lined up, smart in their uniforms.

"Haven't seen this for years," he said, fascination and nostalgia calming the room.

Behind him, through a doorway blocked off by a loose curtain, Ruby could hear the radio in the kitchen. Whispering country music. An American woman singing a sad song, just her faint voice and her slow acoustic guitar. Ruby couldn't make out any lyrics, but knew it was about something tragic – an overwhelming pain reaching up from the past.

And she looked at the scar on Kendall's jawline, lit by the antique lamp in the corner – its bulb warm and red, the tassel rim of its old shade throwing laddered shadows across the wall.

Kendall inspected the photo, then looked up at her. "And two more?"

"Yes."

"Well," he shook his head as though Ruby had missed something obvious, "Frankenfield?"

She nodded. "Maybe, sure."

"He and Scott were best friends. Or more. I mean, they had a bit of a weird relationship."

Laughing, Ruby tilted her head. "You could say that."

"And Frank's alive." Kendall pointed at the small TV in the corner, next to the lamp. "They said on the news he was wanted."

"That's right, he is."

"Isn't that suspicious, though? He's been missing for all this time and now he's back?"

"It's . . ."

"Then again, even if he is as mad as he used to be, why would he kill his best friend?" Kendall seemed to be thinking hard, eyes fixed on nothing, just hovering around the centre of the room. "Do you know where he's been?" he asked, turning to Ruby.

Of course, how could Kendall have known that Frank Enfield never even left town? He'd been sitting in a room for a decade. Scott's prisoner, kept there by coercion alone. No locks. Just blind, dogged loyalty that didn't make sense to any rational mind.

Ruby knew she should tread carefully when sharing information about an active investigation. She'd probably said too much already. But here was that conflict, the divide between professional and personal bridged once again. Kendall was a friend; she trusted him and needed his help.

"It's," she began, resisting the urge to tell him everything, "it's complicated." There was so much doubt here. Frank remained an extremely prominent question mark. But Ruby felt her instincts filling in the gaps. "I don't think he's responsible. It does appear that he was," she thought about the best way to phrase this, "*elsewhere* at all the relevant times." Plus, she'd *seen* the culprit from behind. Only a glimpse, but he wasn't six and a half feet tall. Frank was unmistakable.

Kendall took a big breath, puffing air out with a shrug. "If you're asking me to speculate about who else might have witnessed it, Frank would be at the top of the list."

"Good. OK, who else?"

For the next hour or so, she and Kendall brainstormed some names, producing a shortlist of nine people. Frank felt secure at the top, but those below seemed flimsy. Guesswork. Friendship groups, flings, any vague connection that might put those former students on the playing field at that exact moment. It was too early to send uniformed officers to any homes. She'd need to narrow them down.

Her next move was obvious. Ruby would make contact with them and simply ask if they were there. Having been reasonably good friends with Elizabeth, Will's name was on the list. And, although he was one of the least likely candidates, Ruby had his number. So, she'd start with him.

She left just before 9pm, climbed back into the car and put the scrap of paper on the passenger seat.

Earbuds in, she scrolled down to Will. Hit call. And, as she pulled away, he answered. She explained the situation for a third time – the account now down to three short, punchy sentences. No pauses, no windows for him to ask the hundred questions he had ready to go on the tip of his tongue.

"No," Will said, "I wasn't there."

"Any thoughts on who else might have been?"

"Well." He hummed. "I'd be guessing, but I would agree, Frank seems likely. I remember Elizabeth mentioning it too. And Mary and Adam, they got busy in the changing rooms – you remember?"

"I do remember that." The strange intimacy of adolescent gossip. Back then, sex acts were an arms race. They were neither adults nor children. Still young enough to talk openly about the alluring things they were scarcely old enough to do.

She pulled back out onto the high street, now at the top of the hill, car pointing down towards the coastline. One of the highest points in town.

"But otherwise, no, I'm sorry," Will added. "I wouldn't know."

"OK, thank you, do you have contact details for any of the following—"

Beep. Beep. Her phone lit up, announcing an incoming call in her ear. "Sorry, I have to go."

Ruby answered, expecting to hear Jay's voice – she'd give him these names, get them into the system, see if there were any threads to pull. But it was someone else.

"Hey, Ruby, Ruby Shaw?" It was Detective Warren from the Metropolitan Police. She'd been dreading this call all day.

"Speaking."

He introduced himself again, like she might have forgotten their conversation yesterday. But he'd dropped his sympathetic tone and now sounded professional. Which meant he knew who she was.

Ruby was stationary now, stopped at some more red lights. There were no other cars around. Just her, alone, waiting at the very top of the hill.

Detective Warren went straight to business. "Listen, we've just pulled some CCTV footage from near to Alan, to Alfie Rogers' flat. We've got some good images, I'll send them over."

Ruby looked up at the traffic lights but, when they turned green, she didn't move. Instead, she leant forwards, towards the windscreen, squinting at something. A low cloud, emanating from somewhere down the hill. It was glowing behind the orange haze of streetlights level with the car. Beyond, the black ocean stretched out for infinity, a perfect, clean backdrop for what was quite clearly smoke. A huge plume disappearing into the night above.

"Are you there?" he said.

"Yeah, just . . . just a sec . . ."

Ruby climbed out of the car, standing now on the road. Stunned and staring as though facing an apocalyptic vision, like those nameless extras in a film that get out of their vehicles, mouths open, awestruck by some unimaginable sight in the sky.

She took a few steps sideways, arriving on the pavement. Leaning, looking through the skyline, the rooftops and telegraph

271

wires, she followed the smoke down and saw that, yeah, it was coming from South Street. The station building.

"My God," Ruby said, certain now.

"What?" the detective in her ears seemed concerned.

"The station, the old station building in Missbrook Bay."

"What about it?"

"It's . . . on fire."

"Shit." He sounded unfazed, like this wasn't important. Just a coincidence. "Got your hands full there, hey? Anyway, pictures are on their way over to you, sending," she heard a click, "now."

Ruby turned, went back to the car, the engine still running. "Thank you."

"We think there's more, pulling them together now." Detective Warren continued talking about cameras and evidence as she drove fast down the hill.

Ruby replied with short, distracted sounds.

The roads were clear and, within a minute, she was approaching the scene, discovering just how big the column of smoke was – daunting now she was below it, looking up at the flames pushing a fierce orange glow into the underside of the cloud.

Coming around the final corner, Ruby drove slowly. She saw silhouettes of cars, people, the rectangle of a fire engine parked out the front. Blue emergency lights lost in the chaos and heat.

"Some great views," the detective was saying. "Three cameras on the north side."

Ruby spotted Jay and some uniformed officers on the road. The firefighters unravelling hoses. Pointing, shouting. Gathering onlookers held in place by a line of police, arms spread, herding them all back.

"I'll, uh, I'll have a look," Ruby said, pulling over.

"I'll call back when we do get a clearer shot," Detective Warren said. "Once we align the times. To be perfectly honest, it's not the best at the moment. Pretty blurry."

She climbed out, the smell of smoke and the roar of fire arriving immediately, like she'd fallen into a warzone. The car door hung open behind her, the station building lit up like a bomb had hit it, tornadoes coming out of the upstairs windows, flames crawling tight around the frames. Ruby walked into the road, still dazed, hypnotised.

This was not a coincidence. And it looked absolutely nothing like an accident. Which was a bad sign. The suspect had always been cautious. Sloppy behaviour meant one thing. They were almost finished. It was almost over.

The line was still open, Detective Warren patient through these long silences.

"Great," Ruby said. "Can you see his face?" She was looking at Jay now. He was standing there, neck arched, watching it all burn.

There was a pause. She imagined Detective Warren sitting at his desk, miles away from all this, staring at the photo on his screen. Maybe tilting his head. "No, not really," he replied. "Side of a hooded jumper, half a cheek. Can barely tell the height. But, if I had to bet, I'd say it was a woman."

Jay turned, made eye contact with Ruby. "There she is," he said, striding towards her, a uniformed officer trailing just behind.

"Thanks," she whispered, removing her earbuds to end the call.

"Ruby," Jay said, frustration in his voice.

It felt like a dream, surreal and slow. As though she wasn't here, but rather recalling this moment later, much later, and beginning to doubt the details.

"I have a list," Ruby said, as he arrived. "A list of people who might have been there."

He seemed disinterested, like he had something else to say.

"But I've just spoken to Detective Warren," she went on. "They've got some photos that—"

"Ruby," he said, holding up a cautious hand. A peace offering. Half his face was lit, the other half black, fire in his right eye. "I need you to get into the car." He gestured behind himself, towards some blue lights, silent sirens spinning.

"Why?"

Their long shadows faced off, flickering on the road at their side, dancing along with the flames.

"Just get in and we can talk."

Something crumbled inside, the sound of ceiling rafters collapsing and burning.

"No," Ruby said, her cheeks hot. "This is a waste of time. What does that tell you?" She held her arm to the building, presenting it like a normal piece of evidence as she glanced around the scene.

It was bold. Even from here, Ruby could see one, two, three CCTV cameras. Twenty windows, or more. *Four* CCTV cameras. There was no way on earth whoever was responsible wasn't going to be identified. Arson of this magnitude, this audacity, it really was the home straight. Getting caught was no longer a concern.

Jay frowned. "You think that . . . But why?"

"You can commit injustice by doing nothing."

"We're too far in to be quoting philosophers. Speak plainly."

"The police did *nothing*," Ruby said. "This is retribution for things people *didn't do*. Look, it's happening tonight." She nodded, glaring. "The last two victims. Jay, it's happening *now*. Get on the radio and—"

"Stop," he cut her off. "County head office have records of the comings and goings." He pointed at the fire, speaking to her like she was a child. She needed to pay attention. "Their system said you were the last person to enter the building. *You*. Just over forty-five minutes ago."

"What?"

"Look," palms spread, "please, just get into the car."

The uniformed officer behind him stepped forwards, his hand brushing against the cuffs on his belt. Silver metal, glinting yellow.

It was an arrest. Jay was trying to arrest her. "You don't seriously think I . . ."

She stopped.

Ruby put her hand on her chest pocket, felt her pounding heart. Then, eyes darting, she checked her trousers. Her swipe ID. She pulled the glossy card out and held it in her fingers.

Jay nodded, as if to say, yes, that's it. That's the reason she needed to comply.

"This is a replacement card," she said, waving it in the air like it was worthless, meaningless. "I lost the first one."

She lost it last week. Around the time she went to . . . Click, click, click – the sound of beads clattering on Kendall's wheelchair. The old décor. The faint country music from the next room. All that heavy rain. Ruby had been cold and wet when she first visited. And Zoe had insisted. She *insisted* on taking her jacket.

"Detective Warren would bet it was a woman," Ruby said. "She stole it."

"Who?"

"Oh, I am such an idiot." Hand on her forehead, Ruby closed her eyes. She'd been so focused on these potential victims. She really hadn't stopped to think. "It's her," Ruby said, total conviction in her voice. She looked at Jay again. "Kendall's carer. Zoe Parker."

No one moved. The fire roared.

"She took my jacket." Ruby was smiling. "Last week. My swipe card was in my pocket. That was the last time I saw it. You noticed too – there was something between them. Jay, I'll get in the car, I'll come willingly, but only if you put that out on the radio. Arrest Zoe."

Jay hesitated, a glimmer of trust and respect returning to his eyes. "Are you sure?"

The person running down Will's garden, Ruby's stolen notebook clutched to their chest. They'd seen only a glimpse, from behind, through the kitchen window. And all three of them agreed it was a man. But why? Because he had broad shoulders and short hair? *Zoe* had broad shoulders and short hair.

Ruby thought about those reunion photos Zoe took. Kendall in his wheelchair, Scott and Mary leaning down to pose. Pink fancy-dress scarf, big smiles and drunken eyes. Mary even sat on Kendall's lap. She kissed his cheek. Brazen and without remorse. Kendall had forgiven them. But Zoe? She'd been feeling protective.

Ruby imagined what she must have felt seeing that happen, seeing them together at the party. Having fun. Posing. Mary, who died that very night, leaving lipstick on Kendall's cheek, next to the scar she'd watched Scott create. Zoe knew what Scott did. And she knew what the witnesses didn't do. The answer had been right there in a photo. Just not the photo Ruby had been staring at.

And finally, her mind went back to the imaginary darkroom – the last photo. The one that didn't even exist, hanging, drying now. Coming into focus, crystal clear as the fog fades and the image develops. Someone who cares about Kendall more than anyone else. More than she should. It was a photo of Zoe Parker.

"Jay," Ruby said, "look at me. I'm sure."

The uniformed officer stood patiently as Jay returned to his car, opened the door and leant down for his radio.

Ruby looked into the officer's eyes and, no more than a millimetre either way, she shook her head. It was almost an imperceptible exchange, but she could tell he understood. She was not going to comply.

He sighed as flakes of ash and ember flickered and fell between them like snow. Then the officer tensed his jaw, turned and, standing side on, literally looked the other way. Ruby stepped backwards, retreating from the searing heat, fading away back into the cold shade of the night behind her.

Chapter Seventeen

Ruby pulled over at the side of the road, two wheels on the pavement. Although she was a few streets away, the fire still loomed high behind her, a chugging orange mass in the sky. It was raining now too. Not heavy enough to help, more of a haze, just tiny droplets like gnats floating and shifting in the wind.

She held her phone in one hand, the shortlist in the other. Nine names, eight now she'd ruled Will out. Two more were scheduled to die tonight. Or maybe, she thought, glancing up at the rear-view mirror, they were already dead. There was an undeniable sense of finality in the air. The smoke billowing fast, like a steam engine's chimney at full throttle. A train with nowhere left to go.

No. She had to act as if there was still hope. So, Ruby took a photo of the list – phone camera flashing once in the dark car – and sent it to Jay. A tick glowed on the screen, confirming he'd received it. He was typing.

Thank you, Jay wrote. *Officers heading to Zoe's place now. But we still need to speak to you.*

Considering everything, it wasn't unreasonable to have lost some of Jay's trust. Ruby had spent the last eight hours avoiding his calls and, on paper at least, she understood why he'd felt compelled to arrest her. There was, at the bare minimum, a serious question of misconduct she'd need to answer. Still, she suspected Jay was going through the motions. At present, she couldn't prove that Zoe stole her ID card. That would come later. But he can't have believed Ruby had started any fires. Jay was just doing what he was expected to do. It'd be remiss of him to do anything else.

OK, what now? She opened her inbox, found Detective Warren's email. Scrolled down to the attachment, tapped it. A screenshot from a domestic security camera near Alfie's flat. Zooming in with two fingers, Ruby recognised the street, half the play equipment grainy and blurred in the background. She squinted, tilted her head. While it wasn't possible to identify the person, she agreed, it could be a woman.

And she imagined police breaking through Zoe's front door, shouting as they went room to room, throwing torchlight and armed demands at nothing but a dark, empty house.

That was not the way to find her. Potential victims were the key. Ruby needed to work out where she was going, not where she'd been. Sighing, she looked back to the names. Despite being in the same year at school, most were effectively strangers. First up, Frank Enfield. Decidedly unfindable. Next, Allison Isaac. Ruby was fairly sure Allison was a doctor. It was a start.

Earbuds in, she swiped to her contacts, found Lauren, hit call. Travelling now at a tentative speed, responding to an emergency with no destination, Ruby pulled off the side of the road and drove.

"Listen, hi, yes, hello," she said, cutting Lauren off. "Long shot, but do you have a number for Allison Isaac?"

"Um, no," she said. "But I could get it, why?"

"I figured it out." Ruby had slight pride in her voice. She was excited to tell Lauren that this morning's affirmation had come true. "The connection."

"And?"

"You remember Scott pushing Kendall off the wall?"

"Yeah?"

"Every witness. Anyone who was there, anyone who saw the attack. She's killing them all."

"Who is?"

"Zoe Parker, Kendall's carer. She was at the reunion. You probably met her?"

"I . . . I did. Are you – are you sure?"

"Possessive and controlling, but yeah, it blindsided me too. We've got a list of possible names." Ruby checked her mirror – quiet roads tonight. "Two left. And time isn't exactly on our side. I need to work out who else was there and . . ."

It was unmistakable. Just like last night, in the dark, when sound alone told so many stories. No words were needed. Just steady breathing. There was fear on the end of the line.

"I, uh . . ." Lauren swallowed. "I remember it."

Teeth clamped tight, Ruby's posture changed. Spine straight, poised, ready to listen.

"I was there," Lauren added. "On the field. I saw what Scott did."

"Where are you now?" Ruby's hands solid on the wheel.

"I'm at work."

"Good, *stay there*." She glared down at the phone, the closest she could get to eye contact, speaking with authority. "Are you with other people?"

"Uh, well. I mean, yes. Some. I'm not . . ." Lauren moved, lowered her voice. "You don't think she would come here?"

"Honestly, I don't know." Faster now, turning at the lights, coming off the slip road and, foot down, heading towards the hospital.

"Am I in danger?" Lauren asked.

"I'm coming there now, OK."

"*Ruby.*"

Things had changed. The safety of crowds, witnesses, none of that applied anymore. They'd have CCTV images of Zoe's face within hours. Officers were searching for her as they spoke. And Zoe must know it. These really were the final moves. The last two names would be crossed off with the unique and violent audacity of someone who does not care about consequences.

"Just stay calm, I'm going to hang up and call for assistance."

"*Am I in danger?*" she asked again, stern now. Not necessarily scared, she just needed to know.

Lauren deserved honesty.

"Yes," Ruby said. "Lots."

She hung up, did as she'd promised and called 999. There was no need for middlemen, no advantage to her professional connections. This was a crisis anyone could report.

Ruby hit 100 miles per hour along the main road, headlight raindrops like stars flying past the car, warp speed tracer lines disappearing back into the black void behind her. No more than five minutes later, she swung off the roundabout, accelerated up the hill and screeched to a stop in the hospital car park.

Door open, she climbed out, relieved to hear sirens growing steadily louder in the distance. She ran up some steps, towards the turning circle in front of the building and then straight out into the road, causing a very angry motorist to perform an emergency stop. He honked his horn, flailing his arms in disbelief, indignant and shouting now from his opening window as Ruby held up a sorry hand without breaking pace. The words "stupid bitch" turning a few heads nearby. But not hers.

Across the wet tarmac expanse, the big red cross glowing above the hospital entrance, reflected perfectly below, flowing from one puddle to the next as she approached. A giant neon plus sign. This shape meant hope, it stood tall and proud of what it represented. The polar opposite of her little red crosses and their fatal implications.

Two more to go, she thought again. Was this it? Had it all come down to saving a single life? All those crosses, all this failure. But no matter what horrors were in store tonight, Ruby would die before she let a single drop of red ink anywhere near Lauren's face on that photograph.

Inside now, through automatic glass doors, lights bright and white, Ruby headed for reception, weaving around a hunched, pregnant woman whose partner, hand on her back, seemed startled by the flagrant queue jumping.

"Doctor Lauren Coates," Ruby said to the confused woman at the wide desk. "She's a surgeon. Which floor?"

"Excuse me, ma'am," the receptionist said, "there's a queue. If you'd like to—"

"It's fine." Ruby turned, removed her phone as she stepped aside. She called Lauren. No answer.

Just as the expecting couple arrived at the desk, Ruby swung back and, with remarkably composed force, explained who she was and demanded the receptionist's attention.

She was displeased, but lifted her phone and called the relevant department.

"Is Doctor Coates with you?" she asked, speaking to a colleague somewhere else in this building, somewhere above. "OK. Yes, thank you." She hung up. "Doctor Coates was here earlier, but she left."

"What?"

"She was here but now she isn't. If you'd—"

"Where did she go?"

The receptionist seemed alarmed, looking at something behind Ruby. She turned. Uniformed officers were arriving, gathered between the two sets of automatic doors. Four of them. She recognised one immediately. It was the man from the fire. Stepping

282

into the foyer, he noticed her, tilted his head and turned over a hand. Not again. She couldn't ask for another blind eye.

"Ruby," he said, with end-of-shift exhaustion. "I need you to come with me."

"Stay here," she replied. He couldn't comprehend the urgency and there was simply no time to explain. "Zoe might still arrive."

"Please . . ." Now he seemed disappointed in her. Exasperated. But he didn't intervene as she walked across the lobby, a wide circle leaving enough distance between them in case he changed his mind. "Come on," he said as, facing him, she stepped backwards through the automatic doors and shrugged. What could she say?

And then she was in the cold night again. He had the decency not to pursue. Returning to her car, Ruby tried Lauren once more, checking over her shoulder, phone to her ear. Still nothing. Then she called Will, asked if she'd been in contact.

"No," he said. "Why?"

"Lauren was there." Ruby passed the ambulance station tunnel. "She's on the list."

"Shit. She's at work."

"No, she's not at the hospital anymore. She . . ." Ruby stopped at the top of the car park stairs. "She's afraid. Oh, I think I know where she is." She ran down. "It's OK. Stay at home in case she comes back. Call the police immediately if she does."

"Why would she leave the hospital?"

"Because I scared her." Ruby was sure Lauren had gone to the old dockyard. It wasn't too far from here. "I'm going to go and get her. Don't worry."

Yet more weight added to this. Her heart pounded as she climbed back into the car, ending the call. Years ago, Ruby had envied Lauren, maybe even hated her. Now, tonight, she was someone Ruby would consider a friend. She started the engine, thinking that this was a noble, heroic endeavour. Saving the life of your ex-boyfriend's new partner. She blamed the adrenaline for these ridiculous thoughts, for this grandeur, for the odd pleasure she felt when she imagined the symbolic closure of her actions. But more than anything, their redemptive backstory made the idea of Lauren getting hurt somehow doubly unsettling. Ruby wanted to grab her, hold her, protect her from the encroaching harm of this cruel world.

She came off the hospital roundabout, hit the industrial back roads that led down towards the shoreline.

At first, Ruby had thought leaving the hospital was reckless. A well-lit, public place. But perhaps, all things considered, somewhere secluded would be the safest bet. At least in the short term. Still, as she drove, she checked out of the windows, half expecting to glimpse the beginnings of death in the undergrowth. Discover some disturbance, a trail that led through hazard lights and broken glass all the way to something that would be, once again, her fault. But, to her relief, she saw none of these signs.

Ruby turned onto the closed-off road and mounted the grass verge to pass a metal barrier arm, ignoring all the rust-peeled warnings. "No Entry". "Trespassers Will Be Prosecuted". The word "DANGER" printed bold. Driving along a line of wire fencing now, overgrown plant life, brown and peppered with faded litter – shadows cowering at the edge of headlights. And over the cliff on her right, and down, the ocean below dark enough to seem like nothing.

She arrived at a concrete barrier and stopped. There was no way through. Besides, most of the main vehicle access beyond had crumbled away – driving along there wouldn't be wise. It was only another hundred metres or so to the footpath that ran down to the dockyard. She could walk the rest of the way.

Engine off, lights out. She was up on the cliff, exactly where Alfie had been when he captured every season with his camera.

Now she could see it, down there. The old navy jetty, set against the black splashing waves. A huge, sprawling rectangle of concrete, bigger than she remembered. Strong, unmovable and menacingly dormant in the dark.

Ruby scanned along the abandoned buildings below, vague shapes cut out by the faint glow of night light glinting on long puddles, catching brick edges and the sharpened teeth of smashed glass in window frames. Just silver lines, wet surfaces glittering back at the moon.

And she sighed when she saw a tiny amber square. Right at the far end on the ground floor of the final building. The furthest one away. Almost invisible. She wouldn't have seen it if she hadn't known to look. That was candlelight. Warm in the cold room Lauren goes to when she's vulnerable and wants to hide. Ruby was relieved she was safe but also oddly happy with the intimate vindication of guessing correctly that Lauren would come to a place like here at a time like this.

It was quiet now the rain had stopped. The town over the hill behind her was silent. All Ruby could hear was the breeze and the sea's endless rhythm echoing on the rocks. She tried calling Lauren again. But still, straight to answerphone. Probably no signal. A walk, then. With a calm breath of slow air, Ruby opened the car door, put one foot out onto the gravel but then froze. A new sound.

Gradually standing, she moved around the door, closing it, eyes wide and leaning to—

Shit. It was a car. Someone was approaching at the other entrance up ahead.

Ruby sank down, crouching, crawling forwards to hide behind a mound – elbows in the grass, she peered through the long, curling brambles – suddenly silhouettes when headlights came into view. They swung round, aiming right at her, far away and small but still glaring in her eyes. And then they disappeared.

Silence again – spots in her vision drifted free, snapping back when she tried to focus. The next sound she heard was a car door slamming. Loud out here in all this open air. Ruby looked back down towards the dockyard, chest pressed against the earth, heart beating into it. She could smell the grass, she could hear her own heavy breaths.

Zoe had followed Lauren. Ruby glanced back again and saw a glimpse, just a head, a turning shoulder. A hooded figure calmly, but purposefully, walking across the tarmac, towards the zig-zag steps, towards the footpath that led down to the docks.

"No," Ruby whispered as she stood up, hands jittery and powerless, reaching forwards into the panic as though she could grab something from here.

Should she shout, at least *warn* her? It was too far. The only person who'd definitely hear would be Zoe. And then her walk would become a run.

Fumbling for her phone, Ruby . . . stopped.

Her head snapped round, back to Will's car. She went straight to the boot, opened it, grabbed the sawn-off shotgun, turned and ran towards the verge.

Passing her legs over the low barrier, Ruby knew if she went this way, she could make it onto the dockyard first. As the crow flies, she was closer. But only just.

All she had to do was climb down. But, God, it was dark. And steep. She shuffled her shoe to the edge, peered over. More cliff than hill. There was a ledge, then the possible path disappeared from sight. Waves churning around the unseeable rocks below. Twenty feet? Forty?

She imagined Zoe walking down from the other side, every passing second eating into Ruby's slight advantage. There was no other option.

Holding the shotgun with her broken hand, Ruby sat, lowered herself, then leapt down onto the first outcrop. She thumbed the torch on her phone and pointed it at her feet. It was precarious, but she found something like a route to follow. Having committed, she knew this was it, she couldn't get back up. The only way was down. The path crumbling, stones sliding, tumbling off into the void as she jogged along the shelf. But it was narrowing. Slower now, shoulder pressed against the tufts of ragged grass and rocks at her side, Ruby leant left into the vertical earth, edging along to ensure—

Something gave way and she fell backwards, rolled over, sliding on her front, hip, then her back. Flat rocks beneath were breaking free, bouncing down the cliff face all around her and she realised she was sliding too fast, no control, no possible way she could—

Suddenly she was falling – not in contact with anything but air – stretched long and then, *crunch*, she landed hard on something vaguely flat. Crumpled in a seated position, still gripping the shotgun, elbow on the ground, badly winded as grit and pebbles rained on her hair and clothes.

Ruby looked, discovered she was level with the dock buildings, lower than their roofs. And then down, now just a few feet to the sea, she caught the eerie sight of her phone beneath the water, torch still on, dancing side to side as it sank – a majestic orb that lit the bubbles and green rocks and black mussel shells and swung like a leaf, but then it was gone. And the sea was nothing again.

She pushed on. Her left ankle was sprained, but not, it seemed, broken. Weak, though, over the slippery terrain, the spray getting to her, cold water on her hands and face. She had to wade the last part when the waves rose, shoving her against the solid rocks. Arriving at an old rusted ladder protruding from the wet wall, slick with moss, she climbed. She could barely see it, but went up quickly.

Finally, she was on the concrete, on her knees and then her feet, turning, the abandoned buildings on her left, the sea on her right. And she ran, the awful weight of a bad dream dragging her down, hobbling, both legs throbbing from the fall, further out, limping away from the land behind.

She kept checking left as she went, between each of the buildings, hoping and fearing she'd see Zoe approaching on the other side. Or, worse, she'd see her up ahead and arrive in time to do nothing but witness something she'd been too slow to stop.

Then, down through a narrow alley – the moon shining between broken clouds, bright enough to cast a shadow – a long and moving impression of a person was coming. She was mirroring Ruby's route.

Whimpering now, desperate and knowing they'd arrive at the same time, she sprinted through the pain, the small square of candlelight in that final window swaying in her blurred vision. Nearly there. And then she was.

She passed the doorway, came to the edge of the building and stopped, readying the gun. A good stance. Zoe would come around the corner any second. Footsteps and a shadow and—

"Stop," Ruby yelled. "Stay there." Standing straight, gun aimed. "Don't move."

But it wasn't Zoe. It was a man. And, even before she saw his face, she recognised him. Frank's stature was unmistakable. But Ruby didn't let the confusion cloud her clear, adrenal thoughts. Explanations were not relevant. Not yet. For the second time this week, she held Frank Enfield at gunpoint and demanded he listen to her very carefully.

Frank was just ten paces away on the pitted concrete. He didn't seem surprised or even concerned to see Ruby. But he did as she'd said and stood still.

He was holding a pistol. Single hand, aimed low. Probably one of those missing guns from Scott's house, she reasoned. Or not. It didn't matter where it came from. What mattered was that he . . . "Put it down," she said.

"Ruby?" Lauren's voice, emerging from the open doorway behind her, sounded tiny. Ruby didn't look, just sidestepped, putting herself between them.

Frank was calm as he pulled his hood back.

"So," he said, "you figured it out?"

"Please lie on the ground."

"I told you this would happen." He seemed tired. Almost bored. "I've seen it." Blinking with his slow, sunken eyes, he said, "Death."

"Down." Ruby aimed at his chest, finger on the trigger, hands wrapped tight around the shotgun.

"You don't understand," Frank said. "It has to happen." He looked past Ruby, over her shoulder. "She has to die."

"No," Ruby leant for his eyes, caught them as they drifted back to hers, "no one has to die. You just need to *slowly* put—"

"I wonder if this has already happened?" He frowned. Genuinely curious. "It's already too late. This is just . . . a memory."

There was a moment of peace. All three standing, waiting while he decided what he was going to do.

"Frank, please." Ruby saw his posture change, getting ready to move. "Don't," she said. "Don't do it."

"Yeah." He nodded. "I know how it goes. It's like this. It's like—"

His hand rose and the world was flashing, terrible strobe lights and loud searing pain and the shock and horror of being shot at and Ruby realised she was flinching and ducking her head and clenching her teeth and firing back, pulling the trigger again and again and again on empty, lifting her knee and shielding her face in clumsy, futile desperation as rounds still cracked from Frank's stretched arm as he lurched in the smoke, shooting off into the sky like he'd been shoved but he was reeling now, his gun spinning free from his grip, thrown away as though it was hot. It sounded like a drum kit had been kicked over and, in the silence that followed, Ruby saw him curled into himself, a wounded animal collapsing, falling off the edge of the earth as she fell sideways in the other direction, into the wall, sliding down. Sitting now.

No more than three seconds had passed since the first shot.

Chapter Eighteen

Ruby was on the ground, legs out straight, back against the concrete wall. Strangely calm, aware of the cold but not really feeling it. Just the sense of hot metal, cooked ocean air beginning to cool. In the dark, it reminded her of Bonfire Night, of fireworks and the ambient smoke that lingers in your nose and clothes long after it's gone. Winter festivities, black skies full of lights and songs.

Her left eye stung – water must have splashed on her face. She blinked, wiped with her wrist and realised it was blood.

Lauren was crouched in front of her, doing something to Ruby's chest. Fast, busy hands. Pressing against it now. Too firm. Leaning her head away like a stubborn child, Ruby almost pushed her off. She needed some space. But she didn't, because Lauren was speaking. So, she squinted, tried to listen as, gradually, the sound of waves and breeze breathed back into her ears.

"—a lot," Lauren was saying, "this artery, but it's above. It's above."

Confused, Ruby looked down, hesitated. "What?" she heard herself say.

"It's high. It didn't hit your lung."

Air whistled between the dockyard buildings behind, through open windows – something clonking nearby. An old door, moving in its frame, knocking along to no discernible rhythm. Not like the sea's tempo, which was, as always, predictably perfect and slow.

"That's good," Ruby whispered. She fiddled with the collar of her jumper – something was stuck there. Uncomfortable, like an itchy label. Then – sudden eye contact – she grabbed on to Lauren's wrist. Clung to it like she might fall if she let go. The shock making it all surreal, all too real as Ruby became completely aware that she'd been shot.

It was difficult to tell exactly where, though. Or how many times.

"Hold this." Lauren released her hand, took Ruby's and pressed it against her neck.

Hot but shivering, Ruby was holding a rag or an item of clothing now, like a wet tea towel. She tilted it aside, red fingers trembling, tried to take a quick glance at the damage. It was too high up to see the actual wound, even if she arched her neck, doubled her chin and pulled her jumper to—

Blood pumped out – an astonishing, breathtaking amount free-flowing down her front.

"Ah," she said, pressing the cloth back into place.

It didn't hurt. Which made it feel more severe, not less. Either a crucial connection had been severed or it was simply far too traumatic to elicit something as trite as pain.

Also, she noted, with surprisingly detached clarity, her left arm didn't appear to work anymore. She tried to lift it but it didn't move. Just stayed there, flopped near her thigh. It was all so matter of fact. So clear. Just information. Knowledge about terrible things that, even from the bird's eye view of seminal shock, were *happening*.

"I came here," Ruby said, blinking slowly. She leant her head to one side, jaw putting additional pressure on the back of her hand, pressed into her sticky flesh. "You told me this is where you go sometimes. I remembered . . ."

Lauren didn't reply.

"Did I do it?" Ruby asked. "Did I save you?"

Lauren glanced over her shoulder, looking towards the water.

"Is he gone? Is he dead?"

"I think so," Lauren said, turning back to Ruby.

"I really thought it was Zoe." She swallowed, grimacing at the taste. It took a moment before she could speak again. "I was so sure. But . . . big Frank from school." She smiled, something like a sigh or a laugh on her breath. "Frankenfield."

Lauren, hands on her knees, pushed herself up and stood, turned, stepped across the concrete to check over the edge.

"He was going to shoot you," Ruby said.

"Yes."

"It was him . . . Frank killed them. I don't understand. I don't . . ." Her eyes were dipping. She felt liquid trickling down her forearm, the elbow of her jumper swelling like a blister.

Ruby sat up slightly, back straight against the cold wall and took a few slow breaths, composing herself. Then she stared up at Lauren. She was standing at the brink of the old concrete jetty. There was no barrier, just the sea below, beyond and stretched out between black and blue, with shards of white that always moved. Night-vision moon spread on the water.

The dark coastline curved off forever ahead of them. And, up in town, Ruby looked across the hillside's twinkling lights, like sparklers, swaying tracers when her head lolled and she blinked and focused. The tower of smoke coming from the station building seemed faint now. Distant. It could pass for a cloud or even something less than that. Something imagined, something remembered.

Again, Ruby tried to make sense of it all. Wondered *why* Frank would do this. Maybe it wasn't about Kendall. Perhaps she'd been wrong about everything.

"But he came here." Ruby heard herself speaking. "He came here to kill you . . ."

It was bad that she couldn't get her thoughts in line.

"A bad sign," she whispered.

The early glimmers of delirium appearing, inviting her mind to dance the night away. To turn and spin with dreams that shed the endless burden of meaning and sense and carry you off into a dark land of hope and fear. To see a few things that might happen and many more that never could.

Frank came here, she thought, led by the light of faith serenely beaming. Ruby smiled. Even now, in this state. Even now, bleeding out on the ground, that song was stuck in her head. Her mind always ready to quote the lyrics. Always able to make them fit.

"Shit," she mumbled, "it's still stuck in my head."

Even now. Stuck there. That humming. O holy night. The stars are brightly shining. That's what they'd heard. That's what Kendall remembered from that awful day.

But there were no stars tonight. Yet, still, she listened. Not to the waves or the wind, not to that door knocking away in its old wooden frame. No. Ruby listened to the song. Because she could hear it.

Another alarming thought as she traced the sound and looked up at Lauren's back.

Lauren wasn't moving. She wasn't calling for help. She was just standing there, staring out across the water. And she was humming.

Right there, just a few metres away on the old dockyard concrete, Lauren Coates was humming that song. And steadily, just like on the 999 call, it became a whistle. A casual tune to serenade the haunted void that follows death. This time, Frank's.

"No," Ruby said. "Oh, no, no."

The music stopped. Only waves below, breeze behind as Lauren bowed her head and took a breath.

"It's you," Ruby whispered. She tried to stand, but ended up slumped even lower, knees together, propped up on the elbow of her useless arm, hand still pressed to her neck.

After a long while, Lauren turned around, sighed and said, "I'm sorry."

Chin on her chest, the back of her head awkwardly against the wall, Ruby wanted to speak but she couldn't. It was just a whimper. A sad, pitiful little sound.

"I so nearly told you last night," Lauren said. "I just . . ."

Ruby found her voice, but only had a single word to offer. "No."

"I was so close. I had to finish it."

It took Ruby three failed attempts to ask, "Why?"

"You know why."

"But they didn't . . . they didn't do anything wrong."

"He . . ." Lauren winced, shook her head. "Scott hit Kendall so . . . many . . . times. And they all just stood there. No one helped. Every single day of my life I see that. I feel it."

"Lauren, no."

"He pushed him. He pushed him and he fell. For no reason. It was . . ."

Again, Ruby shifted her weight, sat upright on the ground.

"And then, at the reunion . . ." Lauren staring off into nowhere – back into her memories. "They were taking photos with him. Smiling and posing, like . . ." Ruby could only just make out Lauren's face in the dark, snarling at the ugly image in her mind. "Like it didn't matter. They were making *fun* of him."

"No. No, they weren't. They'd forgotten. Kendall had forgiven him. It was fine."

"It was *never* fine."

"Why the others? Why not just Scott? I mean, Mary? Little Adam Ward? He was always smiling. He was . . ." Ruby groaned, almost shouted like she was trying to shoo the horror away, "he was *harmless.*"

"We don't need to dwell on all this. Let's just—"

"No. *Fuck.* Fuck off. Tell me why."

Lauren sniffed, got herself ready. If Ruby wanted the truth, fine, she'd get it.

"It was . . ." Lauren's eyes were wide, irises floating on the white, lids and lashes well clear of colour. There was nothing like empathy in there now. That switch she mentioned had been flicked. "The first one, Mary, honestly, it was impulsive. After the party. Spur of the moment."

"What did you do?"

"I followed her. Walked with her. We were talking. I asked if she felt bad, seeing Kendall after all this time. And she . . ." Lauren's lip curled again, more in disgust than anger. "She didn't really know what I was talking about. I said we tried. God, I tried so hard. I wanted him to be better. Kendall was *meant* to be walking in time for the party, so everyone could see. I told her that I . . . I can't take it anymore, I can't keep seeing him like that. I said, I explained, Kendall is why I went into medicine in the first place. Everything I've done since then has been . . . I just want to fix it. But three surgeries and he's still in that chair. And everyone saw. Mary said . . . she said, 'Fourth time lucky'. She was just feeling awkward, making light of it. Making a joke at a time like that? I was pouring my fucking heart out and she made a joke?"

"But how could—"

"There was this big rock, and I just . . ." She exhaled. "It was so easy. She didn't suffer. And I didn't regret it. Not even slightly. I felt . . . nothing. Then . . ." Even in the low light, Ruby could see her smile. "I didn't know I could sleep so well."

"Then Scott?"

"Yes. Another dose of *pure* catharsis."

"And then . . ." Ruby's chin quivered. "Elizabeth was a *mother*. She was so kind. And she—"

"Stood there and *watched it happen*."

"They were children."

"Alfie was a teacher. An adult."

Ruby remembered that afternoon in Will's spare room, when they'd looked at their full school year photo together. Lauren had so casually planted the target in her head. It was subtle manipulation. Elegant. The man behind the camera. Maybe there was more. Little hints, gentle nudges in the right direction. How hard had Lauren worked to install the idea of finding Alfie? Hard enough to make it seem like Ruby came up with it all by herself. She felt used, like a fool.

His rainbow bookshelf. His new lease of life. His skull smashed open on the—

"I don't want to hear any more," Ruby said, scrunching her eyes closed.

"You think I'm crazy?"

"No." Ruby looked up again. "Just . . ."

"Evil? What's evil is a police force letting Scott get away with everything."

Just over Lauren's shoulder, glowing in the middle of town – the smoke still rose from a tiny speck of amber. The station building burning away. It looked like newsreel footage – a warzone's pilot light. A deliberate catastrophe that stunned onlookers were yet to understand.

The statement from an anonymous student who'd urged police to take action. That had been Lauren's fledgling exploration of justice, long before the concept became so tragically distorted in her guilty mind. Then came the snowballing nature of mayhem and violence, which ends up, by the mere fact of its own grotesque existence, justifying itself. Because it's either righteous, or the wanton acts of a monster. And Lauren couldn't live with the idea of being precisely the latter.

No. It was simpler than all of that.

"You're a very bad person," Ruby said, blaming the shock for making her say obvious, basic, even childish things.

"I've never claimed otherwise."

"You're selfish. It was all for you. Not for Kendall. He wouldn't want this. You haven't made anything better, apart from your own stupid fucking—"

"There's no point trying to justify anything to you. But keep in mind the kind of person who can stand there and not intervene. Who's to say what else you'd be capable of? There's a poster in my room. Marcus Aurelius. 'And you can also commit injustice by doing nothing.'"

That's where she'd seen them, the words she echoed to Jay earlier this evening – cheeks red from the fire's heat. And red again with this cascade of explanation. Hindsight so bright it hurts to stare.

Lauren took a step closer, standing over Ruby, the low grey light coming off the wet ground glinting on her eyes. Though they were different now. Still totally devoid of all the empathy that plagued her waking hours, but Ruby noticed something even more unsettling on Lauren's face. She looked happy. Content. Blinking, soft transitions between lethargic peace and relief as though appreciating some newfound beauty in the world. The way it all seems after an intimate engagement with something you'd never even believed was real.

"Must feel good," Ruby said. "To turn it off. Dehumanise." She smiled, recalling last night's pitch-black conversation. "Ignore the stakes and get the job done."

"It feels wonderful."

Ruby's hand, still keeping the wound at bay, had begun to ache. Ironic that this injury, a low-ranking veteran among countless new entries in the catalogue of pain, hurt so much. And strange to think that Frank Enfield, some big guy from school, was responsible for almost all of them. A seatbelt tugged too tight, a punch thrown too hard and now their turbulent relationship had escalated up into the realms of lethal force. Now, he was dead, in the sea.

Perhaps it would have been better for Ruby to have stood by and done nothing. What injustice had her actions prevented? Who had she saved tonight? Because meticulous Lauren would have had a plan.

"How did Frank know to come here?" Ruby asked.

"We don't need to speak about this anymore."

"Tell me."

This seemed to be a source of regret. As though she was reluctant. It was just a dirty job that *someone* had to do. Besides, like the virtuous brutality of major surgery, this had all been for the greater good.

"Frank was pretty cut up about Scott," she said. "I heard him rambling in his hospital bed. Kept saying he was going to kill whoever was responsible. I think he'd lost it."

"You. *You* allowed him to escape . . . Why not just kill him there?"

"Look, Ruby, we don't need to—"

"*Why?*"

"It was . . . it was too close to home. Too many eyes. And he was a helpful distraction. Sometimes chaos is good." Another mask on Lauren's face. Or, no. Wait. This was real. A human being *was* peering out of that empty shadow with genuine remorse. "I am sorry for lying to you, though." She actually meant it. And then Lauren sighed and said, "OK . . ."

She reached into her jacket pocket and pulled out a handgun. Ruby heard Gemma's voice in her mind. Scott was always armed. And here it was. All three guns accounted for. Despite this dire situation, Ruby's brain still treated her to a drop of dopamine – like a single tear of joy lost in a vast and churning ocean – the simple, fleeting pleasure of finding an answer to a question.

"That's Scott's gun."

"Yeah." Lauren looked down at it, turned it over. "Fucking bullies, hey?" She laughed, but it sounded hollow. "I guess, in a way, we're all Scott's victims." She gestured back towards the water. "Especially Frank."

"You lured him here?"

"I told him that I was responsible, I knew he'd come."

"You were going to shoot him?"

Lauren nodded at the room behind Ruby. "There's a window back there. Considering he knew what I'd done, it seemed the safest bet. I was ready. Had him in my sights. But I heard you arrive and . . ." She looked down at the empty sawn-off shotgun near Ruby's foot. "Well, you know what happened then."

"And what happens now?" Ruby asked.

"You were right. There were seven names. Frank was the sixth."

One more to go . . .

Ruby's remaining blood surged as panic took hold. She'd wondered just hours earlier if this was it. The climax of her incompetence. Of all the things she'd forgotten, was this the one that mattered most? Did *she* see it happen? Had her name been on the list this whole time?

And she came willingly. She *ran* here. Ruby had served herself up like an animal without the faculties to even comprehend what slaughter means. What sacrifice awaits. She felt so small, so utterly lost and alone. There was nothing left besides doubt and fear.

"Yep," Lauren said, with terrifying finality, eyes wide and ready to finish this monumental task. "Very nearly done now. One more." She held the gun in both hands, nodded at it. Then she gripped the handle, finger on the trigger. And she breathed.

"Please."

"It was always going to be the hardest."

"Don't."

"I'm so sorry, Ruby. It's only fair. I know you tried. And I know all the things you'll say to stop me. But don't. It'll honestly be easier if we don't talk."

"I . . ." Ruby's voice was weak, breaking out like she was on the verge of tears. "No . . . I wasn't . . . I didn't see . . . I— I didn't."

She was hyperventilating, shuffling backwards, back against the wall, heels pushing her back and back but there was nowhere to go. Even with all these reasons, she was still trying not to cry. Mouth stretched out in dismay, like a nightmare's silent scream that wakes you shaking in your bed. Ruby lifted her jittering hand, setting her life free as she bowed her head and begged.

"Close your eyes, Ruby."

She did. She tensed every muscle in her body and said, "I wasn't there. I wasn't there. I wasn't there . . ."

"Oh, I know," Lauren said, reassuringly. "But I was."

Ruby looked. And, in one swift motion, before she could say another word, Lauren put the barrel of the gun in her mouth, aimed up and fired.

Ruby turned away and the next sound, the thud of flesh and bones on concrete, was quiet, muffled like something underwater. She felt herself fall to the side, slipping down and saying, "No," as though it might change reality.

When Ruby opened her eyes, she saw that she was lying down, level with Lauren's body, spreadeagled on the ground, her head eclipsed by her chest. No movement. No life. As perfectly still as the world beneath her.

Trying to stand, Ruby's vision narrowed, a sudden head rush as she got onto one knee – left arm slack, swinging, right hand pressed to the wound. But, instead of rising, she tilted and fell. Now she was lying in exactly the same position, but on her other side.

She sighed. It had sapped all of her energy. She manoeuvred herself round, trying to use the wall for balance. But her final attempt was anticlimactic. Teeth clamped, growling for power, Ruby instructed her muscles to move and they simply didn't. Not enough blood. Or maybe what she'd said was true. She really had lost it. The very thing you need to get back up again. That ability, the courage or resolve or whatever you want to call it, was gone.

She whispered the word "Help," but not even she heard it over the sound of gentle waves below. Water lifting and dropping, out-living us all with indifference and ease.

It seemed too obvious, too plain, but Ruby felt sad. Not only had she failed, in every conceivable sense, she was also bleeding to death. And no one, not a single soul on this earth, knew where she was.

Right here, ribs on the hard ground, she could hear her heart beating in her neck, pulsing through her skull like she was wearing earplugs. Overwhelmingly loud. A fast and foetal clock struggling against the inevitable weakness of a rapidly draining resource.

She thought about crawling. But, even if she could, she didn't really want to. She was empty. All she wanted to do now was rest.

Time passed. Perhaps a minute or two. Maybe a week. A year. A thousand long and lonely lives before Ruby realised she had closed her eyes. And that was OK.

No bright and guiding light to walk towards. Just black as the jumbled thoughts of early dreams entered centre stage, taking her by the hand and leading her back in time. Maybe to school. Or to Giles, where she could ride her bike and smile in circles that would never end.

And with her final fading thought, Ruby noticed total silence had, with divine force, driven the tide away. Even the wind had fled. She did not believe in heaven. But still she enjoyed the illusion of its promise when it arrived. At one point, it even felt like she was rising into the air. Carried in the strong arms of some angelic being that she knew, from the bottom of her dying heart, couldn't possibly be real.

Chapter Nineteen

On the last day of school, students wrote on each other's shirts. The girls wrote nice things, like, "Best of luck for the future", or, "I'm going to miss you so much". Lots of messages about the good times they shared, about staying in touch and hoping college proves just as fun as school had been. Best friends forever. Whereas the boys treated the tradition with far less reverence, employing a more toilet wall graffiti theme – warm wishes interspersed with explicit sexual demands and cartoon genitalia.

But Ruby didn't know what she should write on Elizabeth's shirt. Though, it didn't feel important, because she knew they wouldn't drift apart. Not like the others. This wasn't goodbye. Just the opposite. They were greeting the start of a new chapter in their lives.

So, Ruby wrote the word "Love" on Elizabeth's collar. And that was enough.

They were sitting in science, right at the front of the class. Top set. Ruby was staring idly out of the window, into the courtyard.

Across it, through thick pollen air, clear sky sun, beyond butterflies and hovering bees that sneak in and out of flowers as though they're not welcome, she saw Scott. He'd been sent out of English and was now standing, arms folded, visibly disinterested in whatever Mr Hunter was saying. Lots of animation, pointing back towards the classroom, shouting about a misdemeanour that must have been extreme even for Scott. He was often getting told off, but this one seemed serious.

"I wonder what he did?" she said.

Turning away from the glass, Ruby faced Elizabeth, sitting next to her at the raised science desk. Her tie was short, white shirt already adorned with handwritten notes, "Love" clean and bold near her neck. She looked good today. Prettier than usual. When Ruby asked why, Elizabeth told her it was for the photo. And Ruby felt sudden anxiety because she hadn't prepared.

"No," she said. "That's not today?"

Must be a mistake. The full year 11 photo had already been taken. A long time ago. This was summer. This was, yeah, Ruby glanced around, it was the last day of school.

"All done," Elizabeth said.

Ruby looked down at her shirt sleeve. Elizabeth had written on her forearm in stark red ink. Thick marker-pen letters.

"What does it say? I can't . . ." Ruby squinted at the words but she couldn't really read them. It was something about being children, having no idea what the future would hold. The message was long and it seemed to be about death?

"OK," Elizabeth said. She held the red pen up, waved it side to side and smiled.

Then, with dipped eyes, tongue poking out in concentration as though she was applying make-up, Elizabeth placed the thick felt nib on her temple and started drawing a straight line down her face, over her brow, over her wide-open eye, across the bridge of her nose, cheek, ending at her jaw, just below her ear.

"What are you doing?" Ruby said. "Don't do that."

She tried to take the pen but Elizabeth snatched it away.

"Wait." And Elizabeth held it in her fist, gripped it tight like a knife, put the nib on the other side, at her hairline, and drew down again, firm now, dragging it across her skin to create a cross. Then, head flopped to the side, flesh dead and white, she turned to Ruby, as though presenting herself. "See."

"Stop."

"It's fine. Your turn."

Elizabeth placed her hand on Ruby's shoulder, gently leant into her space, pen ready, nodding for permission to draw.

"No." Ruby pushed her off, stood up and stepped away from the desk.

And now Mary was leaning round, from behind Elizabeth.

"What's the problem?" Mary asked.

Ruby saw that she already had a smudged cross on her face. She looked out the window – Scott had one too. Was that why he was being told off?

"See," Elizabeth said. "Everyone's doing it."

And the bell was ringing as Ruby backed out of the door and ran into the corridor and went through the crowd. She was pushing through the rumble and voices, bumped left, turning. Shoved right, turning back, turning full circle and then outside, up the stairs, towards the expanse. It went on forever. The playground was full. Busy. The criss-cross of uniforms. Pupils all around her, dense, like a sweaty mass of shoulders and chests at a concert.

Someone barged into her. "Sorry," Ruby said, stumbling.

There were too many people.

"Excuse me," she said. "I have to go, my dad's picking me up. Please could I get by?" But no one seemed to care.

Head down, she tried to weave, but she was too small and they were pressing into her and she turned again and again and looked around at the flaring light glistening off the windows above. Flashing. The clouds too fast.

Panicking now, Ruby rose onto tiptoes, spotted the gates. "Please," she said. "I need to get through. Please. I need to—"

Thud. A man pushed her – a giant – and she tripped, fell to her knees, palms slapping onto the concrete. Cowering lower, she went onto her side and shielded her head. Everyone was here, they could see her lying on the ground.

"Are you OK?" Will asked, kneeling.

"I can't get up," she whispered, more embarrassed than anything.

Little Adam had climbed high on the wall, near the playing fields. He leant over and drew a cross on his face. Even Alfie, looking out from a window, standing in his office in the sky – a rainbow beaming behind him. He gave her a quick nod. And then clicked the lid off a red pen. Ruby looked away now.

And she was face to face with Kendall, or someone just like him. He was lying on the ground with her and she stroked his cheek.

"What happened to everyone?" she asked.

"You forgot this." A shadow. She turned her head and saw Frank Enfield. It was him. He'd pushed her over. Frank was holding a pen. He crouched and put it in Ruby's hand.

"No, I don't want to."

Ruby rolled onto her back, looked up through the infinite walls of black legs and blazers and heads staring down at her, to the sky, flooded with colour, the majesty and confusion. The last day of school. Their whole lives spread out ahead of them. All the hope and fear.

"My dad's picking me up," she said. "Is he here?"

"Hey." Lauren was suddenly above, eclipsing everything, too close and in Ruby's face, the top of her skull broken open and she was dead and she was saying, "It's dark enough now." Her voice wrong, too deep, too fast. "They're taking the photo. Ruby, they're taking the photo." She shook her. "They're waiting. You need to wake up. Ruby, you need to wake up and *cry*."

But when the camera flashed, they saw that Ruby's tears were blood and everyone was screaming and they were screaming and they were—

Awake. A binary switch. The difference between on and off, yes and no, now and never. New senses. Ruby could feel a firm bed beneath. She knew time had passed – somewhere just shy of eternity. There is a light, must be white, but no more now than a blood-orange glow on the back of her eyelids.

". . . dressing on the side," a voice was mumbling. "Heart rate seems . . . Ruby?" Things were moving. "Can you hear me? Ruby."

They kept saying her name, but no one was listening. More time passed. Another taste of forever.

A heavy blanket on her lower half. She opened her eyes. And, above, she saw a strip light – the hospital ceiling bright with life.

"Morning," a man said.

Ruby turned her film reel vision and saw that it was Giles. He was sitting at her bedside, a magazine in his hand. It flopped and he shuffled forwards, touched her leg.

She looked. Her index finger pinched by a clip, a pipe leading off and up to a drip.

"Hello," Ruby whispered.

"You're full of drugs," Giles said.

"Awesome."

She closed her eyes again, just for a second, opened them and found the evening. The room was darker now, a warm lamp nearby turned corners black, made caves beneath the beds. Windows glossed and wet with rain. The smell of flowers that weren't for her and chemicals that were. Nurses milled around in the doorway, holding clipboards in a rectangle of white. Long shadows. A red fire alarm, a green exit sign.

"You alive?" another man asked. "OK to talk?"

She considered the room. Jay was sitting at her side. "I think so," she said.

"You've been out for a while."

"Was . . . was Giles here earlier?"

"Yes," Jay said. "All afternoon. You spoke to him for hours."

Ruby had no recollection.

"You don't remember?"

She shook her head.

"He brought you flowers."

Ruby smiled. They *were* for her.

"What *do* you remember?" Jay asked.

"I was . . . I was at the dockyard . . ." Ruby told him what happened and, at the end of her account, she said, "I couldn't . . . I couldn't stop her . . ."

"Is that all?"

She didn't have to say it, Jay could tell Ruby had no idea how she got here. Why she wasn't dead out there on the concrete.

"Your good friend Frank," Jay said. "He carried you. Up the stairs, along the main road. All the way. Doctors reckon it was touch and go. Minutes."

"He's OK?"

"Well, he's seen better days but, sure, he's alive."

Ruby nodded, then rested her head back on the pillow. She felt nauseous. Not from drugs or blood loss or any other physical, trivial thing. Just despair.

"I fucked it all up," she said. And she clenched her jaw, lips together like a toddler acting braver than their years. "I got it wrong."

"Don't be like that." He leant closer, patted the mattress near her knee. "Frank's not dead. Because of you."

"I shot him."

"In the hip. And the wrist." Jay nodded, eyebrows up, as though to imply she did this deliberately. "He'll be fine."

"Worse than I thought then. I'm not even a good shot."

He laughed.

"Sorry," Ruby added, aware of how she must sound. "Ignore me. I'm just speaking shit."

There was no point in telling him how she felt – nothing Jay could say would change it.

"So, as for Miss Coates." He opened a folder, licked his thumb to leaf through a couple of sheets. "CCTV near Alfie's place. Lauren clear as day. Same from the station. Got her coming and going."

He came to a piece of paper and pulled it out, raising it as though she might like to see, then decided he'd be better off just telling her what it said.

"Clothing fibres at the end of Will's garden," he explained. "Lab said they matched, but confirmed they could have been there a while. We were half-right. Our suspect *had* brushed past that fence pole."

Ruby imagined Lauren, wearing her dark-blue jacket, passing through there any number of days earlier. She'd seen tools near their back door. Lauren had even said that she must get round to finishing the fence. But then, if that crucial evidence was not from the intruder, who had they seen?

"So, who broke into the house? Who stole my notebook?" Ruby said. "That wasn't Frank."

"It wasn't, no. Frank left Scott's house, as per the recordings . . . He hired a private investigator to steal it. That's why he was in the bank, withdrawing the money. That black car you saw. That burglar. It was some guy called Trevor or something. He was no one. When it proved useless, Frank took matters into his own hands and came after you."

"But . . . but he *wanted* to be arrested? He came willingly."

"He's provided an admirably detailed statement." Another sheet of paper that Ruby didn't look at. So, Jay did the honours. "He thought ending up in prison would be the best way to, I quote, 'get close to the killer'. That's something at least. Frank had faith in us. Then, discovering he was being hospitalised, he changed his mind. We're thinking Lauren swapped his drip and told him to run." Jay read a few more lines. "Goes on to say they were in contact after that and she promised to help him figure it out. Frank added that he didn't trust her. Smarter than he looks. When the moment came, Lauren confessed, told him where to go. And off he went."

"I want to speak to him." Ruby began to move, tried to sit up.

The nurse near the door looked over, didn't shake her head but the message was clear.

"Tomorrow." Jay said, clocking the concern. "Rest some more." He placed the folder on the cabinet near her head. "If you want to read." Then he stood up and left.

The following day, Ruby woke early and, once more, turned to see someone at her bedside. A seamless shift, men recast as other men in this dreamy haze she was yet to escape.

Giles became Jay. And now, sitting in the same spot, Jay had become Will.

Will now. Will from school, perched and coming forwards on the plastic chair to touch her shoulder and force a smile. He offered her some water. She took the cup and drank. Thanked him. Croaked as he carefully passed it back to the cabinet. And then they spoke about everything imaginable before they finally landed on Lauren.

The topic was prefixed with a mutual moment of quiet reflection. Solemn weight, even veneration. For each other, not for Lauren. No doubt Ruby and Will had plenty of lonely hours ahead of them. Bouts of rumination, long nights where they'd wonder how Lauren's deception, sophisticated though it was, had fallen so far beyond their perception. They'd been blinded by charisma and confidence, lied to, tricked away from even suspecting they were being manipulated. Those sleights of hand, the casual control an expert illusionist has over every bit of your attention. You see only what you're shown.

While Ruby had audited some of her own missed chances, she probably had many more soundbites, snippets of dialogue that'd come to her in the shower, or in bed, leaving her to wince and cringe and wish against that immovable wall of regret.

But Will? He'd closed his woollen eyes for a thousand kisses, he'd slept with her in every way you can. For him, the past was set solid in the coldest stone, casting a shadow far too dark to find anything like retrospective consolation. So, he'd earned the right to speak first.

"I'd actually toyed with the idea she was cheating on me," he said, sniffing, wiping a tear. "She'd be gone at strange times. Working shifts that weren't on the calendar. I was scared. Because I thought . . . I thought about all the possible explanations. And, honestly, cheating was the worst one I considered. I didn't even . . . not for a *moment*."

"We can't have known. She was . . ."

"It's messed up as well because I still . . . I still love her. I can almost wrap my head around what she did to them. It's unforgivable, but a part of me can imagine her being capable of violence. What she did to herself, though? I just . . . it doesn't compute. That she was . . . that she could. I'm sorry you had to see that."

It flashed again, the gun in Lauren's mouth, eyes locked ahead. Ready. No hesitation. There was one level of distress. The physicality, the indelible scorch marks such gore leaves behind. You have to see far more than Ruby had to grow numb. But, also, more so, Ruby was plagued by what it represented. Lauren left this world believing she'd won. She stood proud as she blasted all possible glory out the back of her head without a second thought. There would be no trial. No conviction. Absolutely no closure.

"It was all so fast," Ruby said. "I wish, I *wish* I could have stopped her."

"That's very noble of you."

"No. It's not . . ."

Will understood. He eyed her, wary but not surprised.

"Purely selfish reasons," Ruby added. "I . . . I tried my hardest and . . . anything positive that came of this . . . It's indistinguishable from luck. I failed, Will. There's no simpler way of saying it."

Ruby was braced for his response. But he was uncharacteristically sympathetic. Perhaps this shared trauma had softened him, taken the edge off what she'd expected him to say.

"I wonder," Will said, having given this some thought, "if there's any version of events, any outcome, where you wouldn't feel like you'd fallen short?"

Ruby smiled. It was a fair point.

Later that morning, once he'd gone, Ruby got out of bed. Her left arm was strapped to her chest, her right hand back in its brace, where it belonged. Add a pair of sprained ankles, one swollen to almost comic proportions, and every limb was hindered in some way.

Doctors had explained she'd been shot three times. One bullet took a chunk out of her collarbone, another slotted itself neatly in her humerus but it was the third, which skimmed her neck, that contributed to the extensive blood loss and caused most of the concern. All three were, according to Frank's statement, meant for Lauren.

Up the hall, clicking and squeaking along on a crutch, Ruby found Frank's ward. She went in and sat down next to his bed, propping the crutch against the wall.

Glancing at her once, Frank looked away without saying a word. He just lay there, staring in the opposite direction. She'd imagined he would start proceedings. But now, with no prompts, no way into this conversation, Ruby realised she didn't know why she was here. What did she even want to say? Eventually she settled on "Thank you."

And then she started talking. Rambling. The painkillers had dulled her slow blood, inhibitions melted away like butter, warm and smooth. She was able to smile, just thinking aloud, reflecting on what had happened as though she was chatting to a friend. Catching up with an old chum from school.

She spoke about Lauren. Perhaps Frank might care to hear that every bit of her apparent virtue was little more than desperate repentance. A feverish attempt to repay a debt to karma. But Lauren, Ruby said, had fallen so quickly into moral bankruptcy on the night of the reunion and, instead of more guilt, she'd found solace in bloodshed.

Ruby must have been talking for more than five minutes and, even though he didn't react, she could tell Frank was listening.

"Lauren wanted to fix Kendall," Ruby said. "Undo all of Scott's damage. All the harm she hadn't prevented in the first place. She even told Kendall he'd be able to walk into the sports hall for the reunion. Surgeons and their God complex. Guess failing weighed heavy on her too. Oh, I know how that feels."

She looked out of the window.

"All her anger," Ruby said. "The fury she felt. Enraged that Mary hardly remembered. No one else had suffered like she had. It was projection, I suppose. Because she was just as bad." Ruby shrugged. "She believed their inaction on that day, on the field, she . . . she thought it justified a death sentence. A judgement she executed. She even . . . she even applied it to herself."

Frank exhaled, sounding irritated.

"You saw through her, didn't you?" Ruby asked, scratching near the dressing on her neck – the tape tugged her skin when she moved. "Pretty clever." Flattery. "You beat me to it."

No answer.

She thought about all the power Scott had over him. Even from the grave. Commanding Frank to kill, to avenge his death.

"Why were you in that room?" Ruby asked. "You know Scott was not a good person? He wasn't trying to help you. I understand you were loyal to him but . . . revenge wouldn't have made anything better."

She looked at the bandages around his torso, on his hip. Frank's big arm set in a thick white plaster cast. That night at the dockyard, she'd fired both barrels without aiming, without caution or care. Pure survival mode. It wasn't calculated mercy that meant Frank was alive, despite Jay's charitable suggestion. It was, as she'd said, luck. And, without it, they'd both have died there, right next to Lauren's body. Cold and still, unable to explain what would have been a harrowing crime scene to discover.

"I'm sorry I shot you," Ruby said. "I guess we're even?"

She and Frank had saved each other, without even realising it. And all this, all of Ruby's efforts, the totality of her investigation, it had amounted to a single life. Here he was. Frank Enfield. The only surviving name on that list.

"Funny, isn't it?" she said, smiling, maybe finding some poetic beauty. "So funny how it all pans out, after all these years, how it's just "

"Ruby," Frank said, then he turned to look her in the eye for the first time. "Fuck off."

And he looked away. The conversation was over.

She bit her lip, blinked because this hurt. Chewing her thumb, she stared out of the window, fingers jittery. And now, twitching in her chair, she understood what she was doing. She knew why she was here, saying all this. It was pathetic. Ruby was fishing for gratitude. And he was giving her none.

◆ ◆ ◆

Three weeks later, Ruby was all packed up and ready to go. Her injuries had begun to heal but, alone in these fevered nights, she'd found herself wondering if time could ever repair a heart so broken. Or, in her most shameful moments of private melodrama, if she even had enough left to find out.

She'd been staying at Giles's since she was discharged from hospital, sleeping in her childhood bedroom. Well past tossing and turning, she'd greet most dawns from her back, unfazed as another day crept in through the curtains. She'd watch the sun on the walls, plain now, magnolia. Fresh bedding and a large folded towel. Despite the luxury reserved for guests, Ruby felt comfortable here, secure, perhaps even at home.

The debriefs and paperwork and statements, it had all just passed her by. Meaningless formalities. A conveyer belt of empty ceremony. Ruby sitting in an office, head bowed, watching herself from a thousand miles away. Nodding at unheard things, agreeing or not, saying she understood even when she didn't. She was suspended, reprimanded in some way that fell short of losing her job. There was a form, which she didn't read.

They'd set a date for when she'd return to work back in Australia. It fell neatly within the recommended timeframe she'd been given for recovery. Assuming physiotherapy went well, she'd retain full use of her shoulder and, the doctor had literally touched his wooden desk to add, she wouldn't need any more surgery.

Giles, to his credit, had taken good care of her but, as she'd suspected, he had no interest in self-pity. Or, maybe, he hadn't even noticed. Ruby knew better than to feel sorry for anyone, let alone herself, and there was plenty of physical pain to hide behind. In fact, they'd hardly discussed the case at all. Perhaps Giles was cautious about opening fresh wounds or maybe even he understood it was still too raw for his brand of head-up, eyes-forward pragmatism.

When she'd arrived and he showed her to the spare room – her room – he mentioned in passing that she would have been more than welcome to stay here since day one.

"I know," she'd said. "But . . ."

But. She didn't finish that sentence and neither of them pushed the door. Revisiting the reasons she hadn't, Ruby found yet more regret. Things might have gone differently. Staying at Will's place was, on reflection, a mistake.

In the new light of her sober mind, the unspoken explanation seemed ridiculous. The idea of working with Giles nearby had felt terrifying. Dialled up by jetlag, ambition or a misguided desire to appear autonomous, the stakes were too high. Risking failure alone was one thing, but in front of him?

"Are you staying at your dad's?" Will had asked in the staffroom on that first day.

"Absolutely not."

Ruby hadn't paused to *truly* wonder why.

It was like schoolwork. Any time she didn't get top marks. Young Ruby, smart in her uniform, shirt always tucked in. She'd wait eagerly at her desk as the teacher walked the rows, placing sheets of paper down one by one. And she'd grab hers, look down, searching for ticks in the margin, praying for a big letter "A" circled at the top. Only, with a sinking heart, to find nothing of the sort. And Ruby would have to ball it up and stuff it in the bin. She could never let Giles know. It had to stay buried. Neither of them could bear the sight of those little red crosses.

Now, Ruby carried her suitcase down the stairs, parked it near the door – shoulders and luggage heavy, defeated. She went into the living room. Giles was sitting on the sofa, waiting. He had insisted on giving her a lift to the airport.

"Ready?" she asked.

Giles checked his watch. "Leave in five."

So, she went in and sat down next to him.

Ruby got her phone out, placed it on the coffee table. The TV was on, but muted. The news had just begun. A silent reporter, headlines scrolling along the bottom of the screen. She watched for a few seconds but then . . .

A text message. Electric words on glowing glass, guiding her eyes down. It was from Eduardo. She'd already confirmed when she'd land and he'd replied, *I'll be there x*

Maybe Ruby was smiling. Or giving something away, enough for Giles to probe again at the subject.

"Tell me about this guy," he asked.

"Eduardo?" Ruby leant forwards, slipped her phone into the front pocket of her rucksack. "He's . . . he's a couple of years older than me. Funny. Quite chilled out."

"Do you love him?"

"No."

"Will you?"

Ruby thought about their camping trip, the drunken kiss on the second night, the goosebumps it sent down her sides. And she remembered that afternoon, standing in the sun, next to the van, when death arrived to summon her home. She wondered why she'd agreed. Because, whatever Ruby had been looking for, whatever she'd hoped to find, it evidently wasn't here.

"Maybe," she said.

Ruby looked back up at the TV. And then, that unique feeling of seeing yourself on camera, recognising the person and discovering, within a second, that, yes, it's you. That is what you look like.

This morning's press conference had been her final professional engagement. The dust had settled and the police were ready to talk. There she was, on stage with Jay, on hand to share a story interesting enough to write about, to click on and, who knows, maybe even read.

Still muted, she and Giles watched the images – their soundtrack echoing in her mind. There was one point, towards the end, when someone on the back row stood up and posed a question specifically to Ruby.

"Do you think you could have done more?" the journalist had asked.

Having been silent until then, she was caught off guard. And, as she leant down towards the microphone, still unsure how she might reply, Ruby hesitated. Because an interesting feeling came over her. This was an opportunity.

No one else heard what Lauren said. They didn't understand her reasons, her motives. That all-important "why" had been, as it so often is, lost amid the noise. Taking stock of the truth was like counting snowflakes in a blizzard. These reporters, the whole world looking at her through all those lenses. They were *listening*. She had their attention.

Ruby could have said anything. She could have told them Lauren was just getting started, that she was hell-bent on killing everyone and Ruby's bold, brave, heroic actions had saved countless lives. A tiny edit, a little white lie to rewrite history.

It would be the hollowest of victories, this success that lives exclusively in the minds of other people. Of course, she'd have known. But, given time, settling on the warm ground of her fading memories, it might melt away until, eventually, it'd be as good as true. Like the tree that never fell.

In that moment, on that humble stage, Ruby had felt powerful. The weight of temptation like a loaded gun. It had seemed like a chance to salvage something, to cling on to whatever she'd been searching for – this feeling of triumph, of success, the comfort blanket of excellence she needed just to feel safe. A way to reclaim what Lauren stole.

Or she could have been honest. She could have said that she had, through the random whims of chaos and good fortune, saved a single ungrateful life. A sincere confession, if she were to listen to the worst interpretation that whispered in her ear late at night, would be that her efforts had caused demonstrable harm. Ruby could have simply stated for the record that, all things considered, it might have been better for her to have done absolutely nothing.

"I . . ." she began, looking out into those shadows, across the sea of faceless questions and cameras. One of them flashed. And they waited. For some reason, Frank came into her mind. His last words to her from his hospital bed.

Could she? Could she have done more? No. She'd tried her best.

But Ruby didn't say any of those things. Instead, she just pulled the small microphone closer to herself on the desk, leant in and said, "This isn't about me."

And that was it. They moved on.

Now the silent news cut to another story. Something else that mattered just as much, or even more, to someone far away. A victory, a loss, a triumph or a tragedy. Whatever it was, Ruby didn't care. And that's the bedrock. Giles used to tell her this when she was small. Worrying about what other people think of you is beyond a waste of time. Because they don't.

It was time to leave.

Giles lifted the remote, aimed at the TV and turned it off.

Done. The case was over. And now Giles was able to pass his judgement. Ruby looked, waiting for him to fill this empty silence. But he didn't say anything. Not for a long time. And then, casually, Giles patted her leg and smiled.

"Well done, Ruby," he said.

Then he stood, went to grab his keys. But she didn't move. She couldn't. Ruby just sank back into the sofa and closed her watering eyes, breathing it in. Feeling it arrive all at once, everything she thought she'd lost, everything she'd ever wanted, as she blinked and sighed. As she sat and cried. Even when Giles came back, standing in the doorway now waiting for her. Ruby just sat there on the sofa, crying. She didn't even care if he saw. It really didn't matter. Because these were tears of joy.

ACKNOWLEDGEMENTS

Thanks go to editors Hannah Bond, Leodora Darlington and Celine Kelly for all their hard work, experience and wisdom. And to the rest of the team busy behind the scenes at Thomas & Mercer. As always, I'm also indebted to my agent, Clare Wallace, for her endless advice, expertise and encouragement.

ABOUT THE AUTHOR

Photo © Kayt Webster-Brown

Martyn Ford is a journalist and author from the UK. His debut middle-grade children's book, *The Imagination Box*, was published by Faber & Faber in 2015 to critical acclaim and went on to become a trilogy. This was followed by 2019's stand-alone title, *Chester Parsons is Not a Gorilla*. His first novel for adult readers, *Every Missing Thing*, was published in 2020, followed by *All Our Darkest Secrets* in 2021, and *Any One of Us* in 2022.